Something in Between

Books by Melissa de la Cruz
available from Harlequin TEEN

Something in Between

MELISSA DE LA CRUZ

Something in Between

seventeen FICTION
FROM HARLEQUIN TEEN

ISBN-13: 978-0-373-21238-5
ISBN-13: 978-0-373-21250-7 (Target signed edition)

Something in Between

Recycling programs
for this product may
not exist in your area.

Grateful acknowledgment is made for permission to include the following
previously published material:

For my husband,
for everything,
including my American citizenship.

tiger cub

Remember, remember always, that all of us, and you
and I especially, are descended from immigrants and
revolutionists.

—FRANKLIN D. ROOSEVELT

1

The truth is, immigrants tend to be more American than people born here.

—CHUCK PALAHNIUK, *CHOKE*

FIRST YOU HAVE to hollow out. Suck your belly button back against your spine. Pull up toward your rib cage. Maintain eye contact. Remember to breathe. Feel your muscles tighten. Make yourself compact. Lift up. Fly. Attitude is everything. Believe you can do that stunt. Stay tight. Smile. Keep everything together as you're twisting through the air. Trust yourself. Trust your team. Let doubt creep in and you'll fall—plus, you'll let down the whole squad, and that's the worst thing you can do as cheer captain, other than bossing everyone around like an aggro queen bee.

There's no one more intense than a cheerleader—although according to every Hollywood movie ever made, we're a bunch of ditzy, boy-crazy backstabbers. *As if.*

Don't they get it? Cheerleaders are part of a team, and a good team trusts each other. Because the only thing stopping you from cracking your head open on the gym floor is your teammates.

Cheer makes you tough.

Loyal.

Strong.

"Hit. Hit. Hit. Pull!" Coach Davis shouts, her voice echoing against the gym walls. We jump three times in a row, extending our arms and legs into perfect toe touches, then tuck, flipping backward onto the mats.

Everyone sticks the tuck except for Kayla. She's been struggling with her tumbling even though she used to be one of the best tumblers on the team. Her mind has been somewhere else for a while, worried about her parents, who aren't getting along too well. I make a mental note to ask her how she's doing after practice, maybe offer to help her brush up on some moves before she gets put on probation or kicked off the squad. She's my best friend, but we haven't hung out much since I've been studying for midterms and trying to get my college applications done.

"Keep your feet together, Santos," Coach barks at me. "They're wobbling on your landing."

I nod even though I'm annoyed that she singled me out and didn't say anything to Kayla. I know Coach is bringing me down a notch on purpose. She doesn't want me to end up with an oversize ego. That's why I got voted captain in the first place—I know you have to sacrifice yourself for the team, for the stunt, or else everything falls apart like a crumbling pyramid.

Sometimes the other girls tease me. *You're so perfect, Jasmine. You do everything right. You were junior class president. Cheer captain. Honor Roll. Volunteering. Don't you ever get tired?*

Never, I say with a smile. Except the truth is I'm *always* tired, but I can never admit it, not to my friends, especially not to my family.

"Let's run through the routine until the end of practice," Coach orders. She walks over to the sound system to start the music.

Most of the girls start taking their positions, but Emily crosses her arms. "I'm *exhausted*. I don't know if I can do this anymore." Her cheeks are flaming red on her Irish complexion.

"Don't be a drama queen," Deandra says, whipping her dark braids like the queen of the Nile. She looks like Halle Berry, but prettier with gorgeous naturally thick eyelashes. "You're only tired because you stayed up texting Brandon all night."

"He likes my texts." Emily grins. She raises one eyebrow like she's holding on to a juicy secret. "Creative emojis."

I tell them to hush. It's my senior year and last chance to win at Nationals. If we want to win this time, the whole team has to be serious about practice. We don't have any time not to be on point.

"Positions!" I yell out.

Coach nods and I count down to begin the routine.

"Five, six, seven, eight!"

Music blasts from the speakers.

Our routine begins with high-intensity tumbling. We sprint across the mats, propelling our bodies through the air, hitting our handsprings, layouts, and tucks right on the beat. The girls are getting even more pumped as they move into formation for the flyer stunts. I step up onto my bases, let them propel me up into a barrel roll, and fall back into their cradle. The stunts are getting more and more complex and one of our flyers loses her balance during a dismount on a pyramid, smacking against her back spotter and sending her to the ground. The bases help the spotter back up.

Coach stops the mix. She's frowning.

"We got this! Come on, ladies!" I shout. "Again from the beginning!"

We practice our routine over and over until all of the flyers are hitting their stunts. Our muscles ache and our arms are slick with sweat, but the better we get, the more pumped we are, so by the end of practice everyone is cheering louder, staying tighter, and flying higher.

That's more like it.

We're about to go through our last run when Mrs. Garcia pushes through the swing doors and power walks toward us. Her scuffed pleather heels thump against the wood floors. Weird. What's the college counselor doing at cheer practice? Everyone else must have noticed her too, because they're all chatting and whispering instead of getting into their positions.

Coach catches her eye and turns to us. "Ladies! Listen up. I want you to pair up and practice your back walkovers, back tucks, then cool down with stretches and splits, holding each side for thirty seconds each. Spot for each other. Start slow. Keep them controlled."

As she joins Mrs. Garcia, I pair up with Kayla and help her slowly ease into a backbend. She tries to kick up with her foot, but can't catch the momentum, so I help guide her through the move.

Kayla Paredes is curvy, with a tiny waist, curly dark hair and a quick smile. Boys have been worshipping at her feet since we were twelve, but she tires of them easily. She's fifth-generation Mexican American, which means she learned Spanish in class just like I did.

"Movie night on Friday?" she asks. "My house?"

I'm about to say no, I have to study, but it's been ages and we need to catch up. "Perfect," I tell her. "I'll have to clear it with my mom, but it should be okay. Let's make chocolate-chip cookies."

"With extra chocolate chips." Kayla grins. After a couple

minutes, Coach calls out for me. "Santos! Mrs. Garcia needs a word with you."

Me? Is something wrong? Uncertainty creeps into my stomach. It's October and I've been trying to narrow down my list of colleges. Did I miss an early application deadline? I've been going to Mrs. Garcia's office every couple of weeks since junior year to make sure I'm on track. Could she have forgotten to tell me something important?

I help Kayla up before walking over, trying not to look too worried. Coach winks at me as she passes by on her way back to the group, and I'm relieved. This can only mean something good.

"I have something special for you," Mrs. Garcia says as she hands me an envelope. She folds her arms, a slight smile turning up the corners of her mouth.

My heart begins to beat when I see a fancy logo printed in official navy blue ink on the top right corner: *United States National Scholarship Program, Department of Education.* Somehow, I know I'm holding my future in my hands. The one I've worked so hard for. The one my parents have dreamed of ever since we moved here from the Philippines when I was only nine years old. Danny was a toddler and Isko was still a newborn. I remember holding Danny's hand on the plane while my mom cradled Isko on her lap as the plane rushed down the runway, lifting off toward America.

I wrote about it in my application essay, how one of my earliest memories is of looking out the window in our first house in California, at the bright lights and the stark silhouettes of palm trees, and how different it was from the view of the green and wet mountains in our house in Antipolo, where it was always muggy and raining, and we often kept the mosquito screens closed. I've come to think of America as an open window—open to new possibilities, to the new life promised to those who journey from far away to reach its shores.

The National Scholarship Award is one of the most prestigious in the nation, bestowed upon only the top high school students, the best of the best, who are chosen not only on their grades and scores but on their personal essays and teacher recommendations. It's a bit like applying to college, I guess, but it's even harder than getting into the Ivy League. I worked so hard on my application and I wanted it so badly. Now that it's here, I'm shaking.

Mrs. Garcia puts her hand on my shoulder, startling me back to the present. "I'm so proud of you," she says like I'm her own daughter.

I tear the envelope open, nearly ripping the letter apart.

As I unfold the letter, my eyes drift to the signature at the bottom. It's actually *signed*—not printed—by the president of the United States. I return to the top and begin reading the body of the letter:

Dear Ms. de los Santos,
I am pleased to offer you a National Scholarship Award in recognition of your outstanding academic achievement. The award includes a financial grant covering four years of tuition to the college of your choice. Only three hundred students out of thousands of highly qualified applicants are chosen each year, making the award one of the most competitive in the nation.

You are among a select group of astonishing young people, people who by the ages of sixteen and seventeen have not only succeeded academically but have conducted innovative medical research, played with the Los Angeles Philharmonic, competed in the Olympics, launched companies, volunteered for interna-

tional social service organizations, and more. National Scholars go on to attend our nation's top universities and use their gifts to improve both our country and the world.

It is my distinct pleasure to invite you to attend the National Scholarship Recognition Program to celebrate your achievement and meet with government officials, educators, musicians, scientists, business leaders, and past scholars. You will also have the opportunity to visit historic museums and monuments, as well as attend recitals, receptions and official ceremonies as guests of the Department of Education. Please complete and return the form included with this letter. Additional details about the trip to Washington, D.C., will be sent within the following weeks. Congratulations! I'm looking forward to seeing what you'll do to make a brighter future for our country.

Yours,
The President of the United States

I can't even breathe. This is the happiest day of my life. Everything I've given up—the hours of sleep, the driver's license (because my parents wouldn't allow me to learn), all the parties I never attended, all the fun I never had, all the boys I never kissed…

Nothing compares to this scholarship.

Mrs. Garcia shuffles against the gym floor, leaving small smudges on the wood. "This is a huge deal, Jasmine. There hasn't been a National Scholar from our town as long as I've been here. It's the highest honor a student can be awarded."

A full ride to any college of my choice. My parents won't have to worry about not being able to afford tuition. It almost takes my breath away. I can see it so clearly. My future.

College. Graduate school. I don't know yet what I want to do, but I do know that winning at the meritocracy is my

American dream. A successful career and a handsome husband. A family. I'm old-fashioned that way, maybe because I'm Filipino, but ever since I was a kid I've wanted a family of my own and a marriage like the one my parents share. Corny, I know, but hey, I'm an American girl, and I want it all.

I worked hard for this, gave up *everything*. Some of my friends tease that I'm seventeen going on thirty-five. It doesn't matter now. What's certain is that I'm not going to be stuck with my parents' limited options. My mom graduated top of her class in the Philippines, but in America she cleans up vomit in a hospital, and my dad, the smartest man I know, drives a bus for a living. But they always believed if their children became American like I am now, the sky's the limit.

And here it is. The sky is on fire.

This is it. My year. *My shot* (thanks, *Hamilton*).

The exhilaration is almost as good—if not better—as sticking a killer landing at Nationals.

2

It was my father who taught us that an immigrant must
work twice as hard as anybody else, that he must never
give up.

—ZINEDINE ZIDANE

"WHAT WAS THAT all about?" Kayla asks when Mrs. Garcia leaves. She raises her eyebrows and waits expectantly.

I can't hide my elation, but I want to tell my parents first. The news is too precious, too hard-earned to share with even my best friend right now. It's not that she won't be happy for me; she'll be ecstatic. But Mom and Dad deserve to be the first ones to hear.

"Just some good news about college apps," I tell her. "She thinks I'm eligible for a Regent's at the UC schools." The Regent's Scholarships are California's answer to the National Scholarship Program. They cover thousands of dollars of tuition a year for the top percentage of applicants, and I'd known I've been eligible for a while as UC applications are due at the end of November.

"Well, duh, I could have told you that," she says, as I pull the scholarship letter out of my sports bra and slip it into the front pocket of my backpack.

When practice is over, we run into Lorraine Schiana leaning against her car with a couple of boys in the parking lot.

She's twisting her dark red hair around one of her fingers. Lo is drop-dead gorgeous but never looks as if she's trying. You know the type. Glamorous. Bohemian. Like a rock star's famous girlfriend. She's a total scene queen, always dating a different hot musician at least a year or two older, and dyeing her hair these *amazing* unnatural colors—pink, blue, lavender, and silver. Right now she's wearing her hair au naturel, as she told me all that dye was drying out the ends too much. We've been friends since junior high, but Lo started running in different groups once we got to high school and my class load meant I didn't have as much free time as I'd like. Even though we're not as close anymore, I still love her. Her world always seems so much bigger than mine. She knows so many people and has so many fun things going on that it makes me feel a little jealous sometimes.

As I pass by, I give her a little wave, not wanting to interrupt her conversation.

Kayla leans over and whispers, "Who are those guys? Dibs on the one in the Bob Marley shirt."

It's like the boys can sense she's talking about them because they train their eyes on us, which makes Lorraine look over too. "Hey, Jas," she says. "What up, girl? Haven't seen you in a long time."

"The usual," I say, smiling back. "What's up with you?"

"Hanging out with these losers." Lorraine gestures to the guys at her side. "This is my boyfriend, Julian. That's Dylan. They play in a band together," she says.

Julian is African American, incredibly good-looking, with cappuccino-colored skin and dreadlocks. He's wearing a red beanie and has tattoos all over his forearms. Kayla smiles at Dylan, the surfer-type boy with messy blond hair wearing mirrored aviator sunglasses and a T-shirt with Bob Marley's face on the front. I can tell she's already developed a massive crush on him.

"Cheerleaders, huh?" Dylan asks.

I sigh a little. "Good guess. How can you tell?"

It's not like we're wearing our uniforms or anything, and I don't like the way he said *cheerleaders*, as if we're just chicks who shake their pom-poms. Our squad won Regionals last year. We're just as much athletes as the guys in helmets we supposedly "cheer" for. (They lose every year. Our squad has a better winning percentage. Burn.)

Dylan smirks. "Dorky white tennis shoes are pretty much a dead giveaway."

"Leave her alone, Dylan. She's a friend of mine," Lo says.

"My older sister was a cheerleader," he says somewhat apologetically.

"It's okay," says Kayla, who's practically drooling over him even though she's trying to appear disinterested. "Where do you guys go to school?"

"We graduated last year. Dylan's at Valley College. I'm taking some time off and focusing on music," Julian says. "I might go back to become a sound engineer. I'm still figuring things out."

Lo tosses her hair over her shoulder. "Want to come over on Friday?" she asks. "I'm having a few people over for a kick back. It'll be chill. My parents are out of town."

"I don't know," I say, hesitating to commit, even as I feel Kayla's intense stare on me. "Midterms are coming up and you know what my parents are like. And Kayla and I already have plans that night." To sit at home and bake chocolate-chip cookies, but I don't mention that.

"We can change them!" Kayla chirps.

"Yeah, come on, Jas," Lorraine says. "It'll be fun. Hang out for a change."

"Fine. Maybe. Message me the details?" I hate letting people down and I do miss Lo.

"Will do," Lorraine says. "See you guys then. Bye, Jas. Bye, Kayla."

Kayla seems shocked Lorraine even knows her name but recovers quickly. "Cool, thanks, Lo." She looks at the boys. "Are you guys going to be there?"

Julian seems amused. He exchanges glances with Dylan. I'm not sure what they're trying to say to each other. Boys. I can never read them.

"Yeah, we'll be there," says Julian, and Dylan nods.

"Excellent," says Kayla.

Kayla and I walk to her brand-new pearly-white Dodge Charger, which her parents bought her for her seventeenth birthday. We throw our backpacks onto the backseat and plop into the front seats, overheated and exhausted, although I can tell Kayla's in a good mood from the party invitation and meeting those guys.

I'm catching a ride to the hospital where my mom works. I don't know how to drive yet, and it's kind of embarrassing, especially since I live in LA (okay, Chatsworth, but no one ever wants to admit they live in the Valley).

Daddy always promises to teach me how to drive, but there hasn't been any time in either of our schedules, especially since I've been training so hard at cheer. Right now I don't really have time to go anywhere besides school and practice, so I don't mind too much.

Kayla turns on the ignition and rolls the windows down. "He was cute, right? Did he seem into me? Dylan?"

"Who can tell behind those aviator shades?" I say, teasing her on her "bad boy" taste. As she drives out of the lot and down the highway next to the school, I change the subject. Once Kayla gets going on boy-talk, she'll never stop, and I want to bring up something more important. "Hey, your tumbling is looking really good," I say.

Kayla rolls her eyes. "Thanks, but I don't need false compliments."

I search Kayla's face for a hint of sarcasm, but I don't see any. "I wasn't being fake with you," I say.

"It's not about whether I can do the movements," she says.

"Of course not. You've always been one of the best on the team."

Idling at a stoplight, Kayla turns to me. "I don't need you to make me feel better about myself, Jas. You could just ask what's been going on with me. I feel like you barely exist outside of practice anymore."

"I'm sorry," I say, and I really am. I know Kayla's needed me and I've neglected her. "I'm a terrible friend."

"You're not. I know how important being the best is for you, so I understand that you need to work so hard. But don't forget that I'm here for you too."

I lean my head on Kayla's shoulder. "Thanks, K. So what's been going on with you? Are you still going out with that guy? What was his name? Jason?"

"Girl, we really do need to catch up. I only went on, like, two dates with him. If you can even count them as dates… On the last one, he took me to an arcade, then expected me to *watch* him play video games. I said I was going to the bathroom and ditched him to play mini golf next door with one of the guys who works at the arcade."

We both start laughing at her story, and I know that Kayla

has forgiven me for being so absent lately. "I know you've noticed that I've been missing my marks more than normal," she continues. "But it's not because of boys."

I stay silent. I know Kayla well enough to understand that she's not going to quit talking until she's said everything she needs to get out. Talking is her way of processing things, while I tend to keep things bottled up inside until something's bothering me so bad that I finally explode in tears.

"My parents are separating. Dad moved out last week. He's living in his own apartment in Simi Valley." She takes a deep breath and her upper lip quivers.

"Oh my God. What happened?" I ask, feeling the bottom drop out of my stomach. I knew things were bad at home, but not this bad. No matter how old you are, your parents getting divorced is still every kid's nightmare. I feel awful for her.

Kayla shakes her head. "I don't know. I think Dad had an affair, but they're not saying anything. I guess Mom doesn't want Brian and me to hate him for forever." Her little brother is Danny's age.

"Of course not. But that's terrible." I lean over and give Kayla as much of a hug as I can while she's driving. "I'm so sorry, K. I don't know what to say." I feel my eyes watering.

Kayla gives me a little side hug back and wipes her eyes too. "It's okay. I'm glad I told you."

"Do you want to have movie night at my house instead? You can get away from your place for a while," I suggest.

"You mean on Friday? I thought we were hitting Lo's party after the game..."

"Ugh, I don't know," I say. "It's not a party anyway. It's a *kick back*."

"You know a kick back is just a code name for a total rager. Right? I can't go without you."

"Yes, you can," I say. "You don't need me."

"We're going to that party," she says determinedly. "It's senior year, Jas. It's about time you had a little fun."

Dylan has no idea what's coming at him. What Kayla wants, Kayla gets. Especially when it comes to boys. Then she drops them like flies and they leave sad comments online, asking why she never texts them back. I wish I had her confidence in that arena. It's not that I'm shy around guys, but with my parents being so strict along with my tough academic slate and all my extracurrriculars, I've never really had the time or opportunity to have a boyfriend.

Kayla whips around the corner into the parking lot of the hospital. "You *have* to come. I need you to be my wingwoman. Just tell your parents you're staying at my house. It'll be the truth. I'll drive us back after the party."

"I don't know," I say. "You know them. My mom will call while we're supposed to be at your house, asking to talk to your mom, trying to pretend that she's not checking up on me."

I want to go to Lo's. I do. But I also don't want to lie to my parents, no matter how much we disagree. I know everyone thinks I'm one of the good girls, but I can't afford to mess up like other kids. I'm an immigrant in this country. My dad always told me we have to work *twice* as hard as anyone else just to get to the same place, which is why I work four times as hard—because I want to succeed.

"What's Lo going to say?" Kayla asks. "You told her you'd be there."

I stare out the window at the palm trees lining the edge of the parking lot. Why do I feel guilty for just *thinking* about doing things most teenagers do? "No, I said *maybe*."

"Why do I even bother?" Kayla says, clearly annoyed. "Your *maybe* always means *no*."

Fair enough, but if I didn't always say no to things, I might not be getting the biggest yes of my life now—the golden ticket in my backpack. The one that will bring me straight to the top of the heap, where I belong.

3

The land flourished because it was fed from so many
sources—because it was nourished by so many cultures
and traditions and peoples.

—LYNDON B. JOHNSON

I SAY BYE to Kayla and hope she's not too irritated with me, and promise I'll think about going to Lo's party, then I head into the hospital. My mom has been working there for a few years now. She's what they call an environmental service worker, which basically means she's a glorified janitor. She has to do everything from mopping the hallways to washing dirty sheets. I feel bad for her, especially this year. Her job is already hard, but the hospital administration changed a few months ago and they started laying off some of Mom's co-workers, which means she's doing double the work she used to do. I know she's worried about losing her job too.

I started volunteering at the hospital in the gift shop when I was a freshman, then I assisted the nurses, but a year ago I started interviewing patients for a storytelling project. It's part of a research study to see how connections and being heard can affect the healing process, especially for elderly patients. Apparently patients need personal interactions, especially during recovery, and these moments can even alleviate physical symptoms. Hearing my mom talk about how sad it was that so many of the people at the hospital never had anyone visit made me excited to help out. I wrote about my experiences for my essay for the National Scholarship too. Patients need to know that people care about them, that someone is listening to what they have to say. For many of them, that someone is me.

Trying to shake off disappointing Kayla, I head through the doors to the ER lobby. Gladys, an older woman with curly white hair that she wears in ringlets close to her scalp, sits behind the counter where new patients fill out their paperwork. She's talking to an older gentleman wearing a fancy navy blue suit standing next to a tall boy who looks like he's around my age. They look like father and son, except the son has dark, chestnut-colored hair and his dad's is more wheat-colored.

While the boy listens to his father, I sneak a peek at him. He's tan, although maybe not so much tan as a natural golden-brown color. He must be mixed. Caucasian dad, Latina mom maybe? I can tell because I'm pretty mixed myself. Filipinos are a little of everything. (I'm Filipino Chinese Hawaiian French.) This guy has deep brown eyes and cut-glass cheekbones, and he's wearing a navy suit with a green tie and brown dress shoes. Although his clothes are perfectly put together, his hair looks like he's been running his hands through it too much. When he smiles at something his father says, I notice a dimple on one cheek. He glances over and catches me staring, and I blush, because he's really cute. My heart rate immediately goes up and I'm lucky I'm not hooked up to a machine right now.

His father shakes Gladys's hand. "Thank you, Mrs. Robertson. I appreciate your help." He walks toward the elevator but the son lingers behind. "Go ahead, Dad. I forgot something."

I say hi to Gladys and she hands me the folder with the list of today's patients who've signed up to be part of the project. The boy is still standing next to me. When Gladys gets up from her chair, she raises an eyebrow in my direction, then makes herself look busy at the filing cabinet.

I can feel him looking at me, but he doesn't say anything, so I finally do. "What did you forget?" I blurt.

"I forgot to get your number," he says, his voice low and rich.

My blush deepens, and when our eyes meet, I feel a spark inside, like I'm all lit up from within. He smiles at me from under his long, floppy bangs. It makes me want to run my own hands through his hair, which looks so thick and glossy and inviting. I've never felt so attracted to anyone before, and I'm a little shocked at how much I want to touch him—a shoulder, an elbow.

Somehow I find myself digging for my phone. I don't know why, but I can't remember my number, let alone my name right now.

Gladys yells from the window. "Jazzy baby!" she calls. "I've got another patient for you!"

I'm mortified, but the boy's smile grows wider. He takes my phone from my hand. I didn't even realize I was holding it.

"Tell you what. Why don't you text me? That way it's up to you. I can tell your mother taught you never to talk to strangers." He punches in his number, takes a quick, goofy selfie to go with his contact info and hands it back to me. His fingers are warm, but dry. My hand feels electric.

I pocket my phone, trying to look as cool as he does. I shrug, as if I could care less.

When he's gone, Gladys comes back to the window with an amused expression and a slip of paper with another name for me. "What did he want? Although I can guess," she teases.

"Who is he?" I ask, ignoring the teasing.

"Congressman Blakely's son. His dad represents our district. They were here visiting a relative."

I take a surreptitious look at my phone, at the mug shot he just took. He's smiling like a doofus. A very handsome doofus who does things like take a girl's phone on a whim. ROYCE BLAKELY, it reads. Royce? What kind of ridiculous name is Royce?

Gladys smirks. "Cute, isn't he?"

I roll my eyes. "He'd be even cuter if he didn't wear a suit. Who wears a suit in LA?"

"Be careful what you say," Gladys says, tapping the counter with a pen. "When you're older, you'll want your man to dress better. Some can get pretty lazy. After enough years together, you could find yourself begging him not to wear sweatpants to the Christmas party. Like I know I'll have to do with Bob again this year."

I laugh and say goodbye to her, then take the elevator up to the floor where they keep the people who have chronic illnesses or have to stay at the hospital for long periods of time. Mom makes friends with a lot of these patients, since she cleans their rooms every day. When she comes home quieter than normal, I know she's lost one of them.

Most of our family still lives in the Philippines, so I understand what it's like to be away from people you love. But at least I know they're still alive. I can't even imagine what I would do if I knew I would never be able to visit them again. It's been a few years since we were back in Manila, and I miss it. I miss my grandparents' huge house in the province, where at any time of day you can find neighbors, friends and relatives gathered at the courtyard tables playing mah-jongg or cards. Their house is like the community center for the village, always open and welcome to all.

I look down at my phone again. His name is Royce. Seriously? Am I supposed to call him that? *Why don't you text me? That way it's up to you*, he said. He's not a stranger. He's a congressman's son. I mean, you're supposed to know your congressman, right? I can be a good citizen.

jasmindls: Hey it's me, I send.

I get a text back immediately.

royceb: jazzy baby?

jasmindls: The one and the same, Rolls Royce.

royceb: original. ☹

jasmindls: Is that your real name or did your parents just really want a car?

royceb: if you must know, I'm named after my uncle who died.

jasmindls: Oh god! Sorry. My bad.

royceb: no, it's mine. my uncle's alive. 😈

jasmindls: 😧 You're evil!!!

royceb: actually he just got in a car accident, that's why we were at the hospital.

royceb: so you have a problem with my name huh?

jasmindls: I dunno I kind of like fancy cars.

royceb: cool. 😎 so should I call you Jazzy for short?

royceb: or do you prefer Baby?

jasmindls: It's Jasmine, thank you very much.

royceb: nice to meet you Jasmine.

jasmindls: U too GTG TTYL, I type as I reach my floor.

royceb: ✌

The nurses are chatting around their workstation as an employee pushes a food cart down the hall past me for the early bird dinners. Usually, I try to snag a Jell-O cup for myself. I'd never admit it, but I actually *like* the hospital food. But this time, I leave it. I was starving earlier, yet for some reason, I'm not hungry anymore. I'm excited and queasy-feeling, and I suspect it may have something to do with the boy who's texting me.

I see my mother rounding the corner in her dark blue scrubs, dragging a bucket full of water and a mop behind her tiny frame.

"Mommy!" I say, skipping toward her. I never call her that except when I want to make her happy. It's sort of a Filipino thing, and right now I'm bursting with news about the scholarship. "Guess what!"

But before I can say anything else she sets down the mop and leans against the handle. "Are you busy?" she asks. "I need you."

I shake my head, disappointed not to have her full attention, and my good mood dampens a bit. She seems stressed. "What's up?" I ask.

"Can you come help me with a mess? You don't have to touch anything. I just need you to make sure no one walks on it."

I nod and follow her. When the pressure becomes too much sometimes, when I feel like I'm about to burst with anxiety over my grades or get mad that I've never had a social life, I think about my mom and what she's sacrificed for us so that we can have a better life. I'm so grateful to her and my dad for everything.

She leads me down the hallway into a large room. There's a nurse bustling about the bed, giving a small, frail woman with white hair a sponge bath. I look down to give her privacy, but the woman complains loudly, "Nothing special to see here, honey. When you're this old, there's no such thing as dignity. Your body falls apart like a junky car, but you still have to have the mechanic take a look at the insides. Funny how young people are so modest when they have no reason to be. If you've got it, flaunt it, I say."

I raise my eyebrow at my mom, who suppresses a smile. This patient is a feisty one, that's for sure.

The nurse quiets her down while my mother begins mopping up urine from the floor. Since I'm not allowed to touch anything hazardous, I squeeze the water out of the mop for her. Even though I've been volunteering at the hospital for a few years, I still don't know how Mom does her job. There's no way I could clean up after people like this all day long. I have mad respect for her. She's stronger than anyone I've ever known. Deep down, I think she knows that about herself too. Mom doesn't suffer fools and she was always the one who told me I could work my way up to the top. She's always believed in me, that I could do anything, be anyone I wanted to be.

By the time we're done, the nurse has left the room and the old lady is starting to talk again, something about meeting Frank Sinatra. She's staring out the window at the tall buildings across the street, so I can't tell whether she's speaking to us or just to herself.

Mom nudges me with her shoulder. "Why don't you interview her for your project?"

I check to see if the hospital room is on the approved list

first, and notice that this patient was the last-minute addition that Gladys just handed to me.

Pushing the mop bucket out the doorway, Mom says, "Meet me at the parking lot at the end of my shift."

I nod and pull up a seat next to the bed. The stories this old lady could tell sound like they'd be interesting, especially as she was describing to the nurse how she met Frank Sinatra backstage and he gave her a kiss on the cheek.

"Hi, I'm Jasmine de los Santos," I say. "I'm here to interview you for the study you signed up for? I'm hoping to compile the stories into a book as well, and plan to share it with everyone at the end of the year."

She gazes intensely at me, and I notice for the first time that her eyes are a milky blue, like the sky behind clouds. "I suppose you want to know my name?" She has a slight accent that's hard to place.

I nod. "That would be helpful to start."

"My full name is Amelia Florence Marsh," she says, in the tone of voice as if she's the queen of England.

"Mrs. Marsh..."

"*Ms.* Marsh, actually, though I suppose that's confusing since Marsh is my married name. I'm a widow."

"I'm sorry," I say, backpedaling.

"No need to be sorry. What do you have people call you when you never divorced but you're also not married anymore? Anyway, I go by Millie with my friends. And we're going to be friends, aren't we? I can always tell."

I smile. "Millie, I couldn't help but overhear your story about meeting Frank Sinatra. Do you want to start there?"

Millie arches one perfectly plucked gray eyebrow. "Sure. I was a young girl then—around fifteen probably."

"So what did he say to you?"

She purses her lips as she looks up to the ceiling like a little kid who's been keeping a big secret for a long time and just can't wait to tell someone, even though she also doesn't want to be in trouble. "He told me I'd be just his type if I was just a little older," she says with a throaty laugh. "Oh, that Frank."

I laugh with her. "Did you meet other famous people?"

"Of course. We lived in Beverly Hills, and it was only natural in my husband's line of work. But I'm not some kind of vulgar name-dropper, if that's what you're thinking, missy. The memory just reminded me of being young again, of having a body that worked for me instead of against me. Being old's terrible."

"Sorry, I didn't mean to offend you," I say, although I like that she's a pistol.

Millie wipes her forehead with the back of her hand. "No, I'm sorry, darling. I'm an awful wretch when I'm sick. I shouldn't have snapped at you. I just don't feel well. At my age, everything stops working. They're supposed to tell me if I have something wrong with my heart, but I think the only thing wrong with it is that it's old."

"I should let you get some rest." I begin to stand, but Millie reaches out and grabs my forearm, pulling me back down.

"Please stay. It would be nice to talk a little more."

I smile at her. She reminds me of my auntie Girlie—scrappy yet gentle. I feel slightly homesick for the Philippines. Even though I wouldn't want to move back there to live, I miss my big family. My grandparents and cousins and aunties and uncles—all of them coming and going through the big house—all that noise and laughter and light.

"So you live in Beverly Hills?" I ask, wondering if maybe Royce is from there too. With a name like that...

Millie adjusts a pillow behind her back, sitting up and settling in for the long haul. "That's right. Should I start there?"

I nod, and Millie begins to unravel her tale. I listen patiently, giving her my full attention, even as I'm eager for the day to end so that I can get home and tell my parents my good news already. They're going to die when they find out about the National Scholarship. I can't wait.

4

I had always hoped that this land might become a safe and agreeable asylum to the virtuous and persecuted part of mankind, to whatever nation they might belong.

—GEORGE WASHINGTON

ON THE WAY back home from the hospital, Mom is quiet and tired. I want to tell her my news, but decide to wait until she and Dad are together. That way it'll be more dramatic and special. So instead of talking about that, I tell her about Millie.

"I'm so glad she signed up for my project," I say. "She was a cool old lady. Did you know she founded her own construction company? She was a building engineer."

Mom nods approvingly. "See, I told you, girls can do anything."

When we get home, I dawdle behind her as she walks up the driveway. Shockingly pink bougainvillea flowers spiral around the trellises and lean against the outside of the house. My mother loves bright flowers. They make her feel more at home in America. She plants them every year: hibiscus, ylang-ylang, azalea, birds of paradise, verbena, scarlet larkspur, night-blooming jasmine. Our house may be small, but Mom makes sure we always have the neighborhood's best garden. It's her pride in life besides her three children.

I walk through the door and kick off my sneakers, exchanging them for a pair of light blue *tsinelas*, comfy slippers to wear around the house. Mom is already in the kitchen talking loudly to Lola Cherry on the phone as she cuts up yellow jackfruit and bananas to make *turon* for dessert. Lola Cherry isn't my grandmother. She's my mother's cousin's aunt, but we call her Lola—grandma—anyway. She's as close to a grandmother as I have in the States. We haven't seen my real Lola since I was thirteen and my brothers were seven and five years old. My brothers don't even remember her that well anymore—they don't remember much about our native country. Danny and Isko can only speak English, and my Tagalog is so atrocious, my mother scolds me for "losing my culture." I hate when she says that kind of thing. As if she wasn't the one who decided to move to America in the first place. I'm not complaining though. If my parents had stayed home, I would never have earned this scholarship. And getting to meet the president? The leader of the free world? Forget it.

I weave around Mom and grab a piece of jackfruit, then bite into its sticky flesh, letting the sweet juice linger on my tongue. She shoos me away from the kitchen, pretending she's annoyed at me. I can't wait to tell everyone my big announcement but decide to hold off until dinner is over so I have everyone's full attention. I want my brothers to hear too. I love them almost like they're my kids and not just my brothers. It's funny. When they were really little, when we first moved to America, my mother's *pinay*—and closest—girlfriends would call me *maliit na ina*—little mother—because I was so protective of the boys.

My brothers and I are very different though. Not only because I'm a girl. It goes deeper. Since I'm the oldest, I've always felt more pressure to be successful. I have to show them the way. And I also have to act like a bridge between them and my parents. Danny and Isko are pretty much 100 percent American. It's as if my parents are first-generation immigrants and they're second generation. But I'm stuck somewhere between both of them, trying to figure out how to help them understand each other.

The sounds of my brothers playing video games in the back of the house float down the hallway. Dad is watching the local news. I kiss him hello on the cheek and sit on the couch to watch with him. The anchor introduces a video clip of a politician from Los Angeles slamming an immigration reform bill that's just been introduced in the Senate.

Suddenly, I recognize the man on-screen from the hospital.

It's Congressman Blakely. Royce's father. He's talking about how a path to citizenship shouldn't be granted to undocumented immigrants at all. If they entered the country illegally, he says, then they don't deserve to be Americans. Oh great, he's one of those politicians who think illegal aliens are as good as criminals, and deserve punishment rather than mercy. I shift in my seat, thinking of Royce, and wonder if he agrees with his father. I sort of hope not.

My family got their green cards when we moved to America, but none of us are American citizens yet. I don't think I can apply to become a citizen until I turn eighteen next year. But the minute I do, you can bet I'm taking the oath. I can't wait to vote.

Dad shakes his head and starts pontificating to the air. "If that congressman had to grow up in a different country, he would understand better why people come here. These politicians know nothing of true hardship."

"Easy *lang*, Dad," I say, meaning *take it easy*. "Don't get too riled up. It's bad for your heart."

He looks up at me and clicks his tongue. "*O-o na.* Have you done your homework yet?"

"I just got home! You know I do my homework after dinner." My parents. I swear, school is all they care about. They never ask about Kayla, or cheer, or my hospital project. It's always, how did you do on your test, did you get an A, did you get all your work done?

Dad turns off the television. "As long as you know your job. You're lucky to not have to get up at five in the morning to do chores, then walk three miles to school or swim half a mile in the monsoon season like I did when I was a boy." This is my Filipino dad's version of the classic American dad tale of "walking home for miles in the snow uphill."

Before I can tease him for repeating the same story over and over again, Mom yells at me, "*Neneng!* Take your shower and tell your brothers to set the table. The adobo's almost ready."

I walk down to my room, toss my backpack onto the ground, and flop onto the bedspread. It's fluffy and off-white with textured fabric in the shapes of flowers. It looks like a bed for a princess without the fussiness. Mom and Dad let me redecorate my room for my birthday present one year. I researched what I wanted for months. Dad complained about how long I took to choose everything, but I think Mom enjoyed the redecorating. She never had her own room in Manila, so I didn't mind letting her give me her opinion on just about everything. Even though there were times when she drove me completely crazy.

No, Mom, I know it's hard to believe, but I don't *want yellow bamboo floor mats to go on top of the carpet.*

Anything we couldn't afford to buy, Mom either made herself or got help from her crafty girlfriends. I decided on a creamy light pink and off-white color scheme with black accents. I hung pictures of my family's last vacation to the Philippines, and shadow boxes with pretty colored-glass bottles inside them on the walls. I keep my sand and rock collection inside the bottles. They're filled with little pieces of places I've been since I was a young girl. There are red lava rocks from Taal Volcano near Manila, where Dad and I fished for giant *maliputo*. In a light pink bottle, there's a clump of regular everyday dirt, the first soil I stepped on in California. The newest one, a turquoise green bottle, holds white sand from Boracay Island.

Dad didn't want to spend the money to go to the fancy beach, one of the most popular in the Philippines, but Mom insisted that all of us go for a few days the last time we were there. I remember her making a big deal about the trip, almost like she thought we would never get the chance to go again.

Then I have a pin board where I write down inspirational quotes I've discovered in books or online. My favorite is the one from President Roosevelt about how we're all descended from immigrants and revolutionaries.

But the most important thing in my room, the thing I could never travel anywhere without, my secret good-luck charm, my talisman, is a small piece of amber-colored glass my grandmother found inside a big balete tree when she was a young girl. She gave me the glass for good luck before I left for America. It was a secret between us, because Mom doesn't like her mother's superstitions. I love the story Dad tells about how Lola Baby demanded that Mom and her entire family travel to Dad's village a whole month before their wedding because she was convinced that couples who are about to get married are prone to accidents, so they shouldn't travel before the wedding.

I hear my brothers shouting, barely muffled by the thin

walls. Rolling off my bed, I get up and walk into the hallway. They're still yelling as I open the door to the room next to mine, which they've shared ever since we moved to California. They're playing *Call of Duty*. The bullets are ripping through the television speakers. It's so loud I can barely hear myself think.

"Danny! Isko!"

They can't hear me, or are pretending not to.

I quietly sneak up behind Isko and pinch his neck.

"Ack! *Ate!*" Isko complains. They both call me "big sister." Mom and Dad do too—it's another Filipino thing.

Not wanting to take his hands off the controller, Isko twists his neck to try to get me to stop while Danny laughs at him. On the screen, I watch Danny shoot Isko—his side of the screen turns red with blood. Isko throws down his controller, whining, "You made him kill me. He always wins anyway."

Isko's only nine years old. He's the baby and the one who takes after Dad. He's skinny and has little chicken arms and legs. Danny and I tease him sometimes, calling him our little runt, but Isko isn't just short. He's short even for a little *pinoy* boy. What he doesn't have in height, Isko definitely makes up for in personality. If he enters or exits a room, you'll always know. He's louder and more dramatic than anybody else, which really means something when you come from a Filipino family.

"Thanks, *Ate*." Danny grabs the controller from Isko. "You should do that more often."

I smile at them with fake sweetness. "You guys need to help Mommy set the table. Dinner is ready."

"I thought it was your turn." Isko pouts.

"I still need a shower. Get going. She's about to start calling for you."

Danny switches off the television and both boys sulk down the hallway, pinching and punching each other, as they head to the kitchen.

Danny's the classic middle child. I know he feels like he can't live up to the same expectations my parents have for me. He's smart, but Dad gets down on him because Danny's always drawing and doodling instead of doing schoolwork. He's really good though. Way better than you would expect. You'd never believe he's only eleven years old by looking at his drawings.

"*Ate!* Go take your shower. I don't want to wait for you to eat my dinner," Dad shouts from down the hallway.

"All right! I'm going, Daddy!"

Heading toward the bathroom, I think about the day our family moved to California. We boarded a big jet plane at the Manila airport. Daddy was worried sick about our belongings not showing up in Los Angeles. It's crazy how much our lives have changed since that day. I don't remember much about life there now, mostly that we were hot all the time, and sweaty, since the Philippines is near the equator. I take my shower, washing off all the sweat from practice, letting the water fall over my face and shoulders, warming my skin, relaxing my muscles. The shower is my sanctuary, the one place I can be alone and think without interruptions.

I think about the National Scholarship, how it means I can most likely go to any college now—and the reception will be the first time I'm away from home and on my own. I've traveled with the cheer team, but we're always together. I imagine Washington, D.C., and the fancy reception and all the people who will be there—diplomats, activists, congressmen and women, scientists, artists, the president and the first lady. I'll be around people who actually run the country, people who influence history and who have the power to make other people's lives better. I hope I'll be one of them someday. I don't really know what I want to do yet—something to do with medicine or law, but I'm still unsure.

I decide I'll tell my parents my good news by showing them the letter and letting it speak for itself. Then I'll ask them to fill out the acceptance form with me tonight, so that I can send my information back as soon as possible.

As I'm brushing my hair, my phone buzzes. It's a text from Royce.

royceb: hey good-looking.

So cheesy! But I'm charmed anyway. I can't help but grin as I text back. I forget about seeing his dad rail against illegal immigrants on TV.

jasmindls: Hey yourself.

royceb: are you around this weekend?

royceb: wanna hang out?

jasmindls: Maybe.

It's not that I'm playing hard to get—I do have a lot of studying to do, and Kayla wants to go to Lo's party, so that doesn't really leave me with a lot of free time. I feel a flutter in my heart at the thought of seeing him again. Weekends are difficult, but maybe there's another way.

royceb: maybe?

royceb: did you google me or something?

royceb: i swear that wasn't me in the angry bird costume scaring the children. 😈

jasmindls: LOL are you sure?

royceb: Okay, okay, that was me. The pigs made me do it. 😈

He's funny, I think as I type back.

jasmindls: **Weekend's tough but I volunteer at the hospital on Mondays and Wednesdays.**

royceb: okayyyy. Not quite what I was hoping.

royceb: But I do hear the hospital cafeteria is delightful. 😕

That makes me giggle out loud.

jasmindls: 😇

Glowing, I head to the kitchen. Everyone is gathered around the stove, spooning rice and adobo into their bowls. I slip the scholarship letter under a book on the counter and grab a bowl of adobo for myself.

Mom notices I filled the bowl only a little. "What? You don't like my cooking?"

Isko perks up. "Don't you know, Ma? Jasmine is on a *diet*," he says. "So she won't get *taba* like you."

"How can such a *little* boy have such a *big* personality?" Mom says, pretending to be annoyed that he called her fat, even if it's an endearment. Filipinos don't think being fat is the worst thing in the world, probably because it's a Third World country where many people are starving.

I pat Isko on the head, which I know he hates more than anything. Isn't that a big sister's job? To drive her little brothers crazy?

Danny doesn't say anything to back me up. He's at the table sketching some kind of magical beast. Dad doesn't even look up from his bowl.

"Mommy, I told you, I have to watch what I eat during

the season. Otherwise they won't be able to throw me up in the air."

"I don't understand you girls and your diets. In the Philippines, I never had to watch what I ate and I stayed skinny as a stick. I guess you think our kind of food will make you fat, but look at the Filipinos you know. We're skinnier than Americans!"

Danny sighs. *"In the Philippines..."*

Mom ignores him. "When I was growing up, all of the children played outside all the time. We made up outside games and ran around our compound and climbed trees. At least Jasmine dances," she says to the boys. "You're always glued to the television."

She always calls cheer "dancing" even though she knows better. I don't think she ever got over the fact that I stopped doing the traditional Filipino dance classes in junior high. But I had to drop something to be able to keep my other extracurricular activities and still get all my homework done.

She walks over to Danny and grabs his sketch pad. *"Tsk.* And *you.* No drawing at the table during dinner. You're as bad as your sister with her phone."

I self-consciously check my pocket, to see if Royce has sent a new text, but he hasn't. The thought of seeing him at the hospital next Monday gives me serious butterflies. I've had crushes before, and I can already tell this is the worst one yet. I'm really into him and I've only known him for, like, five seconds.

Isko stuffs a pork chunk into his mouth. "I like hearing about the Philippines," he says, nudging Dad with his elbow. "Tell us the story about how you and Tito Boy used to fight spiders!"

Dad puts down his empty bowl and leans back in his chair.

He loves telling this story. Tito Boy died a few years ago at his construction job in Manila, so I think talking about him helps Daddy remember his brother.

"Tito Boy and I would stay up all night before spider-hunting season opened. As soon as the first light came up, we hunted for El Tigre spiders in the jungle. They're the best ones. We'd keep them in little boxes, any kind of small container, and let them out to crawl on our hands. Then we'd put them on long sticks, watch them crawl toward each other, knock each other off or fight to the death. We'd yell and scream for our favorite. Mine had only seven legs from a fight it survived. But let me tell you, that spider beat a hundred other spiders before I released it into a tree, retired to a new life. If only we could all escape this life with so few scars."

By the time Dad is done with the story, Mom has brought over the turon for dessert. Danny and Isko swarm over the plate, grabbing two for each of them. Despite the warm sweet smell of burned caramel, I'm too excited about the scholarship to eat any dessert. I can't wait any longer.

"Mommy, Daddy, I want to show you something," I say, standing up and walking over to the book on the counter. I slip the envelope from underneath and hand the letter to my father. I'm grinning ear to ear. I'm so proud of myself, of my parents, of my entire family right now.

I can't wait to hear them cry and scream and cheer when they read it.

I did it! I want to shout. *I did it! I'm a National Scholar! And I couldn't have done it without you!*

5

I take issue with many people's description of people being
illegal immigrants. There aren't any illegal human beings
as far as I'm concerned.

—DENNIS KUCINICH

DAD OPENS THE envelope slowly. Mom leans over his
shoulder. They are completely silent as they read the letter. I
expected my father to jump up from the table and hug me,
and my mother to scream and start calling all my aunties to
brag about me. But neither of them say anything.

In fact, they look like they just received the worst kind of
news instead of the best news ever.

Okay.

Maybe they're so happy they're shocked into silence?

"Isn't it amazing?" I reach over and pull the acceptance
form from the envelope. "Don't worry, I can fill everything
else out myself, but I need a copy of my green card. Mrs.
Garcia will let me use the copier at school, but I have to get
it done soon so they know I'm accepting the scholarship and
going to D.C. for the reception."

They look at each other with concern. I'm so confused by
their silence. Isn't this the moment they've been waiting for
my whole life?

What's going on?

"Danny, Isko. Out! We need to talk to Jasmine alone," Mom says. "Take the *turon* with you."

I feel a chill down the back of my neck. Something must really be wrong. Mom never allows the boys to eat in their room, let alone play games after dinner before their homework is done. I suddenly feel outnumbered. I want to call them back to stay with me.

What is it? Are they worried about the plane fare to D.C.? But the letter says the program will cover all hotel and transportation costs for the weekend trip. Oh, maybe they don't want to allow me to go to D.C. alone? Is that it?

Mom pushes the dishes to the side of the table, not meeting my gaze. "We have something to tell you, *neneng*, and you have to believe us when we say we've always wanted the best for you," she says. "We've tried to do everything right."

Dad just keeps staring at the letter like the words don't make any sense. I thought he would be the proudest of me, of what I've done for our family. With this opportunity, I'll be able to take care of my parents someday. I'll be able to give them the lives they wanted to give me.

"What do you mean?" I ask.

"We should have told you sooner, but we didn't know how," she says.

I sense a glimmer of what my mom is trying to tell me, and I feel a cold shock all over my body. This isn't just about letting me go to another city on my own.

"What are you saying?" I ask. "What do you mean *tried*?"

"I don't like your tone, young lady," Mom says.

"Sorry, Mom, I just don't know what's going on. Aren't you happy for me?" I don't understand why she's reacting this way. Almost as if she's annoyed that I won this scholarship.

She's the one who pushed me so hard—they both did—but the way they're reacting isn't making any sense.

"Are you mad that I didn't make the top-ten list?" The accompanying paperwork mentioned that the top ten scholars were invited to spend the summer interning at the White House. Maybe Mom is disappointed I wasn't one of them? "Nothing will ever be good enough for you," I say, almost on the verge of tears. "It's not fair!"

"You don't know what fair is!" she retorts.

Dad doesn't want any of this. "Stop fighting! Right now." His eyes have tears in them. "Jasmine, it's not about you not making the top ten. This is an amazing achievement. We're incredibly proud of you. You know that."

"Okay," I say.

"But there are things that are out of our control that we haven't told you about, and it's time we were honest with you," he says. His face is grave, and so sad that I can't bear it.

I run through the reasons they might be acting so strangely. Did Dad lose his job? Is he sick? "You're scaring me, Daddy."

"It's not what you think. I'm not sick and neither is your mom."

He knows me so well. "So what's going on, then?" I ask, my breath catching in my throat. Whatever it is, it's bad.

"You can't accept this scholarship. I'm so sorry," he says, putting his hand over mine to comfort me. Mom is about to say something but he hushes her.

"But why not?" I ask, stunned.

"Because you don't have a green card, Jasmine. None of us do. And that means you're not eligible for this award."

"I don't have a green card? I don't understand. Of course I do. We all do, don't we?" It's like my dad is talking nonsense.

He puffs out his cheeks. "When we first moved here, we

had work visas that allowed Mom and me to work for Tito Sonny's export business, remember that?"

I nod. We called him Uncle—*Tito*—even though we're not related. Tito Sonny is a friend of the family who gave my parents jobs working in his discount store, stocking shelves and keeping inventory. He imported Chinese and Filipino items and sold them to the expat community. The items were cheap knickknacks—velvet paintings of Jesus, cheesy 3-D paintings of waterfalls, ceramic Buddhas, that sort of thing.

"But that store closed years ago and Tito Sonny went back to the Philippines," I say, remembering now.

"Exactly. When the store closed, our work visas expired. Tito Sonny thought he would be able to sponsor us for green cards, but he couldn't even sustain the business. We thought it would be easy to find other jobs and new visas, but that hasn't been the case."

I vaguely remember a few years ago when my parents were always tense, right after the store closed. There were a few months when neither of them worked. I thought we were just worried about money back then. I didn't know they were also worried about being able to stay here legally.

"So what does that mean?" I ask, still stunned. "We really don't have green cards?" The news is starting to sink in.

"We never did, just temporary work visas. Right now we don't have any proof of legal residency. That's why we stopped visiting the Philippines. We didn't want to get trapped there. Not after building a new life here. We couldn't take away your home. We didn't think you would have to prove legal status for a college scholarship. We were hoping…"

"So wait. What are you saying? I'm not legal? We're not in America legally? Oh my God."

Dad nods and looks like he's about to cry, which makes me want to cry too.

"But if I'm not legal, how could I go to school all these years? How can any of us go to school?"

"Ma and I didn't choose California only for the palm trees and sunshine. We came here because it's easier on immigrants generally. Schools can't report undocumented students, and they don't do a lot of workplace raids."

"But how do you guys work?"

"We have fake papers. The hospital and the bus company don't sponsor work visas, not for the kind of jobs we do." Unskilled jobs, they mean. Menial jobs.

"What…" I feel tears welling in my eyes. Why didn't they tell me earlier? Did they not trust me? "Please tell me you're joking." I just can't accept this. This can't be the truth.

"No, we're not joking, Jasmine," Dad says. "We thought a college scholarship would solve everything for you, for our kids. We didn't know most of the grants and loans are for citizens or green-card holders."

So that's why the two of them had been sort of muted lately when I kept blabbing on about college and financial aid forms. I'd tried not to think about it too much, assuming they were just busy.

"We never wanted this for you. We're so sorry. But you're a smart girl," Mom says, trying to touch my hand. "You'll find a way, *neneng*."

I pull away. I know they tried their best, but their best isn't enough in this case. This is my future, what I've worked so hard for, and I'm furious. "No! I can't! There isn't any other way if I don't have a green card. Getting this scholarship *was* my way!"

"Stop!" Dad isn't crying anymore. He slams his open hand

against the table. "You should consider yourself lucky. If someone finds out our papers are fake, our entire family could be deported. Your mother's already struggling with her supervisor asking questions at the hospital. If all of us aren't careful, our luck will run out."

Deported? Oh my God. I didn't even think of that. It's not just about not being able to go to college. We might lose our entire life here. The cold that's settled around my body turns to ice. There's no way I can go back to live in the Philippines. I can barely speak Tagalog. My life is here. In America.

I grab the letter away from them and scan the application. "But why can't I accept the scholarship money? We have papers, you said. I'll just use the fake ones. I don't care."

"No, absolutely not," Dad says. "You'd be lying to the government. To the president of the United States."

"I seriously doubt the president will *personally* be looking at my application…"

"It doesn't matter, Jas. We have to be careful. If you get caught, are you going to go back to Manila by yourself?"

"So what was the point of me studying so hard, then? If I'm not eligible for loans or a grant, I won't even be able to go to college. Everything I've worked for is totally wasted." I've given up so much to be the best, to be number one. I've never had any fun outside of school. Sweet sixteen and never been kissed? I'm seventeen now.

Mom looks down at her lap. Her frustration has been replaced by a pained expression. It's a face that I've rarely seen on her. "We were hoping something would come through— the latest immigration reform bill maybe." She puts her head in her hands. "Or maybe you can go to school in the Philippines."

Anger keeps working up inside me until I can't stop the

rush of words coming from my mouth. "No! No way! I don't want to go to the Philippines! It's *your* home. Not mine. You're always talking about taking advantage of opportunities here. But haven't you heard? There aren't any for illegal immigrants."

Rage radiates from my chest near where I'd held the letter so close to my heart. I'm shaking. How could my parents hide this from me for so long? How could they bury their heads and just expect everything to turn out for the best? If they had told me earlier, I could have gotten help. I could have done *something*.

I'm *American*. We're *resourceful*, aren't we?

Mom has started weeping quietly. Dad seems shocked at my yelling. I know I've pushed it too far, but I can't help the words ripping from my tongue.

"Why didn't you tell me?" I yell. "I can't believe you guys kept this from us for so long!" My knees are locked too tight. I feel dizzy. I just talked back to my parents.

"Jasmine!" Dad stands from his chair and reaches to steady me.

It feels like there's no ground beneath me, like everything I've ever done has been a lie. Like Los Angeles has never really been my home. I'm breaking apart, shattering. Who am I? Where do I belong?

I'm not American. I'm not a legal resident. I don't even have a green card.

I'm nothing. Nobody.

Illegal.

6

FRIDAY NIGHT. Our football team lost again, but we cheered them on anyway. We change out of our cheer clothes at Kayla's. She's excited and nervous, bouncing up and down as she curls her lashes and puts on her lipstick. I'm edgy too, but I'm not ready to tell her what my parents told me the other day. I'm too embarrassed, and if I don't tell anyone, maybe it won't be true. To be honest, I just want to forget about it for a night. Just thinking about it makes my head hurt.

Royce and I have been texting a little, and the other day he sent me a friend request on Snapchat and on Facebook. I accepted both. He hasn't posted a new story on Snapchat, so I scroll through his FB feed again, impressed and annoyed at the same time. There are all these photos of him skiing in Mammoth with friends and boating in Newport with his family. When he smiles, his teeth are blindingly white, like an actor in a commercial. He's way too handsome to be any good for anyone. Especially me.

His life looks like a cooler version of a Ralph Lauren ad. I squint at a photo of his mother. She looks like a less bombastic Sofia Vergara.

Is your mom Latina? I text him right then, out of the blue. Because I'm curious and jealous at the same time. Because just a few days ago, I thought I was just like him. Mixed race. Hyphenated American. But *American*.

royceb: My grandfather is Mexican. Mom is Mexican-Italian. Why do you ask? My dad is Norwegian-German by the way. English-Irish too I think. Who knows? Aren't we all just American?

Not me, not anymore, I can't help but think. Annoyed, I don't text him back. What's the point? He's just some cute rich guy I'll never see again. Let's be serious. Guys like that don't date girls like me. They only *hook up* with girls like me, and I'm not about to be anyone's booty call. Not even for someone as cute as him...

Besides, his dad is a congressman who thinks all undocumented immigrants should be deported. Frightening. Another reason to steer clear.

Kayla comes out of the bathroom and sees me holding my phone. "Who's that?" she asks, looking over my shoulder.

"Remember I told you about that cute guy I met at the hospital the other day?"

She perks up. "Yeah. Hey, you should invite him to the party!"

I'd thought of that earlier, when he asked what I was doing this weekend, but decided against it. "No."

"Why not?"

"He lives on the other side of the city all the way in Bel-Air. By the time he gets here, the party will be over." In truth, I was embarrassed about inviting a rich Westside kid over to the Valley. I look at all the photos on his FB page again. It confirms everything I assumed, from the way he dressed to the confident way he'd gotten my number. He's a total player, and I've never even had a boyfriend. Besides, what if he thought the party was lame? That *I* was lame?

"God, Jas, you make it sound like Bel-Air is a different planet," says Kayla with a sniff.

Kayla drives us past Lo's place. Cars are bunched in the driveway and along the curb; kids are milling on the streets. I told my parents I'd be staying the night at Kayla's house. After the blowup at the dinner table on Wednesday, they let me sleep over without asking any questions. I'm glad I'm going to this party and doubly glad my parents have no idea where I am. I'm going to have fun—the kind of fun that I'm never allowed to have.

I deserve to let my hair down. Maybe even meet a boy. (*But I've already met a boy,* I think.) No matter. I'll have fun anyway. Dance a little. Get outside of myself.

"Look at all the cars," Kayla says. "We're going to have a good time. *You're* going to have a good time, right?"

"Sure," I say. "That's why I'm here."

"There's a bag behind my seat. Can you get it for me?"

I reach back for the bag. As I pick it up, I hear bottles clink. I turn to her, trying not to sound accusatory. "I didn't know you were planning to drink."

"It's only a couple of beer bottles. Barely anything. Don't worry. If I drink a little at the beginning, I'll have a chance to sober up before we go home."

I haven't even thought about drinking. My parents would *kill* me if I took even one sip. Filipinos believe "nice girls" don't even think of drinking.

Our house has been quieter than normal since the news. Most of the noise comes from either Danny and Isko shouting at each other about dumb little brother things like who will grow up to be the tallest or smartest. No one has told my brothers anything.

Even though they've figured out I'm fighting with Mom and Dad—which happens like *never*, so they know it's about something serious—I don't have the heart to tell them what it's about. I can't. It seems wrong to worry my brothers when they're still so young. I don't want them to have to live in fear like I am now. I think of those scruffy guys we sometimes see ambling outside the Home Depot, and how we felt bad for them, because they would take any job, do anyone's dirty work—they were illegal and had no choice. Is that who we are now? Is that where I'm going to end up?

Instead of sulking, Mom has gone into full-on detail cleaning mode—like washing the miniblinds and wiping down the doors, which she does to keep herself calm and focused when she's too emotional. When her life feels like it's spiraling out of her grasp, she has to find something to control. That would usually mean telling her kids what to do, but she feels guilty, so now she's spending her energy on cleaning and cooking. We always eat well when she's bothered by something. If the problem is really big, she cooks *bibingka*, my favorite rice cake. The buttery, sugary coconut scent means one of two things. It's either Christmas morning, or Mom's stressed out. Let's just say it's not Christmas and there's a *ton* of bibingka in the house right now.

School's not much better. Everyone's talking about colleges, even the slackers who didn't really care about school until a week or two ago. Now everybody's obsessed with their lists—ranking first, second, third, *seventeenth* choice. I'd always dreamed of going to Stanford, and had planned to apply to a few schools back east as well, although I'm worried that's too far from my family. I was supposed to apply to Cal Berkeley and UCLA too, with UC Santa Barbara as my safety. I'd taken the Regent's Scholarship for granted just a few days ago, but what's the point of applying to the UC system if I don't have any papers? If I'm not a citizen or a green-card holder, I'm not eligible for federal or state grants or loans, which makes the UC schools just as expensive as private colleges and totally out of reach.

Maybe it doesn't matter anymore, because if I'm not legal, I don't even know how long I can stay in this country. Maybe I should just go home right now and cry myself to sleep. Why am I even here at this dumb party?

I'm about to say forget it, let's go back, when Kayla finds a parking spot. "Here," Kayla says. "You can hold my keys."

Walking across the street are two boys from school, Carl Thompson and Alan Chen. "Science geeks?" Kayla whispers. "Shouldn't they be studying at home so they can get into Harvard or wherever they're going?"

"What's wrong with that," I say, bristling and feeling jealous of those guys, who still have their future ahead of them.

Kayla laughs. "We're cheerleaders, Jas. We're *supposed* to have social lives." We're at the house now and she eyes a group of boys hanging out in the front yard. She whispers again. "Isn't that Sam Curry?" She points to our quarterback from last year who graduated.

"You should know. Didn't you date him?" I tease.

"Oh yeah, right." She tosses her hair over her shoulder and laughs.

"Anyway, aren't you here for Dylan?" I remind her.

She giggles. "Just keeping my options open. That dark-haired boy over there with Sam is cute."

I glance across the yard, but I'm not really paying attention. "Whatever," I say.

He's not even half as cute as Royce. Ugh. I should really stop thinking about him. That's not going anywhere.

I want to go inside and sit down with a glass of Vitamin-water and listen to gossip, but it's so crowded that I realize I won't be able to hear anyone talking. "I thought this was supposed to be a kick back?"

"It is," Kayla laughs, turning the door handle. "Let's go find Lo."

"Okay." It occurs to me that when we left for this party, I wanted to try to chill and blow off steam. But now I'm just trying to avoid my feelings. I'm a cheerleader. I like peanut butter and pizza. Nicki Minaj and Miley Cyrus. I grew up on *Gossip Girl* and *Sex and the City* reruns. I believe in life, liberty and the pursuit of happiness. Freedom of speech. Every Olympics, my family gathers around the TV and we join the chant: "USA! USA! USA!" I love my country. I love America. Being American is as much a part of me as breathing.

Except it turns out I'm not American where it counts.

On paper.

Kayla and I enter the living room. A drum kit, amps, and mic stand have been set up in a corner of the living room. The band's name, Bob Marley Lives, is on the kick drum and on a spray-painted banner made from a sheet that hangs on the wall.

Lo sees us right away. "I'm so glad you came, Jas." She turns to Kayla. "Hey," she says. "Drinks are in the kitchen and the garage. Help yourself."

"Thanks," Kayla says. She's already not paying attention, I can tell, and is looking for Dylan. She wanders toward the kitchen.

Lo has already turned around. The bass player is asking her whether or not she has some kind of cable or other. Lo smiles at me as she runs past to go find it. She's so beautiful. Carefree. Focused on music, life and friends. The bassist stands there and sort of smirks and raises his eyebrow like he's sort of just stuck standing there until Lo returns. I smile back.

There are people here that I recognize from school. Veronica Lucas, who was veep when I was class president last year, waves hello. She's now senior class president. Darla Anne Tucker, who's in the California Scholarship Federation with me—the club for kids who have high GPAs—stands next to her. Mark Arias, Billy Ogasu, and Len Anderson, whom I know from Math Club, are all wearing checkered flannel shirts and have round pins on their collars with the band's logo. Normally, I would join one of those groups, but right now all I want to do is melt into a chair, which I do and sit down by myself.

Julian, Lo's boyfriend, is sitting on a couch, tuning a guitar. He has it connected to his iPhone. He runs the pick along each string, making minor adjustments until he's happy. Then he gets up and sets it on a stand and checks the microphone. "Hey! Hey! Check! Mic! One…two… Check. Check. One two!"

People start streaming into the living room and I see Kayla with Dylan. They already look like a couple, giggling and whispering in each other's ear. She drops a half-filled drink in my hand, winks at me, then turns back to him without getting my approval, which I don't know if I would have given or not. He's older than her and I hate to see her sidetracked, because I've seen her lose focus before, when her grades dropped last year. I worry she's burying her feelings about her parents' separation in yet another new guy.

Kayla can be pretty vulnerable when it comes to looking for affection. She teases me that I'm the only girl on the squad who's never made out with a guy, let alone hooked up with one. Guys have been interested, but I've never been that into anyone before. Which makes me think of Royce again, which is annoying.

It's not like my parents let me date either. My mom was a chaperone for her own sister when my auntie Riza was already *twenty-three years old*. It's a wonder anyone gets married in the Philippines. They force you to have a chaperone on dates even when you're an adult, then they ask you why you aren't married yet.

I take a big gulp of the drink Kayla handed me. Some kind of punch-and-whatever concoction. I drink it all and set the cup down. Lo returns with a cable for the bass player. The group of boys who were in the front yard come inside too, and the dark-haired one glances at me as they crowd into the room. There are so many people crowding in that I push myself from the chair and move over to a wall. I look at the boys again. Maybe I should make out with one of them, just because. The dark-haired one is sort of cute.

The music is about to start. Lo takes one of the mics. Kayla is in the front of the room, clapping. Dylan holds a guitar, a sky blue Telecaster. Julian just stands there, and the drummer clicks his sticks together.

"Thanks everyone for coming," Lo says into the mic. She's holding a basket. "Yes, I'm taking advantage of my parents being gone. We need your support for Bob Marley Lives. They're going to play a Greenpeace rally in San Francisco and need some travel money. So pass some cash into this basket I'm sending around!"

I take a few dollar bills from my purse and toss them into the basket. I try not to look at my phone to see if Royce has texted me again, but of course I check. No new texts, probably because I didn't answer his. I sort of wish I'd invited him to the party now.

The music starts, and I listen to a few songs. But I can't relax or escape my thoughts, and so I make my way to Kayla and tell her I want to go home. She downs the last of her drink, shoots a glance at Dylan playing guitar, and sets the bottle down on the bookshelf next to us. "Come on," she says, taking my hand and leading me away from the crowd of partygoers surrounding the band. "We need to talk."

"What? Why?"

She leads me to the upstairs bathroom. On the way up, I watch a group of guys pushing each other out the front door. The party is starting to get louder and louder. People are yelling drunkenly over the band.

Kayla pulls me inside the bathroom, then closes the door, shutting out most of the sound from the party. "What's up with you?"

"Huh?"

She lifts up her hair, trying to cool down her neck. It's stuffy inside the bathroom. "I'm not going to lie. This party is getting a little crazy. But I know you. There's something else going on. You never go to parties, and suddenly, here you are at a party. You like that guy from the hospital, and you're never interested in anyone, so that's a big deal, but then you don't invite him out tonight. And you've been really quiet all day."

My parents warned me not to tell anyone. It's too dangerous. I know I can trust Kayla though, and I start to tell her, but right then, we hear a banging coming from the first floor.

"Ugh," Kayla says. "Hold on a sec." She opens the door and peeks out.

I don't hear music anymore. "What's going on?" I ask.

Kayla comes back in. "Lo turned the lights off. Everyone's quiet. I think the police are here to shut it down," she says.

"The police!" I panic. "What are we going to do?"

Kayla shuts the door. "I don't know. I'll figure out something."

Oh God. Thoughts of police turning my family over to immigration officers all because I went to a dumb party start spiraling through my imagination. If any of us are caught doing something illegal, we could be kicked out of the country. How could I be so stupid as to come to this stupid party?

"I can't get caught by the cops!" I say, panicked.

I don't realize how much I'm raising my voice until Kayla puts her hand over my mouth. "If you don't stop shouting, they're going to hear us." She paces the tiny bathroom floor. We can hear loud knocking from down below. "Okay, I have a plan," she says.

Kayla opens the bathroom door and pulls me into the hallway. I try to go back to the bathroom, but she drags me along. She's taller and stronger than I am, and I can't resist her. "Why are we going out there?"

The knocks are getting louder. "Open up!"

Hiding beside the front door, Lo spots us upstairs and points to the kitchen, gesturing for us to go that way. Kayla pulls at me. "*Come on*, Jas. I don't have time to explain. Do you trust me?"

I'm too scared to run from the police, but I trust Kayla more than anyone. Probably even more than my parents right now. She's been there for everything. The tears after a B minus. The schoolgirl daydreams about our crushes asking us out to winter formals and the prom. Not that I ever got to go, of course. I wasn't allowed. My parents are too protective—they wouldn't even let me go to the junior prom. Kayla went, of course.

Before I have a chance to respond, she pulls me down the stairs. The band's instruments are lying on the floor, which is littered with empty red cups and crushed cans. We pass through the living room to the kitchen, where through the window I spot partygoers hopping over the back fence and fleeing through Lo's side gate.

"Let's get out of here," Kayla says.

"But you can't drive," I whisper. "You've been drinking."

Kayla puts her arm around my shoulders. It's supposed to be calming, but I feel anything but calm. "I had *two* light beers," she says. "I get more buzzed off my grandma's rum cake on Christmas Eve."

"I just want to be safe," I say.

Kayla can tell I won't budge. "Fine," she says, shrugging her shoulders. "If you had your license this wouldn't be a problem…"

"This isn't *my* fault. I didn't call the cops."

She takes her phone out of her purse and taps on the screen. "Are you texting your mom?"

"For real?" Kayla asks. "Of course not."

She extends her forearm, showing me Dylan's number next to a silly smiley face scribbled on her skin. I guess boys are never really as grown-up as they might seem. We start giggling a little, then catch ourselves.

The knocking finally subsides and Lo returns to the kitchen. "Where's Julian? It's not even the cops. Just one of my cranky neighbors. I doubt they'll actually send police out here for a stupid noise complaint."

I exhale. "Oh man, everyone must have assumed…"

"That the cops were here. Yeah, I know," Lo says, finishing my sentence. I expect Lo to get mad that her boyfriend ditched her, but she just looks disappointed. "It's ruined anyway. No one's coming back."

"That's not true," I say, even though she's right, the party's over.

"Thanks for coming, Jas. I'm sorry it went down this way."

I give her a hug. "Thanks, Lo. We can help you clean…"

Lo waves me off. "That's okay. My parents won't be back until the end of the weekend. Do you guys have a ride home?"

Kayla looks down at her phone. "I texted Dylan. He's going to drop us off at my place."

"That was fast," Lo says.

"What's that supposed to mean?" says Kayla.

Lo shrugs.

Kayla frowns.

Sensing tension building between them, I try to end the conversation. "We don't want to keep you up. Let's wait outside, Kayla."

"He's outside anyway," Kayla says.

Lo crosses her arms. "Is Julian with him?"

"How should I know?" Kayla asks, pushing past Lo toward the front door. I give Lo a little wave to say I'm sorry. I don't know what's up between her and Kayla. I didn't think Lo was the territorial type.

As I follow Kayla outside, Dylan pulls up in a beat-up, rusted-out Camaro. "How are you going to get your car back?" I ask her.

"He'll pick us up in the morning. Then I'll take you back home."

"Isn't your mom going to notice the car's gone?"

"Probably not. Since Dad left, Mom doesn't really care

what I do. She doesn't have the same expectations of me that your parents do for you, Jasmine."

"Yes, she does," I tell her. "Stop talking like that." I guess sometimes I am lucky—my parents can be pains about rules and they're way too strict, but at least they've always pushed me to do well.

When we walk up, Dylan gets out and puts his arm around Kayla, leading her to the passenger side. I follow behind them, thinking over what Kayla said about expectations.

Until now, I thought everything I did—the grades, student council, cheer—was because my parents expected me to do it. Watching Kayla flirt with Dylan in the front seat, I realize that's not quite the truth.

I did all those things *for me*. I did them because *I* love them. Because they make me who I am. I *like* studying, I like doing well in school. Academics have always been easy for me, and I like pushing myself and topping everyone else. I'm super competitive and I always have to win. Whether I get to go to D.C. or not, I *am* a National Scholar.

I'm not going to lower my expectations of myself because the law and some politicians say I don't belong. I deserve that scholarship. The United States Department of Education thinks so too.

I'm going to figure out a way to go to Washington, D.C. The president will be expecting me.

7

IT'S A WEEK after Lo's party and I still haven't figured out how to put my plan to storm the Capitol into action. Royce and I have been texting again. He saw pictures of me from the party that Kayla posted on Instagram and tagged me in, and said it looked fun. But he never showed up during either of my volunteer shifts at the hospital, so maybe he was mad I didn't invite him? Who knows. I have other things to worry about right now anyway, but I am disappointed I didn't get to see him.

I haven't really talked to my parents. I guess we're living in détente and denial right now. We're learning about the Cold War in AP European History, which makes me America and my parents the Soviet Union, I guess?

After cheer practice on Wednesday, Kayla drives me to the hospital again. She's a different person since she's met Dylan— bouncy and giddy and girlish. I'm happy for her. He seems all right. I thought he was too cool for school, but he's sweet to her. On Monday he was even nice enough to drive me to the hospital when Kayla couldn't because she had to pick up her brother from after-school care. Now that her dad's moved out, her mom needs more help.

"Did Dylan say anything about me by the way?" she asks. "The other day?"

"He says he's totally in love and wants to marry you," I joke. "I don't know. We didn't really talk about you."

"You didn't!" she squeals. "Why not!"

"All right, we did. He thinks you're a 'cool chick.'"

"He likes me, right?"

"He wouldn't drive your best friend to a hospital if he didn't," I say.

Kayla beams.

I hug her goodbye and go visit my favorite patient. I've known her for only a week and a half, but Millie is already high on my list. She told me the other day that she's an immigrant too. Her family moved from Germany when she was a teenager, which is why she still has a slight accent.

"You look great today. Your cheeks are so rosy," I tell her when I arrive. Sitting down next to her hospital bed, I notice that someone has styled her hair, and I can see the Beverly Hills socialite she used to be.

"You flatter me too much," Millie says. "I was never what they call a great beauty. But I'll tell you, I never lacked attention from handsome men either."

"Was your husband handsome?" I ask, taking out my notebook. "You said he did something in politics. Right?"

"Yes, he worked for the city. And he was very good-looking! I would have never married someone I wasn't completely attracted to—both intellectually and physically."

I think about how handsome Royce is—and funny and smart too—and feel myself beginning to blush, which Millie quickly notices.

"I'm sorry, Jasmine. That's always been a trait of mine. I'm terribly forthcoming. I think my husband loved that about me. My mother always said I never had enough tact."

"My best friend Kayla's like that too, although she's *too* honest about some things. It gets her in trouble."

Millie gestures for me to open the window blinds. "You don't strike me as someone who'd keep her opinions to herself though."

Opening the blinds, I consider what I mean about Kayla's honesty. "I try not to lie. And Kayla lies about stupid teenager things, like where she's going or which boy she happens to be dating that minute, but she's honest about how she feels. I wish I could be more like her in that way." I wish I could tell Millie about my family's situation. I think about it all the time, and the secret is starting to weigh on me.

"You'll learn. In some ways you get braver as you get older. That's why old biddies like me get away with saying whatever they want."

We laugh together.

"We're supposed to be talking about you," I say, sitting back down. "What made you fall in love with your husband?"

"He was a dreamer, I suppose. People tend to think of politicians as pragmatic, doing what's sensible, what's realistic. It's all a myth. Every single one is an idealist. Politicians are more about all kinds of crazy ideas than they are about what actually works."

Does Millie know Royce's dad, I wonder. Would she call him an idealist? I consider asking her, but I try to remind myself of the purpose of the project. This interview is to help Millie heal; it's not for me. She's here due to some heart trouble, and she told me she'd been in and out of the hospital for months now.

"What kind of politician was your husband?" I ask.

"A district attorney."

"How did the two of you meet?"

"He helped us with a permit we needed for one of our buildings," Millie straightens herself in her bed.

"Do you miss your work?" I ask, because she sounded a little wistful.

"A little. My sons run the company now." She leans up in her bed. "Could you help me adjust this pillow? I've had a kink in my back all day." As I shift her pillows behind her, Millie turns to put her hand on my shoulder. "I've had something on my mind lately, Jasmine. May I ask you a question? It's only a little personal."

I nod. "Yes. Of course."

"What's your happiest memory?" Millie asks.

I think for a moment, scanning through my happiest moments. My grandmother giving me the amber glass. Being named cheer captain at the end of last school year. Falling asleep on a mattress on the floor my first night in America, snuggled up to Danny, his little toddler's body warm against me. I was scared, but I was also so excited to begin a new life.

Before I can even answer her, Millie starts up again. "Do you ever sense a little silver sliver of sadness around your happy memories?"

"I'm not sure what you mean..."

"I do. There's something about remembering that just isn't the same as the real thing. No matter how happy it makes you feel. When you remember something, you have to recognize that the moment will never happen again."

Millie looks out the window, her expression pensive, like she's remembering something that happened long ago. "Never mind about that anyway," she says. "I shouldn't bother you with an old woman's regrets. What about you? Tell me about yourself. You're a senior, aren't you? Where are you planning on going to college? Is there a boy you're seeing? Good news? Bad news? Future plans?"

My stomach turns. Only a week ago, I would have been excited about these questions, maybe even telling her about Royce. Things have changed. Boy, have they changed.

"Oh, you don't want to hear about my life," I say. I recall my dad warning me to keep mum on our "problem." But why couldn't I tell Millie? It's not like she would call immigration on us, would she? She's my friend, and so is Kayla.

"Sure I do. I find most people interesting. You just have to dig a little to get to know someone. Come on. What's bothering you?"

I decide to take a chance. I can't keep it bottled up inside anymore, and who knows, maybe Millie can help. She's a dynamo who owned her own company. Maybe she could help me figure out what to do. "I've been invited to go to Washington, D.C.," I say. "But I probably shouldn't."

"What do you mean you shouldn't? Why are you invited there in the first place? You're a little too young for office. You're not secretly planning to take over the world?"

Her words actually make me laugh a little. "It's not that," I say. "I just don't know how I'll get there."

I take a deep breath and tell her about the National Scholarship Award and the president's letter. I tell her how my dreams came true only to be shattered by the discovery that I'm here illegally. "I can't believe it. My parents hid the truth from us, and my brothers still don't know. I don't know what's going to happen now. What am I going to do next year?"

As soon as the words come out of my mouth, I get nervous. Can I really trust her? What does she think of me? Why would an elderly Beverly Hills socialite care about an undocumented Filipino girl like me?

Now I feel silly for even thinking about asking her for advice.

Millie wrinkles her forehead like she's thinking really hard. "But you still want to go to Washington, D.C., for the reception?"

"Yes. But what's the use? They'll just laugh me out of the White House."

"You really think in this day and age, with everything that the presidential administration stands for, that they would just kick you out? A beautiful young girl like you who's so smart, she got accepted for such a high honor in the first place?"

I shake my head. "There are lots of people who live in detention centers until they're deported, told to never come back to America. Mom told me a story about one woman who lived here her whole life but was born in Mexico. They deported her for not paying a traffic ticket. And she doesn't even know Spanish. She got a job working at a telemarketing company because she's a native English speaker, but her life completely changed. She lost all her friends. Her belongings. Everyone she knew. Now she can never come back to America. We can't risk it. *I* can't risk it."

Millie considers this. "I suppose you're right. This is a dangerous time to be an immigrant. Still, being brave, following through, and meeting the highest politicians in the land might not be a bad idea."

"You really think so?"

"I know so. You should get on that plane. You won that award fair and square."

I did. Millie's right. I deserve to go. I worked so hard for it. "Okay." I feel hopeful for the first time in days. I'm going to make this happen.

Millie smiles and holds up her hand. I'm about to slap her a high five when she looks over at the doorway. Concern passes over her face. I turn around in my seat to see Mom standing in the hallway, quietly sobbing.

Oh no! I run to my mom.

"Neneng," she says, barely getting the words out. "We have to go."

I put my arms around her. "Are you hurt? Do I need to call Daddy?"

"I've been fired. We have to leave before they call security."

"Fired?" I say, frozen suddenly. "What happened?"

Mom glances at Millie. "I shouldn't have even said that much. I'm so embarrassed." She wipes mascara streaks from her cheeks.

"Please don't worry, Pilar," Millie says, sitting up in her bed. "You're one of the best staff around here. I don't know what I'd do without you. Is there anything I can do or say to help?"

"No, Ms. Millie. It's already done. Thank you," Mom says. She turns to leave and I'm following her, not knowing what I'm going to say, thinking all of my problems mean nothing in comparison to hers, when Millie calls to me.

Mom stops and looks back. "Jas, say goodbye to Millie— you can't come back either," she says.

"I can't?" I ask, a pit forming in my stomach.

"No."

"But what about the project?"

"They'll find someone else to interview the patients for the study."

I'm stunned. "I really can't come back here?" I guess I could still put the book together. I'd been meaning to gift it to the patients at the end of the year, but how will I get it to them if I can't come back?

Mom shakes her head.

Millie is alarmed. "Oh my goodness, that is terrible news. Keep in touch, will you, Jasmine?" she says, writing her number on a napkin next to her bed. "I want to finish our... *interview.* I feel like we were just getting to the important part of our talk. I'll be out of here next week, but you can always call me. And let me see what I can do. Maybe I can help you and your mother. I've been known to pull a few strings."

"You would do that?" I say, taking her information, not quite believing I've been kicked out of the hospital as well.

"I can't make promises. I'll do my best. Call me, okay?"

In the car, Mom's silence is deafening. She doesn't start the engine. She's no longer crying, but she's shaking like she'll lose it any second. I'm afraid to ask why she was fired, because I think I already know.

I'm scared and numb. Until now, I never worried about my family. We never had much money, but we're better off than most. Happy. My parents love each other. Mom makes Dad a heart-shaped meat loaf every Valentine's Day. I'm not worried there. But lately I keep thinking we'll soon be living somewhere on the outskirts of Manila, and I'll be stuck refereeing seven-legged spider fights between my brothers.

I won't be a student anymore. I'll probably end up working for some resort hotel, or become a waitress or underpaid secretary like many of my cousins. I'll fade away in a country that I don't really understand. Not like America, which is my home, my life. Though I'm also starting to think I don't really understand America either.

"What happened?" I finally ask.

Mom sits for a long time before answering. "They found out I'm a liability."

"A liability?" I say. "What do you mean? Did someone die or get hurt during one of your shifts? You're always so safe, so thorough."

"They found out I don't have documentation," she whispers.

We're still sitting in the parking lot. A woman passes by the car and gives us a concerned look. "How? Why would they even check? You've been working at the hospital for years," I say.

I grip my seat. This is exactly what I was scared of, and now it's happened. *How could my parents be so stupid?*

"My supervisor called me into her office," Mom says, taking a deep, heaving breath. "She told me I'm a good worker but that she can't ignore the paperwork this time. Not in this 'political climate.' Something about one of their big donors asking to make sure all their workers are legal."

It gets worse. It turns out my mom's papers were flagged, and some so-called expert claimed they're forgeries. They told my mother she could be legally deported and the hospital fined for hiring her.

"I'm sorry, Mommy." I hug her, which makes her start crying again.

"I tried to reason with them. I told them this was a mistake, and I could fix it. But they didn't want to hear it. They just wanted me out—but that wasn't the worst, Jas."

I can feel myself getting angrier. How could they humiliate my mother, a woman who works twice as hard as anyone else, for not having the papers they were apparently willing to overlook for years?

Mom continues her story. "'Go get your daughter,' my boss said. 'We don't want two illegals in here.' After all you were doing for them, *neneng*. After you've been working so hard on their project. After all you've done for the patients. I'm so sorry."

I've never felt so ashamed. And now I'm terrified for our entire family.

What happens to illegals in this country?

I'm afraid we're about to find out.

8

YOU KNOW HOW people say "life goes on"? Well, life does go on. I take my midterms, I go to cheer practice, I become a bit of a robot, keep my head down and try not to think about the future and what it will or won't bring. I don't know what to do about the National Scholarship. When Mrs. Garcia sees me in the hallway, she reminds me that I have to turn in the acceptance form so the foundation can make my travel arrangements. I tell her I will soon.

Kayla and Dylan are hot and heavy and I rarely see her outside of practice. Royce and I have sent a few more texts back and forth, and he mentioned he's been busy with school, which is why he wasn't able to visit me at the hospital. But that he *was* there last Monday, and was looking for me but didn't see me. I didn't want to tell him I'm not allowed there anymore—it's too painful. So I lied and told him my project is over and I won't be at the hospital again anytime soon. Which is sort of the truth.

He sends me a Snapchat of himself falling off a kiddie

scooter, to show that he's bummed about that, but I don't send him one back.

It's like Kayla said—I do sort of believe he lives on another planet. One with no problems.

I did well on my midterms, except for an uncharacteristic B+ in AP Calculus. Don't know if it was because I was stressed, or an honest mistake on the equation. Dad doesn't make his usual joke about B's being Asian F's. No one thinks anything is funny in my house lately. In European History, Kissinger has just convinced Brezhnev to attend the SALT talks, and the Cold War is thawing.

I wish it would at home too. Mom hasn't worked for three weeks now. It's eating at her. She's spending a huge amount of time reading the news online, watching TV shows, calling all kinds of people about our situation. Lawyers too, even though it's clear we can't afford any of them.

Dad's home for dinner for the first time all week. He picked up some extra hours driving buses on the evening shift, since Mom isn't working anymore. I used to complain that we *had* to eat at the table, but now I realize how much I miss having everyone gathered together, talking and laughing and stuffing our faces with Mom's food.

Mom and I made Dad's favorite dinner—a whole fried chicken and *pancit* with minced green onions, shredded cabbage, carrots, pork tenderloin, peeled shrimp, and soy sauce, working silently beside each other to prepare it. Even though I'm watching my weight, I heap a second helping onto my plate.

"It's nice to see my family for a change," Dad says. He squints, peering at Danny and Isko. "It's awfully quiet at this dinner table. You boys must be up to some mischief. I know you too well."

Isko giggles and Danny kicks him under the table. "We're not up to anything," Danny says. "Huh, Isko?"

"Nuh-uh. Not us," Isko says. "We're not up to no good."

Cutting off a piece of fried chicken, I correct him. "You mean you're not up to any good."

"Yeah!" Isko says. "That's what I mean."

"Dumb little brother. She's tricking you," Danny says. He stands up, takes his plate to the sink, and returns to the table. "Can I be excused?"

Not looking up from his plate, Dad tells him to sit down. "Spend some time with your family. You act more like a teenager than your sister."

"Leave him alone," Mom says. "You don't have to compare them."

"I just want to spend some time with my children. Is that so terrible? I wanted to spend every minute with my father when I was Danny's age. When he came home from harvesting sugarcane, I would pull his boots off his feet. It was an honor to take off his shoes. And now I can't even get my boys to eat dinner with their family for more than fifteen minutes."

"Okay. So does that mean I have to stay?" Danny asks.

"Sit down," Dad says.

Danny sulks over to his seat and plops down on the chair. From under his butt comes the sound of a long, gassy explosion. *Pfffffffft!*

Danny jumps up. "Aw! Man!"

Isko doubles over, laughing so hard he's gasping for air.

Danny picks up the whoopee cushion from his seat. He throws it at Isko but misses. It lands on top of the pancit. Dad's face turns red.

At first we think Dad is going to yell but then both Mom and I try to stifle our giggling, and soon we can barely keep the laughter back. It's the thing that cracks the Cold War, and Dad laughs too. It's then that I realize nothing has changed, really. We're still our family. We're still here in America. At least for now.

"It's not my fault that Danny's a stinkatron," Isko says.

Danny fights back. "You're the gas master!"

"Stink-a-zilla!"

"Fartzilla!"

"Hey, Isko. You know what they call King Kong's little brother?"

Isko, shaking his head, smiles mischievously.

"King Krap!"

"Okay! Enough! Out!" Dad yells, shooing them away from the table. "Water your mother's garden. Then you go to your room and finish your homework."

Danny starts to complain that there's an art project he wants to finish, but Dad won't accept any arguing.

I take the dishes to the sink and begin rinsing them while Mom and Dad sit at the table talking. It's mostly small talk at first. After a few minutes, though, I can hear them arguing with each other even over the running water. "This isn't the end," Dad says. "There are plenty of undocumented workers in this city. You don't even need papers. Work under the table."

"I liked working at the hospital." Mom pouts. "Cleaning houses or offices isn't going to pay enough. And there won't be any benefits."

I put the dishes in the dishwasher loudly, letting them know I can hear everything they're saying, but Mom doesn't lower her voice.

"I have to work a job that pays at least as much as the hospital. Or else we'll lose the house. We have two boys who will soon be eating everything in sight. How will I keep up with them?"

When I had asked them earlier how they bought the house in the first place, they said anyone can buy real estate in America if you don't need a loan. Tito Sonny had loaned them money to buy the house and over the years they had been able to pay him back.

I finish the dishes and sit back down at the table. I hate hearing my parents argue about money, but I want to be part of the conversation. I don't want them to hide anything from me anymore.

"I could start working," I say. "I'll give up cheer and get a job." If they can work with fake papers, so can I.

"No, Jasmine," Dad says. "You have to focus on school."

But why? I think. Why focus on school if we can't afford to send me to college anyway? Not without a scholarship, and we all know I can't get one if I'm not a citizen or a legal resident. All the federal and state aid grants require a social security number and proof of legal residency or citizenship—of which I have neither.

I'm going to miss the UC application deadline that's coming up, but I can't worry about college right now. With my mom out of work, I have to do something. I can't let them lose the house. I can't let my little brothers suffer. I've been so selfish this whole time, thinking about only my own dreams and fears. In cheer you can't let one person take on the weight of the whole team. It's the same with family. Everyone needs to support each other.

"Why not?" I ask. "I can do it."

"Absolutely not," Mom says. She reaches across the table and grabs my hands. "You need to keep your focus on school.

There must be scholarships or grants other than government ones. Maybe we can take out a private loan or something."

She's in denial, I think.

"We'll figure it out. You deserve to go," she tells me.

"And you deserve better than cleaning up other people's messes, Mom," I say. "You could get a different kind of job."

Dad scoffs. "That's not going to happen without citizenship. Or at least another set of fake papers."

"I'm tired of lying," Mom says. "We need to do things the right way."

Mom tells us that she's found several lawyers who help undocumented people, but they're all shady. "It's a scam. They want too much money. Isn't there an alliance out there of lawyers who want to help people like us who are already here and have been for years?"

"Better to leave it alone," Dad says. "Fly under the radar. These issues are debated on the news every day. Politicians never solve the problems. They just talk. Worrying about it isn't going to fix anything."

"What if your boss finds out you're illegal?" Mom asks. "How do you know my supervisor won't call your boss? How do you know they won't send someone to the house? Is that how you want to live? Just waiting for the hammer to fall?"

"There's no hammer," Dad says. "We just got unlucky. Thousands of undocumented workers live in Los Angeles. What are they going to do? Deport all of us? Take a month off. You need the break."

"No," Mom says. "We need the money. I'll get another job. I've done it before. I can do it again. It just might take time to find the right one."

Despite our arguments, I love how my mother can be so

tough. She may have a little breakdown, but then she's back up on her feet, fighting for herself again.

I'm a fighter too.

I go back to my room and turn on my computer. With a start, I realize that tomorrow is the last day to turn in the acceptance form for the National Scholarship, as the awards dinner is next weekend in D.C.! I have to go. I earned it, like Millie said. But how? I can't fake a social security number. Maybe I'll just say I need more time to turn in the acceptance form, but that I still want to go to the reception? If giving them the wrong information on the form is too risky, at least I'll still be able to meet the president.

I pull the award letter out of my jewelry box. There's a contact email at the top. *Suzanne Roberts*. Liaison for the United States Department of Education.

I immediately type out an email apologizing for being so late and wondering if I can still attend the dinner. Can they schedule a last-minute flight for me? Am I too late? Did I miss the greatest opportunity I've had in my whole life?

Send.

"Jasmine!" Dad yells. "You left your backpack in the middle of the living room! I could have tripped over the damn thing!"

I go back to get it. Dad has just kicked Isko off the television and changed the channel to MSNBC, when it's suddenly announced that a new immigration reform bill could give millions of undocumented workers legal status. This is the bill my parents were talking about earlier.

Dad's excited and turns up the volume loud so we can all hear.

"Pilar! Come here!" Dad shouts.

"Why are you turning that up?" Danny asks. "The news is so boring."

Dad ignores him, and the boys run out to play video games as Mom comes into the room.

The TV news anchor has a large forehead. His foundation has been heavily applied and his eyes are bulging from his head, probably due to those crazy clips they use under their hair to stretch the skin smooth (I've seen YouTube tutorials, natch). He looks like a pale pink fish. "Possible good news for undocumented workers in the US," he says in his dull pseudoexcited voice. "Our political analyst Jessica Hart has the full report in our special segment 'Immigration in America,' brought to you by Carl's Jr. and Watson Worldwide Construction."

Jessica wears a starchy bright yellow dress. All I can focus on are her blindingly white teeth as she greets the news anchor.

"Wasn't she the weather girl last week?" Dad says. "How can she be a political analyst?"

"Be quiet," Mom says.

Jessica stares into the camera. Her face is suddenly serious. "Immigration Reform Bill No. 555 passed the Senate last week, which means there's only one hurdle left, and that's a rather big one in the climate of the current House of Representatives."

The screen shows Latino field workers and housekeepers.

"Why do the news stations always show Latinos?" Dad complains. "There are a lot of immigrants in this country. Filipinos, Burmese, Turkish, Nigerian, Iranians, Chinese, Ethiopians..."

"Dad!" I say. "I can't hear."

He throws his hands up. He can never win when Mom and I are around.

Jessica is still talking. "The bill, according to Washington analysts, includes tightening border security on high-risk rural areas where drugs and undocumented aliens are routinely smuggled…"

"The same old story," Dad says. "It's not my fault this country is addicted to drugs! You can't blame me for that. Even the radio reported that immigrants were the least likely group of people to commit a crime." He starts shouting at the TV. "Check the facts!"

Mom elbows him.

Jessica continues reading from the teleprompter scrolling the words for her. "Section 2011b establishes registered provisional immigrant status, granted to eligible aliens who apply within the application period and pay the fee, including any application penalty fees, both of which may exceed $500…"

She's still talking when I hear a beep go off on my phone, signaling that I've gotten an email. When I see who it's from, I raise my eyebrows. Suzanne must work late, because I've never gotten a response that fast. I open the email, preparing myself for bad news since her answer is so short.

Ms. de los Santos—
We're so happy to hear from you! I'm ready to book your flight from LAX to Dulles. Please send me your information so I can do so. And there's plenty of time before the grant forms are due. I can answer any questions you have about it either over email or in person when you arrive. Looking forward to meeting you.
Suzanne Roberts
Department of Education Liaison
P.S. Remember to pack warmly! It's starting to get chilly here in D.C.

I'm barely listening when Dad begins making sarcastic comments about extraterrestrials. "Aliens, huh?" he says. "You think those guys who crash landed in Roswell could afford that fine?"

Mom and I both shake our heads. Now Dad just wants to show off.

"To be eligible," Jessica says, "aliens must have been physically present in the United States since January 1, 2012, except for certain limited absences."

"Thank God," Mom says, sighing. "There's hope for us."

"This is good?" Dad asks. Though he's usually the positive one, he seems unconvinced. "We've been here long enough, but we'll probably go bankrupt just applying to stay here."

"There are also criminal grounds for ineligibility," Jessica adds, "including felony, multiple misdemeanors, and other crimes. Aliens must pass background checks and be financially sustainable above the federal poverty level."

"You see?" Dad complains. "They'll make us go bankrupt, then kick us out anyway."

"Stop it," Mom says. "This is good news!"

This is great news. I'm smiling, actually. For the first time in weeks, I feel like there's a real way out. This means something, even more than the trip to D.C. The bill is a ray of hope. If it passes and becomes law, we can apply for green cards, and once we get those, after five years, we can apply for citizenship as well.

"I have some more good news," I blurt.

"About what?" Mom asks.

"I'm going to Washington, D.C., next weekend for the National Scholarship Award."

I realize that for once I didn't even think about asking for permission.

Dad turns down the volume on the television. "Excuse me? And just how do you think you'll do that? You don't have a social security number."

"I didn't say I was going to fill out the grant acceptance form," I say. "But they don't need documentation for the recognition dinner and weekend activities. I can go to those at least. I'll just have to figure out the rest later."

"I don't know," Dad says doubtfully. "How will you get on an airplane?"

To my surprise, Mom backs me up instead of supporting Dad. "You stop worrying," she says, touching him on the shoulder. "She's right. She should be able to go to D.C. Be happy for your daughter! Besides, I still have our passports from the Philippines. Jasmine can use that for identification. She doesn't have to tell anyone about her status."

I smile. Dad will always go along with Mom's approval. Now I just have to figure out what to wear to the fancy dinner.

"Just think," I say, buoyed by the thought of actually being able to go on the trip, "once that bill passes the House, I can go wherever I want without having to worry. I'll legally be in the US. We'll all be."

Please, God, let it happen.

9

When I discover who I am, I'll be free.

—RALPH ELLISON, *INVISIBLE MAN*

THE NEXT DAY, I stop by the college counseling office to tell Mrs. Garcia I'm leaving for the National Scholarship reception on Thursday. "That's wonderful, Jasmine, have a good time. Like I told you before, I'm so proud of you," she says with a huge smile. "But I have to tell you… A couple of your teachers mentioned that you haven't seemed like yourself the last few weeks," she says. "What's going on?"

"I guess I've been kind of busy," I say, hesitant to reveal anything more.

Honestly, I'm upset to hear that. I've never had teachers complain about my performance. Apart from the B+ in Calc, I'm still pulling the usual A's. Although I have been a little quiet in class, not raising my hand or offering my opinion on things, and I guess they've noticed. It's not that I'm disengaged, it's that I'm consumed with finding a way out of my family's mess.

Every spare moment I'm not at school, I'm online, trying to determine how we can fix the situation we're in, how illegal aliens can become legal in this country. If the new reform bill doesn't pass, the news is terrifyingly grim on that front. My family is breaking the law, and apart from leaving and trying to come back under proper work visas, there's not much we can do. In my parents' minds, they weren't doing anything wrong but were trying to do the best for their children, to give them a new, American start in life. Do I blame them for that? I don't know.

I can understand the other side too—that Americans who were born here, or were born to American parents, don't think we deserve to be here. I get it. But it doesn't make it any easier. I thought we were here legally, and to think that we're as good as criminals in the eyes of the law...it's stomach-churning. I feel so helpless.

But I can't share any of that with my college counselor. "Regionals are coming up soon," I tell Mrs. Garcia. "And we really want to win Nationals this year."

"Of course, and senior year is a lot of pressure too," Mrs. Garcia says. She's across from me, and she reaches for my hand. "You know I'm here for you," she says, giving me a squeeze. "Are you sure that isn't all it is? You seem worried about something."

"Uh..." I'm so overwhelmed I don't even know where to begin. I thought this was going to be a happy moment, telling her about going to Washington, D.C., but now all of the stress of the last few weeks is bubbling up again.

I live in fear that the tiniest little thing—like going to a party and getting caught drinking underage—could get my family in trouble. What if I get caught jaywalking? Littering? I suddenly wonder about Mrs. Garcia. Is she an immigrant? Are her parents, or grandparents? Does she have to deal with people thinking she doesn't belong here too? But everyone in America is from somewhere else, right?

So maybe we're all aliens, like Dad was joking about during the news. He says if we were from the great beyond, we would have fewer problems because everyone would at least want our technology. Mom, of course, says that even space aliens would have trouble finding jobs in America.

"I'm sorry, Jasmine. I didn't tell you about your teachers to stress you out more. That wasn't my intention at all," she says, leaning forward in her chair. "How's everything else going? Did you turn in your UC app?"

"Not yet," I say.

"Well, don't delay, the deadline's coming up and the sooner you apply, the better your chances."

"I know, I know."

"I know you'll get it done," she says. "And remember, if it becomes too much for you to handle, there are people who care about you. You don't always have to rely on yourself. There's an entire community here for you."

"Thanks, Mrs. Garcia, but I'm okay."

Mrs. Garcia squeezes my hand again. "You know where to come if you want to talk."

"I do," I say, thanking her.

Dad said schools are safe zones for illegal immigrants, but I'm not ready to tell her about my status. Not yet.

After school, I tell Coach Davis I have to go to D.C. to accept my award while the girls warm up. She's excited for me, though she knows this is a minor bump for the team.

"It's a difficult weekend to miss," she says. "We've got a football game and pre-Regionals this weekend. We have a real shot at Nationals this year, but it's up to you girls to get us there."

"I know—I'm sorry. I'll put in extra time in workouts and practices when I come back."

"I know. But I need someone to lead the practices while

you're gone. And I'll have to pull up a flyer from the JV team to take your spot. I'll ask Courtney to be interim team captain when you're in D.C.," she says.

I get that she has to name a captain while I'm away because the team needs one. But I'm surprised that she's chosen Courtney, a junior, to lead in my place.

"Why not Kayla?" I ask. "She's got seniority. She puts in the time…"

"I don't think that's a good idea," Coach Davis says.

"She'll be disappointed," I add.

"Too bad," Coach says. "Kayla hasn't been on point lately and she's even missed a few practices. The other girls won't look up to her like they do you. What's going on with her? Do you know?"

"Yeah," I say. "Her parents split up." *And she's got a new boyfriend*, but I don't mention that.

Coach nods. "That's rough. I hope you're there for her."

"I am," I say. Even though I haven't seen her outside of school lately. She's always with Dylan, but I know I'm just using that as an excuse. I've been avoiding her too. I want to tell her what's going on with me, but I'm embarrassed. Of the two of us, I've always been the one who had her life together—the tighter family, the better grades. I can't tell her I'm a mess, that it's all a big lie. I have too much pride.

I don't agree with Coach's choice for captain. I think more responsibility might help pull Kayla back toward the team. Everyone likes her. They'll listen to her, but Coach won't change her mind. I hope Kayla doesn't take the news too hard.

After Coach tells the team about my award and how I'll be heading to D.C., all the girls come up to congratulate me and give me hugs.

"Don't forget us when you're rich and famous," says Deandra.

"The little people," agrees Emily.

Courtney, who's almost six feet tall, laughs at that. The others beam—everyone's so happy for me.

"I'd never forget you guys!" I tell them. "Otherwise you'll throw me off the pyramid and won't catch me!"

"Girl, you got that right," they say and laugh.

They're all here, except for Kayla. She doesn't come up to hug me or congratulate me. And that's how I know she's mad.

After practice, I wait for Kayla to change out of her cheer clothes. Walking out of the bathroom stall, she brushes by me and opens her backpack on the locker room bench.

"Why didn't you tell me about the scholarship?" She doesn't look up from the floor. "I have to find out with everyone else?"

Right. I never told her about it. I'd meant to, but then with everything that happened, it just slipped my mind. I feel my cheeks burn. "I don't know. The day I heard the news, I wanted to tell my family first, and then I sort of forgot…"

"But if you're going to D.C. this weekend, haven't you known for, like, almost a month already? Did you think I'd be jealous or something? That's messed up."

I walk over to her and sit down on the bench next to her backpack. "No, it's not that. I'm sorry. Things have been weird. At home, I mean. I didn't even know I was going to D.C. until a couple days ago."

Finished stuffing clothes inside her backpack, Kayla zips up the sides. "Things are weird at home for you? At least your parents don't hate each other."

I gently grab her arm, turning her toward me. "There's a lot going on that I haven't told you about. First of all, my mom lost her job at the hospital."

Her eyes widen. "Oh my God, Jas, I'm so sorry. Is she okay? Why didn't you tell me?"

"I was embarrassed. I know I shouldn't be, but I just… Ugh. And I'm so sorry I haven't been there for you as much as I should have been. I told myself you were busy with Dylan and you didn't need me. But I'm here now. Tell me what's going on with you too."

Kayla sighs. Tears are building up in her eyes. "I just thought you didn't care. You've been totally MIA for the last few weeks. Things have gotten so bad at home. Dad's gone, and Mom spends as much time out of the house as possible. And I'm stuck watching Brian on the weekends. I hate everything. I just want my life to go back to normal."

I feel the same way, but I don't say anything. Instead, I hug Kayla until she's done crying. Then I go to one of the stalls to get a wad of toilet paper so she can wipe her eyes and blow her nose.

"How's Dylan?" I ask. Talking about boys always makes Kayla feel better. She instantly lights up.

"He's good." She sniffles. "I really like him. He's not like any other guy I've dated. He's really chill and easy to hang out with. I just…feel like I can totally be myself around him."

"That's amazing," I say, feeling wistful. It's not as if Royce and I have been in contact lately. We sort of lost the thread— okay, fine, I dropped it. I'll probably never see him again.

"What are you going to do on your trip?" Kayla asks.

"There's a tour of the Capitol, and there's this fancy reception for the National Scholars. And I'm supposed to meet the president, I guess."

"The *president*?" She wipes her nose, then throws the tissue away. "Wow, Jas, that's huge. How fancy is this dinner? What are you going to wear?"

"I don't know. I haven't thought about that yet."

Kayla pulls me up from the bench. "We have to get out of here," she says. "We're going shopping!"

By Wednesday afternoon, I've got my bags completely packed. I stuffed a little blue glass bottle inside my suitcase so I can scoop up some dirt from the capital to add to my collection.

We're on the way to the airport. My brothers stayed home with one of Mom's friends. Dad and Lola Cherry are along for the ride. Lola Cherry is in her seventies, wearing large Jackie O glasses, and has the demeanor of someone who was quite the looker in her youth. She dyes her hair black and wears bright red lipstick, but like the typical Filipino matron, lives in comfortable housedresses and flip-flops.

I've been sort of dreading this moment when I leave them. It's the first time I'll be on my own anywhere, and I know how Mom can be. She's worried and talking a hundred miles an hour. "You need to be careful out there. Washington, D.C., is filled with strange old men. You keep them away from you. Button up your blouse. And no makeup."

"A chaperone is picking me up at the airport," I say, nibbling my nails. "You're overreacting."

"I don't know this chaperone," Mom says.

"Me either," Dad says. "He could be a space alien for all I know."

"Daddy," I say. "Just stop. You're being silly. And it's a girl."

Lola Cherry sits in the backseat, snickering. "If you were smart, Jasmine, you would take me along," she says.

"Why? So you can flirt with all the old congressmen?" Dad says.

Lola clicks her tongue. "I don't flirt," she says. "I don't

have to say a thing. They'll come to me because of my beauty. They'll take me to dinner on the town. I want to see this Washington, D.C., nightlife."

I laugh. I should probably take Lola Cherry—she'd probably have more fun than me.

"Lola Cherry!" Mom says. "You're not helping. These people have no scruples."

"I know," Lola says, winking at me.

I grin back.

"Ay," Mom says. "I knew we shouldn't have let you come with us."

"So you can keep torturing your daughter on your own?"

"I'm not torturing her," Mom says. "She needs to hear these things."

"Mom," I say. "I'll be *fine*. It's perfectly safe. This is a huge award. There's a ton of security. Nothing will happen to me! Quit worrying. And you know what? That reform bill is going to pass the House. I can feel it. Everything will be okay." My heart begins to beat faster, as I think about everything that's at stake.

"That bill better pass," Dad says. "Or the UFO is going to pick us up and take us away."

"Dad, quit with the space alien jokes," I sigh.

"Don't tell me you're getting tired of them already."

Mom joins in. "We're all getting tired of them."

Finally, Dad pulls up to the drop-off area at the airport. We say our goodbyes and Mom actually cries, which makes me cry too. Lola gives me a hug and tells me to put in a good word to any congressmen or senators who look like movie stars.

"If any look like Elvis, get their phone number for me," she says.

I hug her tightly. I love my crazy family. I wish my brothers were here. "I love you so much," I tell Lola.

Mom complains right away. "What about me?"

"Stop," I say, kissing her cheek. "You know how much I love you. We're practically the same person. I'm going to be fine. I'm going to meet the president of the United States." I kiss Dad goodbye too.

Lola's eyes brighten. "You didn't say you were going to meet the president! He's the best-looking of all!"

"I told all of you," I growl. "You just don't listen! I'm going to be late for the plane. I love you!" I add, and run off into the terminal and to the security checkpoint.

10

There was nothing but land; not a country at all, but the
material out of which countries are made.

—WILLA CATHER, *MY ÁNTONIA*

"MS. DE LOS SANTOS?" asks a young African American
woman with straightened hair cut in a cute bob outside the
terminal at Dulles International Airport. She's holding a sign
with my name on it.

"That's me," I say, with a big smile.

"Suzanne Roberts," she says, shaking my hand. "National
Scholarship Recognition Program Hostess and Department
of Education Liaison. Right this way. You'll be meeting some
of the other students shortly."

For being so young, Suzanne is all business. Her skirt and
coat are a deep royal blue and her blouse is white. She's perfectly put together. Not a wrinkle anywhere on her clothes
or a hair out of place. There's an insignia on her uniform for
the program that looks like a blend with the presidential seal.
I note the way she holds herself. The way she walks. She talks
as if she graduated from some etiquette school in Switzerland where they teach you how to carry yourself with poise.
She has a constant smile that seems real and not polished at
all. She's instantly likable. I want to be like her someday and
tell her so.

"You're sweet, thanks. I hear your essay and self-assessment was a particularly great read for the committee. Congratulations."

"Thanks so much—it's so nice to hear that. Are you on the selection committee?" I ask as we walk through the terminal.

Suzanne smiles. "No, those are all highly regarded scholars in the fields of education, law, medicine, the advanced arts, and other areas. Maybe one day. I was a previous scholarship recipient. I'm a congressional aide and for now, I'm just happy to assist the program's candidates during their time here in Washington, D.C."

"Cool," I say, because it is. I can't wait to meet everyone, to start making connections, to start being part of this great network that runs our country. For a moment, I feel like myself again, the person I was before I discovered the truth about our status.

I'm sitting in the backseat with two other students while Suzanne drives a black sedan toward the Ritz-Carlton on Twenty-second Street.

"This is Richard Morales," Suzanne says, nodding toward the tall boy sitting in the front seat who has such large shoulders, he barely fits inside the car. "He's from Arizona. And an incredible jazz musician, I hear."

"What instruments do you play?" I ask.

Richard cranes his neck around to look at me. "A little of everything, I guess. But my favorite is the saxophone." He curls his fingers and begins playing invisible notes. He's already totally lost in his own imaginary world of music.

The other boy sitting next to me extends his hand, which I shake. His pale fingers are bony and long. "I'm Simon Se-bastian," he says in a nasally voice. "Did you know the Martin Luther King, Jr. Memorial was made in *China*? And that the FDR Memorial has a statue of his *dog*?"

"No," I say. "You know a lot about Washington, D.C...."

While Simon continues to rattle off random trivia, I peer out the window for a glimpse of anything recognizable. I have the window rolled down a little so I can see better, and I'm shocked by how much colder the fall weather is here. Wrapping my coat tighter around me, I imagine myself walking across the campus of George Washington University or Georgetown, watching the auburn leaves falling off the branches of the old trees. I could belong here.

The buildings are so stately and old-fashioned. I've seen all the buildings on television before, of course, but I'm amazed by their size and significance upon seeing them in in real life. But when we finally see the Capitol dome, lit up like an earthly moon, I feel a pang, like it's not for me. I want so badly to feel like part of this country. It's the only home I know.

The Ritz-Carlton is a collection of dark buildings and many windows. It feels like a beautiful fortress. The ceilings are tall and lovely inside the hotel. I want to just sit in a chair and take it all in, stare at everything and everyone. Instead, I follow Suzanne to check-in, where we are each given a room. I'm sharing mine with a few girls, but they've already been there all day. Suzanne tells us to hurry. We're the last group of arrivals.

She hands each of us a small folder, "This is your itinerary. Inside you'll find where you're supposed to be. I will be your guide through most of your stay here. The first Honoree Reception is in about two hours. Get some rest and meet me in the lobby at five, and we'll walk to the main ballroom together."

I'm relieved to hear that Suzanne will be with us the entire way. It makes me feel secure as I find my way to my
room, which is just as elegant as I hoped. They've given
us a two-bedroom suite with heavy floral couches and tables that shine like someone has recently polished them. In
vases set next to each bed there are bouquets of white roses,
which fill the room with a flowery scent that reminds me
of Mom's garden.

I toss my suitcase to the side and plop down on a bed in the
room that doesn't have clothes and jewelry strewn all over the
place. It's a dream, really, and the nicest hotel room I've ever
been in. If this is a taste of my future, I want it.

I text Mom.

**I'm here and in my room. Going to a reception in a couple
hours. I have a chaperone named Suzanne. She's smart
and nice. Love you. Talk soon.**

No reply; she must be busy.

I hear my roommates enter, but they all disappear into the
other bedroom without saying hello. It sounds like they all
know each other, and probably no one wants to room with
the new girl. Fine, more room for me.

After showering, putting on my makeup and brushing out
my long hair, I open my suitcase on one of the beds, unzip-
ping the sides carefully to not catch any of my clothing. On
top lies the dress I bought when I went shopping with Kayla.
I put it on and fluff out the wrinkles. It's as bright as a yellow
gumamela flower, with an open back and a braid that twists
over my shoulders and down to the bottom of the dress's
flowing fabric. I'm dark for a Filipino, nut-brown like my
dad, and the color pops against my skin. From my suitcase,
I take the amber glass my Lola gave me and feel the smooth

sides between my fingers. Preparing my nerves for the dinner, I stick the stone inside my clutch and head out for the reception. I'm so ready for this.

The ballroom is decorated in layered white and gold bunting, and there are vases of white flowers everywhere. It's like a wedding—everything is so pretty, and I can't help but look around, wide-eyed and happy. The event is black-tie, so all the guys are in tuxes and the girls are in long dresses. The room is buzzing, lively. It's clear everyone is thrilled to be here. There's an hour before dinner during which we eat cheese and crackers and Suzanne introduces us to as many dignitaries as she can recognize. I stick close to her, as do Richard and Simon. We're all a bit subdued, and when people congratulate us, we just smile and nod. I meet so many people, it's hard to keep track of who's who.

"Jasmine, may I introduce you to Senator Armstrong, Speaker of the House."

"To Dr. Holly Villa, of the National Health Organization."

"To the Honorable James Macgregor, Ambassador to Switzerland."

"To Eugenia Rosenberg, editor in chief of the *Washington Post*."

My head is swimming and my cheeks hurt from smiling so much. When it's finally time for dinner and speeches, we go to look for our table, which is right in front. The head of the National Scholar Foundation speaks first and introduces the top ten scholars. They each give a short speech about their talents and ambitions, many of them in the scientific and technological arenas. In between, Suzanne engages us all with questions, but I can't concentrate. The whole night is overwhelming, almost unreal to me. Then I cut into the chicken, which is rubbery and hard, and I fall back down to earth for a moment. Dad always says we eat better at home than most people do in restaurants, and he's totally right.

Simon and Richard chat excitedly at our table. The other honorees seated with us include three girls who I find out are my elusive roommates. There's Mallory Lynch, a preppie redhead, and Nina Chandra, a gorgeous Indian girl with a hilarious sense of humor. They're both from Maryland. Then there's Carrie Mayberry. She's a classic all-American beauty with thick sandy-blond hair and cornflower-blue eyes who happens to be a Junior Olympics gymnast, a world-class sailor, and has already landed an internship with the *New York Times* and is a total shoo-in to Columbia, her first choice.

Carrie seems to be the leader of the three girls. Every topic of conversation revolves around what she thinks or whom she knows. Carrie is from D.C., but all three girls know each other because Nina and Carrie go to a boarding school together and Mallory plays on Nina's water polo club team. All of their parents seem to be involved in politics somehow.

The girls are totally ignoring Richard and Simon, which doesn't matter because the boys don't even notice, they're so engrossed in a super nerdy discussion about binary numbers.

"Are you excited to go to Columbia?" I ask Carrie, trying to make conversation. "Do you like New York?"

She crosses her arms. "Do I *like* New York? The city isn't the kind of place that you like or dislike. New York is bigger than any single person. It's the only place to live really."

"Oh," I say. "I guess that's how Manila used to feel to me... that it's more than a city."

Carrie doesn't respond, and Mallory politely picks up the conversation. "So you're from the Philippines? Did you grow up there?"

"My parents were born there," I say. "I grew up in LA."

Both are technically true.

Nina leans forward. "Where in LA?"

"Uh, Chatsworth," I admit.

"Where's that?" asks Mallory.

"It's in the San Fernando Valley," I tell her.

"That's *not* LA," Carrie cuts in with a laugh.

"Yes, it's the Valley," I say coolly. "And the Valley is still part of Los Angeles, last I checked. Everyone thinks LA is just Beverly Hills and West Hollywood, but it's much larger and more diverse than that. Besides, we have the best soup dumplings in the Valley. Better than New York's Chinatown, according to the Michelin guide."

She yawns.

Snobs are the worst. Especially elite snobs like her, who think they're so sophisticated when really, they're closed-minded. They live in their fancy bubble and think that's all there is to life. I turn away, but she's not done with me yet.

"So, Jasmine, since your parents are immigrants, what do you think of that new immigration bill that passed in the Senate last week and was just introduced in the House? I normally don't follow those things, but I wanted to know who I'd be talking to at tonight's reception."

I must have a confused expression on my face, because Nina jumps in to explain the situation to me. "The congressman who's the lead opponent against the bill is speaking tonight. Some people think he could be president in a few election cycles."

Oh, wonderful, a president who hates immigrants.

"What's the bill about again?" Mallory asks. She seems genuinely interested.

"I think it's about giving out citizenship to a bunch of people who have to pay a $500 fine for sneaking into the country in the past. It's basically just a slap on the hand if you've lived here for a long time," Nina says. "But I guess they have to do something for these people."

"Personally, I think that whole argument about immigrants being productive members of American society is pretty weak," Carrie says. "Anyone who entered the United States without proper documentation is technically a criminal. They aren't *law-abiding* people. Obviously."

"What's that supposed to mean?" I say, raising my voice a little. "Playing by the rules isn't always about what's right. There have been plenty of laws that weren't right. Why should someone be law-abiding when the laws are so stacked against them that the system makes it nearly impossible to follow those laws? Ever heard of Rosa Parks?"

No one says anything. Mallory and Nina sit back in their chairs, looking uncomfortable, but Carrie studies me with a calculating expression. I look down at my plate, relieved as the murmur of conversation throughout the room turns into a hush.

My hands are shaking so hard after my outburst at the table that I almost knock my water over and don't hear the introduction of the evening's keynote speaker. It's a politician who looks familiar, and he takes the podium to speak briefly. He congratulates us and says we exemplify the best of America, and we show that all Americans need an education before they can contribute at the higher levels of citizenship. He says we are model citizens from hardworking families who value a degree of being American that many have lost focus on. He calls us the heroes of our generation—the most diverse generation.

I don't feel like a hero at all. Sure, I feel hopeful, that somehow I'm going to find my way through this mess. At the same time, I think of Mom and Dad and how they should be here instead of me. They both deserve this more, since they worked so hard to put me here. Millie too. If it wasn't for her encouragement, I don't think I'd be here either.

I applaud when the politician finishes his speech. He nods to us as he walks to a table to sit with his family.

The politician's wife is wearing a long, gorgeous, sweeping black dress with a full skirt. I saw the same dress in Vogue this month. She's styled her chestnut hair in a low chignon at the nape of her neck that makes her look like a First Lady. The couple is joined by a young man who glances my way. I recognize him from somewhere.

Oh my God.

How could I have not put two and two together? Congressman *Blakely* was the speaker. Duh. Royce's dad. Mr. Anti-immigration. How did I not recognize his face? It's not like I haven't seen him all over the news since I first spotted him at the hospital.

And there's *Royce.* Looking incredibly handsome in a crisp black tuxedo. He scans the room and our eyes meet. It's like I'm zapped by lightning—everything in me is on fire when he looks at me.

I have to look away. It's too much. I feel almost ill from excitement.

My phone buzzes immediately. It's a text from him. I need to go all the way to D.C. to see you?

Oh, hey, fancy seeing you here, I send, trying to seem casual.

My heart is racing. The shock of seeing him takes my breath away. I don't know whether to stare a hole into the tablecloth or check out Royce again, but my decision is made up for me when the host announces that dinner is coming to a close and Suzanne comes to the table to sweep the group up for the next event on the itinerary. We're scheduled for another meet and greet with more dignitaries for dessert. I follow Suzanne to an area where there are many black couches, chairs and small tables. Caterers come around with bottles of water and trays of tarts and tiny little cakes. I decline. I surreptitiously look for Royce but don't see him anywhere. My hands are trembling and I tell myself to calm down. Why does he affect me so much?

I peek at my phone. Why not? Other honorees are. There's a message from Kayla: I'm not the team captain while you're gone? I feel like quitting.

Oh no. She can't! I type back. **I'm so sorry. I tried to tell coach it was the wrong choice. Don't quit. We need you.**

She doesn't text back.

I send her another text and another, but she's gone radio silent. I text her that I'll call her when the reception is over.

I stuff the phone back in my purse. When I look up, Royce is standing in front of me, holding two glasses of champagne.

Oh.

My.

God.

He's so incredibly handsome, and even more so in that tux. The sharp black lines of the jacket and his crisp white shirt look good with his dark hair, which he's slicked back from his forehead. His brown eyes are warm and shining, and I forgot about that dimple on his cheek, which softens the striking edges of his face and makes him look like a mischievous boy. I remember the goofy selfie he took that's still on my phone, and the Snapchats he sent of himself belly flopping into his pool and falling off a surfboard. He may look like the star of a teen soap opera, but he's a goofball, like he doesn't take anything too seriously.

The butterflies in my stomach relax. Being near him is enough to calm me down, it seems. It was the wait, the anticipation that was killing me. Still, it's hard to breathe.

"For me?" I ask, taking the proffered flute with a smile, relieved that my voice sounds even. "Is this allowed?"

"If I say so," he says. We clink glasses.

I take a small sip. It's sweet and tart. I take a bigger sip.

Royce is looking at me so intensely, I feel nervous again. I'm not sure what to say to him. This is the problem when you text a lot but don't see each other in real life. We met only once, so it's weird. And there's the whole thing with his dad thinking illegal immigrants are ruining this country—what if Royce thinks the same way? I really, really hope he doesn't think the same way.

"How come you never mentioned that you're a National Scholar?" he teases, a glint in his eye. "Congrats by the way."

"Thanks. You too!" I say, assuming he's here for the same reason I am.

He flushes, and I worry I've said the wrong thing—and it turns out I have.

"Oh, I'm not one of you guys. I'm just here with my dad."

"Um, okay. That's cool," I say, to make up for my faux pas. I look down at my shoes.

But Royce seems nonplussed and just shrugs. "Yeah, it was a last-minute thing. My dad wanted me to go." His smile disappears.

I look back up at him. "He forced you, huh?" I tease. "Hard life."

He rolls his eyes. "You've heard one of my dad's speeches you've heard them all. Plus the food is always awful."

I groan. "It really was. That chicken was disgusting."

"Of course I still ate the whole thing," he says with a grin.

"So did I!"

We laugh, and he puts me so at ease that I almost snort when I giggle.

"I'm glad I'm here though, I was beginning to think I'd never see you again," he says, a serious look on his face.

"Oh," I say, blushing furiously, not knowing quite what to say. I feel bad he thought I was avoiding him, which I was, but not for the reason he might think.

I try to find my composure and change the subject. "Your dad made a good speech though."

"You really think so?"

"Yeah." I do. I don't agree with the congressman's politics, but I agree with what he said about education and striving.

"Hey, you want to meet him?" Royce asks suddenly, as if to make up for acting so jaded before.

"Your dad? Sure," I say, even though I'm a little scared. What if Congressman Blakely can tell that I don't have papers? That I'm practically the enemy? Of course this is an irrational, paranoid thought, but I have it anyway. Then I tell myself I *should* meet his dad, because once I have, maybe I can go out on a date with Royce without my dad getting upset that he didn't meet Royce first. As if meeting one parent counts somehow?

Am I getting ahead of myself? Why do I think Royce and I are going to date? Royce whisks away our champagne glasses and before I can think more on it, we're next to Congressman Blakely, who's deep in conversation with another important-looking person.

"Dad," Royce says, touching his arm.

The congressman doesn't seem to hear his son.

Royce bounces on his heels a few times. He shoves his hands in his pockets and leans toward me. "He does this sometimes," he says. "Watch this." He turns back toward his dad. "Congressman Blakely, Majority Leader, may I present Jasmine…"

"De los Santos," I say.

The congressman turns now, all smiles, as if a light switch automatically flips as soon as a stranger is present. He takes a split second to survey me. "Pleasure to meet you, Jasmine. You're one of our honorees from California, aren't you?"

I'm amazed at his knowledge. There are three hundred of us. "Yes, the Los Angeles area," I say. "Pleased to meet you, Congressman."

"The honor is all mine. May I introduce you to Senator Lauren Silverton from Wisconsin?"

I shake the senator's hand, which is soft and perfectly manicured. She's one of the few women in the Senate, and I'm ecstatic to meet her. "It's an honor," I tell her.

"We're so proud of you," she tells me with a warm smile. "You and all the honorees are the bright lights of our country."

The two of them beam at me. Royce's dad says, "I heard you wrote a great essay. We need more students like you making America great."

"Thank you both. It's wonderful to be here," I say, noticing Royce smirking.

"Dad, Senator, if you'll excuse us," Royce says.

They nod and smile. "Yes, lovely meeting you," the congressman says, turning away.

And that's it—nothing scary about him. It's odd though, I thought I was meeting Royce's dad, but it turned out I was just meeting the congressman. I'm not sure my dad would think this counts as a meet-the-parents moment, it was so impersonal.

Royce hands me a new champagne glass once we're far enough away from his dad. "So, here you are."

"Here you are," I say, taking a sip.

"IRL," he says.

I raise my glass. "We're not blue bubbles on our phones anymore!"

He smiles, and when his cheeks flush, he looks even more handsome. It's almost painful. My stomach is doing that thing again, and for a moment we're just standing there, smiling at each other, as if we're the only two people in the room. Everything else recedes and goes out of focus. There's only him and my beating heart.

Royce finishes his drink and sets it on the nearest table. "So," he says expectantly. "What are you doing after this?"

11

The most courageous act is still to think for yourself. Aloud.

—COCO CHANEL

ROYCE HAS TO do a little glad-handing for his parents but promises to meet me in the hotel lobby after the event, so I go back to find Suzanne. She introduces me to the person she's talking to, who turns out to be the dean of students at Stanford University.

The dean is one of the more youngish bigwigs here, and he's not wearing a tux, just a black jacket and no tie. He has a slightly disheveled, casual California air that makes me feel right at home. When he asks me about my academic interests, I tell him about the storytelling project I was working on at the hospital, and how I'm drawn to both law and medicine but haven't made a choice just yet. I don't mention that the project is over; I still plan to put that book together and get it to the patients somehow.

"Have you thought about where you're going for college?" he asks.

"Actually, my first choice is Stanford," I tell him, feeling shy.

He raises his glass. "Good girl. We'd be lucky to have you." He reaches in his pocket and hands me his card. "If you have any questions about the school, let me know. Happy to answer them."

I'm so giddy, I almost stutter my goodbye, and when he leaves, Suzanne tells me he was her professor, and one of the youngest deans at Stanford. "He's brilliant—he could have made millions in Silicon Valley, but he'd rather teach and mentor students," she says. "Not enough of those kind of people out there."

I think deeply on what she says. For the longest time, I've thought of success as something that means financial wealth and social status. Something that I needed to earn for myself, and for my family. But here was someone who had chosen another path. Albeit, a prestigious one, but far less lucrative. Suzanne introduces me to a few more people, then the party begins to die down, and people head out of the ballroom.

"There's usually an after-party for honorees somewhere," Suzanne says. "It's practically tradition. One of the local kids always hosts it. I'm sure you can ask around."

"Thanks. I'm meeting someone in the lobby. Maybe we'll end up there."

"Great! Have fun—see you tomorrow," she says with a cheerful wave.

I follow the crowd to the lobby, keeping an eye out for Royce.

Gorgeous oversize paintings of bright flowers hang on the shiny, deep red wood walls. A huge chandelier hangs over a mahogany baby grand piano being played by an older gentleman wearing a navy suit. He plays with so much passion and tenderness, it's like he's the only one in the room. He deserves to be playing in a concert hall, not a hotel lobby where everyone is treating his music like background noise.

I check my texts while I wait, then realize I'm just like everyone else who's taking the music for granted.

Kayla still hasn't responded. I call her. She doesn't pick up, so I leave a voice mail. I really hope she's okay. She can't quit the team, I won't let her.

Mom has texted a few times. I know she wants me to call, but I text her instead and say that the other girls in my room are going to sleep and I don't want to bother them. I tell her I'll call her tomorrow.

I don't want to think of anyone but Royce right now. It's hard to breathe again, just thinking of him. I've never been affected by someone's presence so much, although he's not even here and he's making me feel this way. What is it about him?

Okay, so I *have* kissed boys. On the cheek. I played "I never" in sixth grade a couple of times, and I "went out" with Jarred Agovino for a month in junior high. We held hands. But ever since high school, I haven't had time for boys and I've never had a *real* boyfriend. My parents used to say I couldn't date until I was sixteen, but there wasn't even a reason to *forbid* me to date. Nevertheless, Mom doesn't need to know about Royce right now. No one needs to know about him. There's nothing to know anyway. We're just friends. *Let's see where this goes*, I tell myself, trying for deep, calming breaths.

Royce finally arrives, and there's a group of boys trailing him. They're rambunctious, slapping each other on the back and laughing a little too loudly. The pianist gives them a sideways glance, then returns to caressing the keys.

When Royce sees me he walks right over and I swear his eyes light up. I can feel my heart pounding so hard in my chest. *I get it now*, I think. *I get it.* What all those sappy love songs and romantic movies are trying to say about love, trying to capture this kind of moment, this kind of feeling. I didn't really understand before. No one's ever made me feel this way. It's like lightning, like everything is suddenly wonderful, like the world is actually the great place that Louis Armstrong sings about and life isn't just a drudge of chores and routine.

Life can be magical.

When he's standing in front of me, I have to crane my neck a little to look at him directly. I hadn't realized how tall he was. I barely come up to his shoulders.

"Hey," he says, shyly.

"Hey." I smile. "Are these your friends?" I say, turning to look at the group.

"Nope," he says tersely, his expression changing. He tries to move us away from them. "Come on, let's get out of here."

Somehow, the magic of the moment is gone, and everything goes back to black-and-white after being in Technicolor. Because one of the boys with the group, the one with his bow tie untied and his collar open, giving him a bit of a rakish air, the one who looks a little like Royce, except he's handsome in a too-pretty kind of way, like his lips are too full and his hair is too bouncy—you feel me?—isn't happy that Royce is trying to leave. He laughs and slaps Royce on the back. "This is the girl? You surprise me, Roycey. She's not your usual type."

My cheeks start to burn. What does that mean, I'm not his usual type? I'm not Caucasian? Blonde? Rich?

"Shut up, Mason. She's one of the honorees. You're probably not half as smart as her—and we all know you're definitely not as good-looking," says Royce, in a teasing voice, although his eyes are stormy.

The other boys clap and hiss at Mason, mussing up his hair and pushing him around. "He told you," one of them says, letting out a low whistle.

I stand there awkwardly, annoyed and humiliated. Maybe I should just excuse myself and go upstairs to my room. It's going to be a busy weekend anyway. I don't want to miss the tour of the Capitol in the morning. I have more self-respect than to spend one of the most important nights of my life being insulted by some spoiled rich kids. This is exactly why I didn't want to meet up with Royce in LA. I didn't want to see how truly different he was from me, and I didn't want to meet his friends in case they were like this.

"Don't you guys have an after-party to crash?" Royce asks, looking bored.

"All right, all right. I get the picture. You want us to leave you alone. Although you still haven't introduced us," the rude boy says.

Royce's voice is steely. "Jasmine, this is my brother, Mason. Mason, this is Jasmine."

His brother! Great, just great. But I hold out my hand to Mason. I'll be the bigger person. "Nice to meet you."

Mason takes my hand, and his palm is sweaty. Ick. "My little brother doesn't usually go after the smart girls. Hey, if you get bored of him, give me a call, will you?" he says, winking at Royce and patting him on the shoulder again. "I'll see you in the morning, dude. Breakfast with Mom and Dad. That is, if you don't have too late a night, huh?" He leers.

The guys follow Mason, laughing and joking boisterously as they leave the hotel. Royce looks down at his shoes. "I'm sorry about that."

I shrug. "Like you said, they're not *your* friends."

He looks up at me and smiles. It's like we understand each other. "I thought about taking you to dinner, but then I realized I met you at dinner and we both ate *all* of our chicken. So..."

I smile. "What do you have in mind?"

Royce seems nervous all of a sudden. He shakes out the sleeves on his jacket so they cover his wrists. "It probably doesn't sound very fun, especially since it's your first night in Washington, but I thought maybe we could just hang out on the roof. There's a great view up there."

I hesitate, feeling shy again. Then I think about what Kayla would do, how confident she is with boys. I try to emulate it. "Sure. That sounds cool." Really, he could ask me to watch boring old C-SPAN and I would gladly leap at the chance.

"Yeah?"

I look over at the pianist. He's playing a slow, meandering song—a moonlight song. "Yeah," I say. "I can come up for a little while."

"Great," Royce says, clapping his hands together, a big grin on his face, like a little kid excited to show off a new toy.

I wonder what's so cool about the roof. Also, what are the five hundred different ways my mother would kill me if she knew what I was doing right now—going somewhere alone with a boy?

Royce takes us up to the roof. There's a heated, glassed-in terrace where we can see the whole city. We sit on a bench and look out at this amazing view. Everything is sparkling and pretty—the monuments are lit up, and it feels like the world is at our feet, like we can do anything, be anything. It's corny, but precious all the same. I'm glad he took me up here. It's so quiet, I can hear us both breathing.

"Nice, right?" he asks. "Not everyone knows about the terrace. It's my favorite place in D.C., because no one is ever around. I come here all the time when we're in town, to get away from my family. My dad prefers to stay in a hotel rather than rent a house when congress is in session. He's a little spoiled that way."

"It's beautiful up here." We both stare at the lights and the view for a long time, just enjoying the silence. "I can't remember the last time I felt this relaxed," I tell him.

"You award kids are all type A, huh?"

"Yeah, I guess," I say. "There are only twenty-four hours in a day and I already feel like I'm using twenty-seven."

Royce loosens his tie so that the ends hang down, and he undoes the top button of his shirt. I can see a hint of his throat and Adam's apple. It feels so intimate somehow, it makes me blush again. Thankfully, he doesn't notice.

"I guess girls like you always need to be in control, huh," he says, leaning back in a languid pose.

"What do you mean? Isn't that a good thing?"

"It's not what you're thinking. I like those kinds of girls. Except they always have so much going on it's hard to get them to make time to see you." He gives me a sly side-eye.

Ha. "So you like girls like me, do you?" I tease.

"Maybe," he allows. He's the one blushing now, and I feel my cheeks growing hot as well.

"Can I be honest with you?" I ask, changing the subject. For some reason I feel comfortable with him—he's easy to talk to.

"Sure," Royce says.

"This is the most downtime I've had since I can remember," I say. "I've always judged myself by how much I can achieve. How good I am at things. It's what I do. I never have any time just to appreciate things."

Royce sits up a little, adjusting his pants so they cover his ankles. "It's good to be busy. At least it means you're good at something, unlike me."

"That can't be true," I say. "Why would you say that?" He looks so crushed for a moment that I know he's not being falsely modest like some people can be.

He shrugs. "I guess it doesn't matter either way, really. I'm the son of a congressman and my family has money. My life is all set up for me." He turns to look at me directly. "Look—I know how bad that sounds. Like I'm complaining about my privilege. I get it. People like you and all the other honorees have worked so hard to get here. But I'm just here because of my dad."

I'm about to say something, then decide to listen instead.

His shoulders slump. "I guess sometimes I just want to know that what I do matters. That people aren't judging me by who my parents are, but by who I am."

I nod sympathetically. "Who are you, then? Who do you want to be?" I ask him, thinking I'm asking the same questions about myself.

Royce knits his brows and looks out at the view. I've caught him off guard.

"Sorry. I didn't mean to make you uncomfortable," I say.

"No, no, it's not that," he says, leaning back again, and when he shifts, his knee brushes against mine, and the heat inside me builds. "It's just that no one has ever asked me that before. I don't know how to answer."

I turn to him and look him right in his dark eyes. "What are you interested in? Sometimes it's easier to figure out what you want to do when you figure out what you like."

He stares at me. "I never thought of it that way. You're so wise—you're sure you're only seventeen?" he teases.

"Well?"

He runs his fingers through his hair again, messing it up. "I like to read. I didn't learn how to for a long time. I'm dyslexic, and for the longest time everyone just thought I was just slow. So when I finally learned how to read, I couldn't stop. I felt like I had to catch up."

"Who's your favorite writer?"

"Ah, it's hard to choose," he says. "Saul Bellow maybe. Or Norman Mailer. Did you ever read *Armies of the Night*?"

I shake my head. "I've heard of it though. It's about the sixties, right? The protests against the Vietnam War?"

"Yeah. There's a line from it that's never left me. 'There is no greater importance in all the world like knowing you are right and that the wave of the world is wrong, yet the wave crashes upon you.'" Royce looks out at the view, pensive and still. The space between us is so tight and close it feels as if I can hear his heart beating under his shirt. Can he hear mine?

"I always liked it, about how it's so hard to be brave and stand for what's right when everything's against you, you know?" he asks.

I do know. I take my phone out of my bag and start typing.

"What are you doing?"

I flush. "I, um…it's silly…but I collect quotes. I write them down and I post them in my room on my corkboard."

"Not to Pinterest or Instagram?" he teases.

"No, because they're just for me," I say.

"Are you going to put my quote on it?"

"*Your* quote?" I tease. "You own it?"

"Well, yeah, I mean, I had to read the whole book." He smiles back. "But I'll let you borrow it."

"Okay, so you like to read. Does that mean you want to be a writer, then?"

"Yeah, like a journalist, I think," he says with a flash of a smile. "Like Mailer was. And you know, like those guys who bust cover-ups and that sort of thing."

"You're not just a writer, you're a crusader. An activist."

"I don't know about that," he said. "But whatever I do, it's definitely not going to be politics." Whenever he says *politics*, his mouth makes a hard line, like it's distasteful. "What about you?"

"Law or medicine," I say automatically. "I want to make a difference, but I don't know exactly in what arena yet."

"Cool," he says. "You've got time, you'll figure it out."

"Yeah, isn't it funny? You already know what you want to do, and I don't, and I was the one who gave you advice."

He laughs. "I guess I do know what I want. I just don't know if I can do it."

"Why not?" I ask, concerned at the look on his face.

"I don't think my dad would be too impressed, honestly."

"Oh." I feel bad about that. My parents will be happy with whatever I choose. Royce looks uncomfortable so I try to change the subject, sort of. "Your dad seems busy," I say.

"Yeah, it's a crazy time for him, especially with a vote on this immigration bill coming up soon."

"Right." Wrong subject. I really wish we could talk about something else right now.

"The leadership of the party wants him to move up the ranks. I think they want to test whether he could be a real presidential candidate someday," he says proudly.

Yeah, ride that anti-immigration platform all the way to the top, I think but don't say.

Just my luck, that the first boy I've ever been really interested in is related to someone who has dim views of people like me. "That must be exciting for you. About your father being groomed for president, I mean." But I move away from him, stand up from the bench, and walk out of the enclosed area. I need a little cold air right now.

Royce follows me outside to the edge of the rail. "Not really. The busier Dad gets, the more I feel like a prop in his perfect political life. He carts Mom and I out to his parties. His speeches. Mason usually refuses to go, and my sister's too young."

"Do you agree with him about the immigration bill? That undocumented immigrants shouldn't have a path to citizenship?" I ask, staring out at the view and too nervous to look directly at him. I have to know, before we get any closer, before anything happens between us. Do I want something to happen?

I sneak a peek at his face. Yes. I want something to happen. He's not just handsome, he's sweet and smart too. *Please say you don't agree with your dad. How can you agree with your dad when you love that quote from* Armies of the Night?

Royce turns around and leans back against the railing, the city lights illuminating his chestnut hair and high cheekbones. "I'm not sure. To be honest, I don't really care about politics that much," he says.

It's not the answer I want, but at least he didn't say he agreed with it, and maybe he can't be disloyal to his father.

"Hey," I say, wanting to change the subject and suddenly realizing something. "Are you related to that family on TV?" He has the same name as them, sort of. Maybe there's a connection.

"*Royce Rolls* you mean? Only the most famous reality show family in Hollywood?" he says drily.

I try not to squeal, but the show is my guilty pleasure. I'm obsessed with the Royces. "Bentley Royce is my favorite," I say, meaning the hellion wild child with the smart mouth and the vulnerable streak.

He rolls his eyes. "Yeah, unfortunately we're distant cousins. Royce is a family name."

I shriek. "God, you're so LA! You're related to celebrities!"

He laughs. "If you can call them that."

I smile back, but a draft of cold makes me shiver in the night air. I'm wearing only a thin wrap with my dress. Because the event was held at our hotel, I didn't need to bring a heavier coat.

Royce notices and removes his jacket and puts it on my shoulders. "You look cold."

"Thanks." His coat is soft and warm, and has a wonderful masculine smell. I snuggle deeper into it, feeling as if it's his arms that are around me.

"I have another confession to make. Two confessions, actually," he says.

"Yeah?" I'm not sure what this is about.

"First," Royce says, "I knew you were going to be here. My dad gets a list of the honorees, and when I saw a Jasmine listed, I had a feeling it would be you. I've actually known you were going to be here for a while."

"You did?" I ask, intrigued.

"I know all about you," he teases.

"Oh yeah? What do you know?" I say, the fluttering back in my stomach.

"Junior class president. Varsity cheerleader. Probably going to be valedictorian, am I right?"

"Stalker," I say, thrilled.

He laughs. "Yeah, I deserve that. It's sort of why I told my dad I'd go with him to D.C. this time." He smiles and gazes at me intensely, the way he did at dinner, when our eyes first met.

"Why are you looking at me that way?" I ask.

"I was just remembering something. You know that,

throughout the whole event, you never stopped smiling? You looked so happy."

I roll my eyes. I must have looked like a hick from the sticks. "So?" I ask. "What's wrong with that?"

"Nothing. It's just that I could tell you didn't care about who was looking at you or whom you needed to network with later. You were just *there*, living in the moment, appreciating everything. I can't remember the last time I felt like that."

I nod. Despite all the problems my family and I have been going through and all the uncertainty that faces us right now, I *was* happy at the award reception. I was glad to be in that moment, glad that I was able to attend. My parents taught me that—how to feel grateful, how to feel joy. I'm proud of them suddenly, and proud of myself too.

"So what was your second confession?" I nudge him with my elbow.

"I don't know if I should tell you this one." His voice is husky, and he's way too close now; his shoulder is bumping against my arm and when he turns to me, I can see the gold sparkling in his brown eyes.

"You already said you would," I remind him, wondering once more if he can hear how loud and how fast my heart is beating.

"Maybe I changed my mind," he says.

I move away from him deliberately, teasing him.

"Fine. I'll tell you. Are you sure you're ready?" He follows me, closing the space between us once again.

I huff. "I was born ready."

"I think I need a drink first," he jokes.

"Stop stalling."

"All right, all right," Royce says, putting his hands up.

"Remember when we met at the hospital and I asked for your number?"

I nod.

"It wasn't the first time I saw you. I'd seen you a couple days before—you were interviewing one of the patients. The door was open and I heard you talking to this old guy, asking him about his life, making him laugh. I peeked in and saw you. I thought you'd come to my uncle's room next, but you didn't. When I saw you two days later at the check-in window, I decided that was my chance, so I took it. I had to make destiny happen."

"Destiny, huh?" I say, my voice soft and low. "Like a fairy tale. Is that what this is?"

Royce is towering over me at six feet compared to my five feet three inches, and when he leans down, I can see his thick dark lashes over half-lidded eyes. He pulls me toward him by the jacket arms, and then his own arms are around me, and I tilt up my chin up and close my eyes.

Because I know what happens next. I've seen the movies, I've sung along to all the love songs.

This wonderful boy is going to kiss me.

A kiss I've been waiting for, for a very long time.

Here's a secret: waiting is worth it.

12

I smiled at him. America, I said quietly, just like that.
What is it? The sweepings of every country including
our own. Isn't that true? That's a fact.

—JAMES JOYCE, *ULYSSES*

WHEN I OPEN my eyes the next morning, I forget where I am. Am I late for school? Light streams through the windows, blinding me. I can't see a thing, and the alarm is going off. My heart feels like it's beating through my chest. Where am I?

Then I remember. I'm in the Ritz-Carlton. I'm in Washington, D.C., for the National Scholarship Program.

Finally, I lean way over, trying to get out of bed. I haven't gotten any sleep; I was with Royce all night. We kissed up there on the roof for a while. Until after midnight, actually. I touch my lips as if I could touch his by touching mine, smiling to myself a little. I'm away from home for the first time, I got a little tipsy on champagne, and I kissed a boy. And not just any boy. A sweet and handsome boy. One of the nicest guys I've ever met.

Royce couldn't be more wrong about himself. That he's Congressman Blakely's son is the *least* interesting thing about him.

I check my phone. Kayla left a message, thankfully. She says she won't quit the team, she was just emotional, but she's okay now. Good. I want to tell her all about my night with Royce, but it's way too early back home to call.

There's also a text from Royce at half past midnight, after he walked me back to my hotel room when we left the roof. I smile to myself and text him back, tell him I'll see him later. Then I hear the sounds of girls chattering in the bathroom on the other side of the suite.

Ugh. Mallory, Nina, and Carrie. My roommates…

I pull the pillow back over my head, dreading talking to them. When I got back last night, they were all in the other bedroom, Carrie on one bed, Nina on the other and Mallory in a pullout, with sleeping masks pulled over their eyes.

While the girls talk, I finally take the pillow off my head and look around the suite, my eyes adjusting to the daylight. It's a disaster, with clothes strewn all over the couch and the floor. There's only one bathroom, despite the two bedrooms, so I grab my things and sit on the couch to wait for my turn in the shower.

Carrie steps out of the bathroom. Mallory and Nina follow behind her. All three of them look perfectly put together. Plucked and filled-in eyebrows, tousled hair, classy boots that go up over their knees. Carrie slips her bag over her elbow and looms down at me. "So, I heard you were with Royce Blakely last night."

I nod warily. "Do you know him?"

"We've hung out," she says, with a possessive air. "I've known him for a long time. Our parents are friends."

She's so eager to point out that he's from her circle. I want to ask Carrie what she means by "hung out," but she's the one with the twenty questions it seems. "So did he take you somewhere nice? His dad knows everyone in Washington and gets the best tables."

I really don't want to answer Carrie's question, but she's not going anywhere until she gets an answer. Meanwhile, Mallory and Nina just stare at me, googly-eyed. I must look awful, I barely got any sleep.

"No, we just stayed here," I tell her. "He had to go to an early breakfast with his family." I don't know why, but I'm feeling defensive about this all of a sudden.

"You stayed in the hotel? Why didn't you guys come to the after-party?" Carrie asks, looking overly confused. Then she elbows the girls with a knowing smile.

I feel my cheeks burning, as if I should be ashamed, even though I didn't do anything wrong. Carrie and the girls are acting as if I did something tawdry and scandalous, when last night was one of the best and most magical nights of my life.

"Guess you guys had a party of your own, huh?" Carrie snickers.

Thank God Nina interrupts. "Let's go, I need coffeeeeee."

"Fine," Carrie says. "Let's go."

As the girls file out of the room, Carrie stops at the door and turns back to me. She's not done sticking her knife in yet. "I'm just trying to watch out for you, Jasmine," she says disingenuously. "Royce Blakely isn't what he seems like. I've been there. He's a total player. Trust me on this one."

The door clicks shut.

I've been *there?*

What does that mean?

Were they…? Did they…?

Ugh. Why would she say that? She's just trying to get into my head. She can't mean he was her boyfriend or something. How could that be? He lives in LA and she lives in D.C. She's probably just jealous.

Determined not to let Carrie ruin my beautiful memory

of last night, I go to look out the windows. Morning light bursts over the beautiful, busy city, highlighting people bundled up in coats, hurrying to their jobs, and early-morning traffic. The hotel is only a few blocks from the White House to the southeast, and just a few blocks north from Constitution Gardens, the Vietnam Veterans Memorial, Washington Monument, Potomac Park.

Half an hour later, I've showered, dressed, and eaten, and I barely make it to the tour in time. Part of me can't wait to see Royce again, no matter what Carrie said about him, but the other part wants to be able to see this place on my own, to not worry about anything other than enjoying the present. I've also remembered to bring along my empty little glass bottle, for my own souvenir.

The tour group approaches the outside of the Capitol and I feel myself getting emotional. My eyes burn with tears. Why am I like this? Is this awe of the history before us? Am I anxious about whether or not the reform bill will pass? Or does it have to do with last night?

Suzanne is leading our small group, peppy as a cheerleader at her first football game. She doesn't look tired. No bags around her eyes. Does she even sleep? She must be so busy running the scholarship program, rushing from meetings to parties to cocktail hours. You know who needs sleep though? Me.

Guilt washes over me. What would my parents think if they knew I'd been alone for most of the night with a boy?

I try to stop thinking about Royce and focus on the tour. I'm amazed at all the artwork inside the Capitol. The architecture. The sound of footsteps in the wide halls. The rotunda is my favorite place. I gaze up at the Apotheosis of Washington like I've been frozen into the center of everything.

"It was painted at the end of the Civil War," Suzanne says. The other students and I crane our necks.

"Who is that up there?" Richard Morales asks. "God?"

"The guy in the royal purple coat most toward the center?" Suzanne laughs. "Not quite," she says. "Try George Washington. As you know, he was the first US president and commander in chief of the Continental Army during the Revolutionary War."

"But who is that with him?" Richard asks. "Those aren't people from the Constitutional Convention. Only men signed the Constitution. Women were still second-class citizens in those days."

"You've been doing your homework," Suzanne says. "Figures from classical mythology. Everyone up there is exalted. That's Liberty and Victory on either side of him."

Some of the students have lost interest. I knew they would. Half the students in our group go to private schools. They've been here before and so act bored, except when they spot certain political figures power walking around the Capitol.

Carrie, Nina, and Mallory are turning their backs on the art and noting who's walking by our group. When the Secretary of State passes through the hallway, Carrie whispers to one of her friends, "My mom threw a fundraiser for her last year when she thought she'd run for president."

"Remember that night? I thought I was going to hurl right in her lap," Nina says.

Mallory joins them. "You almost did."

I wander away from them, trying to take in the immensity of the fresco. The way the painter did the perspective makes you think the Capitol's rotunda reaches all the way up to heaven. It's overwhelming. Even though I've never been to the Sistine Chapel in Italy, I imagine that looking at this is a little bit like they describe looking at Michelangelo's painting of God and Adam. I'm thinking about a lecture my AP Art History teacher, Mr. Lee, gave once about this weird thing that happens when people look at great pieces of art and start to feel sick. Like they're going to pass out.

But I think my symptoms are more from last night. I'm still light-headed and not quite awake. Staring up at the painting, I hear a few voices chattering behind me.

"You remember that party. Don't you?" Carrie asks.

A boy's voice responds. "Yeah, that was epic."

I turn around. It's Royce. He doesn't see me, and I duck away. My head hurts and now my heart does too. Of *course* he knows Carrie.

I was so stupid to assume Carrie was lying to me. How could she not know Royce? He must spend a lot of time in D.C. with his dad. He and Carrie have probably known each other for years. Maybe they've even dated, like she hinted. He was at that "epic" party, right? Ugh.

Suzanne has moved into one of the corridors. Royce is still chatting with Carrie and her private-school clique and I hear them laughing, telling inside jokes. I don't recognize any of the names they throw around, or the places they talk about. I haven't been to Vail or to Jackson Hole, have no opinion on whether Parrot Cay is overrated or if the service at the Breakers is better than ever. They're like a real-life version of Rich Kids of Instagram. I bet they'll talk about private planes next. Their whole insider vibe makes me want to puke.

Carrie invites him to go to some party with "the group" later and he says sure.

"Can you believe we have to do this?" Carrie sneers. "I've been on private tours of this place, where they take you to the places the tourists can't go. I wish we could go find a bar or something."

Her friends titter, but I don't know if Royce agreed with her or not and I don't want to stay and find out, so I purposefully lag behind, gawking at a row of female portraits. I don't belong here. I don't belong with them, with him.

Of course, right then, when I'm feeling the most alienated and out of it is when Royce finally sees me.

"There you are," he says, beaming. He doesn't look any worse for wear. His eyes are a little hooded, maybe, but they just serve to make him look mysterious rather than tired. "Hey." He gives me a sly smile, like we share a secret. Images from the night before begin to flash: Royce kissing my forehead, tracing kisses from my nose down to my lips and my neck, Royce putting his arms around me, and how good he smelled, so clean and boyish. It hurts.

My heart rate is going up again, but I try not to let it show. I nod hello but don't return the smile.

"Those are the first female US senators," he says, meaning the paintings. "Rebecca Latimer Felton and Hattie Caraway."

"Interesting," I say, even though I try to make myself sound bored. My skin feels electric at the sight of him, which makes me madder. I thought I knew what last night was all about, but this morning, I'm not so sure. He moves in that circle of rich, connected kids and speaks their language. I'm not part of that world; I'm just a visitor for the weekend. I walk away from him.

"Hey. Where're you going?"

I don't turn around.

He catches up. "Is something wrong?" he asks. "I came to the tour to see you. I'm sorry I'm late."

Royce is only on the tour because he wanted to see me. But I'm too upset about what Carrie said and how chummy he was with them. I can't look him in the eye. "It's nothing. Look, I have to catch up to my group. Let's talk later."

"Okay." He sounds hurt.

I don't look back, but I can imagine him standing there with his hands in his pockets, like when he was waiting to talk to his dad the night before. I'm mad at myself too. Sure, I'm a National Scholar, but it just occurred to me that Royce is from one of those families that probably funds scholarships in their name. Why didn't I think of that to begin with? What's he doing with me? Shouldn't he be with Carrie and those kinds of girls? It's obvious he should.

Still. It's hard to walk away from him.

The group of honorees gathers at the Washington Monument before lunch. I try to stop thinking about Royce. I convince myself it was just a one-night thing. People make out all the time—it didn't mean anything to him, and it sure doesn't mean anything to me. As if.

Oh my God, I need to stop lying to myself. I can't stop thinking about him. I like him so much, and if he doesn't feel the same, I don't know what I'll do.

I try to concentrate on the docent who's giving us all the juicy details. These are the facts: It's an obelisk. It commemorates George, who is up there with the gods in the rotunda. It's due east of the reflecting pool. It's made of marble, granite, and some kind of blue metamorphic rock called gneiss, which is related to the German word *gneist*, which means *to spark*. I walk up to the Washington Monument while the docent is still talking and put a hand to the marble. It feels softer than I imagined. I run my hand along the bumpy texture, then pull out my phone and text Mom.

I'm touching the Washington Monument. It's bumpier than I thought.

She doesn't answer for a little while. I picture her putting her phone down and yelling to everyone in the house. "Can you believe it? Our baby is touching the Washington Monument!" This thought makes me smile along with the idea that Dad is probably saying something stupid like, "Tell her not to bring it home. It's too big for the yard."

Finally I get a text.

I'm so proud of you. Your father wants to know if you've met the President yet and if so, see if he will pass a bill to keep the neighbor's cat off the lawn.

Whatever, Mom. I love you, I write, smiling.

We walk along a semicircle path, cross a street, and pass through the World War Two Memorial, where I see Royce again.

His dark eyes meet mine, but I turn away as soon as he starts walking toward me. I pretend to be interested in what Suzanne is saying.

How can everything change so fast?

Because he's not for you, I tell myself. *You're not from his world, and he wouldn't understand yours.*

It's not just that he's rich. It's everything. Carrie is just one example. What did his brother say? *You're not his usual type.* So what was he doing with me, then? Slumming? *A booty call?* I wish I had more experience with boys so I could figure it out.

I follow close behind Suzanne past the Reflecting Pool and toward the Lincoln Memorial. I look back at the water and see the monument perfectly reflected upside down. I think it looks like a great sword in the earth and wonder why anyone would put it there. Suzanne reminds us of the 1963

March on Washington, when a quarter of a million people gathered around the pool for one of the greatest speeches in modern history.

Suzanne has part of the speech memorized and recites it as we walk. "I still have a dream, a dream deeply rooted in the American dream—one day this nation will rise up and live up to its creed, 'We hold these truths to be self-evident: that all men are created equal.'"

I've always loved that speech, was so proud to be from a country that produced Martin Luther King, Jr. But now I know better.

We're not all created equal. There are the Carries and Royces of the world, high up in their gated mansions and their fancy schools, and then there's me and my family, who are just struggling to keep our footing. Though our paths may cross momentarily, maybe it's better to stick to our own circle, so we don't get hurt when we crash into each other.

Because that's what's happening here, isn't it? I've crashed into Royce, and I'm bound to get hurt.

13

THE GROUP TOURS the Jefferson Memorial after a boxed
lunch of plain sandwiches and potato chips. I'm not angry
at Royce anymore, just sad and confused, and now I miss
my family. I just want a bowl of Mom's adobo and to pinch
Danny and Isko on their ears. Just the other week I was feeling homesick for Manila, but now I can't even imagine going
back. LA is my home.

I walk inside the memorial. It's magnificent. Bright lights
illuminate a passage from the Declaration of Independence
etched into the stone of the dome. While the other students
walk around the statue, I read the inscription. As I begin reading, I start to tear up again.

There are those words again:

*We hold these truths to be self-evident: that all men are created
equal.*

*That they are endowed by their Creator with certain inalienable
rights, among these are life, liberty and the pursuit of happiness.*

But who really gets to pursue their happiness? Do those
words even apply to me anymore? My family moved here for
a better life, a chance at the American dream. *Give me your*

tired, your poor, your huddled masses yearning to breathe free, it says on the bottom of the Statue of Liberty. That was us. America is a beacon of hope around the world, promising a better way of life, if only you can make it here.

I've been thinking about the scholarship. I may be here enjoying a tour of the Capitol and looking forward to meeting the president later, but I keep getting a sinking feeling in my stomach as I look at all these gorgeous buildings. If I can't accept the scholarship to go to college and later grad school, then what's the point of all this? If my family can't live without fear of losing their home and having their entire lives uprooted, then my coming here hasn't done anything to make our situation better.

I tune in to what Suzanne is saying. "Thomas Jefferson was just as important to this country as George Washington. Consider the immensity of this statue. Now think of the immensity of just one of the documents he wrote and how it influenced not only the creation of America, but both you and me this very day. This man wrote the Declaration of Independence. Can you get any more important than that? This is the challenge we all face. What can we do to better ourselves and this country? What can we do to be remembered? Who do we want to be?"

The group moves on, but I linger, and I hear a step behind me. I glance sideways. It's Royce. We've been shadowing each other the whole tour. I was acutely aware of where he was the whole time, and he must have been aware of me too, because here he is now, even though I was pretty cold to him back there. I feel bad for blowing him off earlier.

"I know what I'd do," he says.

"What's that?" I say, still staring at the statue. Trying not to lose my resolve, I count eight buttons on Jefferson's vest.

"I'd tear that statue down and put up one of me," he says.

I snort. "Of you? That's sort of egotistical, don't you think?"

"Not at all," Royce says. "I think I'd look pretty good. I wouldn't have that hipster haircut though."

"Ha." I let out one single laugh, then purposely cut it short.

"You don't believe me?" Royce asks.

"No," I say as I walk around the statue. I'm not looking at Royce, but he follows me anyway. I kind of wish he would leave me alone. He makes me feel too many things—excited, angry, sad, happy. Ugh.

"Do you know why I'd want a statue of myself?"

I shrug like I don't care.

He tells me anyway. "Because it's something my dad will never have."

I feel myself softening. "What makes you so sure there won't be one of him?" I ask. "Maybe he'll have one twice as big. You never know."

"I doubt that—there always seems to be someone mad at him. Don't you follow the news? They say he's a surefire deal breaker on most things. He may be the house majority leader, but he's not inventing a new America, or writing some declaration of anything that's going to change the ideals we're built on. He'll never have an 'I Have a Dream' type speech either."

"Now you're being harsh," I say, though I'm not sure how much I like his father either. The group heads out for the steps, and I should really follow them.

"I'm just telling the truth. I'm tired of being in his shadow. You have no idea what it's like."

"And you have an idea of what my life is like?"

I start to walk away, but Royce catches my arm. "I didn't

say that," he says. I look up at him. His eyes are sincere. Soulful.

"You didn't say it, but you were thinking it," I respond. "You don't know how hard I had to work to be here. You and your rich friends think this is all a joke, some kind of boring sixth-grade field trip, but it's not."

"I don't think that," he says. "And my sixth-grade field trip was to Sacramento." He tries not to smile.

"Whatever."

Royce glances over at Carrie and her crew, who have stopped on the steps now and are pretending not to stare at us. "Is that why you're mad at me all of a sudden?" he asks quietly. "Because I know them?"

I shake my head, even though he's got it on the nose.

"I can't help who I am," he says. "Or who my family is. Who my dad is. Or who I've grown up around."

I know. I know that, just like I can't help who I am and who my family is—or isn't—but I don't tell him that.

Last night, we didn't do anything more than kiss and talk… and talk and kiss…okay…*a whole lot* of kissing. I'm not upset about that—it's more that I know I'm nothing to him and won't *be* anything to him. I'm just some girl he met during another boring event in D.C. He's probably been with so many girls.

"Carrie Mayberry said you're a player," I blurt. And to be honest, wasn't that what I thought too? Even before Carrie said it? When I looked on his Facebook page?

"She said what?" he says.

I start to walk away, but he catches my arm. "Are you serious? Are you really going to judge me based on something *Carrie Mayberry* told you about me? Even after last night?'

"What about last night?" I snap.

He looks around, his hand still on my arm. We're practically alone, save for a few tourists. The award group has left the monument and is milling around the bottom of the steps. He stares at me. "You didn't think…" He can't seem to finish a sentence.

My cheeks are so hot, I feel like smoke is coming off them. Is he really going to say it to my face? That it was nothing to him? That it didn't mean anything? Maybe he's right and I'm overreacting. We just kissed after all.

"Nothing," he says, clearly irritated. "Forget it."

"Yeah, that's what I thought." I shake his hand off.

Now it's his turn to look angry. "No, you don't know anything. If you didn't think last night was amazing, then there's nothing I can do to change your mind. I feel like I've known you all my life even if we just met. I've never told a girl I'm dyslexic, or that I used to have so many tutors everyone called me names and made me feel stupid. I've never been with anyone who didn't care who my father was, or wasn't using me to get to him."

I'm staring at him. My head is spinning. "Royce…"

His hands are in fists by his side. "But for all I know you have a boyfriend back home, and *you're* the one who's playing me."

I'm so shocked I can't respond for a moment. "You're worried about *me*?"

"Why not? You're beautiful, smart, funny," he says, like it's the most obvious thing in the world.

"You think I'm beautiful?" I whisper in disbelief.

He blushes. "I think you're incredibly beautiful," he says, his voice low and husky like last night.

I don't have low self-esteem and I know I'm pretty, but

no boy has ever told me I'm beautiful. It's so romantic, I almost swoon.

"You must have a dozen guys trying to date you, if you don't have someone already. So yeah, I'm worried about you," he says defensively.

"Well, you shouldn't be. I have no one but you." I don't mean to sound like a loser, but I also don't want him to think I just kiss every guy I meet at a party.

"Really?" he asks, raising his eyebrows, and his eyes are lighting up again.

"Yeah." I'm softening. God, he is a sweetheart.

"So you 'have me,' do you?" A small smile begins to form on his lips. I want to touch them again, the way I did last night, when I traced them with the tips of my fingers. So I do. My fingers flutter and he reaches for my hand, holds it in his and presses it to his lips. "I can't stop thinking about last night," he says when he releases it and puts his arms around me.

"I can't either," I say.

"I couldn't wait to see you," he murmurs. I can smell him, that earthy, masculine scent underneath the sharp clean smell of soap and aftershave. I want to breathe it in forever. And this time, it's my turn to pull him close. I pull him by his lapels so that he has to lean down.

"I woke up thinking about you," I tell him. It's strange—before last night, we barely even knew each other, but now he's so important to me. When I reach up to kiss him, he meets me halfway, and soon we're kissing at the Jefferson Memorial.

"All right," I say when we catch our breath.

"All right what?" he asks, still cupping my face in his hands.

"After I meet the president this afternoon."

Royce looks confused. "What about it?"

"I'll have two free hours before the farewell dinner."

You can get a lot of kissing done in two hours.

14

My fellow Americans, we are and always will be a nation of immigrants. We were strangers once, too.

—BARACK OBAMA

THE PRESIDENT IS taller than I expected and more handsome in real life than on television. He greets us in the Oval Office. Each group has five to six minutes with him. He's smiling the entire time and acts interested in everyone.

"You must be Jasmine de los Santos," he says when he gets to me. I'm shocked that he knows my name. I'm not even wearing a name tag.

"That's me, Mr. President," I giggle. I can't help it. I'm too giddy.

"What's so funny about your name?"

"I don't know," I say. "I just can't believe I'm getting to meet the president."

I'm totally starstruck. I've never been so pumped to meet anyone in my whole life. After he finishes shaking my hand, I ask him how he knows my name.

"I was a student just like you," he says with a smile. "I read your scholarship essay. What was the title again?"

"'Something in Between,'" I say. I'm in total disbelief that the president remembers something that I wrote.

The president continues talking about my essay. "My father was from Kenya. Growing up, I think he felt some of the same things that you wrote about in your essay. And I did too. There are times when being biracial feels like living in two different countries at the same time. I never thought I would even *see* the inside of the Oval Office, to be honest."

Wow, the president *is* like me; he even said so. "Do you think I could sit in your chair?" I ask.

The president looks taken aback but he smiles gracefully. "You mean right now?"

I laugh. "No. Not that way. I mean, do you think someone like me could be president? I know I wasn't born in the United States so that will never happen but..."

All of a sudden the president gets serious. "You know, Jasmine. The law—as it is now anyway—may prevent you from doing certain things you want to do. But don't ever let an accident of birth keep you from what you want to do with your life."

It's almost like he knows that I'm undocumented.

The honorees behind me look annoyed that I'm holding up the line, but I know this might be the only time I ever get to talk to the president. "Can I ask you one more question?" He nods. I take a deep breath. "What do you think is going to happen to the immigration reform bill?"

"Ah," he says, shaking his head. "This may not make you feel better, but I find that the public stances of politicians on these things don't always match their personal ones. They use these kinds of bills to make statements about themselves. It's not always about what's good for the country."

"So you don't think the bill will pass," I say quietly.

"Whether I think the bill will pass or not isn't the point. It's that people like you—brilliant, young, educated minds—will turn the tide of some of this country's backward thinking. This country depends on you. You know, America has a long way to go, but we're still sending top-notch kids like you and the other honorees to best schools in the nation. And you're all going on to do great things. Whatever you do, it will make a difference."

"Thank you, Mr. President, thank you so much," I say in disbelief as he turns to greet another student.

I want to text Mom, but I can't just yet, because the Secret Service is holding our cell phones. I want to scream. I want to do another victory lap. I just had a meaningful conversation with the president of the United States. I feel like I'm in this surreal state, levitating above the room, looking down on myself, at everything, at the president by his desk, at Carrie, who's grinning just like me when she meets him.

We're all equals in here. The president doesn't care about private schools or public schools or where we come from. He cares that *we* care, that we're trying our best, making something of our lives, and most of all, that we're not giving up, even if threatened with obstacles completely out of our control.

If only I could convince the entire Congress of those things too.

Like clockwork, after I get my cell phone back, I get a text from Royce.

royceb: how did it go with the Big Man?

royceb: did he know your name? I love when he does that.

jasmindls: Yes he did and I have a new crush, sorry. 😊

royceb: huh, I might have to do something drastic then.

royceb: and the Secret Service ain't no joke. 😵

jasmindls: Don't worry I'll visit you in prison.

royceb: will you bake me a cake with a file in it? 😇

jasmindls: Better. I'll jump out of the cake. 😈

royceb: now you're talking. 😎

jasmindls: Like Marilyn Monroe and JFK.

royceb: she baked him a cake?

jasmindls: No she sang him happy birthday. In a tight dress. 😲

royceb: uh huh, I could live with that. 👍

jasmindls: Perv.

royceb: You started it!

jasmindls: Let's get going then! ♥

jasmindls: Your two hours start now. Where should we meet?

At the restaurant there's a view of the street from the table, which is surrounded by potted trees with little lights in them twinkling everywhere. Royce arrives while I'm sipping water from a glass. He picked the place, told me to meet him there. He asks if I like his choice and I tell him I do.

"It's like Titania's garden, don't you think? With all the lights?" he says.

"From *Midsummer Night's Dream*. Yes. Exactly. You're such a romantic," I tease.

He smiles broadly, not at all embarrassed, and I like him even more than I did already. "So is it safe to let the president live?" he says, scooting so that he's next to me in the banquette.

"Why not? He seems like a nice guy," I say. "And anyway, he's already married."

He slings an arm over the seat, his hand dangling over my shoulder. "Yeah, I suppose you're right. So what did you think of the Oval Office?"

I mull my answer as I move closer to him as well. So this is what attraction means—wanting to be as near as possible. "It was..." I say, pausing, not able to think of the right word. "Presidential."

He cracks a grin and gives my shoulder a squeeze, then lets his hand stay there. "What's your family like? Are they anything like you?"

"Why do you ask?" I say coyly, feeling warm all over.

When he runs his knuckles down the side of my arm, I feel goose bumps underneath my sweater sleeves. "Just wondering if they speak in riddles like you."

"Like you?" I counter, because he plays the game as much as I do.

"No way. I'm an open book."

"They're like me and not like me, I guess," I tell him. "My parents grew up in the Philippines, in another culture. They're very strict. But we have the same sense of humor. We get each other."

"You're lucky."

"I know I am. I'm always thankful for that." I lean against him, thinking of what he said the night before and at the Jefferson Memorial. "Can I ask you something? How come when you talk about politics you always get this look on your face?"

"What look?"

"This look," I say, trying to imitate him. "Like it's repulsive."

"I don't know," he says. "I guess maybe it's because my dad

expects me to go into it like he did. His dad was a politician too. He was a congressman, and my dad took over his seat."

"Old money, huh?"

"I guess. My dad's family does all right, but it was my mom's side of the family that funded my dad's first campaign. My grandfather came from Mexico and started a steel company."

"So he was an immigrant," I say, smiling to learn that his grandfather wasn't too different from me.

"Yeah, he started out selling oranges by the highway, is the family legend, but in his lifetime became one of the biggest industrial manufacturers in the state," he says proudly.

A waiter comes by and we just order drinks, since there's a group dinner with Suzanne later on.

Royce reaches for a piece of warm bread and tears off a piece. He chews thoughtfully. "Anyway, yeah, I guess I'm not into politics. All that dirt, all those compromises, the bubble of big spending."

"Still, it's still a way to help people outside of that bubble. There are other people out there who get forgotten, and they need a voice too," I say.

"Have *you* ever thought about going into politics?" Royce asks. "You definitely have the willpower and intensity. I'd believe anything you say."

He's so sweet that I can't help but smile at him. "You don't have to go into politics to change the world. You just have to work hard." I wonder if that's my father talking now, or maybe my mother. I'm not sure.

"You really believe that?"

"Is it naive of me?"

"No," he says thoughtfully. "It's idealistic. Optimistic.

That's cool." He removes his hand from my shoulder, and I'm a disappointed for a minute until he places it on my knee.

I used to look at couples snuggling in restaurants who couldn't keep their hands off each other and wonder what that was all about. Now I understand. I can't stop touching him either. I run my fingers through his soft hair, pushing it out of his eyes like I did last night.

We disengage a little when we finally get our drinks— iced teas—green for him, black for me since I need the caffeine. When the waiter leaves, Royce has a different look on his face—more determined, but not as self-assured as usual.

"I thought more about our conversation last night, about how I want to go into journalism. But my parents will never go for it. Probably 'cause I'm not smart enough. I think I could be good at it though. When I want to find out something, I don't let up."

"Stop putting yourself down. You'd be great at it, and you're more than smart enough," I say. Then I change tack. "But the thing about journalists, though, is that they have to tell the truth, right?"

"The facts, I think. Truth is relative." He can tell I'm testing him. He's clever and has his guard up, an eyebrow raised.

I guess I *am* testing him. "Okay, the facts, then." I move a little away from him to take a sip of my drink so that he has to remove his hand from my knee.

"What are you getting at?" he says, although I have a feeling he already knows.

"You never explained how you know Carrie," I say. "Or why she would say that about you." *Royce Blakely isn't what he seems like. I've been there. He's a total player.*

Royce meets my gaze steadily, then sighs. "Carrie and I

kind of had a thing the summer before junior year," he says moodily.

"What do you mean by *a thing*?"

"We made out at that party she was talking about this morning. I was pretty wasted when it happened. After, we went out a few times, because I could tell she expected it. But I wasn't feeling it and told her. I wasn't up for dating long-distance either. She wasn't too happy about that."

"You guys seemed pretty friendly today." I try not to feel jealous, but I am. So he *did* go out with Carrie. She's his type, most likely. His brother even said so, said that I wasn't the usual kind of girl that Royce liked.

"Today was the first time I've talked to her in over a year. I was on my way to find you, and I didn't want to be rude by ignoring her as I was walking by. Would you have wanted me to do that?"

I think about it for a second. "No. I guess not." I try not to be mad about Carrie. Of course he had a life before me, other girls before me. *Deal with it.* What did I expect? That he'd waited his whole life to kiss me too?

He leans closer again. "You know, I kind of like it when you're jealous." He's actually smiling.

"Who says I'm jealous?" I huff.

"I'm saying it." He's fully grinning now. "It means you like me. And I like you too, Jas. A lot."

I melt. I turn to him, and he puts an arm around my shoulders again. "You smell good," he says, his nose in my hair. "Is that coconut?"

"Mmm-hmm," I answer as he moves from my hair and buries his face in my neck, planting soft kisses there, then works his way back up.

I close my eyes and tilt my chin so that our lips meet. He

kisses me softly at first, but soon our mouths are open, and the kiss deepens. His hands, my hands, they're everywhere. I can't get enough of touching him. I hug him under his jacket, wrapping my arms around his strong back. We're both breathless.

But I pull away when I realize we're not alone, and we're in public, at a restaurant.

"Sorry," he says. "Got a little carried away there." He has a goofy smile on his face, and I want to kiss him again. Maybe I should be embarrassed, but I'm not.

"I have to ask Suzanne if it's okay, but will you come with me to the farewell dinner?" I ask, already texting her.

"Of course," he says.

He pays the check even though I try to hand him a twenty. Suzanne texts me back to say someone canceled, so Royce can join us. We attend the dinner, where I thank Suzanne and say goodbye to Richard and Simon, and we all promise to keep in touch. The whole time we're there, Royce holds my hand under the table, and I squeeze it back.

When we get back to the hotel, I stop before we go through the double doors. I run out to a small grassy patch and kneel in the dirt. I'd forgotten to do this earlier, and it's my last chance.

"What are you doing?" he asks, kneeling next to me.

I show him the tiny bottle and pick up a tiny handful of dirt. "I like to collect earth or sand from the places I've been, and I forgot to do this all weekend."

Royce nods and doesn't ask more questions. He helps me fill the bottle and close the stopper. "There. A little part of D.C. you can take home."

I'm nervous when we get in the elevator. I wasn't sure what the plan was—we didn't say anything to each other, but somehow I know we both assumed we would spend the last night alone together. But where?

Do I go up to his room?

Invite him to mine?

"I have, uh, roommates," I say.

"I don't," he says.

We're suddenly shy now, and he looks just as nervous as I am, which makes me feel better. "Your room, then," I say.

He looks at me from under his dark lashes, his long bangs falling into his eyes and smiles so sweetly. "Okay." He presses his floor number.

Then he pulls me closer to him and we're kissing again, kissing like mad, and a part of me is worried someone else will get in the elevator and another part of me doesn't care at all who sees us.

When the elevator stops at his floor, we're out of there faster than a senator rushing to the House floor to filibuster an important bill. He makes me feel things and want to do things I've never felt before. Every part of me is addicted to him. Being with him is like waking up, like I'm just discovering something new and amazing about the world, and I tell him so when we stop kissing for a brief moment.

We're lying on the bed, on top of the covers, and I'm looking up at him while he leans on an elbow, gazing down at me.

"I like that," he says. "We're waking up to each other." He rubs my cheek. "Your skin is so soft."

"Yours is so stubbly," I tease, when I put a hand on his.

I like that we're comfortable around each other. I thought I'd feel self-conscious with a boy, nervous, worried that I wouldn't know how to kiss correctly, or that I was doing something wrong. But there's none of that. I've been with him for only two days, but I feel closer to him than to anyone.

All night, we make out, order room service, talk, and make out again. I don't ever want to stop kissing him. I wish I could stay with him until morning, but I can't. I have an early flight.

"When am I going to see you again?" he asks, when we get to my door, yawning. His hair is rumpled and his shirt is untucked, but he's as gorgeous as ever, if not more.

"Um, we both live in LA," I say, giving him one last embrace.

"This weekend, then," he says, kissing my forehead.

"Text me," I say.

He reaches for his phone in his jeans pocket. He punches in a message and sends it. My phone buzzes in my handbag and I remove it to read what he'd sent.

It reads, Hi it's Royce, your boyfriend. Let's hang out this weekend.

I can't help but smile. I guess I have a boyfriend now.

15

An ocean could not explain the distance we have traveled.

—JONATHAN SAFRAN FOER, *EXTREMELY LOUD AND INCREDIBLY CLOSE*

IT'S NOON WHEN Dad picks me up from LAX in our old Toyota Camry. I'm a little tired from the flight, but I feel a huge surge of warmth when I see my old dad in his trusty Member's Only jacket (that Mom still buys at Costco), a huge smile on his leathered face.

"*Anak*. We missed you," he says, giving me a big hug before putting my bags in the trunk. "How was D.C.?"

"Missed you too, Daddy. It was amazing." I tell him all about the receptions, and the fancy people I met, and how the president complimented me on my essay.

Dad listens quietly and nods, and I can tell he also feels bad that this weekend is all I'm ever going to get from being a National Scholar. When his phone rings he picks it up, and soon he's deep into a discussion with Tito Charlie about a new kind of karaoke machine he's thinking of buying.

While he discusses all the new bells and whistles of this fantastic machine, I stare at the palm trees blurring by the window. I wonder when Royce is getting back into town. I'm still buzzing from the high of being with him, but I'm also thinking about the research I did on the plane (thank you,

free Wi-Fi) about the upcoming vote on the immigration reform bill, college tuition, and finding a path to citizenship.
Up until now, I'd been discouraged by what I'd discovered,
but my talk with the president really moved me. I can't give
up. If I don't keep trying to change our situation, who will?

At the airport, when Suzanne dropped me off, I'd confessed
that I wasn't going to be able to accept the scholarship. When
she asked me why, I told her things were complicated and left
it at that. She said she was sorry about it, but she understood,
and if the situation changed to let her know. I still have until
the spring to turn in the form and accept the tuition award.

I told her it was unlikely the situation would change that
quickly, it would take a miracle if it did. For now I put it out
of my mind, because as soon as Dad pulls into the driveway,
I catch a glimpse of Mom's garden and realize how much I
missed home. And now home means Royce too. He's local.

"What's that smile for?" says Dad.

"Nothing," I say.

"Hmm. Fine don't talk to your dad," says Dad.

"What! You were the one who practically didn't talk to
me the entire ride home! You were obsessed with your new
karaoke machine!"

"It's a good one. Samsung. Five thousand songs."

Dad cracks me up. "Where's Mom?" I ask.

He frowns. "She doesn't feel well." I know this means
Mom's still depressed about losing her job.

"Mommy?" I yell. "Where are you?"

"Over here," she says from the kitchen. She's putting out
lunch—chicken salad sandwiches and potato chips. She turns
away from the counter and gives me a big hug before sitting
at the table. "How was your trip?" She's smiling but her eyes
are sad.

"Fun," I say. I tell her about seeing the Capitol, about how someone thought God had been painted on the rotunda. I almost tell her about Royce, but I get nervous since it would mean confessing I was hanging out with a boy, which I'm not allowed to do.

"I'm glad you went. It's scary to take risks, Jas," Mom says. "I can't even tell you how afraid I was to relocate our whole family to the United States. Your father and I had no idea how you kids were going to handle the move, but we wanted to give you opportunities that neither of us had in the Philippines."

Speaking of opportunities. I tell her my new resolve. "I'm not giving up on being able to go to college. I did some research while I was in D.C. Meeting the president reminded me that I want to do great things with my life. I can't give up on my dreams."

Taking a big sigh, she leans back in her chair and rubs her eyes. I know she's worried about money, worried about everything.

"There are special programs," I explain. "I can use our low-income status to get tuition fee waivers. There may be a few colleges that can afford to give scholarships for people like me, who grew up in the United States but don't have citizenship. We might have to pay for a couple of applications, but I won't know what's possible if I never try. Most of the state schools are out, because they're funded by the government, but I could try for a some of the private ones, like Stanford." I can't give up on Stanford, I have to keep trying, and if I don't apply, I'll lose a whole year.

"Are you sure? I don't want you to have any false hope. I feel bad for never telling you the truth." She sounds disappointed in herself. It's heartbreaking to hear my mother, who has always been so strong and such a go-getter, to feel like a failure. "What about the reform bill? Will that help?"

"Even if it passes, it could take forever before it becomes law. There are deadlines coming up," I say. "I can't miss them or I might miss out on some of the schools. You don't have to feel bad, Mom. Everything you did—how hard you made me work—wouldn't be worth anything if I didn't keep trying."

I read somewhere that a lot of kids of immigrants grow up quickly and are given more responsibility than other kids. Their parents tend to depend on them, mostly because the kids can speak the language better and can act as a conduit to mainstream American society. The child becomes the parent, and the parent, the child. I feel a little like that now, like I'm older and wiser than my mom.

If I do go to college, my life will become even more different from hers. If I don't go, I know I'll never live up to her dreams for me. It seems like any path I take will lead us further apart. Maybe that's part of what being a daughter means. Maybe that's how the children of all immigrants feel.

Still, I'm determined and happy to have a goal. I like goals. I tend to meet them.

Dad comes in from the living room. He stares at my face, squinting his eyes. "There's something about you I didn't notice earlier," he says.

My little brothers brush past us. "Her face," they both say in unison. "It stinks!"

"You both stink!" I say, stretching out my arms.

Both of them come to hug me. I love my brothers so much I think I'm going to cry as I squeeze them as tight as I can.

Isko pinches his nose. "No, you stink!"

Dad actually comes to my defense. "Your sister does not stink!"

"Thanks, Daddy," I say.

"Well, something stinks," Danny says, twisting away from my embrace.

"Can you please just turn into a cat or something useful?" I say to him.

Dad laughs. "If he were a cat, I'd throw him out. I may throw him out anyway!"

Danny has already disappeared from the room. He'll be buried in his manga in a minute.

"I'm serious," Dad adds.

"I know, Daddy."

He's still looking at me funny. "I'm serious that something is different about you. You keep smiling. What happened in Washington? Were you responsible? Did you meet a boy?"

Eeek! How'd he know? Do my parents have some kind of guy radar? Am I really smiling that much? I kissed Royce a total of one, two—okay, maybe a few more—times. I already know what my dad is thinking. He's so overprotective. "Daddy, I go to Washington, D.C., as an honored guest, and you want to give me a sex talk?"

"I don't trust those people," he says. His voice is getting louder. "You see them in the movies. They're worse than those sleazy Wall Street stockbrokers who hire ladies of the evening every night and snort God-knows-what into their tiny brains."

Oh my God, my parents and the way they talk! It's too much. Ladies of the evening? Who says that? My Filipino parents, I guess.

My parents have always had weird rules about dating. Filipinos are all about family. If you're even *thinking* about dating a boy, they want to meet him. They've always threatened to send me on dates with a chaperone, like they had to have when they were teenagers, but I don't think they would actually go through with it. Although, if they knew I'd been with Royce *alone* during the weekend, they'd probably have to start taking medicine for their blood pressure.

"It was a weekend for high school honorees," I say.

He leans on my mother's shoulder. "Why are you so happy, then?"

"Am I not supposed to be happy?"

Now he knows I'm covering up. I don't know how he figures this stuff out. He's always called me on the tiniest of lies. I should just shut my mouth, become a nun, take vows of celibacy and silence. If I let Dad get what he wanted, I'd be alone forever and never move out of his house.

He trades looks with Mom. "All right. Out with it," he says.

I hold on to the thinnest shred of denial. "Out with what?"

But that's it. He's calling in reinforcements.

Dad stands up and gazes down at Mom. "Your daughter. She has a secret!"

"All daughters have secrets," Mom says. "If you've lost your interrogation skills then just leave her alone! She's old enough to have a life outside of us."

I give Dad a wide smile. This is an unprecedented victory in our household.

He points a finger at me, "We better meet him soon, whoever he is!" and leaves the room as I'm still beaming.

Later that night, after I'm already in bed in my heart-print pajamas, Mom comes into my room. She knocks so lightly, I almost don't hear. I'm surprised she didn't just do her usual barging in, talking at some sonic level. Something must be wrong. She sits on the edge of my bed, asking if I'm asleep yet.

"Not yet," I say. "What's up?"

"So, can you tell me anything more about your trip to D.C.?"

Oh no. She's going to ask if I did meet a boy. The whole day I was sort of glad she didn't ask too many questions. I don't think I can hide Royce from her like I did from Dad. She and I think so much alike.

"I told you guys all about it already," I say lightly. I showed them a few of my photos (although not the ones with Royce).

She lies down on the bed next to me and starts stroking my hair. It makes me feel like a little girl again. Mom's being so nice, I can tell she's about to ask me something else. Something private. I sit up in bed, forcing her to stop touching my hair.

"Did you make any friends while you were there, *neneng*?" she asks.

I *knew* it. She's playing the rare good cop. Mommy-Daddy role reversal. "I made several friends from around the country," I say just to make a point. "Some from LA too."

"Really? What kind of 'friends'?"

"Mom. Come on. You know, with the other honorees. We had a chaperone. We ate together, we bonded. But since you're playing detective, yes, I met 'a boy.'" I can't hide the smile on my face anymore. Mom will understand, and I do want to tell her about Royce. He's too important to me not to tell her about. Especially if I want to be able to see him in LA.

She sits up straight and turns on the lamp, blinding me. "You met a boy from the other side of the country?"

"Sort of," I hedge.

She pauses for a moment, considers a thought, then crosses her arms. "Is he Filipino?"

"Does it matter?"

"No, of course not." Mom shrugs.

I know my parents don't care who I marry, but they do care that whoever I marry shares our values. They always talk about how Americans aren't close to their families like Filipinos are.

"Well," Mom sighs. "I guess it's okay. He still lives on the other side of the country."

I shift on the bed. "I never said that."

"Where does he live, then? Who is this boy?"

"He lives in Bel-Air. He's the son of Congressman Colin Blakely, the house majority leader."

I can tell Mom is shocked. She sort of leans back. I'm starting to fear that this is too much for her to take in. First the scholarship, then the trip to Washington, now there's a boy— and not any boy, but a rich boy with a powerful father who's practically the enemy. Mom shifts her weight, nearly falling off the bed. "You can't mean the congressman who's always on TV trying to kill the immigration bill that the Senate passed?"

"Yeah, but he's not like his dad," I say defensively.

"Are you sure it's safe to know him?"

"It's not like I told him about us. But he's not like that, Mom. I know he isn't. He's nice."

"Oh," she says softly. "What's his name?"

"Royce."

It surprises me that even just the sound of his name coming out of my mouth makes me feel more hopeful, like everything is within my reach.

"What kind of name is that?" she asks. "Like the car?"

I giggle. "I know, right?"

"So you like this boy?"

"Yeah," I say. "I like him a lot." I've never had a boyfriend, I've never been allowed to date. But I'm seventeen years old now, and I think it's okay to admit I like a boy, isn't it? I'm not just attracted to him—I really like him. He's just like me, intense and sort of secretly nerdy. Most of all, I like how he looks into my eyes like he's seeing past the image everyone else sees into who I really am beyond all the things that I do. And he thinks I'm beautiful.

Mom stays quiet.

"I want you guys to meet him," I say. "Because I want to, um...hang out with him. Okay?"

Mom doesn't say a word.

"Mom?"

"We'll see, I'll have to talk to your dad about it."

My stomach twists. Whenever she has to talk to my dad about something, it just means *no*.

16

She cannot stay out of duty. The things one does,
one should do out of love.

—EDWIDGE DANTICAT, *BREATH, EYES, MEMORY*

MONDAY, KAYLA AND I walk together to cheer practice. Our school is a typical California one—the hallways are outside, and people walk through the grassy courtyards to get across campus. Our town is in a valley, so we have a view of the mountains all around. A bunch of football players wave as we walk from the quad to the gym. Not just them. Being a cheerleader means pretty much everyone knows who you are. That's one of my favorite things about it.

We wave back to people we know. Kayla and I aren't in the same classes, so this is the first chance we've had to download since I got back.

I was worried she'd still be mad that she found out about my scholarship at the same time the other girls did, but she seems to be over it. And she's over Courtney being named captain while I was away as well. The squad qualified for Regionals, like we all expected we would. That competition is coming up in December, so we have practice almost every day now.

She links her arms around mine. "So how was D.C.? Is the president cool?"

"Yes but more importantly, you'll never guess who was there," I say.

"Who!" Kayla can smell a good cute-boy story from one hint. She claps her hands and jumps up and down.

"Remember that guy I met at the hospital? The one from Bel-Air?" I say.

"Right, what's his name again? Aston? Martin?" she teases.

"It's Royce!" I laugh.

"That's the one. You looooove him!" she says. "He was there? Tell me everything!"

"Yeah, he was there. He knew I would be there, so he went with his dad to the dinner."

"What!"

"Yeah. So we, um… You know."

Kayla gives another squeal. "Oh my God, good-girl Jasmine de los Santos, you hooked up with a boy!"

"We didn't *hook up* hook up… We just made out…"

She's fully laughing now and gives me a squeeze. "You like him?"

"A lot." *So much.*

"So when are you going to see him again?"

"I don't know. My parents are being weird about it."

"They won't let you see him?"

"I don't know. They haven't said yes or no." I nervously switch my backpack to my other shoulder.

"Well, that's a start. Your parents *always* say no."

"It is, isn't it? Maybe it means they'll say yes." They have to, I think. I won't take no for an answer this time. I'm a senior in high school—I'm allowed to have a boyfriend by now, aren't I? We don't live in the Philippines, we live in America. At least, right now we do. Even in my happiness, the dark cloud of our problem hangs heavily. "So, what's up with you? How are things at home?"

"They suck. Let's not talk about it. And I miss Dylan."

"I'm sorry, K. Is he on tour with the band or something?"

"Yeah, Seattle now."

"When is he back?"

"At the end of the month."

"You'll survive," I say. "You really think my parents will say yes? That I can see Royce?"

"Why not? What are they going to do, lock you up in a tower?" She smirks.

If they could, they would, I think.

My parents don't say yes, and they don't say no either. What they say when I ask for permission again later that week is "Up to you." Usually, when my parents say things are up to me, it means they want me to make the right decision for myself, to prove I'm responsible and can be trusted. I know they think that I'll decide that I don't have to see him. But they're wrong.

"Okay, so if it's up to me, I'm going to hang out with him on Saturday. He wants me to meet his family. I can't drive, so he's coming out here to pick me up and take me to meet them. Actually, just his mom, I already met his dad, but he's back in D.C. right now. So is it okay if Royce picks me up?"

Dad raises his eyebrows and looks at Mom. "Is he a safe driver?" he asks.

"I'm sure he is."

"Pilar?"

"We said it was up to her," Mom says, getting up from the couch.

"You really think this is the right decision?" asks Dad.

"Yes." I won't budge on this. I'm tired of being treated like a child. It's bad enough I can't drive so I have to cadge rides all the time, and Royce is nice enough to offer to drive all the way out here to pick me up just to turn around and drive right back home. It's a long way from the Valley to the Westside—people in LA would even joke that we have a long-distance relationship.

"Besides, technically, I've already been on two dates with him in D.C.," I say.

Dad raises his eyes again and shifts uncomfortably in his chair. Mom just shrugs, like she's tired of this conversation "It's up to you," she says again.

My parents don't say anything more, so it's settled. On Saturday, Royce and I are hanging out. It's a small step, but a huge victory where my social life is concerned.

Of course, when Saturday rolls around and Royce comes to pick me up, neither of my parents are at home. Mom is out cleaning a house for cash, a connection through a friend. Dad pulled a weekend shift. I tell Royce I'm sorry they're not here to say hello.

"It's cool," Royce says as we're driving over the canyon.

I couldn't wait to see him again, and we had to pull over right after we left my house so that we could say hello properly. Here I go again, doing things I never thought I would, like making out in cars. But it's just so much fun kissing him. I don't feel nervous at all around him, like I thought I would be with my first boyfriend. I'm just happy and excited.

He has one hand on the steering wheel and holds my hand with the other. Watching him drive his silver-gray Range Rover Sport, I think he seems much older than seventeen.

He drives fast, changing lanes, maneuvering between cars like the native Angeleno he is.

"I like to drive fast," he says, wiggling his eyebrows.

"I see that," I say, amused.

Royce laughs. "By the way, Dad's still in Washington. You'll meet my mom and little sister though. Mason is back at SC."

I wasn't really fond of Mason when I met him in the Ritz-Carlton lobby but I keep my mouth shut. I'm glad he's back at college for now. Mason is his brother, and in Filipino families we don't talk about the relatives we don't like until we're part of the family. When you're married, you can throw them under the bus every which way. But only after you're married.

There's even a Filipino saying that to court the daughter, you have to court the mother too. I wonder what Royce would say about that, so I ask him.

"Oh, I've got this! Your mom is going to love me, just wait."

"Confident, are you?"

He grins. "If she's anything like her daughter, she's in love with me already."

I laugh but I don't deny it.

We pull up to the house and get out of Royce's car. The gravel driveway leads to a freshly manicured lawn with tasteful shrubs and white flowers. There are magnificent white pillars holding up a balcony over the front door, and two big white chimneys standing proudly over the gray slate roof. It's stately and traditional—everything I would have imagined a congressman's house would be.

Though I try not to show Royce, I'm a little intimidated to meet Mrs. Blakely. It's not because they have more money or a bigger house than my family. Okay, so maybe that's part of it. But it's also because rich people are often so sure of themselves that it's hard to feel as confident in their presence.

Royce's mother probably went to a school that taught her how to do everything correctly. She's beautiful, I know, and I'm sure she's smart and well-read and most likely even knows how to flawlessly fold a fitted sheet. Not even Mom does that—she just sort of bundles them up and stuffs them inside the hall closet.

A little girl who looks to be about eleven years old rushes by on a scooter. She nearly runs over Royce's foot.

"What the heck are you doing, Olivia?" he says.

"Trying to run over your foot."

I can't decide whether to be appalled or to laugh at her honesty. It seems like something Danny would say. She has to be Royce's little sister.

"I can see that," Royce says as his sister heads away from us down the driveway. "Are you not aware that your scooter would actually hurt my foot? I feel pain, you know. Even though I'm your older brother, I do feel pain."

Olivia spins around on her scooter. She giggles the kind of laugh that means she knows what she's doing. I never understood why younger siblings take satisfaction in the pain of their older brothers and sisters. Looks like we have something in common.

"My brothers are like that too," I say.

"Olivia," Royce calls after his sister. "This is Jasmine, my girlfriend."

Olivia rides closer. She stops right in front of me. I finally get a better look at her face. She has long, wavy brown hair with blond highlights, golden-caramel skin, and dark eyes that look exactly like Royce's. She's gorgeous and knows it.

"Royce likes you," she says with an evil little laugh.

"I do like her," he says. "So watch it, Liv."

"Hi, Olivia," I say. "I like your scooter. Too bad you don't have another one. I'd race you to the corner."

"You wouldn't beat me," she says.

"But I'd try."

Olivia lets out a laugh. "We'll see," she says.

She's growing on me.

"You're really pretty. I like your hair," she says.

"Thanks, I like yours too."

"Do you like Royce?" she asks, with the same devilish giggle.

"I do," I say, smiling up at him. He winks back.

"Okay, okay, get out of here, Liv," Royce says. "Where's Mom?"

"In the house. Duh." Olivia sticks her tongue out at him and speeds off.

"This way," Royce says. "Told you."

"I think she's cute," I say. "I was kind of hoping she would chase you around a little bit more with that scooter of hers."

"I don't think so," he says as I follow him through the front door.

He gives me a whole tour of the place. The Blakely house is spacious. There are huge, vaulted ceilings so high I can't imagine how they clean the cobwebs even though the rooms are spotless. The rooms are spread far apart between different wings, and the house sits on a landscaped hill partly covered with solar panels. Even though my house is smaller, I think it's cozier. It's definitely louder. His is much bigger, but I bet Mr. Blakely needs more room for parties and meetings. There's a huge dining room. Massively amazing industrial kitchen. Paintings hang everywhere.

We walk back to the hallway between the entryway and the family room, where I see a large painting of a ballerina wearing a flowing red dress that looks like flames engulfing her body. She's standing on her pointe shoes and reaching out toward something beyond the painting. The painting's passion surprises me, especially because everything else seems to be decorated with neutral colors. I vaguely remember Royce telling me his mother was a dancer when she was younger.

I decide not to be afraid of his mother. She can't be that different than me. We both understand the pain of training and caring for and punishing your body to find grace and beauty. If she was a dancer, she knows what passion means— what wanting something so much you think you might die of want feels like.

Royce leads me to the doorway of the family room, where Mrs. Blakely is cradling a phone between her shoulder and her ear as she sits on a leather chair, watching the stock ticker on the television.

"She's working," Royce whispers, turning around. "We should leave her alone. Let's go sit in our other family room. She'll come around when she's ready."

"You have another family room?" I say.

When he takes me there, I see that it's more of a library. Books line shelves from floor to ceiling. There are couches and chairs. Coffee tables. Odd artifacts in cases. Statues, mostly. Busts of important political figures and old documents framed on the walls. "Mom started collecting these when dad first started getting into politics." He points to a case. "Here's a statue of Theodore Roosevelt she bought off a collector just last year."

He sits on the couch, clearly expecting me to sit next to him. I do, but not too close. Not like we were in the car earlier. I don't want Mrs. Blakely to get the wrong idea about me, and I don't want to mess anything up, especially with his parents.

Suddenly I hear, "May I interest you in something to drink?" I look up to see a housekeeper wearing pressed slacks and a tasteful purple sweater waiting for our reply.

I know immediately that she's Filipino, and she looks like she's in her early fifties. She smiles shyly. I wonder where her family is from. I want to ask, but I worry that it would be weird. A lot of Filipino immigrants work as housekeepers; some of my mom's friends do. My own mother is cleaning someone's house right now, I remember uncomfortably.

"I'm okay, Maria," Royce says. "Our guest might be thirsty though. Jas?"

He motions to me. I'm uncomfortable, but I try not to let my feelings show. It's not fair, but the sight of Maria is unnerving. If I don't go to college, what if I have to work a job like this for the rest of my life? Then I realize that I'm being a jerk. Who am I to judge this woman I've barely met?

Maria comes closer. She has a sort of sparkle in her eye, like she's watching me and not the other way around. This time she smiles more bravely and I like that. I smile in return. Filipinos sometimes do this with each other. It's like we're communicating telepathically. Still, I'm too embarrassed to ask for anything. I'm not used to being served.

Maria looks like she could be my aunt or an older cousin. I shift on the couch, adjusting my skirt over my knees. How is it that I'm dating someone and I have more in common with his house staff than with him?

"Thank you for the offer, but I'm not really thirsty," I say.

"I'll check back in a little while," she says, then leaves us alone together.

"She's only been here a few years," he says. "Her family's from the Philippines too. We found her through an agency." It's almost like he's saying, *She's not illegal.* It's then that I remember I haven't told him about my undocumented status. Should I? Is that something people tell each other?

Before I start feeling too guilty, Royce's mother steps into the room. "Hi, darling, I thought I saw someone with you," she says. "So who's our guest?"

Wait, Royce didn't tell her I was coming over? Has he even told his parents anything about me?

Royce stands up and I do too. "Jasmine. This is my mother, Debra Blakely, the Art Collector.

"Mom, this is Jasmine, the girl I met in D.C."

He doesn't call me his girlfriend, but maybe it's because he's nervous too.

She takes my hand. Her fingers are soft and smooth, but she shakes my hand assertively. "Royce is always calling me the art collector. He's too embarrassed to say I buy and sell stocks *and* art. Two of my loves. Besides my children, of course, though I have to admit I haven't seen much of my two boys lately."

"Pleased to meet you, Mrs. Blakely," I say. "I'm sorry to take Royce away from you."

We all sit back down and his mother leans on the side of the couch next to us. "It's quite all right. I hear he's in good company. He says you're one of the recent honorees for the National Scholarship Program?"

"I am," I say.

"He told me you were Filipino. How nice. Like our Maria."

I don't know how to take her comment. I don't need to have my Filipino-ness pointed out to me. Maybe she's as uncomfortable as I am that I'm the same race as their help? Maybe she doesn't know what to say. So I play nice. I've been taught to smile, to hide my inner fire when not appropriate. *Be polite, Jasmine.*

I smile at Mrs. Blakely.

Royce interrupts our moment. "Aren't you meeting Dad in Washington tonight?"

"Oh, dear Lord, I forgot!" she says. "Thanks for reminding me. I better pack. Nice meeting you, Jasmine. If you need anything, don't hesitate to ask Royce or Maria... Oh, Royce? Liv's coming with me. And can you please tell Mason to call me if you see him? His midterms must have started already, but that's no reason not to call his mother."

"Don't worry, Mom. I'll let you know when he comes home."

After she leaves, Royce turns to me, his eyebrows raised like a little boy. He looks so hopeful and excited, but I can't get rid of the nagging feeling that I don't belong here. We come from such different backgrounds. My mom doesn't even have a steady job right now.

How are we ever going to make this work?

He scoots closer to me on the couch so that our knees are touching. "You all right? You're so quiet."

"Your mom is nice," I say, still working over the *Filipino like our maid* comment and wondering how I should take it.

"Too bad she had to go. You haven't even seen half the art. And once she starts talking about it... In college, she and a bunch of her classmates protested at a museum in Chicago for exhibiting Renoir. I don't know what they had against the guy. 'Aesthetic terrorism' they called it. It was probably just a prank. They wanted attention, don't you think?"

I don't know what to think. Aren't there more important things to protest than hanging a famous, beautiful piece of art on a wall? But I just nod and continue to let him talk and try to feel more at ease in his home.

We're back at my house a few hours later. My parents are home this time and, yep, this is the moment we've all been waiting for. I'm anxious, but Mom and Dad are perfectly normal and greet Royce like I bring boys home all the time.

Mom asks him a few questions about school and what he thought of D.C., and Royce is right. I can tell she's charmed by him. She smiles and laughs at his jokes. She also doesn't mention his dad and what he does, so I count it as a win.

Then Dad corrals Royce into helping him change the oil on his truck. Royce is wearing clean, pressed khakis and a nice blue-and-white-checked button-down shirt, but he swears he doesn't care about getting dirty. We head to the garage, where he rolls up his sleeves and hops under the truck. Apparently my world doesn't seem strange to him like his world did to me. Maybe I'm the one who's the snob, the one who thinks we're so different, when we're not.

"Who taught you how to change oil?" Dad asks.

"My dad hired a mechanic to teach me," he says, filling the oil pan. "He said every guy needs to learn."

"Daddy, Royce is here to hang out with me," I say. "You have two sons to help you with that."

Dad's arm pops out from under the car. He shakes a wrench at me. It looks like the arm isn't attached to a body, which makes me giggle. "If you were a good daughter you would fetch us some lemonade," he says.

"*Fetch*, Dad? Dogs fetch things. Not daughters,"

Royce peers up at me with a pouty face and a puppy dog look.

"Fine," I say, but in truth I can't resist him.

When I enter the kitchen, I find Mom counting the cash from today's work. I think of Maria doing the same job over at Royce's house and feel a mixture of shame and irritation at myself for feeling strange about the whole situation, like I'm embarrassed about her, which I'm not.

Opening the refrigerator, I reach for a big pitcher full of juice. "What do you think of Royce?" I ask, pouring the liquid into a couple of glasses for Royce and Dad.

"He's very nice, like you said, *que guapo*," she says distractedly, even as she notes how handsome he is. She finishes counting the bills, then turns her attention to me. "But you watch out you don't get hurt."

"Is that what your mother told you when you brought Dad home for the first time?"

"Not at all. Your Lolo took Dad outside and was about to chop the head off a chicken. But your father stepped in, took over, showed Lolo that he wasn't afraid of a chicken without a head, or of blood, that he knew how to take care of business."

"Gross, Mom. Are you trying to say Royce needs to impress Dad by chopping off the head of a chicken? The Blakelys live in Bel-Air. They've probably never even seen a live chicken. Well, maybe on TV or something." I laugh, thinking of Royce beheading a live chicken.

I head back to the garage with the glasses of juice. My dad comes out from under the car, wiping the sweat from his head with an American-flag bandanna. He takes big gulps from the glass.

"Thanks," he says, after greedily finishing it. Without saying anything more, he starts to leave.

"Where're you going?" I ask.

"Wherever the next chore is," he says, leaving us alone in the garage.

Royce pops out from under the car too and washes the grease from his hands. He tucks his shirt back inside his pants and finally takes a drink. He's sweaty, and there are grease marks on his clean pants and shirt. "Thanks," he says. "Wow, this is really good, what is this?"

"It's calamansi juice. It's a Filipino key lime, I think?"

He guzzles the rest of it down. "Yum."

"You know that was a test," I say.

"What do you mean?" Royce crinkles his forehead.

"My dad, making you change the oil—that was him trying to see what you were made of."

His face brightens. "Oh yeah? And did I pass?"

In answer, I tiptoe and give him a quick kiss. Somehow, I know he'd behead a chicken for me if he had to.

Long, long ago, I learned the heart cannot live in two places. I had to choose. My heart is in America. Where is yours?

—MARIVI SOLIVEN, *THE MANGO BRIDE*

THE END OF November comes and goes, and the deadline to apply for UC schools passes. I didn't turn mine in, since it seemed like a waste of the application fee. I know I made the right call, but I'm still down about it.

Also, on Tuesday evening, the House of Representatives fails to pass the immigration reform bill.

I'm watching the news with my family, stunned. We'd been counting on that bill passing, and now it feels like yet another nail in the coffin. Worse, it failed largely because of Mr. Blakely's leadership. I feel sick to my stomach. How can I see Royce and his family without thinking of the bill and freaking out about it in front of them? I need to tell him the truth about my situation, but I'm too scared.

I was stupid to think that the bill would ever pass with the way politics are right now.

I'm sitting next to Mom and we're holding each other, staring as a dumb furniture store commercial blasts from the television.

Dad sighs.

"It'll be okay," I tell Mom, who's dangerously close to crying.

"What's wrong?" Danny asks.

He and Isko are confused about why we're all devastated by the announcement. They're concerned about Mom. No one really quite knows what to do when she gets upset. I've seen her this way only a few times in my life.

"We're not supposed to be here," Mom chokes out.

"What do you mean? In this house?" Isko asks.

His eyes are watering. I don't think he's seen Mom so upset before either. "Come here, Koko," I say, holding out my arms.

He comes to me like he did when he was a toddler, and I throw out my arms around him, hugging him as tight as I can.

Danny is usually the levelheaded one, but he starts to raise his voice. "What do you mean we're not supposed to be here?"

Mom sniffles. "We're undocumented. We're not supposed to be in the United States. We're here illegally. We have been for a long time."

"I thought we had green cards? What are you talking about? You lied to us!" Danny shouts.

"Don't talk to your mother that way," Dad says.

"It's not his fault," I say. "We should have told him sooner."

Danny stands up from the couch. "*You* knew?"

I nod. "I'm sorry, Danny." I think about trying to explain to him that I didn't want to say anything because I didn't want him to worry, but then I realize I'm being a hypocrite. That's the same reason Mom and Dad gave me when I found out.

"What's going to happen to us? We can't leave LA!" Danny yells. "I don't want to go back to the stupid Philippines!"

I can tell that Dad's about to send Danny to his room, but he stomps off anyway. As the news starts up again, Isko starts asking a million questions that I barely know how to answer.

He looks at me. "Does that mean we're going to jail?"

"No, Isko," Dad says. He's annoyed. "They don't put you in jail."

"Does that mean we're criminals? Are we bad people?"

My heart is breaking for my brothers. I have no idea how I would have handled this at their age. I probably would have gone completely off the deep end.

I shake my head. "I don't think so. Do you think you're a bad person?"

Isko smiles a little. "Only when I play mean pranks on Danny…"

"I don't think you're a bad person," I say. "We're not criminals either."

Mom shakes her head. "I hate this. We wanted to do things right. We came here on legitimate work visas, but when they expired we couldn't find jobs that would sponsor us." She looks at me pleadingly. "What were we supposed to do? Pick up you three and move you back to Manila? You'd already been through so much. And Dad and I figured out a way to stay. We survived. We made a life here. A good life. Isn't that worth something?"

I let go of Isko and turn to give Mom a hug. "It's okay, Mommy. We're not mad at you. Danny's not mad at you. He's just hurt."

"Do we have to leave?" Isko asks.

"I don't know, Ko," I say.

Of course my brothers don't understand, but now that they're witnessing our broken hearts, they're sad because we're sad. At least that's a start for them.

The news is back. "That same ex–weather girl is still the political analyst?" Dad complains. "I don't understand. Did she go to college for this? I could do her job."

Mom's smeared her mascara all over her cheeks from wiping her tears. I hold her even tighter, remembering how she would scoop me into her arms and hug me tight every time I fell off my bicycle and skinned my knees when I was learning to ride without training wheels.

"Will you stop that?" Dad says. "The weather girl talking politics. Now that's something to cry over."

"If you say that again, I'll put chili powder in your meat loaf." Mom sniffs.

I guess she hasn't lost her sense of humor quite yet.

"I just want to talk about what we're going to do," Dad says. "Crying isn't going to help."

"It's going to be okay," I say again, but I don't even believe my own reassurance.

The bill not passing doesn't mean my family will automatically be deported, but we'll have to continue to lie low. Maybe I'd be better off if we did end up going back to the Philippines. How can I hide the fact that I won't be able to vote because I'm not a US citizen? How will I explain that my driver's license will be a special one for undocumented immigrants? That's not the kind of thing you can hide forever.

If the bill had passed, at least my family would have been able to apply for green cards and then citizenship. We could have become real Americans at some point. Now it feels like everything is spiraling out of control. Like everything I've been trying to do with my life, including dating Royce, is getting grounded before it even has the chance to take off.

Mom's keeping her eyes trained closely on the news anchor.

"The vote wasn't even close," she says. "Why does America hate us?"

"They don't, only some of them do," I say. It's too depressing to sit in the living room with my family. I leave for the comfort of my room, look at the bottles on the shelf and the quotes I've pinned to my wall.

There's the one from *Armies of the Night*, the one Royce let me "borrow."

There is no greater importance in all the world like knowing you are right and that the wave of the world is wrong, yet the wave crashes upon you.

I wiggle my phone out of the pocket of my jeans and text him. I have to tell him the truth about me, and I can't put it off anymore. Especially since I want to confide my fears in him. We've been dating for a while now, and spending every weekend together. He drives over and we hang out at my house, eat at Denny's, go to movies, go bowling. When we hang in his neighborhood, we go to the Brentwood Country Mart and gawk at celebrities. Once we even ran into his famous reality–TV show cousin. She was sweet and we took selfies.

I talk to him every day; he's the last voice I hear before I go to sleep. Sometimes I fall asleep clutching the phone to my ear. He knows everything about me, how much I want to win Nationals this year, that I already wrote my valedictorian speech, because I'm so confident I'll be number one, that I'm worried that my mom still doesn't have a job. Although I didn't tell him why she lost it. And I know everything about him—that he had a dog when he was little and that, when it died last year, he buried it himself in his backyard, and that he wants to get another one but is worried he won't be able to love it the way he did the first. I know that he's turned in his Stanford application, deciding to go Early Decision for the best shot, since he's worried he doesn't have the grades, that he had to take the SAT at a special place because people with learning disabilities are allowed more time, and how embarrassed he was, that he felt like he was cheating or something. He knows Stanford is my first choice too.

So I text him. I refuse to believe he wouldn't support a reform bill like this one, even if his dad was the main architect of its demise. It's *Royce.* Sweet, wonderful, amazing Royce, *my* Royce. He can't believe in his father's politics, can he? He hates politics, he's said so more than once.

His number is the first one on my phone. I send him a quick text.

jasmindls: OMG. The immigration reform bill didn't pass. Can you believe it?

Royce hits me back immediately.

royceb: you're worried about that? the immigration bill? why?

jasmindls: America needed this.

My phone buzzes again. Another text. My stomach churns as I read it.

royceb: maybe, but you know my dad was working against it.

royceb: he went through a lot of trouble lobbying to help kill it and put a lot of hard work into it.

jasmindls: That's what you call hard work? Immigrants work hard too you know.

royceb: yeah, and so does my dad.

I don't know what to say to that. I put on my coat and go outside. I don't want Mom or Dad to see that I'm totally devastated and not just by the news, but by Royce's reaction to it. I knew what his dad's position on the bill was, what Congressman Blakely stood for, and I know that Royce is loyal. It's one of the best things about him.

Of course he's loyal to his dad, to his family.

But it still makes me feel ill. Maybe he doesn't think like his dad does on the issue, but that doesn't mean he would deliberately choose to be with someone who's exactly the kind of person his father has fought so hard to keep out of the country. Once he learns the truth, he'll probably be furious with me for not being honest with him in the first place.

I should have told him when we met in D.C. I should never have let it go this far.

What was I thinking?

My phone buzzes again.

royceb: Jas? Are you there?

royceb: That was rude of me.

royceb: I know immigrants work hard too, but it was an important victory for my dad.

royceb: I'm sorry I snapped at you.

I start typing a reply then hit Delete. I don't know what to say to him.

I always text him back within seconds, but since I don't, he knows something's wrong. My phone rings this time.

ROYCE BLAKELY pops on my phone, with that goofy photo of him crossing his eyes and sticking out his tongue.

I hit Ignore.

I can't do this right now. I'm scared about what happened with the bill, and I'm mad at him too, even if he did apologize.

So instead, I text Kayla. I need a friend, an old friend, someone who'll accept me no matter what.

jasmindls: Are you busy? Want to hang out? I need you.

kaykayla: Coffee? I'm here.

jasmindls: I've got a better idea. Donuts?

We're at the doughnut shop drinking green tea and sugar-free raspberry lemonade. In front of us are four big, fluffy doughnuts, two covered in frosting and sugar cereal, and two slathered in chocolate.

"Coach Davis would kill us if she knew we were about to eat these," I say.

Kayla has the same terrified smile. "I know."

"But you've taught me something, K. It's an important lesson I've had to learn this year. Something I didn't really think about until the last few months."

"What's that?" Kayla asks, considering the doughnut covered with crispy cinnamon-swirl cereal.

I grab a chocolate one and ravenously tear off a huge bite. "You only live once."

As if given permission by my indulgence, Kayla dives in to the doughnut she's been eyeing. I don't think I've ever had so much fun eating something I shouldn't in my entire life. The chocolate is smooth and coats my tongue, and I feel the bliss of a sugar high. These people must make a killing off sad girls.

We devour every crumb within minutes, every bit of frosting and cereal. I point to the corner of Kayla's mouth where there's a chocolate smudge, and she wipes it away.

"I'm sorry," I say.

"For what? Getting me fat?" Kayla jokes.

I pick up my glass of green tea, leaving a ring of condensation on the table. "Well, now I guess I have *two* things to apologize for." I put down the glass without taking a sip.

Kayla looks out the window. "Nah."

Honesty is the best thing sometimes. If you're never honest with someone, then you're pretending to be perfect all the time. That's what people expect from me, and I don't want to be that girl anymore. I'm tired of it, of having too much pride.

But I don't know how to start, and because she knows me so well, Kayla talks first. She says that her dad served her mom divorce papers, so it's official. They're definitely not getting back together.

"I'm so sorry," I tell her.

"It's okay. At least they're not yelling at each other all the time anymore. The house is peaceful for a change. And now that Dad has to see us on the weekends, we actually end up spending more time with him."

"How's Dylan? Is he back?"

"Yeah, and he told me I shouldn't worry about groupies or anything. Not that he would cheat on me, but also that when they're on the road all they do is eat at vegan restaurants and do yoga. They don't party that much. That's not what they're about. It's the music. I guess some rock bands really are different."

"I guess so. He is a nice guy, and he adores you."

"Yeah," she says happily. "He told me not to quit cheer and keep going so we can kick butt at Nationals. But we're not here to talk about me. What's up, Jas? What's wrong?"

My phone buzzes.

"You've got a text," she says, sipping her tea. "Aren't you going to read it?"

I sigh and glance down at my phone. It's Royce again.

royceb: Hey, did you get my text?

royceb: Are you at practice or something?

royceb: Why aren't you picking up your phone?

royceb: I don't get it. Are we fighting over politics?

royceb: Or did I do something wrong?

I shove the phone deep into my purse.

"Out with it," Kayla says.

I'm finding it difficult to get any words out. It's like there's this awful lump in my throat paralyzing my neck muscles.

"Jasmine?" Kayla says. "What's really wrong? Is it Royce? Did something happen?"

"Yes. But it's not just Royce." I have to start at the beginning. "I can trust you, right?"

"Of course you can. Duh!"

"Okay, okay, I know. But this is hard for me to say. You know the day Mrs. Garcia came to the gym during cheer?"

Kayla nods, waiting patiently.

"She gave me a letter telling me about the National Scholarship. But when I went home and told my parents, I found out that our visas expired years ago. That's why I didn't tell you about the scholarship at first—I didn't know what to say. We've been living here without documentation the whole time I've been in high school. That's why my Dad wouldn't let me get my driver's permit. That's why we don't go back to the Philippines to visit family anymore. I'm not an American, Kayla. I'm not here legally."

Her face pales.

"But that's not all. Royce's dad is Congressman Blakely, the house majority leader. He hates illegal aliens and just killed the big reform bill that would have let my family stay in the US."

Kayla is now so pale that she's the same shade as the napkin.

"I saved the best for last. Royce has no idea I'm undocumented." I don't like the term *illegal*; it feels too much like a brand, like a pejorative, like a sneer, whereas *undocumented* just states the fact of our situation without prejudice.

She gets up from the table. For a second, I'm afraid she doesn't want to talk to me anymore.

"Where're you going?" I say. "Don't leave."

"I'm not leaving," she says. "I'm buying more doughnuts."

You can waste your lives drawing lines. Or you can live your life crossing them.

—SHONDA RHIMES

KAYLA TOLD ME yesterday that I shouldn't be embarrassed by our legal situation, that I should tell more people what's going on with me. There's no shame in what happened, it wasn't my fault, and I should let people know so that they can support me, at least. She says I owe Royce the truth as well. I know she's right about everything, but I'm not ready to deal with him just yet.

But being with her reminds me that I do have friends who care about me, and that I haven't asked for any help, even from those who've offered it.

I pick up my phone and scroll through my contacts.

Because there is someone I can call. Someone who might be able to help with one thing.

I dial Millie's number. After a few rings, she answers the phone. She's excited to hear from me. "Jasmine! I was starting to think you weren't going to call." I can hear Millie shake ice in a glass and picture her sitting there, drinking her scotch.

I feel a burst of happiness at hearing her raspy voice again. I've missed my friend and I tell her so. "I'm sorry. Things here—"

Before I can finish my sentence, Isko flings open my door and runs inside the room, then slams the door behind him. Panting, he attempts to hold it shut while Danny pushes on the other side.

I pull the phone away from my mouth. "*Ack!* Get out of here! I'm on the phone..."

Danny finally succeeds in pushing the door open and pulling Isko out into the hallway. As they wrestle with each other, I get up and slam the door.

"I'm so sorry, Millie. My little brothers are being super annoying."

Millie laughs.

I tell her about my trip to D.C., and I thank her for encouraging me to go. We talk about the defeat of the immigration reform bill. She tells me she's so sorry it didn't pass—she knows how much I was counting on it.

"I can't even turn on Facebook," I say. "I hate seeing all the political rants and people hating on families like mine. If people only knew that people they talk to every day are probably illegal immigrants..." I pause, considering my sentence. "Maybe they would be nicer. Or maybe not. Maybe they really think we don't belong here."

"Maybe you should tell them the truth of your situation," she says. "Don't be afraid. Maybe when they see it happening to someone they know, they'll have a change of heart."

I shake my head. "I don't know."

"What about your friends at least? Have you told them? I think you should. If you give them a chance, I think people will surprise you with their kindness."

How can Millie believe in the goodness of people when so many spend so much time hating on each other? She comes from a different time. The news used to be more balanced.

People couldn't just get on social media and say whatever's on their mind without looking people in the face. Although it's an easy way of telling where people stand, I guess.

"I'm just not ready to tell everyone about it," I say. "I know my family isn't. My little brothers don't even understand what's going on. They're in denial most of all. All of their identity is as Americans. To think of themselves as anything else is alien to them."

"Your brothers may not understand for years," she says. "Listen, your story is incredibly moving. It will inspire others if you share it. I was listening to a report last night on the News Hour about the difference between those who have been undocumented immigrants and those who have not. Who's more compassionate on average? Those who have been undocumented, they said. Who experiences more joy in life? The undocumented. Who is better at establishing community? The undocumented. They band together. They support each other."

"You know that, Millie, but other people don't—they think undocumented immigrants are criminals and liars. That they're the leeches of the American economy."

I hear the clink of Millie setting down her glass. "Show them, then," she says defiantly. "Show them the truth of who you—and your family—really are. Shine light on their ignorance."

I think about Millie's words. How can I get the word out? Identifying ourselves could put us at risk.

"I just feel like I'm in a kind of limbo," I say. "Mom is contacting immigration lawyers to see what our options are, but more and more it looks like we're going to either have to hide our status, which will change our whole lives and limit what we can and can't do. Or we have to risk being deported to try to get documentation."

"I really wish you didn't have to go through this. I wish there was some way I could help."

Before I lose my nerve, I get to the point of why I called. "Actually that's why I'm calling," I say. I explain that my mom still hasn't found another job, and that I recall that when we were kicked out of the hospital, Millie had offered to help her.

"Yes, of course! I'm so glad you asked. She can come to work for me. Or my son, I mean. I don't have a personal office anymore, but I think we can find her a place in the company."

"Are you sure? You'll be breaking the law." I'm so happy I could cry.

"Oh, I don't care about her status. There are ways of getting around the papers. I want good workers, people who care about other people. That's your mother. That's you. I knew as soon as I met you in the hospital."

"What kind of job is it? Are you sure she can do it?"

"Of course she can," Millie says. "You underestimate your mother. It'll be mostly administrative office work. She'll be fine."

"I'll tell her to call you," I say. "But I'm not sure she will."

Millie sighs. "Can you give her a message for me, then?"

I promise I will.

"Tell her I'm not offering her a job because I feel bad for her, or because I want to feel good about myself. She's a smart woman, and her job at the hospital didn't let her use her skills. Believe it or not, I've been there before. I want to help her out."

I thank her, and hope I can convince my mom to take this opportunity.

★ ★ ★

It's our last day of cheer practice before winter break. Kayla and I are stretching outside next to each other. Practicing for Regionals has made us so in tune with one another that we do our stretches in unison without even thinking about it.

"I can't believe you still haven't told him," Kayla says.

"I don't know what to say," I say. "What's the use anyway?" It's been almost an entire week now and I haven't answered Royce's texts or calls. I can't even listen to his voice mail messages, even though I miss his voice so badly.

"Oh man, don't ghost him. That's so not your style."

"I know," I say. I don't know what to do, I want to see him, but I'm angry too. *It was an important victory for my dad.* It turns my stomach. "His family hates families like mine. I can't be with someone like that."

Kayla bends her arm over her head. "You're being unfair. What if someone judged you on what your family believes? You don't agree with them on everything. You need to tell him. Give him a chance."

"How can I? What if he accidentally tells his dad? My whole family could be deported." I don't believe it would come to that, but the thought that it could scares me too much. I'd like to think Royce would protect us, but do I really know him?

I lunge with my right leg, feeling the soreness of my muscles. Even though I practice every day—and on the weekends too—the pain never fully goes away. I think I'm going to take a yearlong nap after Nationals.

Kayla lunges with her left leg, mirroring me. "Is he still texting you?"

"Only about ten times a day." I want to delete his messages, but I don't have the heart. I can't read them either though. It's too painful.

"What did you say he looks like again? Dark hair? Tan? Tall?" Kayla starts humming. She sits spread-legged on the grass and reaches for her toes. "He's cute, right?"

"You wouldn't think so. He wears suits all the time."

Suddenly, I hear Royce's voice from over my shoulder. "Not always."

I whip around with a gasp. I'm shocked to see him, but I also want to laugh a little. He's wearing a navy blue blazer and jeans. No tie. His "casual" look. I'm elated to see him but scared to death too. I'm not ready to face him. My heart hammers in my throat even as my stomach drops.

Apparently I have no choice but to be ready as Kayla gets to her feet while I stand there gaping. "I'll tell Coach you'll be a couple minutes late," she says.

"You don't have to," I say. "I'll be there."

Kayla starts walking to the front of the gym as I turn to Royce. "What are you doing here?" I ask, in a rush, already feeling a little high from just the sight of him.

Royce steps toward me. "I wanted to see you. You haven't returned any of my texts or called me back since Sunday night. I would have come over earlier but with my tutoring schedule for finals I couldn't get away until now. Why are you ignoring me?"

"Well, you've seen me," I say, choking on the words and taking a step away from him. "Feel better?" I know I'm being cruel to him, but it's better this way. I can't be with someone like him and he shouldn't be with someone like me. I'm practically doing him a favor.

"Come on, Jasmine. What's going on? What did I do to piss you off?"

"You didn't do anything to piss me off. I'm just moving on," I say, shrugging as if I'm so bored of this conversation.

His face turns red. "Moving *on*? What's that supposed to mean? Everything was going fine and then you just disappear? What the— *Why*? You owe me an explanation at least."

"I don't owe you anything. Not everyone owes you something, Royce," I snap, even though it hurts me to hurt him like this. The jagged twist in my stomach makes me feel so nauseous, I could vomit. But I don't see how we can work things out. Whether Royce believes in what his father does or not doesn't matter anymore. It's too dangerous for me to be with him.

He runs his fingers through his hair. "Look, if you hate my guts that's fine. But it's not like you to not say what's on your mind. You're not that kind of person. I know it."

"That's where you're wrong. You've never known who I really am," I say. *And whose fault is that?* A million thoughts race across my mind. I should have told him. Or once I knew who his dad was and what he believed in, I should've stayed far, far away from him. I should have never gone to meet him after the dinner. I shouldn't have let him kiss me.

"Why are you saying this? I know you, Jasmine. You know me. Why can't you tell me what's wrong?" he asks, looking as stricken as I feel.

But I have to do this. It's better this way. Safer for me, and easier for him. He'll forget about me, find someone else to read his favorite passages from the books he likes to, some other girl to lend quotes to.

"Look, I'm going to be late for practice. I have to go," I say, my voice deliberately cold.

"Your friend just said she'd tell your coach you'd be late."

"Like you know who my friends are. You've never met any

of them!" I yell, which makes me realize I've never seen his school, never met any of *his* friends either. Our entire world is made up only of each other. I never noticed before, because we never needed anyone else. I just wanted to be with him, and he with me. But now it bothers me. Was he hiding me or something?

"I'd love to meet your friends. But you've never introduced me to any," he says. He's right. I haven't, even when he spends the weekend hanging out with me in the Valley.

"Well, I haven't met any of your friends either!" I scowl.

"That's because I don't have friends."

"Oh please." My arms are crossed now and I'm fuming. He has tons of friends, and so many followers on Snapchat (six hundred and two to be exact).

"I mean, yeah, I know a lot of guys, but we're not close. I don't have any close friends, okay? Satisfied?" His jaw is a stern line.

"But you know everybody in D.C....all those kids...Carrie's crew..." I'm convinced I'm right about this.

"Yeah, I might *know* a lot of people, but that's not the same as having *friends*. Jesus, do I have to go into detail as to how big a loser I am?"

"You're not a loser," I say, because I hate when he puts himself down.

"And you're not just my girlfriend, Jasmine. You're my best friend. The first real friend I've had. When you stopped talking to me, I just, I can't..." He growls in annoyance and stuffs his hands back in in pockets. "Whatever! Forget it! Forget I said anything!" He pivots away, obviously embarrassed.

Now he's walking away and I'm the one running after him.

"Royce!"

When I catch up to him, his cheeks are red and his eyes are as glassy as mine.

"Royce, I'm sorry," I say, because I am. Because I suck, because I should have been honest with him from the start. I pride myself on being forthright, and yet I've been unable to tell this guy I really care about something fundamental about me.

I was so worried about getting hurt, but now I know it hurts so much more to be the one causing pain.

"About what?" he asks. "What are you sorry about?" His face is terrible, gray and angry.

"I should have told you the truth about me, when we first met," I say slowly.

"What? Do you have a boyfriend? I should have known." He looks like he wants to punch something.

I laugh, it's so absurd. "No!" I want to hug him. "I told you, you're the only one." The only one I've ever fallen for, the only one who makes me feel the way I do. He's the only one for me, which is why it hurts so much that we can't, that we shouldn't, be together.

He's not laughing. "So what is it, then?" A pause, until it's like he puts two and two together. "Wait, it's because I disagreed with you about immigration reform, right? You don't agree with my dad, so you're mad at me?"

"I wish that was all it is," I say.

He stares at me, really looks at me, and I know tears are running down my cheeks because I can feel them. "I don't understand why the bill not passing would make you so upset. Weren't you born in America?" he asks quietly.

I shake my head no. My throat is so tight I can't answer.

He looks right into my eyes. "Okay, so you weren't born

here. Why do you think I would care about that? Even if you're not American, it doesn't change how I feel about you."

"Really?" I ask, finding my voice at last and wiping my tears with my sleeve. "What if I told you I was undocumented? *Illegal.*"

"You're..." Royce trails off.

I turn away, not wanting to see the look on his face. "See? You think *I'm* a criminal now, right? That we're nothing but a bunch of thieves? That we'll peek in your window at night, threatening to steal all of your mom's precious artwork?"

"I never said I liked my mom's art collection," he says mildly. "You can steal it."

I hate that he tries to make me laugh when I'm upset, but I love it too. He puts a hand on my arm gently, as if to let me know he doesn't want me to go, that he has more to say. I stand there, refusing to face him, but not running away either.

"My parents didn't tell me until I got the National Scholarship," I say. "I never knew we were illegal aliens until a couple months ago."

He steps closer to me. "Jas, I'm so sorry."

"I can't accept the award. I don't have a social security number. I can't get a driver's license. I don't know what's going to happen to us. I didn't want to tell you because I was embarrassed, and I was scared you'd tell your dad."

"I would never do anything to hurt you or your family," Royce says urgently. "You have to believe that. I like you, Jas. I don't care what you are. I don't care about any of that."

I sniff and wipe my eyes again with my sleeve. He's saying all the right things, and I want to believe him, but I'm too overwhelmed by my admission. I feel like a cracked egg, raw and vulnerable.

He looks right into my eyes, and I can see the hurt I feel reflected in his. He looks completely miserable. "Jas, I just want to be with you. I'm sorry I said those stupid things about that bill. If I'd known you were having trouble like that, I would have tried to help. My dad is the one who believes those things, but that's him, not me. I don't even know why I said that to you. I was just trying to sound smart. I'm an idiot."

"You're not an idiot," I say automatically.

"I'm so sorry the bill didn't pass. I didn't know it was so important to you. Is your family okay? What are you guys going to do?" He has both hands on my shoulders now.

I tear up again. "I don't know. I don't know what's going to happen."

"What about us?" he asks roughly.

"Us?"

"I haven't changed my mind about you. But it sounds like you have. Are we good?" he asks, so sadly that I want to say yes, that everything's okay, that nothing's the matter.

But I can't. It's too much. I'm too exposed, dying of shame that he knows the truth about my reduced legal situation. I feel so much for him, but somehow, I'm furious too, at his dad, at his family, at his whole background that's so different than mine. I pull away. "I don't know. I need time to think. Can we take a break? I just need some space right now."

He releases me, his hands going slack at his sides, his face blank. "Uh-huh. Well, how long do you need?"

"I don't know. There's so much going on. Family stuff we have to figure out." I'm flooded with emotion, and I just need time to myself, time to breathe.

"Right." He kicks the pebbles on the ground.

We stare at each other, not quite believing what is happening. Are we breaking up? Is this the end of us?

Finally he says, "I'll be in Aspen over Christmas. I promise not to bother you until I get back. Can we talk then?"

I nod.

"And if you decide you don't want to see me anymore I'll leave you alone, don't worry," he says, his voice so low I have to strain to hear him.

I don't want him to leave me alone, I don't want to break up, and I want to tell him that this is all a mistake, I don't want him to go, I don't want it to be over. But the words don't come, and somehow I nod my head.

"Good luck at Regionals." He turns away then, and I watch him leave, his shoulders slumped, hands jammed in his pockets, and it feels like I've broken his heart instead of the other way around. Maybe it is.

becoming illegal

Give me your tired, your poor,
Your huddled masses yearning to breathe free,
The wretched refuse of your teeming shore.
Send these, the homeless, tempest-tossed, to me:
I lift my lamp beside the golden door.

—EMMA LAZARUS'S POEM,
INSCRIBED ON THE STATUE OF LIBERTY

19

If you find someone you love in your life, then hang on to that love.

—PRINCESS DIANA

A FEW DAYS LATER, the other girls are singing and shouting cheers on the bus to the Anaheim Convention Center. We're on our way to compete in the Regional competition, which is right before Christmas. I keep thinking about Royce, checking my phone, hoping he'll text me, though I know he won't. Why do I need him to give in first? I just do.

There's plenty of room, so we're all spread out on the bus. Kayla leans over the back of my seat. "Are you nervous?"

I take my headphones out of my ears. "A little, I guess."

"I know you're upset about Royce," she says. I told her what happened, how I asked him for space.

I look at Kayla like I'm about to roll my eyes at her. "No I'm not," I say. "Who's Royce?"

"You're a terrible liar, Jas. You always have been," Kayla laughs. She gets up and moves into the seat next to me, putting her head on my shoulder. "I'm going to give you a piece of advice that you've given me more than once this year. So listen up."

"All right," I say. "I'm listening."

"Cheer is a mental game just as much as a physical one. You

have to clear your mind. Focus on the team. Concentrate on your body," Kayla says.

I look down at my phone again. "I know. That's what I say all the time."

"Well, you're obviously not taking your own advice right now. You're all torn up about him. Come on, talk to me. You have to get it out before the competition."

I shake my head. "I'm fine. This isn't about Royce." But she knows me too well and she's right, I am a terrible liar. I hate that Royce and I aren't talking, even though I'm the reason we're not.

"Your family, then? What's going on with the immigration stuff?"

"I really, really don't want to talk about that right now—that's the last thing I want to think about before the competition." I need to put it out of my head, but I'm nervous and panicky and she can tell. Looking behind my seat, I see that the girls nearby are watching us, probably wondering what's going on. "I'm not ready for the whole squad to know."

Kayla throws up her hands. "Fine. *Fine.* Don't say I didn't try to help…"

She goes to the back of the bus to hang out with some of the other girls.

I need to stop thinking about Royce and my own situation and focus on our performance. I put my headphones back in and try to psych myself up and prepare, to visualize nailing every stunt, hitting every landing. But my mind won't clear, and I'm edgy and distracted.

After the bus pulls up to the convention center, Coach Davis checks us in for the Medium Varsity Division I Group while we change into our uniforms and fix our hair.

The morning flies by. We watch a few teams compete,

some of them good enough to make us worry a little, but we know we've got this. Then we stretch for twenty minutes and do warm-ups before the team is called up to compete. Coach Davis asks me to give the girls a pep talk as the competition organizers cue up our music. The girls gather around me, and I look at them, wondering what they would think if they knew I was an undocumented immigrant. Would they care? Would they look at me differently? Would they pity me?

Gathering the girls into a big huddle, I give my speech. "You've all been working so hard toward this moment. Your tucks are tight. Your moves are sharp. We're going to win this thing and we're going on to Nationals!"

Coach Davis signals me to call the girls to the mats.

"Positions!" I shout, and we all run out to the floor, bouncing and cheering, before taking our places.

This is our moment. Our chance to qualify for Nationals.

The music starts up. We begin our tumbling routine followed by our stunts. I plaster a smile on my face, but my rhythm is off, like I'm moving in slow motion.

The bright lights are shining on us and I imagine that everyone looking at me knows my terrible secret. And I remember the hurt look on Royce's face when I told him to leave me alone.

My bases start to pop me up for a simple toe-touch basket toss, but I mistime their movements and begin to jump before they've released me, sending all of us off balance. On the way down, I try to correct my positioning but I've already screwed everything up and come crashing down on my back spotter. It's Anabel, and she picks me up right away. Everyone gets back on the routine like nothing has happened, but I know I've cost our team qualifying for Nationals. I finish the rest of the routine without starting to cry, but once the music is over, I run to the bathroom and lock the stall door.

I can't believe I've let them all down. I'm petrified of having people see me like this. I can't have them know how close I am to crying right now.

I'm sitting in the stall trying to get control of my emotions when someone knocks on the door. "Jasmine?" Kayla asks. "Is that you?"

Trying to hold back my tears, because I don't want her to hear, I gasp an uneasy "Yeah, I'm here."

"Are you going to let me in? Or am I going to have to knock down this door?"

I unlatch the lock, still sitting on top of the toilet in my cheer uniform.

"You can't blame yourself," Kayla says. "Everyone makes mistakes."

"Not on a stupid basket toss," I say. "It's such an easy move."

"Don't be so hard on yourself. We got *second* place. That's not bad. Come out, they're about to give us our trophies. We need you out there."

She's right. I can't hide in here while my team accepts our second-place trophy. I swallow my tears and my pride and get up. "Okay," I say to Kayla. "Let's do this."

The team is waiting for me and we all ascend the podium together. The judges hand us our trophy. I smile and wave to the crowd along with the rest of the girls. I know we're all disappointed, no one more than me, but at least we tried.

Sometimes, it's all you can do.

We link hands and bow, and watch as the first-place team receives a trophy taller than their coach.

Coming in second means no Nationals for us. Everything

I was aiming for, that I had been so sure of three months ago, has completely fallen apart.

My cheer career is over. This was my last chance at glory, and I blew it.

On the way home, I think of the other good thing in my life that I wrecked. When I first met Royce, I thought he was a total player. He was so confident when we met, and no one that rich and handsome isn't a player, right?

But when he told me about Carrie, he also told me about other girls. Sure, he's had a number of girlfriends. (Six. But who's counting? Me.) But he claimed that four of them were girls who walked home with him between grades two through seven. He said they only held hands. No kisses. No actual dates. Because each one walked with him at least twice, he counted them as girlfriends.

That one made me laugh.

The fifth one was a "real" girlfriend, but they only went out for a month.

So I guess he didn't have as much experience with girls as I thought.

It's Christmas vacation, and I can't get him out of my mind as I go between reading trashy novels, trying to get over losing at Regionals, and helping Mom with her work. She started working at Millie's old firm the other day.

I told Royce I needed time to figure out my own life, but all I can do is think of him in Aspen. He's probably at some ski resort with those beautiful European girls who know how to snowboard down giant mountains. He probably won't be lonely for long.

He hasn't texted or called, but maybe that's because he's keeping his promise. It's still early during winter break, and

I'm hoping he'll break down and text me. I'm stubborn. I don't want to be the one to break down first. So I help Mom, babysit my brothers, and decorate the house for Christmas. Kayla tries to cheer me up, and we spend afternoons baking cookies and shopping for presents.

I miss him though. I miss telling him about my life and hearing about his.

Instead, I fill out my Stanford application, and I send them the same essay I wrote for the National Scholarship but tweaked a little to answer their question. Maybe I'm delusional, but I want to hold on to some kind of hope that the future I want is still out there and within reach. I can't lose my focus like I did at Regionals. I have to stay in the game.

Mom's started working for Millie, and while she was nervous at first, she's much more confident now. They have her working data entry, and she practices her typing skills when she's not at the office. At least we're not as worried about money anymore.

I turn eighteen in the middle of Christmas break. Both Royce and I have birthdays within a week of each other, and now we won't be celebrating together like we'd planned. I end up deciding to just have a quiet birthday celebration with my family.

I should have known I wouldn't get away with that. The night before my actual birthday, Kayla and the team surprise me and take me out to CPK, where we get large barbecue pizzas and Chinese chicken salads. They put candles on the molten chocolate cake and sing "Happy Birthday" really loudly. It's a fun night, and I'm glad I have my friends. For a while, I'm able to forget my problems.

At home on the day, Mom decorates the house with party

favors in silver and white, my favorite colors, and Dad lets me blast my favorite music over the TV's sound system. I sit next to Lola Cherry at the kitchen table, watching Mom put the finishing touches on lunch. I've specially requested *lumpia* and pancit. It's my birthday, and I figure I can eat what I want.

"What did you get me for my birthday?" I ask Lola Cherry.

"Same as last year," Lola says like she's bored.

"You're going to hit my brothers with your cane?"

"No. Though they need it."

"Hey!" Danny yells. "I didn't do anything!"

Lola whacks him on the tush with her cane faster than a bolt from the blue. "Don't yell at your Lola," she says.

"I wasn't." Danny rubs his rear, then steps into the safe zone, one cane's length away. I laugh, feeling warm all over.

"Where's your brother?" she asks.

"Why?" Danny says.

"Because he needs one now. It should always be even."

"Isko!" Danny yells in mad laughter.

I laugh as I go answer the door. It's Millie. She hugs me and hands me a present. "Happy birthday," she says. "It's just a little something."

I open the gift to find a leather-bound picture album with gold filigree. "It's gorgeous—thank you so much! Come meet some of my family."

I take her elbow and lead her into the kitchen to meet Lola, but there's no introduction needed. It's as if they're continuing a conversation from another life. How do old women do this? Put them into a room, and they're like sisters.

"I can't believe these knuckleheads," Lola says to her. "They're just like my grandchildren in Manila. Always causing trouble." Then she looks at me, though my brothers are laughing and dancing just out of cane's reach. "Especially this one."

"What did *I* do?" I laugh.

"I understand." Millie sits down. "Who keeps this younger generation in line if not us? I always keep something close, just to threaten them."

My brothers laugh. They're still dancing out of Lola's reach.

"Here," Lola starts to hand her cane to Millie, though we all know she's pretending.

Millie is clearly an expert at this and holds out her hand as if about to take Lola's cane. "You want me to take a swat at 'em?"

"My hand's getting tired," Lola says, and just like that both women are laughing hysterically.

"You know, when I was your age," Millie says to me, "I had a relative like Lola Cherry."

"Was she as beautiful?" Lola says.

Both women start laughing again.

"No," Millie says, "and it was a he. Uncle George resembled a potato, but he could snap your rear hide faster than a buffalo stampede."

"I like him," Lola says. "Does he have a girlfriend?"

Millie bursts into laughter and holds out her hand as if she's going to address that in a moment. "The thing is," she says through her giggles, "he was blind!"

Both women roar. As they do, I set the table and Mom puts the lumpia and pancit in the center along with plates of boiled pork and vegetables.

"That's good aim for a blind man," Lola says in amazement.

"It was," Millie says. "And he did have a brother. He was blind too. They had contests to see how many of us they could whack on birthdays and holidays."

Just when I think both women are done laughing, Lola

says, "I changed my mind. I don't want either of them for a boyfriend. I need a man to see all of my beauty."

Mom hands me a hot plate as the two women howl. "Millie should come keep Lola Cherry company more often," she says with a smile.

Royce never even had the chance to meet Millie or Lola Cherry, I realize, and I bet he'd like both of them. I kept him separate from my friends, my family, not only because I wanted to be alone with him, but also because I was worried about him getting to know everything about me. I was keeping him at arm's length. But I wish now that I'd been much more open from the beginning.

I like you, Jas. I don't care what you are. I just want to be with you.

If he doesn't care where I'm from or what I am, why can't I do the same for him?

It's Christmas Eve when my parents finally hear back from an immigration lawyer. Dad thinks the fees will be too expensive, and even though I was able to get a few fee waivers for my college applications, I still cost my parents more money this month than I normally would. No one told me how expensive applying to colleges would be. It's crazy how everyone expects you to go to the best colleges but then no one tells you how to get there.

Dad sits on the floor, messing with the train track for the toy train that runs around the base of the Christmas tree. "We need to keep looking for a lawyer," he says. "This one's consultation fee is equal to a week's worth of groceries already. If we go to trial, it'll be even more…"

"I already made an appointment," Mom says.

Dad looks up from the track. "So cancel it."

"He's got good references." Mom pauses. She stands up

and turns on the radio to a station playing Christmas music. Little bell sounds tinkle from the speakers. "Anyway, Millie offered to pay the consultation fee."

"Millie can't pay the consultation fee," Dad says. He likes Millie, but he doesn't like accepting money. He's proud, like I am.

"Why not?" Mom says. "We can get a better lawyer this way. Do you want to be ripped off?"

"I'm feeling ripped off right now just having this conversation. Handouts from your boss? I don't want to be in debt to a rich old white woman. Or for you to be either. You shouldn't owe anyone anything. They'll take advantage of you."

I side with Mom. "She's really nice and doesn't deserve that," I say.

"*Neneng*. Butt out. This isn't your conversation."

"This conversation belongs to all of us," Mom says. "Jasmine wants to live in America too. And if you haven't noticed, your daughter is a National Scholar. More than I can say for you."

"I work with my hands," Dad says. "That means I know how this world runs—through hard work." The train comes around the track and falls off onto the carpet.

"We need a good lawyer," Mom says. "You can't fix legal situations like ours with your hands. You've been watching too many gangster movies."

"Yeah, Daddy," I say. "We need to put our best foot forward. If Millie wants to help, then let her. Hasn't she been on our side all along? Didn't she give Mom a job? Just think of it as a Christmas bonus."

"Christmas bonus…?" Dad echoes. He returns the train to the track.

"Listen to yourself," Mom says. "You sound like some kind of Scrooge."

"I *am* some kind of Scrooge," Dad mumbles.

After we're all done arguing—Mom and I insist we won, like always—I decide I'm going to stop waiting and text Royce. I can't blame him for his father's decisions. If he doesn't care that I'm an illegal alien, why should I care that he's the son of a conservative congressman?

I miss him something awful. The truth is, I'm not just his best friend—he's my best friend too. Just like Kayla is, but in a different way. He understands the part of me that no one else in my life completely does. Kayla's smart, but she's not into books and art like I am, and my parents don't like museums—when we went to the Getty, they stayed in the gift shop.

Sometimes Royce and I would just send emails with quotes to each other.

After we went to the beach once, he sent me:

royceb: **Her fair hair had streamed out behind her like gold in the sun. TOWER OF IVORY. HOUSE OF GOLD. By thinking of things you could understand them.—James Joyce, Portrait of the Artist as a Young Man**

I wrote back:

jasmindls: **I am alive where your fingers are—Anne Sexton, Love Poems**

It's nearly Christmas. And isn't Christmas all about forgiveness and making peace with each other? All I can think about is him and when I'm going to see him again.

In the warmth of my bed, I pull my comforter over my head. The twinkly white lights decorating my room create a soft glow through the blankets. I think about what I should write. I try a few different sentences, but none of them seem quite right. I try to look for a quote, but nothing seems to fit.

Finally, I realize it's because there's only one thing to say.

jasmindls: I miss you.

He writes back right away.

royceb: what happened to waiting to talk till after xmas?

I smile. I can imagine him texting me under the table while he's at some fancy party with his parents.

jasmindls: Close enough. Merry Christmas Eve.

My skin tingles when I see his next text.

royceb: I miss you too.

I'm typing a reply when my phone rings. It's funny how we hardly talk to each other—our generation prefers sending messages for hours. But I'm glad he called. It's so much nicer to hear his actual voice.

"Hey," he says.

"Hey. Where are you?"

"Out on the terrace, getting away from everyone, watching the snow fall. I wish you were here to see it."

I smile. He likes looking out at views. "I wish I was there too. I've never seen snow fall," I say. "What's up with your family? Are they bugging you?"

"It's nothing, just the same old stuff. Mom and Dad are arguing about Mason again."

"That sucks. I'm sorry."

"It's nothing new," he says. "Hey, I meant to tell you last time I saw you. I, uh, got into Stanford. Early Decisions were sent out."

"Royce! That's awesome! Congratulations! Aren't you excited?" I say, and I'm happy for him, but the feeling is both joyous and bittersweet, hearing that he's gotten something I want so badly.

"Yeah, I am. Mostly I'm relieved. Probably helped that my dad knows the chancellor," he says.

"You're just being modest, stop! You deserve this." He really does; he works so hard. Maria told me, when I was over once, that he'd won some fancy writing award at his school. He never makes much of his accomplishments like I do mine.

So that's why he drove out to see me that day—he wanted to tell me his good news in person, and he never even got to. "I'm sorry you didn't get to tell me earlier."

"It's okay," he says, and I know he means it. "Hey, do you think your parents would let you come and visit?" he asks, hope in his voice. "We're here for another week. I know you don't know how to ski, but you'll pick it up quickly—you're so coordinated."

"That's so sweet. But probably not. Filipino Christmases are sort of a big deal. We go to Midnight Mass and then we eat salty ham and drink hot chocolate—the thick Spanish kind."

"Man, that sounds nice."

"Yup."

"Well, what about after Christmas? We're here till New Year's."

"I wish I could, but I can't," I whisper. "My parents aren't like yours. They're not going to let me stay with my boyfriend out of town somewhere."

For a while, neither of us says anything.

Then, "Hey, Jas, I'm really sorry about what I said about the reform bill. You believe me, right?" His voice is low and sad.

I think about it. If I didn't believe he was sincere, I wouldn't be talking to him now. "I do."

"I thought about it, about what it means that it didn't pass," he says. "I never realized how much stuff like that affects people. To my family, it's just my dad's career. But it's your life."

"Yeah." I press the phone closer to my ear, blinking back tears. I can hear how much he cares about me, and I wish I'd told him earlier. I was so lonely without him to lean on.

"So what are you guys going to do now? You don't have to leave, do you? That would be crazy. You can't leave, even if you're illegal."

"Undocumented," I snap. "I hate that other word." Even though I use it myself all the time, but for some reason, I want to correct him.

"Sorry, sorry. My bad."

"It's okay. I'm sorry I'm so sensitive. Anyway, in answer to your question, we're going to meet with a lawyer, see what our options are."

"I want to help," he says. "Anything I can do, just ask, okay? I can even talk to my dad. He might know how to help. He knows a lot of people."

I inhale sharply. Wasn't this exactly what I was afraid of?

"He wouldn't report you, if that's what you're worried about. You're my friend," he says, trying not to sound too defensive.

"I know, I believe you, but I think we should keep him out of it for now, okay?" I say.

"Okay." He can tell I don't want to talk about it anymore. "I hate skiing anyway, did I ever tell you?" He doesn't wait for me to answer. "It's too cold and Mason always beats me down the hill."

I laugh, thinking of Royce trying to catch up to his older brother.

"So we're good now?" he asks softly.

"We're good. Come home," I say, and my voice betrays the yearning I feel inside.

"I'll be there as fast as I can," he promises.

20

DAD GIVES ME a ride to Royce's house in Bel-Air on
Christmas afternoon so that I can drop off his present. I know
the drive is far, and I had to beg my dad to take me, but I
really want it to be there for him when he gets back instead
of giving it to him when I see him. There's just something
I hate about giving gifts late. I'd rather it sit at his house for
a week than for him to think I'm some kind of last-minute
shopper—which I am.

I hadn't planned on buying him a gift, since we were fighting, but I couldn't help myself. It's in my Filipino blood. We
love giving gifts. It doesn't even matter if we're upset at the
person getting the gift.

"Where is this boy's house?" Dad asks.

"Just around the next corner," I say, pointing to the street.

The whole neighborhood is decorated for Christmas. The
big, classic houses are absolutely gorgeous. Lights are wrapped
around the pillars and roofs. Even the palm trees look like
they're covered with icicles.

I wish Royce were around to celebrate with my family.
We'd show him a real Filipino Christmas. Mom would give

him warm ginger tea and a thick yellow rice cake for breakfast. Isko and Danny would force him to play video games, and Dad would torture Royce by trying to teach him traditional Tagalog holiday songs. I'm lucky that my whole family gets along with him. The boys are constantly bothering me to ask him over to the house.

Dad lets out a long whistle. "His family can afford to live around here?"

"His grandfather founded some big steel company. And his dad's a congressman," I say. "I've told you that."

"Congressman, huh. They should have to live on minimum wage," Dad says.

"Dad. Please stop. They do a lot of hard work too. Maybe I'll be a congresswoman someday. There's no law against it if we ever become citizens! You never know." I think of what Royce said to me once, how I should be the one to go into politics since I'm so passionate about issues he believes I can sway people to follow my lead.

"If you become a congresswoman, I'll be the first one to move in!" he says, pointing through the window at the houses.

I laugh. "I think you better work on becoming an American first."

When Dad parks on the street, I run up to the door and ring the bell. Royce told me Maria would be there for part of the day. Sure enough, she answers the door. When she sees it's me, she doesn't smile.

"Hello?" she says, a little coldly.

"Oh hi, Maria, I hope it's okay—I wanted to drop off a gift for Royce," I say, trying to sound casual and as if I drop by his house all the time.

"Royce is not here," she says shortly.

"I know—that's why I wanted to drop off his present."

"You have a Christmas gift for Royce?" she asks, almost as if she didn't hear me the first time.

"Yes," I say.

"Did you two get back together?" she asks out of the blue.

Now I realize why she's being so unfriendly. It's obvious she's wary because of what happened between us.

"Oh, did he tell you about it?" I say, trying not to blush.

She doesn't respond, but it's clear that he did.

"Yes, but, um, we're together again," I say.

Suddenly, she breaks into a huge smile. "How nice. Come inside, come inside."

I'd planned to just hand over the gift, but now it feels like I have to say yes to be polite.

"Is that your dad? Would he like to come too? I can make some tea."

I gesture to Dad to get out of the car, but he waves me off. He's too busy eyeing all of the houses.

I enter the house and hand Maria the gift, which she sets on a table in the foyer. She doesn't bring up my and Royce's relationship again, and we make small talk standing there. Because she was so protective of Royce earlier, I don't feel that uncomfortable around her anymore. It's clear she cares for him, and since I do too, now we have something in common other than being Filipino. "What are you doing for the holiday?" I ask.

"I'm going to see some of my cousins tonight," she tells me. "That's very sweet of you to bring Royce a gift."

"Thanks," I say. "He's sweet to me too."

Just then the front door opens. I jump a little, especially when I realize it's Royce's mother. She doesn't see me right away.

"Maria, is that one of your relatives outside?" she says as a driver follows her inside and places two suitcases against the wall. "I thought you were staying until five this afternoon?"

Why does Maria have to work on Christmas? And why is Mrs. Blakely home? It's Christmas Day. Why isn't she in Aspen with Royce and Mr. Blakely? What about Mason and Olivia?

"I am staying until then, Mrs. Blakely," Maria says. "Shall I bring up your bags?"

When Mrs. Blakely looks up, she sees me and raises an eyebrow. "Jasmine? Dear, I wasn't expecting you. Merry Christmas. You and Maria must have a lot to talk about."

I'm not sure what she means, other than maybe she thinks, because we're both Filipino, we'd have a lot to talk about no matter what. It makes me squirm, but I ignore her raised eyebrow and smile. "Thank you. Merry Christmas. I was just dropping off a gift for Royce," I say, pointing to the package on the table. "I hope you had a nice time in Aspen."

"I *dread* Aspen every year. Thank God it's over for now," she says. "I can't stand all the cold and being cooped up inside, and I'm not much of a skier. I'm guessing you've never been to the snow though. Is that your father outside?"

"It is," I say, slightly hurt by her comment. Sure, I've never seen snow fall, but I went tobogganing with friends at Big Bear in eighth grade. It was one of the greatest times of my life, but I decide it's better to play the innocent young (and poor) girlfriend of her son. "Yes. I shouldn't keep Dad waiting," I say, thinking how funny it would be if I said we still had to go catch and pluck chickens for our Christmas dinner (which we don't; it's a joke but I'm sure she'd believe me). "I hope you have a good rest of your holiday."

"Please," she says, "don't be a stranger." She turns to Maria. "Be a darling and help me with my bags, then you can have the rest of the day off. I need to deal with this mess Mason has made of his finals. We just got notice that USC has put him on academic probation again. Apparently he hasn't been going to his classes for weeks."

Mrs. Blakely heads up the grand stairway that curves gracefully up from the foyer. Maria picks up both bags. "Just give me a minute, Jasmine, then I'll take you up to Royce's room. You can put the gift there yourself," Maria says. "That way Mason won't open it."

Why would his older brother open a present that's clearly not meant for him?

"I can help you with the bags," I offer.

"No. That's all right. I'll be right back."

Maria drags the suitcases up the stairs and disappears for a few minutes.

I stay where I am, feeling a bit awkward to be alone in Royce's house without him. The house is lavishly and perfectly decorated for the holidays—I count no less than three Christmas trees, one in the living room, one in the other living room, one by the dining area. It looks as perfect as a magazine spread…and just as impersonal.

"The house looks so pretty," I tell Maria when she returns. "All white and gold."

"Mrs. Blakely has it decorated every year, although they're almost never here for the holiday," Maria explains.

"Meanwhile my house looks like a *parol* exploded," I tell her, meaning the typical Filipino Christmas star lantern that we usually hang in the window. My parents tend to decorate in the typical red and green. Our house is so full of tinsel, you can't leave without being covered in it.

We laugh. "Do you like working here?" I can't help but ask. I'm most likely overstepping, but I'm curious.

"Oh yes, they're very good to me. But Mr. Blakely is gone

a lot. Mrs. Blakely has her work. Mason is…" Maria pauses, thinking of what to say. "Mason is Mason. I worry about Royce and Olivia. They seem to be the ones keeping this family together."

"Why would Mrs. Blakely leave her children on Christmas Day? Are Mason's grades *that* important? What's she going to be able to do about it on Christmas?"

"I don't think that's the only reason she came home," Maria says.

"What do you mean?" I ask.

"Mrs. and Mr. Blakely haven't had the easiest time since he became house majority leader. They almost never see each other. They probably had a fight," she whispers.

Right. Royce mentioned his parents were fighting about Mason, but I hadn't thought to ask him more. I wish I had now.

Maria looks like she's regretting saying anything. She gestures to me to follow her. "Come on. Bring your present." She leads me down a great hall on the second landing to Royce's room. I've only been inside once before. Royce likes to come over to my house. It's easier, since he can drive and I don't have a license.

I walk in and look around. His room is fairly clean for a boy. Well, compared to Danny and Isko's room. There's a wrinkled suit hanging over his desk chair and lots of pairs of dress and athletic shoes that have been kicked onto the ground. On his bedside tables are stacks of books about the military and the history of wars and spy novels, all in various states of being read. I riffle through the pages of a book, stroking its pages, thinking of him absorbed in them.

I walk over to his desk to leave the gift while Maria stands near the doorway. On the desk, I see a picture of him and

Mason from when they were little boys, horsing around on the beach. Mason seems to have Royce in some kind of choke hold, but the two of them are laughing. Mason's only a couple years older, but based on what Royce has said about his brother, they seem so far apart now.

I pick up the picture frame and turn to Maria. "They used to be close, huh?"

"Very," Maria says.

"But not anymore, right?"

Maria considers this. "I think both of the boys want their father's approval, but they show it in very different ways. Mason rebels. Royce tries to follow in his father's footsteps. As much as he can anyway."

"I don't know why he does," I say, putting the picture back down on the desk. "He's nothing like his father."

Maria crosses her arms. "You know Mr. Blakely, then?"

"No. Not really. I'm sorry," I say, realizing how horribly judgmental I just sounded.

"Royce is a good boy," Maria says. "You be good to him." She's serious.

I look her in the eye and nod. Turns out I'm not the only one with a Filipino mother. "I'll do my best," I tell her, setting Royce's gift on his desk. "Will you make sure he opens this as soon as he gets home?"

When I get to the car, Dad's still being a Scrooge. "Filipino maid, huh," he says.

"Maria is really nice," I say, closing the door.

Dad gives the home one last glance as we drive off. "I hope he's not just dating you so you can be his maid," he says.

"Daddy, why do you always do this? No, I'm not going to be the help. Why would he think that? You're being rude.

Maria is nice, though I think Mrs. Blakely thinks I was there just to pry some kind of information out of her. She was surprised to see me."

"This is getting good," Dad teases. "Now you and the Mrs. are cat-fighting."

"I didn't say that! See? This is why I never tell you anything."

"Aha!" Dad says. "So you admit you're keeping secrets! No Christmas dinner for you!"

I lean my head on Dad's shoulder while he drives.

He instantly pretends he feels sorry for me. "Okay, you can have bread and water."

"I love you, Daddy," I say.

"I love you too, *neneng*. Everything's going to be all right."

21

Those who deny freedom to others, deserve it not for
themselves.

—ABRAHAM LINCOLN

WE MEET WITH the lawyer for our consultation the week after Christmas. Freddie Alvarado is Latino, in his midfifties, and has a close-trimmed beard and mustache. When he greets us, he's holding a cup of green tea, which is my favorite drink. Dad, on the other hand, isn't impressed and scowls at everything.

The office is filled with all kinds of photos of labor leaders past and present, including a shot of Mr. Alvarado standing between Larry Itliong and Philip Vera Cruz. I know who the two Filipino men in the photo are because Dad spent some time in the fields. Most Filipinos his age have worked, or have family who worked, in the fields at one time or another.

I can tell by Dad's grimace that he thinks the picture is there to keep any potential Filipino clients happy.

"Welcome, Mr. and Mrs. de los Santos," Mr. Alvarado says.

"Very interesting office," Dad says, looking up and down the bookcases.

"I take great pride in meeting some of the political figures I've admired."

While Mom and I sit on the chairs, Dad remains standing.

"How much are you charging for this consultation? I want to know we're getting a fair price."

"Daddy," I say, mortified. "We already know."

Mom decides to speak up. "We would like to get started as soon as possible, Mr. Alvarado."

"Of course," he says. "You'll be happy to know I've already begun researching your case. I believe with your work records and your children's academic success, you have a good chance to prove you're worthy candidates for a green card that can then lead to American citizenship."

"How much will that cost?" Dad asks.

Mom steps on his foot.

Dad changes his tone. "I mean, what's your well-counseled advice?"

Mom steps on his foot again. I make a mental note not to bring Dad next time. The way he's acting right now, Mr. Alvarado will probably pay *us* to leave the country.

Mr. Alvarado seems to expect this kind of behavior and ignores the foot-smashing on our side of the desk. "I'd like to press for a deportation trial," he says. "Your family also hasn't committed any offenses, especially aggravated felonies."

I'm a little nervous. The memory of running with Kayla through Lo's living room to avoid the police flashes in my mind. Even though there weren't any actual police, I still feel exposed.

"What exactly is a deportation trial?" Mom asks.

"It'll mean you'll be admitting fault that you have been living here without documentation," says Mr. Alvarado. "But I'll be able to argue that you should be able to stay and receive some kind of documentation in the meantime."

I sense my parents are already feeling overwhelmed, so I speak up. "That's a little scary, isn't it? If we lose, couldn't we be deported? Wouldn't it be difficult to get back into the US if that happens? And wouldn't my parents lose all their assets?"

Mr. Alvarado folds his hands. "You must have been researching this process, Ms. de los Santos." I nod silently in agreement. Doing research seems to be my full-time hobby these days.

"That is a possibility..." Mr. Alvarado continues. "It's always risky, even for the most seasoned of deportation defense attorneys, to win these types of cases. That's also why I'm careful when I agree to take on a case. I've won about ninety percent of these types of hearings."

"I can do simple math," Dad says. "That leaves ten percent getting kicked out."

"That's not always the case either," Mr. Alvarado says. "In some cases, there are appeals that can be made to the Board of Immigration Appeals. There are also short extensions via temporary permission to live and work in the US that can result."

"We don't want temporary visas," Mom says. "What about just waiting for a new bill? We could get amnesty. Is there going to be another?"

"Laws are always changing, Mrs. de los Santos," Mr. Alvarado says. He adjusts his bright green tie and buttons his suit jacket. "They depend on politics. And, as you know, politics are undependable. They can also take a very, very long time. In the meantime, any undocumented family runs the risk of deportation. And, of course, any infraction—even something as simple as a speeding ticket—while undocumented could put the entire family at risk of being housed in a detention center if you're all in the car when it happens."

In disbelief, Mom covers her mouth. Dad sits up in his chair. "A detention center?" I ask.

"They do exist, unfortunately. The government calls them family detention centers in the name of keeping families together, but my understanding is that they're terrible, as one would assume, especially for children. I won't let that happen to you. Most of them are used for those caught at border crossings." Mr. Alvarado continues. "In some ways you're lucky. The current administration recently passed laws to speed up the process of hearings. Just a few years ago, there was a backlog of more than 300,000 cases and a waiting time average of 1.5 years."

"One and a half years!" Dad says. "All for a chance at eventual citizenship?"

"It's a quicker process now," Mr. Alvarado says. "And I believe your case will get a speedy hearing. Your daughter's accomplishments and her meeting the president will really help your case. She's a model citizen, as are all the members of your family. It would be even better if you could somehow bring more public attention to your case."

"You think we should go around telling everyone?" Dad asks.

"Your daughter has been named a National Scholar. Surely she must know someone who could publicize her case."

The only person I can think of is Mr. Blakely. Royce offered to ask his dad for help, but I don't really see why the congressman would help us.

"Get the word out," Mr. Alvarado continues. "The more political pressure, the better. The more support from the community. We can use help from all sides."

"But we could still end up in a detention center or deported," Mom says.

Mr. Alvarado looks each of us dead in the eye. "Like I said, there are risks. But you're already technically taking them now. If you win, however, you'll be deemed legal once and for all. You'll be eligible for naturalization in a few years. You'll all be United States citizens."

22

Above all, be the heroine of your life, not the victim.

—NORA EPHRON

MOM AND DAD have been arguing nonstop about whether to petition for a deportation hearing. As important as that is to all of us, Royce's return offers relief from the tension at my house. As soon as he gets back to Los Angeles, he picks me up in his father's sweet little German sports car, which impresses my brothers to no end. He's taking me out to dinner in Beverly Hills to celebrate our birthdays, like we'd originally planned.

I'm so excited to see him that I spent a longer time than usual doing my hair, fixing my makeup, trying and discarding every outfit until I found the perfect one.

He gets more handsome every time I see him. But today he looks even better than usual, because when he holds the car door open for me I notice he's wearing the tie I bought him for Christmas. It has the flag of the Philippines on one side and the US flag on the other. He's got it Philippines side out. The tie was one of those cheesy knickknacks my parents used to sell at Tito Sonny's store. I thought Royce would find it funny, and I was right.

That's what I love about him. Not that he's taking me to a

fancy dinner, but that he's wearing the silly gift I gave him. He's a good sport.

He gives me a long wolf whistle when I take off my sweater before sliding into the seat. I didn't want my parents to see the dress I'm wearing, and I blush a little.

It's a tight-fitting, low-cut, red knee-length cocktail dress that I bought at an after-Christmas sale. Lipstick to match. I was worried I couldn't pull it off—I've never worn anything so outwardly sexy before—but he seems to like it. (Okay, he seems to like it a lot.)

"I didn't think you would actually wear that tie," I tell him, as he settles into the driver's seat. It was just one of those whims. A self-pride moment. Okay, I admit it. I wanted the last laugh. I wanted him to go the extra mile for me, to be willing to be uncomfortable for my sake, to wear a funny tie to prove he cares for me. He's doing a great job.

He fidgets with the tie. "I really like how the flip side is the US flag. It's sort of like us."

"Ha," I say. "Have you thought about relocating to Manila?"

"I'll go if you do," he says lightly. And with the roar of the engine, we're off.

When we're at Spago, I tell him I've never been to a restaurant this fancy, other than the time I was in D.C. for the award. I'm a bit intimidated, but I feel more confident as the night goes on, especially since Royce is so self-assured that we belong there.

The waiter takes our order and leaves, and for a moment we kind of just stare at each other. Then we both look down and laugh. But there's a slight distance between us now, and he's not reaching for my hand across the table the way he used to. He's all the way over there, and I'm all the way over here, and even though we're easy with each other, it's not quite the same.

"I'll start," he says. "Aspen was a bore."

"Liar," I say.

"No. Seriously. I was bored out of my mind. Have you ever felt that way? I mean, gone someplace really fun, someplace you always look forward to going, then when you get there, there's sort of this big letdown?"

"Yeah, sort of, I guess." I admit I'm kind of happy to hear this. If he'd had a great time I probably would have wanted to leave the table right then. "We haven't seen each other in a while, and I was looking forward to *this*. But are you disappointed now?" I ask, because I like to tease him.

"Right now I'm pretty much the farthest from disappointed anyone can be," he says with a serious look on his face. "What about you?"

"Ditto," I say.

He smiles. "It's good to know I'm not such a disappointment to other people like I am to my dad."

"He's not disappointed in you!"

Royce shrugs. "He was when I told him I wanted to be a journalist."

"Oh man, I'm sorry. If it helps, I'm always trying to please my parents too. It's a Filipino thing."

"Then I'm Filipino too." He grins, the shadow leaving his face. "I'm wearing the tie, aren't I?"

"Are your parents okay? You said they were fighting about Mason."

He sighs. "Yeah, they just disagree on what to do about him. Mom thinks Dad should be harder on him, but Dad thinks Mason will shape up eventually. He wants him to transfer out of USC next year, but Mom thinks it's better if he's close to home."

"I'm sorry," I say.

"It's all right. Like I said, it's nothing new. They've been fighting about Mason for years now."

The waiter comes over with our food and refills our waters. I thank him. Royce fidgets again, this time with his napkin.

"So your dad wasn't too happy about journalism, huh?" I ask.

"Nope. He keeps sending me links to all these articles about how it's a dying profession and all these ex-journalists now drive for Uber."

I grimace. "Yikes."

"Yeah, well. Dad wants me to major in political science, which means I'll probably have to intern for him at some point," he says, getting that look on his face again.

"That bad, huh?"

"The worst."

"Well, in other news, I turned in my Stanford application," I tell him.

He raises his eyebrows and he talks all in a rush. "That's great! You said it's your first choice, right?" he says hopefully.

"Yeah."

"That would be cool if we both ended up there," he says. "We could probably room together or share an apartment if we wanted. I think they let you do that. Not freshman year, but later."

"Are you asking me to move in with you already?" I tease.

He blushes. "Oops."

"No, I like that you always make plans for us," I tell him. I do like it. I like that he's so sure of me, of what he wants, and that he wants me. I indulge in a fantasy of the two of us at Stanford, walking the quad, going to the library. Sharing an apartment senior year maybe. How much fun it would be, to wake up in his arms—to be with him all the time. We've only been going out for a short time and already he's got us shacking up. What would my parents say about that?

We're Filipino, and we go to church every Sunday. They don't approve of premarital sex. My dad would probably insist we get married before we moved in together. *Shotgun shack-up*, I think with a laugh.

"What's so funny?" he asks.

I tell him about the image of my dad with a shotgun and he gets a strange, nervous look on his face, and I can't tell what he's thinking. "Don't worry, I won't let him shoot you," I say.

"Gee, thanks."

"Much," I say, and then we're both laughing.

I tell him what's going on with Mr. Alvarado, about all the risks involved with a hearing, and how Mom and Dad have been arguing constantly about what to do next.

"I guess once you throw it out there, anything can happen. You get on the government's radar and that's a two-edged sword for sure," he says, between bites.

"Yeah. Even though I'm dying to visit, I don't want to go to the Philippines to live. There's nothing there for me. My life is here." I push my fish around on my plate, having lost my appetite a little.

"What are your chances?" Royce asks. "When it's said and done, if you don't have near-certain chances, your family shouldn't do it. It's too risky."

"It's awful, isn't it? No one who's been in America as long as us should have to go through this. I've been here most of my life. I can barely remember the Philippines. I used to think

I belonged equally to both cultures, but I'm not really Filipino, and now I'm not quite American either."

"You're who you've always been, Jas. That doesn't change," he says. "Like I said the other night, I really think we should ask my dad to help. He can do a lot, he knows so many people."

"I still don't think that's a good idea," I say. "I don't want to put you in the middle of all this. Do you even trust him to know about my status?" I ask nervously, the butterflies returning to my stomach.

"There has to be some way I can help," Royce says. "Look, I know you think my dad's a bad guy, but he's not really. He would do this for me."

"I don't need anything from you except to just be there for me," I say. I want to reach across the table and touch him, but I don't. I'm still a bit shy after our sort-of-breakup.

"I am," he says. "You know I am. But you need to tell more people what's going on."

Suddenly, I recall someone else saying the same thing.

"What's up?" Royce asks.

"My friend Millie told me that recently. That I need to build a support group. I can't do it alone."

"Great minds think alike," he says. Royce hasn't met Millie, but he's heard all about her.

"You know what though? If I'm only going to be here for a little while longer, I want to make it count. Live it up a little," I say, an idea dawning. Royce is back in LA, and we're back together. We're eighteen years old—what are we doing in this stuffy restaurant?

"Live it up? You? I can't believe what I'm hearing." Now he's the one teasing me.

"Let's get out of here. Take me somewhere." I lean over

and look into his eyes. I reach for his hand and slowly scratch a nail under his palm in a seductive gesture I never realized I was capable of making. Maybe it's because I waited so long to kiss a boy, or maybe it's just because it's him. I think it's because it's him. Like Royce, I know what I want.

His face turns bright red, and he throws the napkin down on the table along with enough cash to cover the meal. No need for dessert.

Royce stands up. "Where do you want to go?"

"I don't know. How fast can you drive?"

Royce grins as I'm hanging on to the side of the car door for dear life. We're going top-down in the Carrera. I've never been more attracted to him. This is it, I tell myself. Speed. The edge. Roaring curves. Mulholland Drive. This is a metaphor for life, and I'm completely trusting Royce with mine.

I embrace every turn, every leap of my stomach. Royce tells me not to worry—he's had speed-driving lessons. I didn't even know you could get those, but apparently you can if you're rich enough.

"I can't believe you've never driven fast on Mulholland," he says. "This is me taking it easy!"

"Don't take it easy," I say, loving the wicked, dangerous thrill. "Go as fast as you can."

"Oh, I will," he says. I love the way he focuses. Eyes on the road. Carefully shifting and downshifting on the curves, then hitting the gears again so we're really soaring. We're going faster now. Faster. The car roars; it was made for this.

When he turns to me, his handsome face is full of joy. He's totally lost in the moment, not caring about anything but the speed, the ride, wind in his hair and the speakers blasting Kanye's "All of the Lights." My heart is bursting for him. This is exactly what I wanted tonight.

The curves come faster, harder. If my parents were here, I'd never see Royce again. The car screeches on a turn and I scream at him to slow down. In my defense, I want to live.

He laughs and shakes his head. "No way! This is what you wanted!"

Damn, he's right. Through the howl of the wind, I manage to squeak out a few words. "The city is so beautiful from here!"

He laughs again. "You want me to watch the lights or the road?"

I laugh nervously and nearly throw up.

"You don't look scared enough!" he yells. "Maybe I should go faster!"

He'd better be joking, or I'll kill him before he kills me, but I stay quiet, gripping the edge of my seat, taking in the dangerous, iridescent beauty of Los Angeles. Below us are cascades of city lights like swirling jellyfish in a sea of bioluminescence. I'm above the darkness and the lights on the swells of this road. I'm a little carsick, but I don't tell Royce.

Somehow I know I need to feel scared. Somehow I know, that tonight, I need to feel everything.

He parks the car at a secluded spot, high on the hill, where we can see the whole city. We don't say a word to each other. We don't have to; we know exactly what we're about to do. He's breathing heavily and so am I, and as soon as he cuts the engine I literally leap into his arms, scooting over from my side of the seat to get nearer to his. With the top down on the car, I should be cold, but he's so warm, and pressed against him like this, so am I.

We're kissing now, our arms wrapped around each other, as if we can't get close enough to each other, and we want—we *need* to be closer. I tug at his shirt, run my hands underneath, so I can feel his skin, and I notice he's trembling.

"What?" I whisper.

"I want you so much," he says.

"Let's do it," I say, feeling so powerfully feminine at the moment, and my hand goes to his belt, and he tugs down on the straps of my dress, and I think, this is it, I want this. I want him. I want this *with him*.

Now he's lying on top of me, his body heavy on mine, and I like its weight, like having him on top of me. I start to unbuckle his belt, but suddenly, and with a drawn-out groan, he stops me. Puts his hand on mine.

"We shouldn't," he says hoarsely. "Not like this, not here."

I wiggle underneath him, and he catches his breath again. I can make him change his mind, I know I can. "But I want to." I want to show him how much I feel for him, how much closer I want to be. Yet I'm a little nervous too, and maybe he senses that because he shakes his head.

"Jas," he breathes. "We can't."

"Why not?" I say, my heart pounding, my breath shallow, but feeling relief as well.

"It's not that I don't want to," he says. "But…"

I know what he means. We're not ready. We just got back together. It *feels* right, but it's way, way, too fast.

He pulls away a little and we both settle down. That's when I realize the seats in the car go all the way down. *So that's how we got in this position*, I think, and laugh to myself.

Royce pushes up on one elbow and looks down at me. His dark hair is plastered to his forehead, and I push his bangs away so I can see his eyes.

"What's so funny?" he asks, looking worried.

I smile to show him there's nothing to worry about. "The seats. I didn't realize until just now that they recline all the way down."

"They have to," he says, with a serious look on his face. "Otherwise how else are we going to have sex in this thing one day?"

"Oh my God," I say, hiding my face in my hands. I almost had *sex* with him. I wanted to, so badly, but I'm glad he stopped us.

When he gently pulls my hands away from my face, I know he's telling me there's nothing to be ashamed of, and I know he's right.

I want to know all of him, and I want him to know all of me. One day we will.

Everything is beautiful in the moonlight.

Never grow a wishbone, daughter, where your backbone
ought to be.

—CLEMENTINE PADDLEFORD

IT DOESN'T TAKE long for Mom and Dad to catch on that I don't want to be at home. At all. Since Royce and I got back together, I just want to spend as much time with him as I can to make up for all that time when we weren't together. We take it slow though, and go back to kissing a lot. He sends me love letters (okay, love emails) and writes me poetry. I take endless portraits of him with my phone. I used to be really into photography, and I am obsessed with capturing every angle of his handsome face. I want to show him how I see him, how beautiful he is to me.

But every moment we're together is an anxious one too. Who knows how long we have to be together? If my family does end up having to leave America, I don't want to lose out on any time left that I might have with him. Tonight, I'm halfway to the front door, trying to sneak out for the evening, when Dad stops me. "Where do you think you're going?"

"Out," I say.

Dad puts his arm across the doorway. "With who? Kayla?"

"You know who, Daddy." I inch closer toward the door. It's not that I don't want to spend *any* time with my family anymore, but come on, I've spent eighteen years with them staying home almost every single night.

"But Lola Cherry's coming over for dinner. You know she'll want to see you."

He had to say that. He knows I love Lola Cherry.

It's probably a trick though. "I already made plans," I say.

"Bring your white boy in for a while," Dad says, resolute. "Lola wants to meet him."

I recall how I wanted Royce to know more about me, about my family. But I know how Lola Cherry can get. Royce has no idea how loose-tongued older-generation Filipinos are.

I try a new tactic. "We have reservations," I say. "And his mom is Latina, by the way. He's not a white boy."

"Sure looks like one to me," says Dad. "And I don't care about reservations. Un-reserve them."

I'm not giving up yet. "We made them a week ago, Dad. Royce said they were really hard to get." I'm stretching it a little—we're just going to the movies and grabbing burgers— but Dad doesn't have to know that.

"So?" he says. "You'll save money if you eat here."

"I wasn't paying," I say, trying to go around him, but he blocks me from leaving.

"*Neneng*. Don't waste that boy's money."

"I'm not. I didn't ask him to spend it!"

I give Dad the eternal look of daughter disapproval, but he doesn't budge. It's so unfair—I've been such a good girl my whole life, and he still won't let me be a regular teenager for a few months. Not that I'm ever going to tell him about Royce taking me drag racing on Mulholland Drive, of course. Or what almost happened after. Filipinos think all brides are virgins, or should be.

Although Mom surprised me the other day. Out of the

blue she said she hoped Royce and I were "being careful" and that "there are a lot of diseases out there" which I think is the code for "make sure you don't get pregnant or catch an STD." I wanted to tell her that we weren't having sex! At least not yet. How does she know it's on my mind? But then, moms always know, right? I was too embarrassed to say anything, but I promised her I was taking care of myself. She seemed okay with that.

Dad is another matter.

"Fine," I say after our standoff. "I'll get him. When's Lola coming?"

"Your mother's picking her up. Show some respect. She's a lonely old woman."

"She's not lonely," I say. "She hangs out with old Filipino women at the home every day."

"Sounds like a hard life to me," Dad says. "If you knew my mother, rest her soul."

I laugh. My dad can always crack me up. I'm glad we're staying in now. I have missed hanging out with my family. I walk out to the driveway, where Royce is waiting in his Range Rover.

He rolls down the window. "Why aren't you getting in?"

"I can't go," I sigh.

"Oh," he says, flummoxed. This hasn't happened before. "Are you grounded or something? Do I have to leave?"

"No!" I say. "They want you to come in and have dinner with us. Is that okay?"

"Sure, of course. Why didn't you just say so earlier?" he says. "You know I like Filipino food."

Just then Mom rolls up with Lola Cherry. Mom gets out and opens the door for Lola, who starts arguing with Mom about something in Tagalog.

"You think I can't open a door?" Lola barks.

"I was already here," Mom says.

"You're treating me like a cripple."

As they walk toward the house, Lola leans on Mom's arm. Suddenly, Lola Cherry sees Royce and me. "*Neneng!* What are you doing outside! Come in here with that handsome boyfriend of yours!"

I wave to her. My stomach has tied itself into a big knot. Oh well, Royce has to meet her sooner or later.

Inside, Lola sits down at the kitchen table with Dad, who's drinking coffee. Mom starts cooking lumpia over the stove. I notice Lola has her curved wooden cane sitting at her side.

"Hi, Mr. and Mrs. de los Santos," Royce says.

Mom claps her hands. "Royce!" she says. She doesn't usually act this way. It's something she's putting on for Lola. She wants to show us off. She turns to Lola. "This is Jasmine's boyfriend, Royce. He goes to Eastlake Prep."

I sit down. Royce continues to stand.

"Where's that?" Lola says.

"It's in Brentwood," I tell her. "Private school."

"Ah, one of those."

"Lola! You went to Catholic school in Cebu City," Mom says before Royce can say anything. We're all talking at the same time.

"St. Theresa's was a long time ago," Lola says. "And the nuns were stupid."

Royce and I laugh. I hand him a Coke. He smiles his thanks.

"Don't say that!" Mom says. "God in heaven will strike us all dead."

"It's true," says Lola. "They were dumb as bricks. They thought we were all good girls, but we were smoking, drinking, and meeting the boys after dark. We could stay out until 6:00 a.m. because those nuns were so old, dumb, and blind." Lola takes off her trifocals. Her eyes suddenly look tiny. "I can't see through these," she says, reaching for her purse.

"Let me get that for you." Royce reaches down.

Lola is quicker than lightning and smacks Royce on the hand with her cane. "Don't touch that. What are you? Some hooligan?"

Royce yelps, pulling away his hand from Lola like she's some kind of poisonous snake who snapped at him with her forked tongue. I hold my breath, waiting to see how he'll react.

"Is that all you've got?" he says to Lola with a raised eyebrow.

Dad starts laughing. "Good one, Royce."

"Lola!" Mom says. "What if he's going to become a surgeon? You can't break his hands!"

Lola opens her purse and takes out a handkerchief to wipe her lenses. "I can't help if he's slow," she says.

Royce winks at me while he rubs his hand.

I smirk at Lola. She pretends to be so innocent, but she's always been a prankster.

"How's your knee?" I ask Lola.

"It's fine, but my dancing days are definitely over."

"Were you a dancer?" Royce asks.

"She likes to think she was," Dad says.

Mom rolls the last lumpia and puts it on a sheet with the others to fry.

"I was a *great* dancer," Lola says. "I may not be a blood relative of Jasmine, but she wouldn't be cheerleading if I hadn't shown her how to shake her hips."

Royce raises an eyebrow and looks intrigued. I try not to blush.

"Oh, come on," Mom says.

"It's true! Tell her, *neneng*. You know the truth."

"Lola was a traditional dance leader for the Filipino community here," I say. "And before that, according to legend—and by legend I mean from the mouth of Lola herself—she also taught ballet at some dance school for fifty years."

"You exaggerate," Lola says. "I'm not even fifty years old…"

"Try more like a thousand years," Dad says, as Danny and Isko enter the room.

"When's dinner going to be ready?" Danny asks.

Isko kicks Royce in the back of the knee. Royce almost goes tumbling to the floor. Poor Royce. He's always so abused when he comes over to my house.

"Isko!" Mom says. "*Tarantado!* Apologize to Royce!"

"Oh, that Francisco," Lola laughs. "Maybe he should wear a black dress for the rest of the day and say Hail Marys. You have black skirts, Jasmine. Maybe you can lend him one."

"I'm not wearing a dress!" Isko says. "It's Danny's fault! He dared me to see if I could make him fall!"

"How about I make you fall?" Dad says. "You and your brother get out of here."

The boys dart out of the room.

I turn to Royce and hug him. "Don't worry. I'll get him back for you later."

"Or I will." He grins. "Don't forget, I have an older brother. I can defend myself."

Lola has her glasses back on her face. "*Neneng*. You didn't tell me your friend was white."

Oh no, I think. Here she goes. Lola may be wild, but she's also still more traditional than my parents in some ways.

This time Royce speaks up. "Italian-Mexican-Norwegian-German-English actually," he says. "Oh, and some Irish."

Lola gives Royce a bizarre look. "Running for politics like your fancy dad?"

I glance at Mom. She shrugs apologetically. She must have told Lola Cherry everything about Royce. And Congressman Blakely.

"If my dad had his way, I would be just like him," Royce says.

"Then don't be a fool. Be like JFK. Now there was an American president! He looked good in a suit too. Charming. Handsome. He was a playboy though. Are you a playboy?"

Royce laughs. "I don't think so."

"You don't *think* so? You sound like JFK already. Maybe you should run for president."

"Nah, that's my dad, not me."

"Lola," I interrupt. "How are your friends in the home?"

"Oh, them," she says. "They're fine. Boring. Same old stories every day. My son's family is doing this. My daughter's family is doing that. My son's family is wealthier than your son's family. My hip is going out. I can't eat pork anymore. I get tired of it all. I just want to watch movies and dance, but this knee hurts too much. I watch some of them dance and I say, 'Hey, you got two left feet. What's wrong with you?' But it does no good unless I can show them."

I sometimes feel bad for Lola. Old people in the Philippines never go to a home. Their families take care of them. But then I remember not to feel so sorry for her, because Lola actually seems to like being social with the other old people. She might complain about them, but they allow her to constantly be the center of attention, which is her favorite thing to be.

Lola turns her attention to Royce again. "Why are you here? Why aren't you taking Jasmine out?"

I give Dad a *told-you-so* look. Royce glances at me and smiles.

"He wanted to meet you," Dad lies. "He heard so much about you."

"Do you want me to hit you with my cane?" she says to Dad.

Dad chuckles. "You look like Charlie Chaplin when you walk with that."

"You say that again," Lola says like she's daring him.

"Tell us about the boys you snuck out to meet in Cebu City," says Royce. "What were they like?"

"You don't even know," Lola says. "There was this military man on leave taking classes nearby. He was in World War Two. There was a scar hole on his shoulder you could put your finger in from a Japanese bayonet. Oh, and there was a French scholar who liked my dancing. Wild days, those were. He came to the ballet to see me once. He was studying birds and politics. Can you believe that? He called me his falconet. You ever see one? Glossy. Blue black. They yell *kek-kek-kek-kek* when they're diving between the trees."

"Stop it, Lola," Mom says. "You're giving Jasmine ideas."

Lola's eyes brighten. "Oh, I don't have to do that. She's young. She has her own ideas. Don't you, *neneng*? I don't need to help you come up with those."

"Not if I can help it," Dad says.

I try to see if Royce is squirming as badly as I am, but he doesn't seem to be. He's smiling, going with the flow.

"Why did you move to the United States, Lola Cherry?" Royce asks.

"Ah. You want to hear this story?" Lola asks. Before Royce can respond, Lola leans toward the table, clasping her hands together as if in prayer. "In the Philippines, I used to... When I was around Jasmine's age, I was quite a looker, just like her. If I do say so myself. There was one night I put on my best dress and snuck out of my family's compound to go to a dance at a bar. There was a handsome man drinking whiskey, leaning against the bar, but he didn't talk to anyone. Well, you know me, I couldn't let him go through the whole night not talking to anyone, so I went up to him and asked him to dance. He agreed, but I was soon regretting my choice because he had two left feet!"

Royce seems enthralled by her story. I guess it is kind of funny. "What did you do? Did you ditch him? Did you whack him with your cane?"

Lola laughs. "I wish I'd had my cane then. I could have taught him a thing or two about rhythm. To answer your question—no, I didn't abandon him. In fact, I discovered that he was Filipino, but he had been born in the United States. His reason for coming to the Philippines was to find a wife. And, well, how should I say this? He found me. So here I am."

"You knew he was the one for you, just like that?" Royce asks. But he's looking at me, not Lola, and I can feel myself blushing and smiling.

"Yes, I knew he was the one. Just like that." Lola nods. "But enough about me," she says, uncharacteristically. I can tell talking about her late husband is making her sad. She turns around in her seat, pointing her cane at Dad. "What are you doing about your citizenship problem?"

I'm glad she's changed the subject, but not really sure I want to hear this argument.

"We came to a decision," Mom says.

I'm surprised. "You did? How come I didn't hear about this?"

"Because you're never home," Dad says. "Huh, Royce?"

Royce's ears turn red and he chokes down the last of his Coke.

"What did you decide?" Lola asks, tapping the kitchen table with her cane. "If you're going back to the Philippines, you can take me with you. I'd rather be buried there than here. I don't like American cemeteries."

"What's wrong with the cemeteries?" Dad asks.

Mom interrupts. "We're going to go through with the deportation hearing."

"We are?" I ask. My stomach heaves.

"Might as well take our chances," Mom says.

Royce and I catch each other's gaze. I can't tell which of us looks more anxious.

24

I'm inspired by failure. The process of defeat—picking
yourself back up again is the hardest thing in the world.

—LOLO JONES

"YOU NEED TO spend more time doing schoolwork," Mom
says the next Saturday night as I'm getting ready to go to Lo's
for another kick back.

"Why? What's the point?" I ask.

Even though our family has been through a lot together,
I'm starting to get bitter about the possibilities for my future.
The more research I do about the success of deportation tri-
als, the angrier I get. It turns out Mr. Alvarado was being
overly optimistic about our chances.

"Quit being so angry," Mom says. "You weren't born in
America. You're not entitled to its privileges."

I can't believe she just said that to me. If that's really how
she feels, then I don't even want to be home right now.

"You don't get it," I say. "I put in my hard work. I did what
you told me to do. And it won't do any good—it won't help
us stay here. Now, I finally have something in my life that
you didn't pick out for me. You can't control me for forever,
Mom. I'm already eighteen."

"You're with that boy all the time," she says. "It's not good
for you to be so serious with someone at this age."

"Are you really going to start calling Royce *'that boy,'* Mom?"

What happened to "be careful" and trusting that I can take care of myself? It's so dumb, because I *know* that she actually *likes* Royce. And too bad, we *are* serious about each other.

When Mom leaves my room, I text Kayla to see if she and Dylan are on the way to pick me up. We haven't seen each other much, since she spends most of her time with Dylan and I've gotten back together with Royce. Coming in second at Regionals, we don't have as much cheer practice anymore—mostly we just perform for basketball games—so it'll be nice to hang out.

Kayla texts back and says they'll be there soon. Royce is going to meet me at the party, since he's coming from some thing he had to do for his dad. I'm excited for him to meet my friends, to see what I'm like around people who aren't my family.

"Hey, guys," I say, when they arrive. Dylan gives me the thumbs-up and Kayla has a huge smile on her face.

"What up, girl," she says. "Wait till you hear their new song, it's amazing."

"Can't wait," I say. I'm a senior in high school, it's Saturday night, and I'm going to have fun with my guy and my friends.

This kick back is much smaller than the first one we went to. Just the guys in the band and their girlfriends hanging out in the backyard, sitting in a circle around a fire pit and drinking a few beers.

I take a seat on a patio chair and drink a little beer, which makes me feel light-headed. I wish Royce would get here already, but I know that he's going to be a while. It's at least an hour drive for him. Maybe less, if traffic isn't too bad and he's driving fast like he usually does. I listen to the conversation, mostly about where the band should tour next.

I don't say much. I'm thinking of the deportation hearing that's coming up. If we win, we get to stay, but if we lose, we lose everything. I've also been thinking how frustrating it is that a law can somehow define who you are or how you see yourself. It's like I'm somehow less of a person because I'm not in America legally.

Maybe my frustration is showing because Kayla knocks me with her foot and mouths *You okay?*

Dylan notices and says, "Yeah, you look bummed. What's up with you?"

I shrug, but suddenly I find myself strangely close to tears. "It's nothing," I say.

"Doesn't look like it," says Dylan with a kind smile. He really is nice. I'm glad he's with Kayla. "You might feel better if you talk about it."

"Jasmine recently found out she's an illegal immigrant," Kayla says after taking a long pull of her beer.

I want to feel betrayed that she's telling people my big secret like it's no big deal, but I know better. She's just trying to do what she thinks is good for me, and I already know she thinks I should be more open about what's wrong. I'm actually surprised she hasn't told Dylan yet, especially since I didn't tell her she couldn't.

"Undocumented," I correct.

"Oh man," Julian says, overhearing. "How could you just find something like that out?"

"Her parents didn't tell her. They were too scared to," Kayla explains.

"Man, that blows," says Dylan. "I can't imagine waking

up one day and finding out I'm not American. That's crazy. Are you okay? I mean, that's a stupid question."

Lo reaches across the circle and puts a hand on my knee. "Jas, we're here for you. Is there anything we can do to help?"

I shake my head.

"So what are you going to do?" Julian asks, concerned.

"I don't know," I say. I smile weakly, but I do feel better having told them.

The back door of Lo's house opens. Her younger brother, Eric, and Kayla's brother, Brian, come into the backyard. Both of the boys are around Danny's age. They're a little bit older but go to the same middle school. Danny mentions them every once in a while, but I don't think they hang out.

"You've got more guests, Lo," Eric says.

I turn and see Royce and Mason walking up behind them.

Mason? What's *he* doing here? Why would Royce bring him?

Brian walks up to Kayla and puts his arm around her. "Hey, sis. Can we hang out here with you guys for a few minutes? You and Lo *are* supposed to be *watching us* after all."

"Yeah," Lo answers before Kayla can. "Whatever. You guys are going to get bored soon enough. And absolutely no beer."

I get up and give Royce a hug and introduce him all around. "Guys, this is Royce, I've told you all about him. And this is his brother, Mason. Royce, Mason, these are my friends," I say, and name each of them in turn.

Lo smiles, Julian tips his beer. Dylan, Kayla and the others wave. Someone hands both the Blakely boys a beer.

I motion Royce over to my chair and he sits down so that I can perch on his lap like the other girls are doing. He leans in close to whisper in my ear. "I'm sorry. I didn't want to bring

Mason, but he wouldn't leave me alone and I didn't want to miss the chance to see you."

I turn and give him a half smile. "It's all right."

He looks relieved. We haven't seen each other as much this week in comparison to the weeks before. Both of us do still have to focus on school. When we're together, he's been quiet lately. I know he's worried about the deportation trial, and I am too. But whenever he brings it up, I don't want to talk about it, and it makes him frustrated. He keeps offering to help, but it's my family's problem—my problem—not his.

Mason is soon engrossed in a conversation with Kayla and Dylan about something, and they all laugh. I think maybe for once he might actually be an okay guy.

Turns out I'm wrong.

After about an hour or so, Mason has drunk so many bottles of beer—and finished his own flask of whiskey—that he's stumbling around the backyard. He's talking about the crazy parties he goes to at USC and how much money he's going to make when he sets up his own hedge fund.

I lean over to Royce and whisper in his ear. "I'm glad you came, but maybe you should take Mason home. He's had too much to drink…"

But the younger kids, Eric and Brian, think Mason is hilarious and practically hero-worship him. They keep asking him questions about college, but in between answers that crack them up, Mason seems to be drunkenly interested in Kayla, which is obviously getting on Dylan's nerves. He tolerates the flirting until Mason puts his hand on Kayla's thigh. She freezes and looks at Dylan, not knowing what to do or say.

"Hey, man," Dylan says to Mason. "Things are wrapping up here. I think it's time to go home."

Apparently, I'm not the only one who wants him to leave.

"Yeah," I say, scooting off Royce's lap reluctantly. "It's getting late. I'll walk you guys out."

But of course it's not that easy.

Mason takes his hand off Kayla and sneers at me. "Oh, you're still here? Little Miss National Scholar? Haven't been sent back to your island yet?"

"What island?" Brian asks, as I'm trying to catch my breath.

"Treasure Island," Mason laughs. "Wherever she's from, it's not America."

"Shut up, Mason. Don't mind him. He's drunk and I'm taking him home," Royce says. He looks at me apologetically, then gets up and walks over to Mason, grabbing his arm. *I'm sorry*, he mouths.

I nod. It's okay. I can handle his douche-bag brother. But I'm bummed, because I'd hoped Royce and I could have some time alone tonight, and that's not happening now. I also try not to be annoyed that he told Mason about my legal status. But I guess they are family.

"Aw, come on," Eric and Brian whine. "Mason's funny. Let him stay."

Lo glares at them. Julian seems like he's about to help her kick everyone out of the house. Kayla has a deer-in-the-headlights look on her face.

Mason violently shakes Royce off. "Fine. Let's go. Why am I hanging out with a bunch of stupid high schoolers in the middle of nowhere anyway?"

Royce shoots me an intense look full of everything he can't say.

Strangely, even though Mason was awful, I'm glad everyone knows about me now. Royce, Millie and Kayla are right, I need to let people know what's eating at me, what's happening to my family. I can't shoulder this alone. There are so many haters out there. I need to start garnering support from the people who do care about me.

25

Feet, what do I need you for when I have wings to fly?

—FRIDA KAHLO

MRS. GARCIA'S OFFICE is freezing. She's wearing a sweater, and I've already cooled down from exercising during PE. I silently count the goose bumps along my arms. My skin is a pincushion.

"Why do you need to see me, Jasmine?" Mrs. Garcia asks. "Have you already heard back from colleges? It's pretty soon if you applied for early admission."

"I didn't apply early. I'm going through some things," I say. "But, um, you said last time that I could talk to you if I needed to?" I want to kick myself for being so vague.

"Of course. What's on your mind?"

I try to tell her, but it's hard. I can feel my cheeks burn and my throat is suddenly dry. I force myself to spit it out. "I found out I'm undocumented," I whisper. "I was born in the Philippines, but I always thought my family had green cards. It turns out they don't. My parents told me we're here illegally." My eyes begin to water.

"Oh dear. I wasn't expecting that," Mrs. Garcia says. She gets up from her desk, comes over, and puts an arm around me. "I'm so sorry to hear that. When did you find out?"

I take a deep breath and try to control myself. "When I got

the National Scholarship," I confess. "I can't accept it. I'm so sorry," I whisper.

"Oh, Jasmine, I'm sorry too," she says, and she removes her glasses. She wipes her eyes as well.

I feel terrible. I know how proud she was of me. I'm her top student.

"I'm so glad you told me. That's an awful burden to keep to yourself," she says.

I nod and take a few more tissues. "I feel so alone. And I'm scared everyone will judge me if they know. Like they won't want me here."

"Is that how the people who know acted when you've told them?" Mrs. Garcia asks.

"No," I admit. Sniffling, I wipe my nose with my sleeve when the box runs out of tissues. "You don't think I'll get in trouble with ICE?"

Mrs. Garcia rummages in her desk for more tissues and hands me a new box. "There are lots of kids who go to this school—and thousands of kids in LA alone—who are un-documented. The sheer number makes it impossible for ICE to deport everyone. You're a good kid. They're not going to bother you."

She's right. I've read the statistics of how many undocu-mented immigrants there are in California, but they didn't seem real to me. They just seemed like numbers, not people. And talking to Mrs. Garcia is the first time that I really un-derstand there are a lot of people out there facing what I'm going through. I'm not the only one. Or the first. And defi-nitely not the last.

The tears start to well up again. How could I be so self-centered?

Mrs. Garcia puts a hand on my shoulder. "Just let it out," she says.

I do. "I don't even know who I am anymore." I really don't. I feel like a ghost in my own country. No matter what I do, I feel like I'm fading, like I'm becoming a shadow. I'm trying really hard to hang on, but I'm not sure I can. "But I wanted to tell you, in case you had any ideas for colleges that give out loans to people like me."

Mrs. Garcia goes back to her desk and looks relieved that she has a task. "I'll start looking into it. There's got to be something for such a talented kid like you."

"Thanks, Mrs. Garcia. I hope so."

At the next practice, Coach Davis calls the squad together for an emergency meeting. She has a big announcement concerning me. Mrs. Garcia made me promise to tell Coach Davis. *Your coach and your team can be a support system for you.*

Everyone is gathered together in their street clothes, chatting and laughing. Seeing them reminds me of how I let them down at Regionals. At the same time, I realize, all of these girls are my sisters. The entire team is family. This, I realize, is my American family. Lexie. Deandra. Emily. Anabel. Natalia. Taylor. Rosa. Kayla. We'd do anything for each other. But even though my sisters and I love each other, I don't know what will happen when they find out the truth about me.

When I told Coach Davis, I barely got a response. She said, "Okay," and then, "Let's go," and we walked down the hall into the gym.

Coach Davis takes me in front of the entire team. "Sorry I'm late, girls, but your captain came to me with an important issue."

"Is she on her period?" Deandra says. "If one more of us syncs up…"

Several of the girls laugh.

I'm terrified. I wish my period were my problem right now.

"It's nothing like that," Coach Davis says. "It's serious, Deandra."

Deandra's always funny. But she sees this is business and quickly apologizes. "Sorry, Coach."

Coach Davis waits for the girls to quiet down. She clears her throat.

I want to die inside a little, but I stand strong, because the team expects that of me.

"I want to say to you something that I've said before," Coach Davis says. "All of you girls need to lean on each other. You have to share your problems. Rely on your teammates to help you out. Don't you?"

"Yes," Kayla and a few of the others say.

Coach Davis continues, "When one of us hurts, all of us feel some kind of pain. When Chelsea lost her brother to cancer, didn't we all rally?"

"We raised $20,000," Deandra says.

Coach Davis doesn't stop there. "When Denise came down with meningitis, weren't we all there in the hospital? I saw all of you at her bedside."

"We do it because we love each other," Kayla says, glancing at me. Both Chelsea and Denise graduated last year, but we still keep in touch.

"That's right. We do," Coach Davis says. "Girls, something else has happened. Right now your captain needs you. I want to say I have never met someone who has been such a good citizen as Jasmine de los Santos. And neither have you. But she's been carrying a heavy burden for a while now. It's a sensitive issue and requires that she can trust each and every one of you not to take it out of this practice. Can you do that?"

Each of the girls nods. Lexie walks up to me and puts her arm around my shoulders, her braids brushing against my neck. "You could have said something, Jas."

"I know," I say, trying to hold back the tears.

"Jasmine only just discovered her family is undocumented, and right now, there's no way for them to stay in this country legally, not with the current laws in place. How she kept this from all of us, I don't know. This news has devastated her family, and she needs our support. So before we start doing anything today, we know what we need to do."

Tears stream down my cheeks as everyone stands together. They come up one by one, and in twos and threes and hold me in their arms. They tell me that they will all carry my pain. "We love you," Kayla says. "You don't have to go through this alone."

I swallow every tear.

"Thank you. I can't say enough how your support makes me feel."

As all the girls gather around me, Coach speaks again. "I also have another announcement. It's why I originally called you to this meeting. The team that beat us out at Regionals. Foothill High School. They've been disqualified."

"Yes!" Deandra shouts.

Kayla puts her hands on her hips. "Why?"

"Apparently they were working with a choreographer months before the season started. Someone reported them last week."

"What does that mean for us?" I ask, hoping against hope that the news is good.

"Since our squad came in second place," Coach explains, "they've bumped us up to first. We're going to Nationals."

I feel like I'm going to cry again. We're going to Nationals after all!

The next day I visit Millie to thank her for encouraging me to come clean with everyone who matters in my life. She's genuinely happy to see me. This, of course, makes me beam, but I'm also worried about her. She didn't sound so good on the phone when she asked me to come visit her next time I had a chance. She said she had something to show me.

"Jasmine! What are you doing here?"

"You said to drop by if I was in the area. I'm sorry. Is this a bad time?"

"No, no, come in, come in. Of course I did. It's good to see you." She looks past me. "Is anyone with you? I'm not feeling too well. And I'm sure I don't look like a dream either."

She's wearing a nightgown during the middle of the day. Is her heart okay? Did she have a bout of pancreatitis again? Is her son taking care of her?

"No. My boyfriend dropped me off. He lives near you. I told him I'd take a bus home." Royce had a family obligation and was sorry he couldn't drive me home after my visit with Millie. I'd told him he was my boyfriend, not my driver, and not to worry about it.

"You didn't have to do that," Millie says, opening the door wider for me to enter. "He could have come in too. As long as he doesn't mind an old lady in a night shift."

"It's all right. He had to run to a meeting with his father. The only time he sees his dad is during *meetings*." After Millie closes the door, I give her a hug, smelling her vanilla perfume. "I'm sorry. Should I have called?"

"No, honey. It's nice to have someone drop by for a change. You know, there was a time people always dropped by. But now, because of all this technology, everyone texts or calls or emails, or sends a message some other way to say 'I'm on my way!' No, this is nice. How often are you surprised by a visit anymore? Come into the kitchen with me."

She sets out a plate of cookies. "Tea?" she asks.

"Water's fine, and I can get it," I tell her, finding a pitcher of water in the fridge and pouring myself a cup.

We sit down at the kitchen table and eat sugar cookies. They're the kind that come in a blue tin box. Do all grand-mothers eat them? Mine did, and Lola Cherry does too.

I tell her my latest news, about the team going to Nationals and about how I finally started telling people about my undocumented status.

"Do you feel better now that everyone knows? Takes the pressure off, at least?" she asks, getting up to fetch more cookies.

"I guess. I don't know." I thought Millie was going to be happier for me, but she seems melancholy.

"Well, this is life, Jasmine. It's filled with tough moments. There are going to be tougher times ahead too."

Even though I don't want to think about those times right now, I know she's right. I need to prepare myself for the idea that we might not win Nationals. Or, even worse, that my family might lose the deportation trial.

"You said you had something to show me?" I ask.

"Oh, Jasmine," Millie says, grabbing her side and doubling over in pain. It must the pancreatitis.

"Here. Come sit down on the couch," I say, putting my arm around her shoulder.

She shakes her head. "No, no. The pain comes in waves.

It'll go away. I must have eaten something too fatty at breakfast."

I hold her until she's able to stand all the way upright again. She rummages in the kitchen drawers, looking for something.

While she goes through a stack of papers and documents, she asks me about our upcoming hearing. "Your mother hasn't told me about a court date. Is there one?" Millie asks.

"Not yet," I say. "I did some research, and the process used to take nearly two years in some cases. The lawyer thinks we will have an expedited date though, which is good, but also bad, because if we lose, we have to leave sooner. But Mom thinks we can't live in fear, that we have to try and win legal status. We have to risk it."

"She's right, your mother," she says. "Without risk, there's no reward." She walks back to the table and shows me a yellowed piece of paper.

"What is it?" I ask, trying to read the faded letters.

"It was my acceptance to architecture school," she says. "I really wanted to become an architect instead of an engineer."

"Why didn't you?" I ask.

"I spent a summer working in Jean Prouvé's office in Paris. It was one of the happiest times of my life. But when I returned to America, I was too scared to do what I loved, so I ended up doing something safer and more commercial. My father was a builder, and I had an engineering degree, so I knew the business already. I wanted to make beautiful structures, work for Richard Neutra and Frank Lloyd Wright. Instead, we put up some boring strip malls. It's the biggest regret of my life."

She takes the paper and folds it back into a square. "Whatever happens with the trial, go after what you want, Jasmine. Don't wait for life to make the decision for you."

26

Remember, no effort that we make to attain something
beautiful is ever lost.

—HELEN KELLER

IN MID-JANUARY, two nights before I leave for Nationals, I'm supposed to hang out with Royce. But he cancels at the last minute.

"I'm sorry, Jas," he says. "I have a dinner for my dad."

He's spending a lot of time with his dad lately. I want to ask him why he can't bring a date. Or is it that he doesn't want to bring *me*, that maybe I'm not good enough for this fancy benefit he's going to? But I don't say anything.

"It's all right. I'll see you when I get back," I say.

"You're going to kick ass," he tells me. "I wish I could be there."

I'm disappointed that I'm not going to see him, but don't let it distract me like I did before. Winning Nationals won't be easy—just like winning the deportation case won't be easy. The case may be out of my hands, but how well I lead the team is something I control. I need to focus for my team, for our sisterhood. Millie's right, I can't let life distract me from what I want.

The plane ride to Florida the next day is filled with turbulence. I hold hands with Kayla, who hates airplanes, until we land in Orlando.

"You all right?" I ask.

"Yeah, I'm good," she says, but she has a faraway look in her eye. I realize that we haven't talked about what happened at Lo's party. I think she was embarrassed that Mason hit on her in front of Dylan.

It's warm here. Sticky. We get to the hotel, which is less than a mile from Disney World, where the competition is taking place. We have a team meeting, then we go to the beach to relax. I scoop up some sand to put in a bottle for my collection. At practice the next day, the girls are nervous, but I tell them to have confidence.

We went to Nationals last year, but only came in third place. This time we have to win it all. "We've done everything possible," I say at our final meeting just before we compete for the Universal Cheerleaders Association National High School Cheerleading Championships. "We've put in the time at practice. We've trained our bodies and perfected our moves as much as we can. It's all a mental game now. You girls got this. I believe in you."

Coach Davis doesn't even have to talk. She simply steps back and watches us prepare. We begin our stretching routine as the other teams compete at the center of the auditorium. The girls are so focused on the moment that no one's talking anymore. I keep my mind off everything except for my stunts and my girls.

After a few minutes of stretching, Coach tells us we're next up to perform our routine. We all get up and check each other's ponytails and shoelaces as the emcee announces Chatsworth High over the speaker system.

I yell at the girls, trying to pump them up. I briefly worry about Kayla, who's kept to herself a bit on the entire trip. But when I catch her eye, she nods, determined, and I know she won't let us down.

"You're all champions. So act like it!"

The girls follow me onto the performance mats. Hundreds of people are watching us standing under the spotlights. We bow, tuck our chins toward our chests, waiting for the music. When the beats blast through the speakers, I count out our start.

We start off strong with our tumbling, hitting all our back-flips and full twists. Our stunt sequence begins, and the bases pop us flyers up into perfect scorpions. Each group sticks their marks right on the beat. We fly through the rest of the routine—tumbling, cheering, stunting—with barely any mistakes. After the music ends, I can't believe how well the girls have done. The entire audience gives us a standing ovation.

I know, even before they announce it over the loudspeakers at the end of the event, that we've won.

27

The most common way people give up their power is by
thinking they don't have any.

—ALICE WALKER

I'M SO HAPPY I can't even describe the feeling. There's
something about winning at a high level that leaves you both
mentally exhausted and in euphoria somewhere over the cloud
banks hovering on the edge of a sunset's pink glow.

When I finally get home, I fall into my parents' arms as
they welcome me at the door. "We're so proud of you, Jas!" I
realize how lucky I am to have them. They know how hard
I've worked.

In the hallway is the biggest bouquet of flowers I've ever
seen. It's from Royce, of course. I'm beaming as I read his
card.

This national championship couldn't have come at a better
time for everyone. Even Lola Cherry is sweet and cheerful
the next time she visits. And I can tell that Danny and Isko
are proud of their cheerleader big sister.

It feels like my old confidence is finally returning. It's different this time though. Before all of these problems happened, I thought I was perfect. I think I secretly thought I
deserved more than anyone else, because I worked so hard.
Now the confidence comes from knowing that I can get

through anything with a little persistence and a lot of love from family and friends.

When I arrive at school on Monday, I start to realize how big my support group has gotten. We're celebrating our championship with a rally in the gym, where we're going to perform the winning routine. The entire school is in attendance. Chatsworth High has never won a national cheerleading championship, so everyone is really proud. Even the kids who look down on cheerleaders and think we're just bimbos in short skirts. The band plays our school fight song. Everyone cheers for us.

Our cheer squad should have its own cheerleaders. Ha. I lead the girls to the middle of the floor to get ready for our performance. It's so loud I can barely hear what Coach Davis is saying to us. When I take my position, I look up and see all of the school administrators, sports teams, and directors looking down at us. As Coach cues up the routine music, I yell out to the team.

"Kayla leads," I shout. "She's captain on this one!"

Kayla nods at me. She's got her game face on. She's focused and ready. Kayla signals for us to begin. We put all our heads down, waiting for the music to start.

That's when I see Royce standing at the corner of the gym. He'd texted me the night before saying he would try to be there and my heart does that tumble-over thing it does when he's around. Even though it's been only a couple of days since we've seen each other, it feels like forever. He's wearing the tie that I gave him for Christmas. He sees me see him and gives a little wave. I can't wave back so I wink at him. Our song suddenly blasts out of the speakers. The entire gym goes crazy.

We start our routine. Everyone hits each mark, just like at Nationals, but you can tell we're having more fun with the moves. We're smiling big and doing little extra shimmies and adjustments to make the crowd happy. We're finally home.

When the performance ends, the leadership crew has us gather around our trophy to have pictures taken while the DJ plays music for the students as they're waiting. I stay still long enough for the photographer to get one picture, then I run through the dancing and singing students, searching for Royce. I try to spot him by looking for the flag on his tie, but I don't see him anywhere. He's already gone. I know he said he had to get to a tutoring session, but I wish we'd been able to say hi to each other. I'm glad he was here, but I wish he'd stayed.

My family decides to hold a celebration at our house after school the next Friday.

At the door, I show our guests where to kick off their shoes. Even though she would never say anything to a guest, Mom would kill me if I let people walk on the carpet with their shoes on. Last night I had to spend the whole evening with her, making sure the house was completely clean for the party. We trimmed the indoor bamboo plants and scrubbed the outside of the pots, dusted all of Dad's elephant statue collection that has spread all over the house, and steam-vacuumed the carpets.

Chatting and laughing, Deandra, Anabel, Lexie, and Kayla place their shoes in pairs along the entryway. Since I know how much food Mom can cook when she invites a few of her lady friends over, I'm not as awed as everyone else when my teammates show up to the literal mountains of pancit, barbecue pork, lumpia, rice, and roasted vegetables. Even though there are a ton of us, Mom has made enough that I'm certain I'll be begging guests to take some food home.

"Where are your brothers?" Mom asks me as she pulls a pan out of the oven. The girls are all gathered around the kitchen table talking to each other. "They're supposed to be helping me."

As soon as she pulls out one pan, I replace it with another. "Probably walking home," I say.

"Yeah, well, they're walking really slow," she says. "Funny how long it takes when you know you have to do some work when you get home. You were the same way."

"I've always done my chores," I protest.

Scooping food from the pan onto a plate, Mom shakes her head. "When your brothers show up, tell them they can't play any video games."

"They're not going to like that," I say, wondering where Royce is.

He's late for the party, and he's never late. That's one thing he learned from his mother. We've been texting each other, and I spoke to him on the phone a couple of times, but I haven't seen him in days. Not properly. It's starting to worry me, even though we haven't fought or anything. He apologized a bunch of times about Mason's behavior at Lo's party, but I told him it was all right, and he seemed to believe me. I guess I should tell him how I really feel about Mason, but I don't want to cause conflict. Besides, I don't want to think about his jackass brother right now. This is my party.

Dad's roped a couple of the girls into playing dominoes. He looks over and starts digging in. "*Neneng?* Why don't you go clean your room? You must have some chores to do."

"This is how you congratulate me?" I ask. "By putting me to work?"

"Exactly. Hard work makes a cheerleader strong," Dad

says, turning back to the game. "Girls, this is where I dominate your futures."

Some of the other girls are already digging in to the food. Deandra seems to have the metabolism of the entire team and goes back for thirds. We don't know how she keeps that small muscular frame so trim. She must be working harder than the rest of us. Or maybe all the clowning around she does burns more calories than I think.

Lexie must be thinking the same thing, because she says, "Did you not eat anything for the last month before Nationals?"

Deandra just smiles and talks with her mouth full. "You can't let good food like this go to waste." She turns to me. "My mother's cooking is terrible. If I had this food around every day, I'd be five times my size."

Royce finally shows up. I practically run into his arms but he just gives me a quick peck on the cheek when he walks into the kitchen. "Hey, babe," he says distractedly. "Am I late?"

"A little," I say. "Where've you been?"

He doesn't answer and seems tense, like he doesn't want to be here. He's never like this. Does he not want to hang out with the cheerleaders? He knows Kayla, of course, but not any of the other girls. He takes a piece of lumpia from the tray. It's his favorite. "I was with Mason," he finally says.

"Everything all right?" I ask. Like I said, I'm not a big fan of Mason, but I try to be cool about it. If one of my brothers was having trouble, I would expect the same from Royce.

"Yeah, yeah, you know, Mason," he says, waving off my words. "So what's going on here? Food and girls? How can a guy want anything more?"

"Whatever," I say, sticking my tongue out at him. I get

jealous so easily. And I'm thrilled to see him. "I need something to drink. Want something?"

"I'm good," he says, and finally grins at me. "You're not wearing your cheer uniform."

"Oh, you liked that, did you?" I put my hands on my hips and pretend to scold him.

He shrugs his shoulders boyishly, and my heart flips in my chest. He sits on a kitchen stool and I lean forward against his back, my arms around his neck, resting my chin on his head. It's the most public we've been with our affection around my family, but I think they can handle it.

As soon as I slip away to get my drink, Kayla walks right up to him. As I pour some tea at the drink table, I listen to them talk to each other.

"Hey, Kayla," he says, stretching out his hand to shake hers. "Nice to see you again."

What a dork. What kind of high school guy shakes hands with a girl he's met before? A politician's son. That's who. It's probably automatic for him at this point.

"You too," she says. "Glad you could make it. How's your…"

"Good," he interrupts. "We're all good. You know?"

"Yeah. I better go check on the dominoes game. Jasmine's dad usually needs to be watched so he won't cheat," Kayla says. "See you."

"Yeah," he says. "I'm sure I'll see you at some point."

What does *that* mean? Why is he going to see her? When? I walk back to Royce, thinking how odd it was that Kayla approached him. Maybe she was just trying to make him feel welcome, but I get the sense that something's going on.

"What was that all about?" I ask.

"Nothing," he says. "We were just saying hi."

I don't know why, but I start feeling a twinge of jealousy in my stomach as I watch Kayla beeline to the opposite end of the room.

I wonder how things are with her and Dylan. I half expected him to be here, even though this isn't his kind of crowd. Still...she seemed weird around Royce. Or was she flirting? I can't tell. My mind is racing. I glance at Royce, my jealousy now a raging green-eyed monster.

Come on, Jas. Stop. Be serious. Your best friend isn't trying to steal your boyfriend.

"Let me introduce you to a few of the girls," I say, and lead him to where my teammates are clustered. "Royce, this is Anabel, Natalia, and Deandra. They're on the team with me."

"Hey, everyone, congratulations on everything... Nice to meet you," he says. He makes small talk with everyone, but then pulls me away.

"What's up?"

He grimaces, looks at his watch. "I'm sorry, Jas, I really have to go."

"You're *leaving*?"

"Yeah." He shuffles his feet.

"But you just got here."

"I know, but my dad..."

I feel everyone trying to look elsewhere, to give us our privacy, but I'm embarrassed nonetheless. I was so proud to introduce him to everyone, but he's not himself, I can tell. He's anxious and won't look me in the eye.

"We've barely seen each other since the week before I left for Nationals. You know, if you leave now, Lola Cherry will be mad she didn't see you. She's not even here yet. Did you even say hello to my parents? Can't you stay a *little* longer?"

He gently removes my hand from his arm. "I really need

to go," he says. "Sorry. I wanted to make sure I came at least for a few minutes. I'll make it up to you. Promise."

He gives me half a kiss, apologizes again. "I'm really sorry."

"Fine, go." I pout. "Call you later?"

"Yes, later," he says and apologizes again.

I want to ask him what he's doing with his dad this time, but I don't want to seem possessive. I don't want to be one of those stereotypical clingy girls. He must have his reasons for leaving so quickly. I need to trust him.

Deandra comes up to me as soon as he walks away. "Where's he going? I was going to give him some of my lumpia. I think I'm finally starting to get full."

"He has to go do something with his dad," I say.

"Really? He's probably pretty busy. I heard his dad's a congressman or something."

"He is," I say, a little annoyed that the only thing people know about Royce is his father's name. I take Deandra's plate from her. "Here, give me those. I'm hungry."

"Oh yeah, sure," she says. "They're really great. Your mom's such an awesome cook."

Just then, I hear Mom yell. "Danny!" It isn't her usual voice. She sounds frantic. Pained. I turn to look, and I gasp. There's my brother, dripping blood from his nose and mouth. His eyes are swollen nearly shut. Isko is helping him walk, nearly falling over from the extra weight. Some of the girls on the cheer squad instantly run over to hold him up.

"What happened?" Mom yells. "Angelo! Get over here, right now!" she says, calling for Dad.

"Eric and his friends jumped him after calling us FOBs," Isko says. "They told us to go back to our stupid island. I tried to fight back, but Danny told me to run away."

"What's an FOB?" Deandra asks.

"Fresh off the boat," I say. *Go back to your stupid island?* Eric learned that from Mason at Lo's party. I'm seeing white, I'm so angry.

Dad carries Danny over to a couch while Mom grabs packs of ice. He winces from a pain in his side where he must have also been punched in the ribs. One of the girls has already brought wet cloths to wipe away the blood. He looks awful. This wasn't just a little school-yard fight. They really, really beat him up. They wanted him to hurt.

I'm so angry, I want to go out and give those boys a lesson even though I'm at least five years older and a good thirty pounds heavier than them.

"Who's Eric?" Dad demands, holding Danny.

I already know.

Isko talks for his brother again. "You know, Lorraine? She used to be friends with Jasmine. It was her brother Eric who threw the first punch," he says, and looks around the room. He spots Kayla leaning against a wall and nods toward her. "But it was *her* brother, Brian, who started it."

28

It takes a great deal of courage to stand up to your enemies,
but even more to stand up to your friends.

—J. K. ROWLING, *HARRY POTTER AND THE SORCERER'S STONE*

KAYLA LEAVES THE celebration right away without explanation or apology. I don't know what to think. I'm so confused, and angry too. The celebration winds down not long afterward, with Deandra taking home the biggest container of food. Dad's furious, but he quiets down as soon as Isko tells the story of how Danny got beaten up. I'll never forget the way Dad looked at me when he heard it was my friends' little brothers who did this. He wants answers. His son is injured.

"I'll find out what's going on," I promise, already getting up from my chair.

"You better," he replies. "Or I will."

"Daddy. I'll take care of it."

I decide to start with Lo before I talk to Kayla. She doesn't live that far away. Deandra offers to drive me, and when we arrive Eric is standing outside their house. When he sees me, he darts around back. I admit I want to shove his head into a wall, but I know that's not going to fix anything.

It just hurts that it's Lo's brother who attacked Danny. I always thought he was as nice as she is. But, then again, kids follow other kids—they're not even thinking about what they're doing or where their anger is coming from. That's probably the problem. I'll figure it out. Lo will tell her parents. Everything will work out.

Deandra promises to wait for me and I go to the door and knock. I'm actually happy that Lo answers.

"Jas! So great to see you. That rally was so awesome! You must really be proud. Is your family happy?"

"They are," I say. "We just had a big celebration. Mom cooked for the squad."

"Invite me to the next one. I love your Mom's cooking. Hey, how's the whole immigration thing? I've been meaning to call. Everything okay?" Lo asks. She opens the door farther. "You know, I'm being rude. Do you want to come in?"

"Yeah, sure," I say.

I don't want to have this conversation with Lo. It hasn't been that long since we've become closer friends again. Lo leads me to the living room, and I sit on the couch next to her. Eric starts walking past the doorway, but when he sees me he splits down the hallway. "God. He's such a spaz," Lo says. "He must be up to something."

"Speaking of your brother..." I say.

"What about him?" Lo asks. She leans back on the couch, giving me a confused expression.

"Yeah. Isko says Eric and a few of his friends jumped Danny today. He came home completely beaten up and limping."

"*Jumped* him? What? Are you sure?"

"I'm sure." I tell her what happened.

"Oh my God. I'm so sorry, Jasmine. I'm going to beat him myself. Eric!" she yells. "Get in here!"

She turns to me. "I'll go get him."

"No, it's okay. But will you talk to your parents? Tell them what happened?"

"Yeah, of course," she says. "I'll talk to them as soon as they're home. Brian was supposed to come over tonight, but I'll tell Dad to not let Eric have him over."

"Thanks," I say. "That helps."

"Wait here. He needs to apologize."

I shake my head. "That's okay," I say. "It's Danny he should apologize to, but I'd give him a day or two to heal."

"I can't believe my brother! God! What a little jerk! I promise he'll learn a big lesson from this one, especially when he has to go begging Danny's forgiveness."

"Thanks, Lo."

"I'm sorry this happened, Jasmine. You know we're not like that."

I nod. I know.

On the way home, I text Kayla. No answer. **Hey, I need to talk to you**, I write, adding, **Why did you leave?** I don't want to just show up at her house. For some reason, I don't feel that's the right move here. She could have left because she wanted to deal with her brother herself. Maybe she was embarrassed or ashamed. I would be. Maybe she didn't think she was welcome at my house anymore, which would be a dumb thing to think, because Kayla will always be my best friend.

I text Royce too. I feel like a broken record.

I write, **Hey, I kind of need you right now.**

Unlike Kayla, he writes back to me right away.

royceb: I'm with my dad, can I call you later? I think I can see you tomorrow.

jasmindls: sure.

He didn't even bother to ask what's wrong. That isn't like Royce. Why doesn't he care?

I text Kayla again. **I'm not mad at you. I just want to know what's going on.**

By the time Deandra drops me off at home, Kayla still hasn't answered me. Inside, Danny is asleep on the couch, his head on Mom's lap. All of the guests have left. What a celebration.

Dad looks at me. "Well?"

"Eric's taken care of," I say. "I'll deal with Brian too. Don't worry."

Mom whispers, "Thank you, Jasmine."

"You're welcome. How is he?"

"He'll be okay," she says.

Mom continues to stroke Danny's head. "I heard back from our lawyer. He called after you left. Mr. Alvarado got us a court date. It's sooner than we all thought."

Kayla doesn't respond to my texts all weekend. It's taken everything for me to not go to her house and pound on the door. Royce isn't much better, even though we hang out on Saturday night and go to the mall. For a little while, it feels like everything is normal between us. He's incensed about what happened to Danny, angry that he didn't stay longer at the party and wasn't able to help, and wants to go over there to beat up the little punks immediately.

I tell him I'm taking care of it. I don't need him to fight my brother's battles. But I do tell him one thing.

"They learned it from Mason," I say. "To tell my brothers to go back to the island I mean. They thought it was funny."

Royce puts his head in his hands. "Oh man," he says. "I'm so sorry. I'm going to make him *hurt*."

"Don't," I say. "I don't want our families to have trouble. Just leave it."

He drives me back to my house and gives me a brief kiss

on the lips. We don't make out like we usually do. I think he feels bad about the Mason connection and doesn't know what to do about it. I can tell that's not the only thing bothering him though, but when I ask him what it is, he brushes it off, says something about family pressure.

When he's gone, I begin to worry that maybe "family pressure" means his parents want him to break up with me, an illegal alien. Could that be it? Or am I just paranoid? I wish he'd *talk* to me. But every time I try to reach out, he clams up.

I haven't even told Royce that we have a court date for the deportation trial. If he can't be bothered to tell me what's up with him, why should I offer any information?

On Sunday afternoon, Lo's parents have a meeting with my parents. It's pretty civil. Eric starts tearing up when he has to apologize. Danny is hilarious, which almost makes me cry.

After Eric apologizes, Danny smugly crosses his arms and smiles. "It's all right," he says, leaning back in his chair. "I know your friend put you up to it. But I actually have to thank you."

Eric wrinkles his forehead. "Thank me?"

All of us at the table stare at him—Mom and Dad, Lo's parents, me—waiting for what Danny will say next.

"Yeah," Danny says. "The entire National High School Cheerleading Championship team kissed me. That ain't ever gonna happen for you! So, yeah, forget about it."

I think Eric was in awe after that. He left pretty wide-eyed. And Danny, though his face still looks like a bruised apple, is pretty much back to normal.

Monday night I'm sitting at the kitchen table, doing a set of difficult problems for Calculus, when I finally hear a text go off on my phone. It's the music I assigned for Kayla.

Shoving away my homework, I pick up the phone with both hands and open up her text.

kaykayla: I heard brian planning the fight with his friends the other day. I didn't believe him though. but don't worry, it's been taken care of. That's why i left your party so quickly. I wanted to catch him before he went to my dad's. I'm so sorry about danny. Is he ok?

I'm furious. How could she have known and not told me? How could she not say anything until now?

jasmindls: Thanks for taking care of the problem. I wish you'd told me though. Danny's okay. He's a tough kid. What about you. What's going on?

kaykayla: not much. dad has a new girlfriend. She's a ho. See you at school.

See me at school? What's that supposed to mean? Kayla suddenly feels like someone I don't know. She's shut me out, and I don't know what to think. Even though her parents have split, Kayla seemed to have been doing okay lately. She applied to the Art Institute in Hollywood and CalArts to study dance next year, and she's planning on getting a place of her own after graduation.

Dad's not happy with her response either. He seems to have a sixth sense about everything.

"It's been taken care of?" he asks. "What's that supposed to mean? Did she take her brother out back and beat him with a switch?"

"That's what I would have done," Mom says, putting dishes into the dishwasher.

The plates and glasses clank against each other loudly. Dad sighs and rubs his temples. "We'll have to tell school officials about what happened. Make doubly sure there's no problem. It'll keep others from copying. We can't have our boys beaten up every week because of what some dumb kids hear from others. What's wrong with these people?"

"I blame the parents," Mom says. "Parents need to know where their children are and what they're up to. They need to keep them busy."

I don't tell them I found out the attack on Danny was planned. That would send Dad over the edge. If he wants to go to the school and complain, that's fine, but I'd rather not be in the middle of it.

How could Kayla not say anything to me about it? What was up with that? She's been acting so shady lately. I'd gotten over my irrational jealousy—I know there's nothing going on with her and Royce. She would never do that to me, and he never would either. I trust both of them. Yet I can't help but notice that both of them have been sort of avoiding me.

What's the deal?

29

Wine comes in at the mouth, and love comes in at the eye;
that's all we know for truth, Before we grow old and die.

—WILLIAM BUTLER YEATS

BEFORE I HEAD off to school the next Monday, I examine Danny's face. Even a week later, it's still bruised from the fight. There's a scab forming by his nose and mouth. Yellowish-blue shadows circle his eyes. I tell him I can cover it with makeup. He groans and squirms away from me.

I don't blame him. He's got a badge of courage.

As for myself, I'm feeling wounded too. At school, I walk with my head down. I focus on schoolwork. I start talking less, hanging around less. Kayla doesn't have the same lunch period as me this semester and she's not in any of my classes, plus we don't have cheer practice anymore, so I don't see her at all. I guess I could text her, but since she doesn't text me, I don't bother. I'm still mad at her brother for beating up mine. I can stand to give her the cold shoulder for a while.

Royce sends a few hello texts all week, but they read like lip service.

royceb: Hey, thinking of you. Everything OK?

I want to text back: "Everything is A-OK! I'm fine! Why wouldn't I be fine? Danny still has bruises and we're all being called FOBs, it's just great. Hooray! Our deportation defense hearing is coming up soon. Sometimes I wish I hadn't pressured my parents to get a hearing so fast. We might all be kicked out of the country we love. Everything is super awesome, Royce! Don't worry about me! I don't miss you! Not at all! You don't want to tell me what's going on with you, so why should I tell you what's up with me?"

But I don't say anything.

I just retreat further into myself.

I look at my shoes when I walk the hallways. I don't say hi to anybody. Almost everyone at school knows about my situation now. I know what they're thinking when they see me.

Ha! You thought you were so smart, and now look at you. You suck. You're no one. You're nobody. You're dirt! You're not from here! Go home! Go back to Asia or wherever you're from!

Except when I do look up once in a while, the faces I see are smiling at me. Friends say hi and stop and talk.

But when I'm alone again, I keep hearing the voices, the negative self-talk telling me that I'm worthless. I keep seeing my brother's wounded face, and Mason's sneer.

I miss my friends, but it seems they don't miss me.

It's almost the end of January and Kayla's still avoiding me at school. When I do see her and bring up what happened between our brothers, she changes the topic or finds some excuse to go somewhere else. So I continue with my routine of going through the motions. Cheer is done as basketball season is over now. There's still the occasional pep rally, but the tension between Kayla and I makes things awkward for the whole team.

The only peace I find is in doing well with my schoolwork. I meet with Mrs. Garcia again, and she tells me what she discovered concerning financial aid for students like me. Most

elite colleges make admissions decisions without considering
the applicant's need for financial aid. Need-blind admissions,
it's called. The only schools that guarantee full financial aid
to "international" (noncitizen) applicants are MIT, Harvard,
Princeton, Yale and Amherst. A few, like Columbia and Stanford, are "need aware" for noncitizens, which means they'll
make an exception and provide aid for international students
that they really want at their school.

"Basically, if they accept you, they'll make every effort to
ensure you can enroll in the fall," she says.

It's a ray of hope, but it's not something I can count on. I
have to get in first, and who knows if schools like that will
want a student like me, National Scholar or not. I just feel
like a burden. I'm glad I'd applied to a few of those colleges
though, including Stanford. I guess I'll find out in April.

I'm walking down the hall from Calculus to English later
that week when Lo stops me.

"Jas. I know you and your family are hurting, but you don't
have to completely shut down. You can respond when other
people talk to you."

I feel awful. "Am I that bad?"

Lo nods. "You're that bad. My brother hasn't caused any
more problems, has he?"

"No," I say. "He sort of follows my brother around now
once he found out that so many cheerleaders came to Danny's
rescue. It's actually kind of funny."

"Yeah. He doesn't stop talking about that," Lo says. "You
hear about Kayla?"

"No. We're sort of not talking right now," I say. "I think
she's embarrassed about what her brother did."

"I thought you guys were tight."

"I thought so too. Do I even want to know what's up with her?" I shift my heavy English textbook onto my other hip.

"Yeah…she and Dylan broke up. It was pretty messy. Happened a few days after my party, right before the band left on tour again."

"Really?" I say, my heart sinking a little at the news. I feel bad they broke up and I can't believe Kayla didn't tell me. When she's having boy problems, I'm always the first person she calls.

"Yeah, Dylan took it really hard. He even threatened to leave the band and skip the tour. Poor guy. Julian's trying to sort of win his soul back."

"Why?" I ask. "Why would they break up? She was so happy with him."

"I heard she's seeing somebody else," Lo says. The passing period bell rings, sending all of the students scattering. "Hey, I gotta go. Please quit acting like a stranger. You're not. You're Jas, and you're awesome," she says, heading for a door at the end of the hallway.

If I'm so awesome, how come my best friend won't confide in me and I can't get my boyfriend to spend any time with me?

Like I said, I don't believe these two things are related, but together, they definitely bum me out.

Valentine's Day is coming up, and as I'm walking home from school on Friday, Royce pulls up next to me. I used to be proud when he would drive up in his Range Rover and lean out the window, beckoning me to hop inside. It was almost like being in a cheesy teen movie, and I loved it. But now I know romantic movies are stupid. They make you think stuff like that is real, that the rich popular boy will fall for the poor outcast. But we all know the reality.

And the reality is, I know what's happening between us now. Royce has been doing the slow fade. Letting me down easy. Not ghosting completely, but letting go little by little so that I'll get the picture.

I got the picture.

Except, I'm so mad at the part of myself that's happy to see him, annoyed that he still makes my heart pound.

He rolls down the window. "Hey, good-lookin'," he says. "Need a ride?"

His tone makes me furious. I turn around and glare at him. I'm too mad to even say anything, so I turn away and walk faster, cutting through the neighborhood park. It's a short-cut anyway.

He stops the engine and gets out. I can't decide whether I want him to follow me or not. He runs to catch up. I walk faster and try to keep myself from looking at him. If I do, I know I'll break down. I won't be able to be mad at him for long. I never can, not when he shows up like this.

"Jas, talk to me. I'm sorry, okay? I know I haven't been around. But I'm here now, aren't I?" he says, directly blocking my path.

I shift my backpack up. It's heavy with textbooks. I glare at him. "So what? You want a medal or something? For showing up to your relationship? You forget I don't give out participation trophies."

I run away from him again, but he catches me, making me stop at the edge of the playground. There are young schoolchildren running around and yelling while their tired mothers chat with each other on the park benches.

"Please hear me out. Jas? Please? Come on," he says. "Don't be mad."

But I *am* mad, and I hate when people tell me not to be

mad when I'm mad. Ugh, I hate him. I hate that he can make me feel so crazy.

"Where've you been all week?" I demand. "All month? Since January?"

He grimaces. "I told you, I had to do stuff for my dad, and I've had family issues."

"Really? That's it? I don't know if you've noticed, but we *all* have family issues. Me especially."

"Well, I've been trying to take care of mine." He moves closer, puts a hand on my shoulder.

"Which means avoiding me?"

One of the mothers looks up at us.

Royce doesn't deny it. His mouth is a hard line. "I didn't know what else to do. It's complicated."

"It's complicated? *Everything* is complicated, Royce," I say, pulling away so he can't touch me anymore. "What does that even mean?"

Royce winces. I can see I've hurt him by not letting him touch me. "I came to find you," he says. "To say I'm sorry that I haven't been around, that's all."

"It's a little too late for that. You know what bugs me about you? You think driving up in your car, pretending like nothing's wrong, is going to make all of our problems go away. But I have no idea what's going on with you. You haven't been honest with me for *weeks*."

"So now what? You're breaking up with me?"

Am I? I consider what to say next. Part of me wants to end all of this right now. Burn it to the ground. Tell him I never want to see him again. Part of me wants to continue just so I can find out what hideous secret he's hiding. Part of me wants to cry. Most of me continues to be stubborn. I'm my daddy's girl after all.

"I didn't say that. You're putting words in my mouth," I say.

Royce crosses his arms. "Like you were doing to me earlier," he says. "Look, I'm not perfect, all right? I'm sorry I'm not the perfect boyfriend you want me to be."

"Who said anything about perfect?" I say.

He shrugs. "You always have such high expectations. It's hard to meet them sometimes."

"What? Are you saying I set too high a bar for you?"

"Sometimes," he admits.

"Sorry, but I guess expecting someone to be around for me when they say they care about me is too high an expectation for you," I snap.

I look over at the park bench, where both mothers jerk their heads back down, realizing I've caught them watching us. Great. Now the neighborhood mommy circle will be gossiping about our fight all afternoon.

I decide to play hardball. "So why are you here? Are you back in town from D.C.? Or were you in Malibu? Don't tell me, you went to New York for the week," I curl my lip. "You're always somewhere, but I never know where. But that's okay, because you don't have that problem, do you? You know where I am, where I'll be. I'm just right here. Right where you can find me. That is, until they kick me out."

Royce looks down at sneakers. Adidas Sambas that I picked out for him. Seeing them twists a knife in my belly.

"Jas, I haven't been out of town. Like I told you already, I've just been under a lot of family pressure," he says. "And hanging out with Mason and stuff."

"Uh-huh."

"Yeah, I have family too, you know. You're not the only one with family," he says unhappily.

"Don't talk to me about family!"

He holds up his hands, frustrated, like he can't do anything right with me at the moment, and he's correct. He can't.

"So that's it? That's your big excuse?" I say.

"What do you want me to say?"

"I don't know. I just wish you'd tell me what's really going on." Then I realize—he did tell me, but I have to read between the lines. He's been spending time with Mason. Mason doesn't like me, and when he hangs out with Mason, he can't hang out with me.

Royce runs his fingers through his dark hair and pulls at the roots. "I'm trying. I hate this. I hate what's happening to us."

"Then stop it," I plead. "Just please, tell me the truth. Mason doesn't like me. That's it, isn't it? He wants you to break up with me. He doesn't think I'm good enough for you."

"I told you, I don't care what Mason thinks!" Royce says hotly. But he doesn't deny it either.

"But it's not just him, is it? It's your parents too. They don't think you should date me. You keep saying you're under a lot of family pressure. Family pressure to let me go, isn't that it?"

"No. No, that's not it. *No!*" Royce says, a little desperately.

"Oh, come on, Royce, just admit your parents don't think I'm good enough for you! You're too embarrassed to take me to your dad's events, and your mom thinks I'm practically the maid!"

"Whoa, *what?*" Now it's his turn to be furious. "You're crazy. Just the other day I overheard my mom telling Maria how much she likes you. And you know I hate those things my dad drags me to—why would I inflict the torture on you?"

"Your mom told Maria she likes me?" I blink.

"Yeah. She said she thinks you're really smart, and that you work so hard."

I go over what he said about how he hates being part of his father's political social life, and I have to grudgingly admit he might be telling the truth about that too.

"Yeah," he says, then gets angry again. "Wait, you really think that's what my family is like? That they would think those things about you? God, you must think so little of us if you do. So little of *me*."

If I'd started to feel a little mollified before, the rage comes roaring back. He does *not* get to win this one. He's the one in the wrong. "Oh, come on, it's not like you think much of my family either. Just a bunch of amusing ethnic people you don't take seriously," I say, practically spitting out the words. "You must feel so proud of yourself for being so liberal and *open-minded*." I'm a cyclone of fury and will stop at nothing until he is utterly destroyed.

He's just staring at me, but I'm not done.

"And what about me, huh? I'm just some booty call you can pick up with when it suits you! I'm your last priority, but what does it matter, right? I'm just some illegal! Isn't that what you called me?"

He's gray and quiet now, and everything is awful. I can feel it. It's ruined. Something beautiful is ruined between us.

He's tired—I can see that now—so tired, and I'm exhausted too.

"If you really think I'm that kind of person, then maybe we should break up," he says finally, without any emotion at all.

My eyes are clear and so are his. Neither of us is crying.

There's nothing to cry about here. It's just the end, and I've been waiting for it since we started anyway.

"Yeah, maybe you're right," I tell him. "Maybe we should."

30

Love does not consist of gazing at each other, but in looking outward together in the same direction.

—ANTOINE DE SAINT-EXUPÉRY, *WIND, SAND AND STARS*

IT'S VALENTINE'S DAY and I don't have a valentine. Instead, I'm leaning back with a gigantic bucket of popcorn on my lap, waiting for the movie to start. I haven't seen Royce since our fight at the playground the other week. I'm still not sure who broke up with whom. Is it my fault? Or his? All I have are questions and no answers. It's not *officially* officially over. Is it? How could it be over? I can't bring myself to check if he's changed his Facebook status. I still have all these feelings for him, and every time I look at my phone, I expect to see a text from him.

I can't figure out if I'm heartbroken, because I'm just numb. I also know I wasn't completely innocent here. I have to live with that. I insulted him, I insulted his family. I said all those awful things. I'd believed they were the ones looking down on me, but it turns out I was the one who was looking down on them. How did we let it get so out of control? I keep replaying the argument in my head.

Why was I so angry? He'd been MIA, sure, but he'd come all the way out to see me. Why couldn't I have just let it be? Why did I have to know what was bothering him and where he was? Why am I such a control freak? Why did I level those horrible accusations?

I don't believe any of that about him, of course I don't. I just wanted to hurt him. I hate myself right now, and I miss him. I miss him so badly I can't taste anything.

Mom and Dad are worried about me, but I haven't told them we broke up. Royce hadn't been coming around a lot before this happened anyway, so it's just status quo.

Now I'm sitting next to Lo in a dark theater. Julian is away on tour with his band, so she doesn't have a date either. I've given up on Kayla. Everything hurts.

"I think you're really going to like this movie," Lo says, leaning over so I can hear her. I try to smile.

While waiting in line for the popcorn, Lo and I talked about her plans for next year. She's going to do a gap year and travel, though she hasn't decided where yet. Maybe Bali or Thailand. Or the Philippines. It's funny. Lo wants to go on a crazy adventure to the exact place that I don't want to go. Don't get me wrong. The Philippines is an amazingly beautiful country, but I'd rather stay here with my family.

I let Lo pick the movie. It's some dumb stoner comedy that I don't really like that much. There are a few funny parts that I halfheartedly laugh at, but all I can think about is Royce, and how much I hurt him. I say the nastiest things when I'm angry, but I never mean them. I wish I could take it back.

Lo gets the sense that I don't really like the movie and leans over to whisper in my ear. "Want to movie hop? This one is kind of a flop."

I shake my head. "I'm not feeling very good. I think I might need to go home. I'm sorry, Lo."

"That's okay," she says. "I'll walk you out."

I set the popcorn on the floor. I'm grateful Lo is so intuitive.

"I'm sorry I ruined your movie," I say. "And our Galentine's Day."

"Don't feel bad at all. That's what friends are for." She knows Royce and I are fighting, but not that we broke up. I haven't admitted it, because telling someone would make it true.

We walk out of the theater together. The light nearly blinds me, and I have to squint to figure out where I'm walking. "You don't have to wait with me," I say to Lo.

"You sure?"

"Yeah. Let me know how the other movie is…"

"Will do. Let's do this again, Jas. I hang out with Julian so much, it's nice to have a girlfriend to do things with sometimes," Lo says, then disappears down the hallway to catch another flick.

I text my dad to pick me up. He writes back that he's already on the way.

That's when I look up and see Kayla come out of the bathroom. She's wearing a flowing, silky top, short white miniskirt, and chunky heels. She's obviously on a hot V-Day date.

I don't move. It would look stupid if I ran and hid.

It takes a couple seconds for her to see me. She seems terrified. I expect her to run off, but she takes a deep breath and continues walking toward me.

I don't smile. I don't run. I don't walk away.

She stops in front of me. "Hey, Jas."

"Hey."

"Listen, I know you're mad at me."

"Am I?" I don't think I'm so much mad as just exhausted.

"Probably. I haven't been a good friend lately," she says. And that's when I see him coming down the bathroom stairs. Kayla sees my face and instantly goes silent. It's Royce, on

the stairwell. I'd recognize his dark hair anywhere. Oh God.
I can't breathe. How can this be happening? This is a nightmare.

Wait! What?

It's not Royce.

It's his brother, Mason. *Mason?* What's he doing here?

Then I put it all together. She's *with* Mason. I have no idea
when or how, but somehow Mason and Kayla have hooked up.
Somehow she's fallen for my boyfriend's brother and dumped
Dylan in the meantime. I don't know whether to be angry
or confused.

Was this the "family issue" Royce was talking about? But
what did I care if his brother was dating my best friend? Why
couldn't he tell me? Why did it have to be so hush-hush?

Mason walks up, slick and smarmy. How can such a nice
guy like Royce have such a slimy brother? How can they have
come from the same parents?

"Isn't this a surprise?" Mason asks, putting his arm around
Kayla. I have to try really hard to keep myself from audibly
groaning. "What's up, National Scholar? Did you see anything good?"

What does Kayla see in him? I don't get it. Dylan's a prince
compared to Mason.

"Haven't seen you around lately," he continues, looking
me up and down. "You and Royce still an item? Or did you
finally kick my stupid little brother to the curb?"

"He's not stupid!" What an awful thing to say about Royce
being dyslexic, as if Royce wasn't so sensitive about it already.

"Only because he has more tutors than God," Mason
laughs. "Poor Royce, trying to keep up with his little honor
student. I hope you don't use very big words." Mason grins.
His teeth are perfectly straight and *too* white. It's like he left

his teeth whitener on for too long. "That's okay. I told him a girl like you would get bored of a guy like him soon enough."

Something he says stirs a memory in me.

That night in the lobby of the Ritz-Carlton in D.C., when I first met Mason, he'd been slimy, sure, but he'd been charming too. He was flirting with me, I realize now. Trying to put his little brother down in front of me. I'd thought he was insulting me, but it wasn't me he was belittling. What had he said then?

My little brother doesn't usually go after the smart girls. Hey, if you get bored of him, give me a call, will you?

Mason hadn't been joking when he said that. He was trying to horn in, trying to pick me up, right in front of his brother, just to show Royce he could.

I thought Mason didn't like me because I wasn't good enough for Royce, but there's something else going on here. Something gross.

I feel sick to my stomach, and I want to find Royce as soon as possible and make everything right between us again.

Call me, Mason mouths. *You know where I live.* Now he's flirting with me in front of Kayla. How he can be related to someone as decent as Royce, I will never understand.

"Come on, Mason. Let's go," Kayla says. She glances back as they're walking away, but I glare at her. I can't believe she's with that loser.

As soon as they're out the door, Dad texts that he's waiting in the parking lot.

I walk to the car and get inside.

Dad turns on the ignition. "How was the movie?"

"It was fine," I say. I'm shaking. I have to see Royce. I can't bear to be away from him for another moment. I text him.

jasmindls: I saw Mason and Kayla. Can you meet me? We need to talk. Please?

It feels like it takes forever for him to text back, but it's really only a few minutes.

royceb: Hey. Where?

I answer right away.

jasmindls: Outside my house. I'll come out to your car.

When we get home, I tell Dad that Royce is heading over and I'm going to meet him out front, because he and I need to talk. Dad knows I mean business, so he doesn't argue. He's tired anyway from getting up so early to drive buses. I can see it on his face. He's weighed down by the upcoming hearing. I don't even want to know what Daddy and Mommy are going through. When I get home, I get out and hug him, then lean against the car and wait for Royce.

When Royce arrives, he unlocks the passenger door so that I can open it. When I get inside, I notice that his hair is messy, and he looks like a little boy in his navy hoodie sweatshirt and long khaki shorts—like he's wearing a school uniform. He's sitting behind the wheel, staring out the windshield at our garage door as I climb in. I want to hold his hand, but I'm not sure if he'll let me.

"So now you know the big secret," he says dully. "They're dating."

"Why didn't you tell me? Is that why you haven't been around?"

He shakes his head. "No, it's not. Although, I guess that's part of it." He keeps staring out the windshield and doesn't look at me. "I told Mason to back off, that Kayla had a boyfriend, but he never listens to me. And he likes a challenge.

He got her number at the party somehow, and she started coming over. She asked me not to tell you. She said you'd hate her for not telling you first."

"Huh." I'm not sure I would hate Kayla, but she knows I don't like Mason. I'm sure she didn't want to hear me disapprove.

"So I didn't tell you. And I was embarrassed about Mason. I hate that I brought him to the party and into your life, that he said those things to you, that he gave those little losers the idea to jump your brother."

I don't say anything. I look down at my raggedy fingernails, which have been bitten to the quick ever since we broke up.

"But that's not really why I haven't been around." He takes a deep sigh. "I've been avoiding you because I've been interning for my dad since after Christmas break," he says.

"You have? But why? I know you didn't want to. You said it would be the worst," I say, confused.

"Yeah, that's why I couldn't face you. I knew you'd think I was weak, and I couldn't stand it if you did," he says, a catch in his voice.

I recall what he'd said during our fight. *I'm not perfect. You always have such high expectations. It's hard to meet them sometimes.*

I don't say anything; I just listen.

He continues. "I thought if I gave in and did what he wanted me to do, he would feel better about helping you when I asked him to. That it would be easier to get his support."

"What do you mean?"

"He's a congressman, Jas, I don't think you understand how powerful he is. He really could help you. He could help your family," Royce says intently.

"So let me get this straight—you've been avoiding me because you're interning for him, and you're interning for him because you think it might help me?"

"Yeah, that's pretty much it. I know, it sounds messed up." He gnaws on his thumbnail. We have the same bad habits. "But also because it was easier to say yes. I was tired of fighting him. I didn't want you to think I was a coward. I'm not like you. You always go after what you want. I thought you would be ashamed of me, that I caved so easily."

"I would *never* be ashamed of you," I say. "I'm sorry you felt you couldn't tell me, and that you would give up your own dreams to try and help with mine. But you don't have to do that. I didn't ask you to."

"Yeah, well." He shrugs.

"I have something to tell you too. The deportation trial's coming up."

He turns and looks at me directly for the first time. I liked looking at his profile, but this is much better. "It is? You never told me!" he says, his eyes flashing.

"I know. I was mad, so I kept it from you."

"So when is it?"

I tell him. It's so soon. Too soon.

"Is it too late to get my dad involved?" he asks.

"I think so."

He puts his head down on the steering wheel.

I reach over and tentatively put a hand on his back. Mason and Kayla and his internship for his dad aren't our real problems. I have to talk to him about what tore us apart—about what I said about his family. What I said about him.

He doesn't shake off my hand, which is a good sign. I keep it there, and put on a little more pressure, so that I'm rubbing his back, trying to console him.

"You broke up with me anyway—why do I care if you have to leave the country," he says, his voice muffled.

"I know you care." I know he does, because I feel the same way. I don't want to leave him. "And if we're broken up, why are you here?"

"You asked me to meet you," he says in a matter-of-fact tone.

"And you just do whatever I ask you to do?" I say, amused.

"Pretty much."

I laugh. It never occurred to me before that I have so much power over him, and that it was equal, if not more, than the power he holds over me.

He was just as miserable as I was. He missed me just as much. At least I had my family, my friends to fall back on. Who did Royce have? His parents are always traveling. His brother is a snake. His sister is sweet, but young. He had Maria, I guess.

Once, he had me.

He's still slumped against the steering wheel, and so I continue to rub his back. I've always liked his back. It's so broad, so manly. It's one of his nicest physical features, and he has many. "Higher," he says. "I have an itch right there. Right between my shoulder blades."

I scratch it. He sighs in relief.

I wonder if this is what it would be like when we're old and married. Having someone to scratch your back. *Who's got your back.*

"I didn't mean what I said that day," I tell him. "About your family. About you. I was just angry and stressed. I lashed out more from my own insecurity about my background than anything you or your parents have done to me. They're great. You're great."

As an apology it's lame, I know. But he's the writer, not me.

Royce doesn't say anything. I can feel him breathing under my hand, like a wounded animal. One that I shot.

"I know I'm always telling you to stop putting yourself down," I tell him. "But I was guilty of the same thing. I put myself down. I convinced myself everyone else was the one doing it, that it was your family that was judging me, that you were judging me, but *I* was the one who found me and my family lacking. I was the one who was embarrassed to be who I was, embarrassed about where I came from."

He raises his head from the steering wheel and looks at me. "Jas..."

"Let me finish," I say. "Because I have to say it. I was embarrassed that I was embarrassed, if you know what I mean. I hated that I felt that way about myself. I work so hard to hold my head up, to be proud of my culture, my background, my history. I would never change my skin color, the shape of my eyes, or the color of my hair, but inside, I was worse than anyone out there who calls me a chink, or a FOB."

He sits up straight now. "Jas, really, stop. I know you didn't mean what you said when we were fighting."

"Do you forgive me?" I ask, hugging my knees to my chest on the seat next to him.

Royce reaches over across the console so that he can wrap his strong arms around me, and I curl into him, feeling safe again for the first time in weeks. He buries his head in my shoulder. "Always," he murmurs. "You don't even need to ask."

I raise my head so he can see me smile. I don't deserve someone like Royce, I think, and then I squash the thought. There's no "deserving" when it comes to love, when it comes to relationships. You just accept the love you get and you count yourself lucky.

And I am so, so, so, so lucky.

"I love you," I tell him. I'd wanted him to say it first, like it was a competition or something, because that's the kind of selfish person I am. But I don't want to be that person anymore. I want to be open and generous and vulnerable, and I want to tell him how I feel about him. I should have said it earlier. I should have said it when he came back from Aspen and he was wearing that silly tie. I should have said it all those times we were kissing. I should've texted it to him a hundred times a day.

"I love you," I repeat, because he's just looking at me, smiling.

"Yeah?" he says, turning pink, a small smile turning up the corners of his mouth. "Well, guess what? I love you too. But you already know that, right?"

I do. I've lived in his love for months now, have basked in it, have been warmed by it, have been supported and buoyed by it.

"I love you more," I say.

"Not possible," he says. "I love you most."

When he leans down, I stretch to meet him halfway and we're kissing again. It's soft and sweet and a little sad this time, licking wounds, trying to find our way back to each other. That beautiful thing between us, it was tarnished a little, and it's going to take some work, some effort, to bring it back to where it was. Maybe it'll always have a scar in it, but scars heal—that's what love does. It breaks things open and puts them back together again.

"You know, I knew you were the one for me when I heard you interviewing that old guy in the hospital," he says. "You listened to him and asked questions, and you were so interested. You were such a good friend to him. It made me realize I didn't have anyone like that in my life—someone who just listens to me. You're beautiful, Jas, but I fell in love with your beautiful heart."

"So you're saying you think of yourself as an elderly hospice patient?" I tease.

He kisses my head.

"Hey, I almost forgot," Royce says when we've stopped kissing and we're just sitting in the car holding hands, listening to the crickets and cicadas. "There was another reason I came out to see you."

"What is it?" I ask.

He opens the glove compartment, hands me a present. When I open it, I see it's a copy of *Armies of the Night*. Inside the book, he's inscribed, *For Jas, my hero. Happy Valentine's Day. Love, Royce.*

"I forgot it was Valentine's Day," I tell him, admiring the book. "I have a present for you too."

"Yeah?" he asks happily.

"I was still working on it, so I have to print it out." But I take out my phone and show it to him. It's a photo I took of the two of us, and over the picture I've written a quote from one of our favorite poems.

I have spread my dreams under your feet.
Tread softly because you tread upon my dreams.
-William Butler Yeats.

He studies it for a long time. "It's beautiful."

"You're beautiful," I say.

"That's my line." He smiles.

We're kissing again, until Daddy knocks on the glass. When

Royce rolls down the window, Dad tells me it's time to go to bed.

"She's not a sucker fish," Dad says. "Go home, Royce."

Embarrassed, I tell Royce good-night.

But I smile all the way to bed.

31

You show people what you're willing to fight for when you
fight for your friends.

—HILLARY CLINTON

I'M WEARING ALL BLACK. Not because I'm in mourning, though I *am* terrified. It's just more professional. It makes me look older. Mom wears a lavender sweater over a nice gray tweed skirt. She really looks like she could own an entire estate. Dad wears his old suit. Even though it's the same one he's worn for years, he doesn't wear it very often, so the navy blue fabric still looks brand-new. He's handsome in it. He could be a doctor or a lawyer. My brothers stand behind us, completely silent. Mom has coached them to be on their best behavior. They don't want to go back to live in the Philippines either.

I think we all look sharp. A real all-American family.

Royce sends me a text: Don't worry. America was made for and by people like you. I love you.

His words make me feel braver about what's going to happen. Our deportation hearing isn't in a courtroom, like I was expecting. We're standing in a small chamber with a long wooden table and lots of chairs. Mr. Alvarado wears a black suit. A representative from the government who specializes in these kinds of hearings chats with him. Next to him is a bailiff. I don't know why there's a need for one. We're not threatening anyone. I mean, I don't particularly expect Dad to go crazy.

The door swings open suddenly, causing the bailiff to shout over our heads. "All rise for the Honorable Judge Reynolds."

The judge comes in wearing a black robe. He carries an armload of papers. Though he's nearly bald, the judge has bushy eyebrows and a fierceness about him that makes me want to disappear. Instead of sinking into my seat, I focus on my posture. I need to look like the National Scholar and National Cheer Champion I am.

Mom and Dad are silent as the judge takes a seat.

"Counsel Alvarado," Judge Reynolds says. "I haven't seen you in a while."

Mr. Alvarado coughs. "I've had to take fewer cases. My back isn't as agreeable these days. Too many years of litigation."

"That's unfortunate. At least you lawyers don't have the problems we judges do. When I first started, I thought the robes were there to create an air of authority and formality. Turns out they're only good for hiding how fat we get from sitting all day."

Mr. Alvarado meekly laughs. It's strange how the judge doesn't say anything to us or look at us. It's like he wants to pretend we don't even exist.

"Shall we get started? I'd like for this to go as quickly as possible," Judge Reynolds says.

"I'm ready," Mr. Alvarado replies.

The government representative nods. His narrow face seems expressionless. I try not to dislike him. I'm sure he's just doing his job. But he still represents everything that doesn't want us here, and that I'll never forget.

"Well, then," says Judge Reynolds as he picks up a paper from the stack in front of him. "The Government asserts that the de los Santos family are in violation of United States law." He turns to my parents. "The purpose of this hearing is to determine whether you are aliens and, if so, if you are in violation of United States law. The Court must also determine whether there are any provisions of law that would permit you to remain in the United States permanently and, if that is not possible, whether you will be leaving the United States under an order of removal or an order of voluntary departure. These questions will be answered after we hear the facts of the case." He pauses. "Clearly—and I say this to move the trial forward as quickly as possible—there has been a violation. That is not in question as I have seen no document that can verify your citizenship or any temporary or permanent status as aliens."

I'm terrified. It's true that our family doesn't have documentation, but how can the judge not even give us a chance to state our case first? It's already feeling like a slap in the face.

Mr. Alvarado turns to Judge Reynolds. "Your Honor, I have presented to you and the federal counsel the work history of both clients. They have exceptional records within their areas of employment. I also have presented letters from current and past employers asserting their impeccable behavior as model workers. I have gathered other witness accounts, including letters from friends—"

"Friends?" Judge Alvarado cuts in. "You know, Mr. Alvarado, that you have to do better than that. I read these 'friend' letters. Are there no written statements from California assemblymen or assemblywomen that you could bring me? How about US senators or representatives, for that matter?"

Representatives? He means congressmen, right? Oh my

God. Royce kept offering to ask his dad for help. Why didn't I accept it? Why didn't I ask his dad to write a letter on our behalf? What was I thinking? Why was I so stubborn? Why do I always think I'm right about everything and that I don't need anyone's help?

"Our friends are important people. US citizens," Dad says.

The judge doesn't like this at all. "Mr. de los Santos, you will speak only when spoken to. There's an order to these hearings, and that begins with me having a dialogue with the counsel you have chosen as your representation. Please honor that."

"Yes, sir," Dad says. Mom gives Dad one of those looks.

The government representative asks for the floor. "Excuse me, Judge. I'd also like to submit documentation concerning the plaintiffs' 'work history,'" he says, getting up and giving a stack of papers to the judge. "Apparently, Mr. and Mrs. de los Santos forged their work documentation for a number of years after their initial temporary work visas expired four years ago, which allowed them to steal jobs that are meant for legal residents and citizens of the United States."

Ugh. That can't be good.

Mr. Alvarado speaks up. "Your Honor, while forgery is never advisable, please take note the unique case we have before us with the daughter being recognized as a National Scholar by the White House. It would be unprecedented—"

"Actually," the government representative says. "School records also reveal that the middle child, Danilo de los Santos, has a history of antisocial behavior. He was recently in a fight at his school. If you allow this family to stay, Judge, you must ask yourself whether this boy will carry out this tendency toward violence into adulthood?"

Danny yelps in protest, and I can barely keep myself from

jumping up and throttling the other attorney. Danny is the sweetest and most sensitive kid out of all three of us. How could he twist the facts about what happened so much to make Danny into a juvenile delinquent? And how did he find out about the fight anyway?

Then I remember—Dad made sure to tell the school to protect the boys from further harm.

"Becoming a National Scholar is impressive," says Judge Reynolds. "However, I don't believe Ms. de los Santos's accomplishments forgive her parents' violation of the law."

Mom and Dad look at each other. I think Dad's about to walk out of the courtroom, but he patiently holds Mom's hand. She can't even look up from the floor.

"Your Honor, I have included many letters from the girl's teachers, her principal, her coach—"

"Yet not one politician has written a statement on this family's behalf," says the judge.

Again, I kick myself for failing to accept Royce's offer of help.

The government representative is still straight-faced, though the hint of a smile in his eyes terrifies me. He clicks a pen and makes a note, then goes back to watching the judge. Judge Reynolds is making his case so easy that he probably won't even have to say anything himself. I don't know whether to be angry at him, the judge, or our lawyer. This doesn't seem to be going in our favor, but I don't know what to do except continue to silently sit and pray. I'm sitting between Danny and Isko, so I squeeze their hands, letting them know that their big sister will be there for them no matter what happens to our family.

"But, Your Honor," says Mr. Alvarado. "A student who is a National Scholar should be a prize in the eyes of this great nation. To turn one away at this point, when she's on the verge of attending one of our great collegiate institutions, would disrupt this very community. Please also take into account the recent National High School Cheerleading Championship Jasmine de los Santos's team won. Not only that, she's the captain. She led her team to victory. What does that say about her future leadership capabilities?"

The judge gets a smirk on his thin lips. He seems to find our case completely amusing. "Oh, I see, Mr. Alvarado," he says, mocking him. "Yes, yes. You're right. Our country is in dire need of more cheerleaders."

I'm instantly ashamed. What do they call the feeling? Belittled? To be made small? No wonder the bailiff is here.

"Your Honor," Mr. Alvarado says. "Jasmine de los Santos has shown great academic promise. You can't ignore her remarkable achievements as a scholar."

"If that's so, why didn't you file for her separately? She's eighteen isn't she?" The judge smirks.

Filing for myself was a possibility that our lawyer proposed, but I rejected it. I couldn't stay in America by myself. Either we all leave or we all stay.

But right now I feel like I'm failing my family. Like everything I've done hasn't been good enough. If I was the prize that Mom and Dad have been polishing, then I've suddenly become tarnished. Was I never good enough to begin with? What kind of people does America want—people who are famous or happen to have friends in high places? Or people who work hard and love their country? I want to run out of the room and never come back. They'll have to find me to deport me, because I'll have vanished.

"The de los Santos family would like to remain in the

country together and not be separated," Mr. Alvarado explains.

The judge seems unmoved.

The man from the government seems like he's chuckling inside.

I feel ill.

Judge Reynolds surveys each of us before resting his eyes on Mr. Alvarado. "You should know that simply working in America doesn't give anyone the right to stay in America, no matter how excellent reports are." The judge sets down the papers. "I am afraid, Mr. Alvarado, there's just not enough credible testimony here. After carefully reviewing the evidence, I rule that the de los Santos family are aliens in the United States of America. I also rule in favor of deportation."

32

*The Guide says there is an art to flying...or rather a knack.
The knack lies in learning how to throw yourself to the
ground and miss.*

—DOUGLAS ADAMS

"WHAT DID I tell you about the lawyer?" Dad says as we all pile into the car. He's the only one talking. Mom probably can't say anything because she'll break down in tears.

"Did you hear how he and the judge talked?" Dad asks himself. "They were golf buddies. I knew it soon as I walked into his office. Alvarado didn't even *try...*"

"It wasn't his fault," I say.

Dad isn't finished yet. "And who was that other man in the room? A lawyer? Or a hit man? Do we have to watch our backs now until we board the plane?"

Mom wipes her eyes. I'm crying too. Everything I've known is gone. Everything. This life has been an illusion. Something I thought I knew. I thought I understood how life works. School. Cheer. Boys. Family. Life. Right? No. Life gets pulled out from under you like some kind of slow death. I can't even think about Royce and I being separated from each other. Not now. Not after everything we've been through.

That's really what this is. Torture. I know I belong here, but the government doesn't think I do. I may look like I belong in the Philippines, but they'll know I'm a fraud too. I can't even speak Tagalog or Ilocano. Neither country will want me.

"I don't understand," says Danny. His bruises are barely visible now. "Do we have to leave right now? Where are we going? We haven't packed our games."

"I don't know," I say to him. "We haven't talked about it."

Dad pulls into traffic. "We'll figure it out. We have family all over the Philippines. Someone will know of a place we can buy or rent. And there are bus driver jobs everywhere. I have a lot of experience. You'll have a good education there. The colleges are good. You boys will like the schools."

"We'll get beat up for talking American," Isko cries. "I don't want to get beat up like Danny."

"Shut up," Danny says. "They like Americans over there. And when they find out cheerleaders kiss me, I'll be the coolest kid at school."

"But no cheerleaders kissed me," Isko cries. "They'll pick on me and cover me with spiders!"

"Will you boys quit?" Dad says.

Mom's still not saying a word. I worry about her. I know that she'll feel guilty for everything. Not telling me about our expired visas. Pushing to have a deportation hearing. Giving me false hope for college. America turns out to be a hopeless, wasted dream. I'm not a National Scholar, because I'm not a *national*.

It's not just my future that I've lost. My past and present are about to get ripped away too. I'll have to completely start over again.

"They're just scared we might have to leave right away," Mom says.

"It will be a few months before we have to go," Dad says to the boys. "Our useless lawyer negotiated that we don't have to leave until Jasmine graduates high school." He turns to Mom. "I'm telling you, she'll get into a top university in Manila, maybe even Ateneo. And you boys will really like it over there."

I finally text Royce. I didn't want to share the bad news until I had time to process it. Since we made up, we've been so solid.

But now I have to tell him.

jasmindls: We lost. We have to leave the country.

He texts back immediately.

royceb: no ducking way! DUCK DUCK DUCK DUCK DUCK

royceb: DUCKING autocorrect i don't mean DUCK!!!

royceb: i thought your case was a sure thing!!!

royceb: i'm coming over right now. There has to be something we can do.

Royce is leaning against his car when we arrive home. I jump out and run into his arms. "I don't want to go," I say. I'm scared to cry again. Crying means defeat, and I'm not giving up.

"You're not going anywhere," he says. I've never heard him curse as much as he has today. "I can't believe it. They'd turn you away because of some expired visa? What is that about? After everything you've done? You didn't do anything wrong!"

"The law says we did," I say shakily. "You should have seen the judge."

My family crosses the lawn to go into the house. Mom and Dad wave at Royce. He acknowledges them. My brothers are joking around.

"You think I can get the cheerleaders to kiss me before we go?" asks Isko.

"I don't know," Danny says. "You have a monkey face."

"Your brothers don't seem to be taking it too bad," Royce says.

"They don't understand," I say, leaning into his chest. "To them, everything's a big adventure."

Royce runs his hands up and down my arms. "It will be," he says.

"No, it will be horrible."

He squeezes my arms. "You can't leave. There's got to be something I can do." He keeps saying that. He's said for months that he can help me, but I won't let him.

"The judge asked us if we knew anyone important in government," I finally confess.

"He did?"

"Yeah."

It's like I lit a fire underneath him. "Okay. We need to move fast, then. Let's go talk to my mom."

"Your mom?" I ask. "Why?"

Royce is obviously surprised by this comment. He pulls away. "Because you're my girlfriend. I thought we were over this thing you have with my family."

"I didn't mean it that way," I say, but I guess I did. I think about the day I dropped off his Christmas gift. I left his house feeling like I could never impress her.

"But isn't your dad the one we have to talk to? He's the congressman."

Royce smiles ruefully. "He definitely is. Except we have to win over Mom first. It's just the way things work in my family."

"Okay," I say. I'm desperate, and he's offering.

"Great, she's in town. Let's go."

★ ★ ★

When Royce and I enter the Blakely house, Maria greets me. "Nice to see you, Jasmine," she says. "I've been wondering where you've been lately."

"Where's Mom?" Royce asks.

"She's in the kitchen," Maria says. "Is something wrong?"

Royce nods. He looks more determined than I've ever seen him. "It's a long story. I'll catch you up later."

We hurry to the kitchen. Even though my family doesn't have to leave the country right away, everything seems to have taken on a feeling of urgency. It's like a timer has been set, and every ticking second means we're closer to deportation.

"Mom. I need to talk to you," Royce says as we enter the kitchen.

Mrs. Blakely is rinsing out a coffee cup. "I have a hair appointment in thirty minutes, Royce," she says, smiling at me. "Hello, Jasmine. Congratulations on your cheerleading championship. Royce told me a few weeks ago."

"Thanks," I say quietly.

"Did I tell you I was a cheerleader at UCLA? Go Bruins! Unfortunately, I was never the captain. But look at you. Smart. Driven. I'm so proud of you."

Is this the same woman I saw at Christmas? She's not looking at me the way she did that day, like something Royce dragged inside from the street onto her spotless white carpet. She's friendlier. Sweeter. She really does seem to like me. Was it all in my head, then? It must have been. I told Royce when I apologized that I was projecting my own insecurity onto her, and this is more proof of it.

"Thank you, Mrs. Blakely," I say. "That's really nice of you to say."

"You can call me Debra," she says, putting the cup away. "We all need to have dinner soon. Anyway, I'm off."

"It's important, Mom," Royce says. "I need you."

Debra stops in her tracks. "Okay. What is it?" She sets down her purse, waiting for Royce to continue.

He gets right to the point.

"Jasmine and her family are going to be deported. We have to help."

33

There is no exercise better for the heart than reaching
down and lifting people up.

—JOHN HOLMES

"WHEN MARIA'S VISA EXPIRED," Mrs. Blakely says,
"we had to help her get an extension, which is much harder to
do once the date has passed. The government tends to frown
on that, but we were able to make it happen."

I'm at a coffeehouse with Royce and his mom. She's meeting with us after her hair appointment. Her hair looks perfect.
She's listened to my story quietly and without judgment. For
the first time, I feel a glimmer of hope, although there's still
more than a hint of desperation mixed with it.

She stirs some sugar substitute into her coffee. "These
things can be a real headache, but in Maria's case we were
able to extend her stay for another five years."

"Only five years?" Royce says, alarmed. "That's not enough
time for Jasmine to get a degree and go to grad school too.
There has to be a solution that wouldn't mean she'd need to
get approvals through the immigration and American court
system for the rest of her life."

"And I can't stay here without my family," I say. "We all
need to be able to stay." I'm adamant about that point.

"Wait, Maria's leaving after five years?" Royce asks.

Mrs. Blakely nods. "She wants to move back to the Philippines and be with her family." She takes a drink. "Your father had to pull some strings to get her a new work visa." She looks at me. "In your case though, you need something to stall the deportation. To file some kind of appeal. And you'll need a judge on your side for that. I think it's called a stay of deportation. After that, you'll need to somehow be eligible to apply for green cards so you can become permanent residents. But I just can't believe the judge wouldn't look at your academic excellence as a reason to keep you and your family here in America."

"It was a nightmare," I say, feeling brave enough to speak my mind after hearing her supportive words. "He was definitely not on our side. He thought winning Nationals at cheer was silly. He made some comment about how America had enough cheerleaders."

"I'm not surprised," Mrs. Blakely says. "Some of these people think a woman's place truly is in the gutter. They've spent years at the top and believe their power gives them the right to decide people's fates. That they *deserve* the power to say who stays and goes."

"Like Dad?" Royce says.

Mrs. Blakely laughs. "Your dad wouldn't get anything done without me."

Royce elbows me. "What did I tell you? Maria wouldn't be here without Mom pushing Dad to help."

"He was glad to help," Mrs. Blakely says. "It's just that he has so much going on. He would have never known if I hadn't pushed the issue. He probably would have just hired another housekeeper. But I like Maria, and she asked if I had any solutions. So here we are."

"Do you have any solutions for Jasmine?" Royce asked.

"Not yet," Mrs. Blakely says. "First, we need to take this to your father. He'll know what to do. There are so many loopholes and ways of doing things. We might have to do a little research. Ask around Washington."

"Dad will do it, right?" Royce asks. "Even if his politics are very conservative."

"Just because someone is conservative doesn't mean they don't help people, Royce," his mother chides. "You know that. Besides, this is your Jasmine we're talking about. Her track record alone means that this is a special case, don't you think? Let me talk to him first, and when Dad gets back in town this week, you and Jasmine should schedule some time to talk to him as well."

A few days later, I've gotten out early from school and Royce and I are sitting in the waiting area of Congressman Blakely's office. It strikes me as funny that Royce had to be penciled in to the appointment book like any other constituent, but I guess his dad's schedule is that tight. Every moment is accounted for, even time with his son.

Mr. Blakely's office is a testament to all he's done in his political career. There are photos of him with two US presidents, senators, foreign dignitaries, celebrities, and of course of him in the House of Representatives, speaking on the floor. There are paintings too, probably commissioned by Mrs. Blakely. There's one of him hanging next to a case that has all kinds of awards of recognition he's received over the years from around the world. Behind him are the US and California flags.

"He's ready for you," says his assistant, a serious-looking guy in his twenties wearing a crisp suit. "Go on in."

As Royce and I enter his office, Mr. Blakely stands, comes

out from around his desk, and clasps Royce around the shoulder. He has Royce's broad shoulders and classic features, but Royce has his mother's eyes.

He tells us to sit, and instead of returning behind his desk, he takes a seat on the chair opposite the couch where we're sitting.

"How's work?" he asks Royce. "I'm told you're quite an asset to the team. That press release you wrote about the water initiative was picked up almost word for word by the press."

"Thanks, Dad," he says, blushing.

I look at him admiringly. I'm so proud.

"Your mother told me what's going on," his dad says. "This is tough business we're talking about. Jasmine is in the process of being deported?"

"Yes, sir," says Royce.

"My entire family actually," I say. "We tried to go through the appropriate process, but we lost the trial."

"And we didn't know who else to talk to," Royce adds. "Mom said to come to you."

"You came to the right place," Congressman Blakely says. He studies me. "How are you doing, Jasmine?" he asks.

"I'm all right, sir."

"I'm sorry about all this. Royce tells me that because of your status, you're not eligible for the National Scholarship anymore."

"Yes, sir." I flush. I hope he doesn't think I was some kind of fraud for having gone to the reception in D.C.

"That's a terrible shame," he says. He doesn't seem to think so. I breathe a little easier.

"Thank you, sir," I say.

"Call me Colin, please. I've told you before, let's not be so formal," he says. "I've been thinking about what we can do about your documentation status since Debra told me about it. Here's my solution. I want to offer you a special chance at something. Have you ever heard of a private bill?"

"No, I haven't," I admit, hope rising in my chest.

Royce, who's holding my hand, squeezes it.

"Several years ago, there was a young man from Uganda who had birth defects to his heart that had never been repaired," Congressman Blakely says. "He was a walking time bomb. Doctors said he could die anytime. How he lived to sixteen, no one knew. But there was nothing they could do. They didn't have the expertise to treat him. The boy was in an orphanage and had no money to travel for health care. He was discovered by Doctors Without Borders. They referred him to one of the programs in the US that was training medical students at a university here. And so they treated him. He recovered."

Mr. Blakely returns to his desk chair and motions for Royce and I to move to the chairs before him. He continues with his story. "Then guess what happened? Over the next few years, he took a bunch of college classes. He wanted to study medicine. Only, he needed to have residency in the US to enter the program. So, Representative Bill Turner from Wisconsin drafted a private bill. Included in that were letters from high-ranking officials from the university and the US government. The bill passed the House and the Senate. No problems. Then the president signed off on it. Just like that, the young man became a green-card holder and then a US citizen. In his case, the private bill only encompassed one man."

I feel light-headed with hope. "So you're saying one of these bills could work for my entire family? You would do that for us?" It's mind-boggling to think it could be this easy, that just because I know Royce, my family could find ourselves moved to the front of the immigration line, the VIP pass to citizenship.

Mr. Blakely nods. "Exactly, Jasmine. We'd center the bill around you—an accomplished young student and her support system. What do you think?"

"I think it's amazing," I say. Wow. This is more than I expected. A private bill. Just for us. For my family. I exchange a hopeful glance with Royce. So this is what he meant when he said he could help me. He could make this happen, because of who his father is.

"It's definitely worth a shot," Royce says with a broad smile.

"I have to say, it sounds good on paper. But it will be tricky," Mr. Blakely says. "First I have to talk to the judge who presided over the case, see if I can get him to have a change of heart and grant some kind of temporary visa for you all. We don't want you to be deported while we're trying to make this happen. That might simply result in another hearing, which means waiting all over again. It could be a lengthy process."

"So she would have to wait for two things?" Royce says. "A hearing to see if she could stay temporarily, and then to see if the private bill passes?"

"Yes," Congressman Blakely says. "In the meantime, there will be a lot of information to gather. I'll have to call the judge. Letters have to be written. Then the bill will have to be drafted. We can try to fast-track this, but that might not work. It could still take six months to a year, and there are no guarantees it will pass. It's an exceptional case. Then again, you and your family, Jasmine, are exceptional. We have to find a way to tug on the heartstrings of my fellow congressmen, senators, and the president. I'd say you have a good chance, but you've probably heard that before."

"Thank you, Mr. Blakely," I say. I can't call him Colin, just like I can't call his wife Debra. Not yet. Maybe one day. I'm floored that he's helping us. I know it's not for me, that he's doing this for his son and because his wife asked him to help. He's doing it for his family, and maybe that means Royce's family really isn't that different from mine.

"Wait a minute. Before you go..." Congressman Blakely lifts his hand to stop Royce and I from leaving the room. "I'd appreciate if you kept what I'm doing quiet, Jasmine. It is very much against my party line. If certain people find out, they could take advantage of your situation to hurt me. And that would do neither of us any favors."

"Wow, your dad is a superhero. Your mom too," I say to Royce as we walk hand in hand on the Santa Monica Pier after meeting with his father. The pier is one of Royce's favorite places in LA. He says it reminds him of his childhood, so we go there often. We're next to the balloon-popping game at the carnival.

This is the closest I've ever felt to him. Not only because he's helping me but because his family knows me, the real me. They know me and want to help me.

"I told you they could help," he says simply.

"Thank you," I say. "I'll never be able to thank you guys enough."

"There's no need to thank me. I'm doing it for myself, you know. I'm very selfish," he jokes. "And you know I don't have any other friends."

I still can't believe it. Just one meeting with his father and all our problems have vanished. It's magic.

"Look at you lovers," one of the carnies says. He holds up

a black teddy bear cradling a heart. "Why don't you do the girl a favor and win her something she'll never forget?"

Royce looks at me. "Think I have good enough aim?"

"I don't know," I say. "I kind of want to go tell my parents the good news."

"Live a little," the carnie says. "No one has all the time in the world. Your time for winning is now."

"He's a good salesman, don't you think?" Royce says.

"Not good enough," I say. I don't feel like playing games right now.

"Sorry, buddy," Royce says to the man.

We continue walking down the boardwalk. The breeze is cool and soft on my skin. Everywhere there are kids chasing each other around, laughing at the games. Several seagulls hover overhead. One lands on a railing. The Ferris wheel turns close by. A few kids scream from their seats as the ride rotates.

Royce had offered to help with my situation from the beginning, and I kept turning away his help. I thought I was being practical, that I didn't want to burden him with my problems when really I was too proud to accept his help. Too self-absorbed to accept his love, because love means letting other people love you too.

While I'm happy for myself, I think about the many millions of people in my situation who don't have the same resources, the same connections, and don't have a voice in the system. *There, but for the grace of God go I.* I'd never really understood what that meant before, but I do now. What if we were locked away in a detention center for years? How would my brothers grow up? What would I be like when I got out? Would my parents' hair be gray?

I'd been thinking about what I want to do with my life,

in case everything worked out, and now I think I know. I want to help these people in some way, to be an advocate for those who don't have one.

"You okay?" he asks, putting an arm around my shoulder.

"What if I'd kept saying no? What if I didn't accept your help?" I ask.

"I'd have probably done the same thing anyway," he says. "I should have done it earlier."

"We didn't know it could be this easy," I say. "And it's not your fault. I'm really lucky."

"I'm lucky too," he says simply.

My mind turns back to the millions of illegal immigrants in this country, waiting and hiding. Trying to stay in America is a game of cat and mouse, a life of working under the table, for less than minimum wage, with no way to report workplace abuses and transgressions. What happens when they get sick? What happens if they're hurt? The sacrifice they're making is enormous.

My story is only one of many.

I feel connected to everyone who has ever tried to move to the United States in search of a better life. Those who have sacrificed so much for the dream of a future they won't get to enjoy—only their children will.

I feel tears welling up in my eyes, and I pledge that I will be worthy of that sacrifice.

34

The main thing is to remain oneself, under any
circumstances; that was and is our common purpose.
—MADELEINE ALBRIGHT

AT SCHOOL, EVERYONE is shocked when they hear the
results of the trial. Mrs. Garcia shakes her head. Coach Davis
is angry. My teammates are livid. Mrs. Lopez, the school
principal, pulls me aside and looks at me with sad eyes. "Deported?" she says in disbelief.

Everyone says the same thing. *But you're a National Scholar.
You're a part of the fabric of this school, this city, this country.* I want
to tell them that the fabric is torn. A hole has been ripped
through this country. People like me pour out of it, spilling
back over the borders because of the way we are all criminal-
ized, instead of only the few who are criminals. But I keep
my mouth shut about the private bill for now.

I wait a day to tell my family about my conversation with
Congressman Blakely. Dad's already contacting family members in the Philippines, planning our arrival. He looks like he
has a gun to his back. We all do. We're feeling like outsiders
in our own community, in our own house.

"What's it going to be like over there?" Isko asks. "Will it
smell different?"

We're eating dinner together. Mom has made fried rice

with shrimp and chicken. I drown mine in chili sauce. Isko and Danny stuff their faces with food.

"Everything will be different," Mom says. "You won't be the minority anymore."

"What does that mean?" Isko asks.

"It means everyone will be Filipino like you," Dad says.

"But I'm American," Isko says. "I'll be the one talking funny."

"You'll look exactly like them, and for your information, Filipinos can speak English. You just don't remember."

Isko pouts.

Danny gives his little brother a look, the one that means all the cheerleaders will love him and not his little brother. I'm glad Danny seems to be getting out of his funk.

"Shut up," Isko says.

Danny feigns surprise. "I didn't say anything."

"You're doing it again," Isko says.

"Will you stop?" Mom says to Danny. "No one wants to kiss you."

Danny laughs while looking at Isko. "Oh yes, they do."

I speak up. "I met with Royce's dad."

"He was finally in town?" Dad says, taking a last bite.

Mom clears the plates from the table. Danny helps, but he still teases Isko by winking when he picks up Isko's plate. Isko growls at him. Mom gives them both *the look*.

"I asked him if he could help us." I push around the last shrimp on my plate but don't have the stomach to finish, I'm too nervous to share my news.

"And?" Dad says. "Did he give you a lecture and a nice send-off? 'Bon voyage! Thanks for dating my son!'"

"No, Daddy," I say patiently. "We had a nice conversation. He wants to try to help. He wants to write a private bill."

I tell Dad and Mom about how Congressman Blakely is going to get the judge to agree to a stay of deportation and issue a temporary visa or something while congress drafts us a private bill. I tell them how it will work.

"The US Congress is going to pass a bill just for us?" Dad asks, his eyes bulging. "And the president will sign it?"

"Yes."

Neither of them looks excited at the news. I don't understand.

"Jasmine, it sounds too good to be true, and here's the thing—when it's too good to be true, it usually is. Think about it. This bill would have to pass the House and the Senate, and the president's desk? That's a lot of what-ifs. Don't you remember that he and his party *oppose* immigration reform?"

"It will work if we get a lot of lawmakers on our side." I explain the stories about other private bills. I've done some research as well. "They're so rare that I don't see why we would be denied. This is what we were missing in the deportation hearing, remember? Having high-ranking officials on our side. Remember how the judge asked if there were any letters from politicians? It's too bad we didn't tell our lawyer we knew Royce's dad. Apparently it's how this sort of thing works. If you get enough politicians on your side you can get what you need—"

"That's the problem," Dad says. "Politicians are the last people to be trusted. And if you depend on them, you find out you're just a pawn in some bigger game of theirs."

"It's not like that," I say. "He's really trying to help. They helped their Filipino housekeeper, Maria—"

"Oh great. Now we're just like the help," Dad says. "They're going to want us to clean their house next?"

Once he makes up his mind about people, I can never get

Dad to listen. It's so frustrating. I get up from the table. "Why do you have to be so difficult?"

Mom is surprisingly quiet as she dries a dish and puts it away.

My brothers have long disappeared to another room, disinterested or too scared to follow this conversation.

"I'm not being difficult," Dad says. "I'm a realist. If our deportation is stayed, and this private bill passes, I'll be the first one to celebrate. But we need to be prepared for the worst. Mom and I are putting this house on the market, and making plans for what will happen when we do have to move back to the Philippines. We can't depend on the imaginary games of politicians. We have to have a concrete plan. We can't live like ostriches with our heads stuck deep into the sand."

"But we don't have to give up so easily either," I say. "Don't you want to stay?"

"Of course I'd rather stay. But sometimes I wish I'd never suggested moving us to this damn country," Dad says. He gets up from the table. "It's made me break all my promises to my children."

There's no cheer practice after school. Just a brief team meeting to say goodbye to the seniors and to let the returning girls know when practices will start up again during the summer. The meeting is already over. Coach Davis left in a hurry. I thought that our send-off would be a bigger deal, but no one really wants to linger. Everyone must feel the coming spring break in the air.

Most of the girls eagerly scatter. Kayla doesn't. She comes up to me. "Hey, Jas, want a ride home?"

We haven't spoken much since the movie-theater incident. I have no idea if she's still dating Mason or not. I'm not mad at her for keeping it from me, but I am annoyed that she asked Royce to do so, and I'm still mad about what her little brother did to mine. I haven't told her how Royce and I are doing, and what he's doing for my family.

"No, thanks, I'll walk," I say.

"Please? We can get a coffee," she says.

Even I can't hold a grudge forever. "All right," I say.

At the coffeehouse, we sit at a corner table and sip Americanos. The caffeine from the espresso wakes me up. I feel like I could go on a five-mile run or a shopping binge in Beverly Hills.

"Have you talked to Lo lately?" Kayla asks.

I already know where this is going. "If you want to know how Dylan is doing, why don't you just ask him?"

"I don't know," she says.

"How's Mason?"

"That's over," she says. "I don't even know why I dated that jerk."

"Yeah, seriously."

"Look, I'm sorry I didn't tell you about Mason. I went out with him because he kept calling, and I was tired of waiting around while Dylan toured with his band. You know how bored I get," she says, putting her hands around her mug.

"Try long-distance when you have to go to the Philippines."

"Yeah," she says. "I guess *that* relationship is over."

Meaning Royce and me.

"No, we're not over," I say, offended.

"Oh. I just assumed that since the Philippines is so far away..."

"You shouldn't assume," I say. "Look, Kayla. Why are we here? What do you want?"

Kayla takes a breath. "I want my friend back. I wanted to tell you I'm so sorry about what happened with our brothers. Brian's been acting out since our parents split, and I didn't know how to handle it. I really thought he was just joking. I was horrified when it happened, and I was so embarrassed. I couldn't face you."

I understand how that feels.

"I miss you, Jas. You're my oldest friend," she says, her eyes watery.

"I miss you too, K," I say, close to tears as well. It's been such an emotional year.

Because no matter how mad she and I get at each other, we bounce back. I can forgive Brian for what he did to Danny, I guess. And we're not going to let an idiot like Mason get in the way. But next time she wants to hook up with a guy, I'm going to make her screen him through me first, and I tell her so.

"I don't want to meet another guy," she says. "I miss Dylan. I made such a huge mistake. Do you think he'll ever talk to me again?"

"Why not?" I say, thinking of everything Royce and I have been through, and how no relationship is perfect all the time. "Everyone deserves a second chance."

35

IT'S MID-MARCH AND we don't hear anything about a new visa, or about the private bill other than Royce telling me that his father's staff is working on it. Except for our relationship, which is growing deeper every day, everything else seems to be up in the air. I'm starting to think maybe Dad was right for not being optimistic about the process. If we do end up having to move back to Manila, Dad says his cousins have a house we can rent-to-own.

Mom starts organizing every room. We all help. A lot of our things will be sold at a yard sale to help raise travel expenses. We just can't afford to move all our things. Mom says we'll get new furniture in the Philippines. We'll truly start over. She's already window-shopping online, setting placeholders for the furniture she's going to buy. She's not as sad when she does this. Somehow I think there's a kind of peace, a calm in the storm when she confronts Dad on the budget for all the furniture. Of course he's more concerned with our house and if and when it sells.

Although immersing themselves in the business of moving helps my parents get their minds off the deportation, I get sad when they talk about selling the house. It's the only place I can remember living. When I think of home, I don't think of the Philippines or even America. I think of our house.

Even if my whole family is readying for the worst, I still have hope for the bill. I try not to constantly pester Congressman Blakely about the process. One night, at a dinner with Royce's mother and father at a restaurant in Beverly Hills near Tiffany's, I ask, "Are these things hard to draft?"

"No harder than any other bill," he says, looking around. "But let's not talk about that here."

His wife gives him a look. I don't know what it means, other than we change the subject to both Royce's acceptance and my interest in attending Stanford. I won't find out whether I'm in until April. I try not to think about it too much. Even if I can stay and Stanford does admit me—two really big *ifs*—I'll still have to figure out a way to pay my tuition. Stanford says it's need-blind even when it comes to international students, but who knows if that's really true? As my dad says, you never know. I can't depend on anything.

"So you applied there too," Mrs. Blakely says. "What are you hoping to study?"

"Political science, I think," I say. "I've been thinking I might go to law school."

Mr. Blakely beams. "An excellent choice!"

Royce smiles at me proudly, and I'm tickled to have impressed his father.

"Are you continuing with cheer?" Debra asks.

I chew on a steamed green bean. "Thinking about it. I do want to compete at the collegiate level. It might help me focus overall. Keep me healthy. But I guess that depends on whether I make the team."

Mrs. Blakely sips her wine. "I don't think that will be a problem."

"At any rate," Congressman Blakely says, lowering his voice. "I did finally talk to the judge about an extension of you know what... I have a pretty good feeling."

I'm quietly elated, but I don't understand why he has to be so secretive about the extension. It's not like any of his party leadership are hiding in the planters next to the dining tables.

Royce prods his dad for more information. "What did he say?"

Congressman Blakely takes a big stab of his steak. "I'm not going to talk exact details. Let's just say I turned up the pressure and if he doesn't take care of this right away, he won't have my continued support when he's up for reelection." He takes a drink of lemon water. "It's all about favors, son. Sometimes you have to put your foot down so these guys don't continue to balk when you need something done."

"Is that what you did with the immigration reform bill?" Royce asks.

Mr. Blakely appears agitated. "We're not going to talk about that right now either."

Still, Royce doesn't give up. "I just thought, since you're helping Jasmine, you might want to explain why you basically killed the bill that would have helped her family in the first place."

I kick Royce under the table. I'm kind of impressed, but I'm also wondering why he's doing this all of a sudden. I don't want Congressman Blakely to think I'm ungrateful and stop helping us.

The congressman sets down his fork rather hard. He talks with his hands, gesticulating forcefully. "Son, I don't *have* to explain anything to you. I'm not going to talk about that here, or anywhere in public for that matter. So drop it, okay? This isn't the place. You sure are aggravating enough to make a good investigative journalist."

"Oh!" Mrs. Blakely suddenly says, waving out the window. "It's Mason! I told him to try and join us if he could."

Royce reaches for my hand under the table. I squeeze his reassuringly.

"I see there are still aliens among us," Mason says when he arrives, and my stomach immediately drops.

"Come on, Mason," Royce says, raising his voice. "Why do you have to be that way? It's not funny."

Mason gives me a little smile. "Ease up, little brother. She's a smart girl. She knows I'm kidding."

"That's enough, Mason," the congressman says.

Dinner continues, awkward and tense. Royce squeezes my hand under the table, a small comfort.

A week later, I see that Royce has left me a voice mail. He rarely calls, since we text all the time, so I know there must be big news. I hold the phone close to my ear as I walk home, trying to block out the noise with my hand.

"The judge is allowing your family a temporary visa!" he says. "I think it's for a year. Maybe more. Isn't this great? It's a first step. Dad says his office has been gathering some great letters from officials, including one from the commission that looked at your essay for National Scholar. Things are pulling together. I would have waited to tell you in person, but I thought you would want to know as soon as possible. Call me today. I want to see you when I can. We need to celebrate!"

I feel this weight lift off my shoulders. When I get home, I start dancing around the house. It's a victory we desperately needed. I run into the living room and throw my arms around Daddy. I tell him and Mom the good news.

"Wait. Is this a sure thing?" Mom asks.

"Royce says so. I don't know why he would be wrong."

"I'll believe it when I see it," Dad says darkly. "Until then, mission is not aborted. We still need to prepare to leave."

"Daddy! Why do you have to be so negative? Come on."

Mom stands there with a hand over her mouth, shocked by the news. I don't think she ever believed the political plan would work.

"Did you hear me, Mommy?" I ask. "We got our extension! One, maybe two years! It's a start, right?"

"Yes, it is *neneng*," she says. "This is good news. Great news! But what about the bill? That's what we really need. There was all this talk, but we haven't heard anything in weeks."

I think about the dinner the other night. Congressman Blakely was acting so strange. What was wrong with talking publicly about the private bill? Everyone would know about us soon enough. What's wrong if people find out that his party sometimes does support immigrants? Wouldn't that be a good thing?

It's not like my brothers and I made those decisions to come here. We just live with them. It's not our fault that we love America, that we want to stay in the only country we know.

It's not our fault that we aren't carrying green cards in our pockets.

American dream

I, too, am America.

—LANGSTON HUGHES

36

America I've given you all and now I'm nothing.
—ALLEN GINSBERG, "AMERICA"

THE BOMB DROPS at 8:37 a.m. during first period Calculus.

Royce sends an accusatory text. DO YOU KNOW WHO DID THIS?

Did what? I reply.

Oops, these... he adds. He sends links to two *Politico* and *Fox News* articles.

I can't figure out what's going on. Is he mad at me? I click on the *Politico* article, GOP Fiasco: Majority Leader Blakely Backtracks After Criticism for Bill Favoring Illegal Immigrants.

My stomach drops as I read the article.

WASHINGTON, D.C.—A once popular U.S. representative has pulled out of writing a rare private bill seeking citizenship for a family of undocumented immigrants residing in Southern California.

U.S. Rep. Colin Blakely has been targeted by fellow lawmakers who discovered the representative's attempt to quietly write a bill that would grant citizenship to an entire family illegally in the U.S. from the Philippines.

Blakely denied the bill existed, and said there would be no rare private bill from him anytime soon. "These rumors about a private bill being written by my office will be stopped here and now," said the congressman in Washington, D.C., early this morning. "While the U.S. is in need of immigration reform of some kind, this office won't support individual efforts with private bills."

Politico has learned that Congressman Blakely had personal interest in the family of five, who currently reside in Chatsworth, Calif. Sources say one of Blakely's sons is in a relationship with a member of the de los Santos family, who are illegally in the U.S. Blakely refused to answer any related questions. "My family is private when it comes to our personal life," he said.

Blakely, one of the most powerful members of Congress, has been rumored to be losing his position within the party. He's been targeted by more extreme members for being too moderate. U.S. Rep. Mitt Schilling of Texas said, "Mr. Blakely went too far with attempting to draft a private bill. Once I found out, I called his office directly. We had words." Schilling didn't elaborate on how he found out about the bill. He did say other congressmen supported the phone call to stop the bill.

"Why he's denying the whole thing is beyond me," Schilling said. "We'll be getting to the bottom of this."

Blakely said these rumors wouldn't affect his tenure as House Majority Leader. "I won't be stepping down anytime soon. I have a lot of work to do. We all do."

Private bills are rare bills in the U.S. that are written in the support of granting individuals citizenship due to unique and insurmountable hardships...

I stop reading. I'm in shock. Just like that, the bill being drafted for my family's freedom has been swept away. Congressman Blakely has denied its entire existence. He's essentially lying to the whole world. Not to mention my family's name has been dragged through the mud as some kind of political pawn in the process.

I get another text from Royce.

royceb: **My dad is in jeopardy of losing his position. You don't understand. These guys are cutthroat and they're going to use it to destroy him. They want Dad out.**

I know Royce is freaking out about his dad being in trouble, but I can't feel anything beyond worry for my family and what's going to happen to us now. But I tell him to pick me up at lunch. We need to talk.

When Royce shows up, I can tell we're both silently building arguments in our heads as he drives. I know where he's going. He's decided to have it out at Stoney Point Park, an outcropping of natural rocks east of Topanga Canyon Boulevard. We have to have this talk or we're done—even if I don't end up moving to the Philippines, which now seems more and more likely.

We get out of the car and walk along the park. Finally Royce speaks first. "Did you do it? It doesn't make sense that anyone else would."

I suddenly don't feel like walking. "Did I do what?"

"Leak the story."

"What's wrong with you? Why would I do that? This is obviously *horrible* for my family." Does he really think I would do such a thing? How can he? It's like I don't know him at all right now.

Also, is it wrong that I want to slap him?

"I don't know," he says, frustrated. "To get attention, thinking it would somehow help generate sympathy for your family. Maybe the private-bill route wasn't going fast enough for you." He runs his fingers through his hair.

"That's ridiculous," I say. "The *Politico* article trashed my family in about five different ways. I didn't even bother with the one on *Fox News*. According to them we're worse than criminals."

"I can't figure this out," he says, making a poor attempt to hide his anger. "You know, if you would have just let me help you from the beginning, this wouldn't have happened. Now my dad is hated even more by Representative Schilling and his goon squad."

I feel my face getting flushed. I hate yelling, so I try to stay calm, though my heart races. "Are you serious right now? All you care about is your dad? What about my family? What's going to happen to us? You think your father's career is going to end over this? It's a *blip* for him. But for me and my family? It'll change our entire *lives*."

I want to throw something at him but there's nothing but rocks and I don't want to hurt him *that* badly. "I didn't do anything, Royce," I say. "Remember, I'm the one who's going to get kicked out of the country."

"You're right, you're right. I'm sorry, I'm upset, I wasn't thinking."

"So it's over, isn't it? The private bill?" I want to cry but I'm also furious.

"It's dead," he says dully. "Jas, this is politics. When things go south you have to abandon ship. My dad did what he had to do." He rumples his hair in frustration. "I just don't understand how anyone found out. The only people who know about this are my family and yours."

"It wasn't my family."

"Well, it wasn't mine," he says back.

"Are you embarrassed that the article exposed our relationship?" I ask angrily. The piece made us sound so tawdry, like I was only dating him so that I could get my hands on a green card. It made me feel dirty.

"No, of course not! I love you!" he yells.

"I love you too!" I yell back.

We're both red-faced. Royce bends his head down. "Jas, I'm so sorry. Of course it wasn't you. I don't know what I was thinking. I'm just scared right now."

"Me too," I say, going to him. "I'm sorry too."

He curses emphatically.

"What do we do now?" I wail. I'm so angry about America and its toxic politics, its public servants who are supposed to help their constituents but only care about reelection.

"We'll figure it out," he says. "You're not going anywhere."

"You keep saying that, but it doesn't mean it's true."

"I'll *make* it true," he says.

We hold each other as if we'll never let go. Deportation is getting more real every day. Somehow I see beyond the Stoney Point rocks in front of us to a mirage of a coastline in the South China Sea, in Manila Bay.

Six thousand miles away from the one I love, and the one who loves me back.

Dare to live the life you have dreamed for yourself.
Go forward and make your dreams come true.

—RALPH WALDO EMERSON

JOURNALISTS SHOW UP at our house for the next couple of days, but no one in our family talks to them so, after a while, they finally leave us alone. There are a few mean-spirited articles online, but soon some married senator is caught sending nude pictures of himself online to a few young female constituents, and the hungry news media moves on.

At school the next day, Kayla tells me she's called Dylan twenty times in the past forty-eight hours. "You really need to give it a rest," I tell her. "Don't you think you're becoming a little obsessive?"

We're walking through a hallway between classes. I'm headed to English, which has been a total bore. Chaucer feels as foreign as America these days.

"I only left five messages yesterday," Kayla says, sliding on some transparent vanilla glitter lip gloss. "I'm starting to think Mason was better than nothing."

"Don't go there," I say. "He's bad news and you know it."

"I know." She pops her lips. "But why won't Dylan forgive me?"

"People need time," I say. "And you dumped him. What do you expect?"

"I thought I was doing him a favor breaking up with him since he was gone so much, you know, so he wouldn't have to miss me," she says, heading toward Calculus. "I guess I just didn't want to be hurt and so I hurt him instead."

I of all people understand that sentiment and tell her so.

Kayla stands by the open door to my class, she has a free period next and can hang around a little. "I miss him," she says.

I squeeze her arm. "Maybe you can let him miss you a little more."

"Why? Do I seem desperate?"

"A little," I say, digging in my backpack for my homework. I can't figure out where I put it. "Okay, a lot."

"So you want me to pull back?" she says. "Play chase the rabbit?"

"Yes, little bunny," I say, finding my homework folded inside my math textbook as if I'm in grade school. I'm so disorganized lately. Although I think it's a good thing I've loosened up. I connect with people better. I don't get so worked up about small stuff.

"Just do me one favor," she asks.

"I don't know," I say, dropping my homework in the bin at the front of the room. "Depends."

Kayla watches me. "What? You don't trust me?"

"Just tell me," I say.

"Will you come with me to Lo's next get-together? I know she's having one this weekend. Bob Marley Lives is playing it."

"Of course," I say. "But you and Dylan really need to have a conversation before the party. Otherwise everything will be super awkward. And you won't be able to talk there that much."

"How can I have a conversation if he won't speak to me?"

"Let me try," I say. "I'll see what I can do. There's a chance he'll be open to talking. Right? Just don't get your hopes up. I mean, what if he's seeing someone?"

"We can fix that," Kayla says, not accepting defeat. She twirls a lock of her curly hair and winks. "See you later."

I say goodbye to Kayla, admiring her for never giving up on what she wants. I've always liked that about her. Then I realize, I could use some of that moxie too. And in my case, it won't just be the affections of a slacker rocker on the line.

It will be our whole life.

When I get home, I tell my dad we have to call our lawyer. I have a plan.

Mr. Alvarado's office hasn't changed. Not a photo has been moved on his wall. Half of them are still hanging crooked. Dad's reaction is the same as mine. He gazes at all the walls and squints disgustedly.

"Mr. Alvarado is Latino," I say. "Why are you expecting Filipinos all over his walls?"

"He could hang a few more," he says. "At least for while we're here. I wouldn't feel so small then." As Mr. Alvarado enters the room, Dad grumbles audibly. Mom shushes him.

"So good to see you," the lawyer says, greeting each of us. I wouldn't blame him for not being nice to Dad. "How are you getting along?"

"We're making plans to leave," Dad says. "It's not very exciting."

"Terrible news about that private bill," Mr. Alvarado says. "I heard about that recently. I'm very sorry I couldn't do more."

"Actually," I say, surprised that I've spoken up, "there's been a development."

"Oh?" he says. "Are you the spokesperson today?"

"Apparently so," Dad says.

I know Dad doesn't want to be here. That's why he and Mom are happy to relinquish this role to me. "Well…" I take a breath, building up my courage. "While we were negotiating with Congressman Blakely about the private bill, he said he'd already gotten the judge in our case to grant us an extension, a visa or something, so that we could stay longer. Only thing is, once he pulled back on the bill, we have no idea what happened with the visa."

Mr. Alvarado takes a moment. "Have you tried contacting Congressman Blakely, then?" he asks.

"Yes," I say. "But his office says it's in our hands. They advised us to wait and not press the matter, actually." I don't mention that the congressman is my boyfriend's dad. Mr. Blakely was sincerely apologetic but it was clear he was also rattled by the leak and there was nothing more he could or would do for my family.

"They said that? Politicians," Mr. Alvarado says, shaking his head. "They duck and hide."

"But the judge already agreed to the visa extension. We're not supposed to be deported, at least, not yet."

"Tell me what you know," he says.

I tell him everything I remember about the judge supposedly being pressured by Congressman Blakely to grant the stay of deportation.

Mr. Alvarado sits back, takes it all in. He coughs, clearing his throat. "I don't know if I can touch this," he says, to our disappointment. "The judge may have already put a stop to this once Blakely backed out and denied the existence of the private bill. I don't see how you would still be entitled to that. I'm sorry. I don't think I can do anything for you."

"Not even to call the judge to see if the visas were granted to us?" I ask, irritated.

"You chicken! You're a little hen!" Dad suddenly says.

Mr. Alvarado is shocked at Dad's words. "I don't know what you're talking about. I'm no chicken!"

"Liar! I see your feathers!" Dad points. "Right there! Under your collar!"

Mr. Alvarado, still shocked, straightens his shirt.

"Dad!" I say, turning to Mr. Alvarado. "Sir, you can see the stress this has caused. You've seen our family in the news. In fact, don't you think the media would be interested in our side of the story, especially when we tell them how our lawyer promised us a victory and encouraged us to ask for a deportation hearing? I think the exploitation of helpless immigrants for profit is a story that some news outlets would be glad to pursue."

Mr. Alvarado's eyes seem to prickle. "Are you forcing my hand, little girl?" he says.

"Call it what you want," I say. "You need to keep your reputation as a pro-immigrant crusader, and we need you to contact the judge and remind him to make good on his promise. You need to tell him you know all about the favors he owes Congressman Blakely, and that he better get us our visa or we'll go to the media and tell our side of the story, about how everyone has been in cahoots. They've been dying for us to talk to them. We've been quiet so far."

"You would do that?" he says.

"We would," I say. "It all depends though."

"On what?" he says.

"On whether you do what's right. We're tired of being pawns."

"And you would make me one?"

I smile sweetly.

When Dad and I get back to the car, Mom's shocked at how I handled the lawyer.

"Neneng," Dad says. "You almost sounded like a lawyer yourself."

"Do you think he'll do something?" Mom says. "He seemed to start listening."

"He has to," I say. "Or we'll talk to those journalists who keep hounding us. They've been wanting us to talk."

"Is that a good idea?" Mom asks.

"It would complicate things," I admit. "But Mr. Alvarado doesn't know that."

Dad starts laughing. "Maybe you should work in a casino, Jasmine. You're pretty good at gambling."

38

If you obey all the rules, you miss all the fun.
—KATHARINE HEPBURN

ROYCE TAKES MY hand and I feel his warmth. Every time he touches me, there's a spark between us. I smile to myself— I am so in love with this boy.

We're at his house. His parents aren't around. Just us hanging outside by his pool in the evening, lazing in lounge chairs. Everything about this backyard is perfect. The pool. The fountains. The furniture. The meticulously landscaped trees and bushes. A line of statues and columns.

"What was it like growing up here?" I ask.

"Just like growing up anywhere else," he says. "It's just home. It's all I've known. I guess it is a little like living in a bubble though, and the older you get the more you can't see that it's a bubble. Mason still doesn't realize the bubble is going to pop one day."

I want to tell him what I've figured out about Mason but let him finish his story.

"Anyway, one summer—I think I was ten or eleven— Mason and I were sitting on opposite edges of the pool, and he poured a bucket of water over one of the maids. He wasn't trying to be funny. He was being mean and he knew it. You want to know the saddest part? At the time I thought it was funny too. We laughed our asses off."

"You were kids," I say.

"Privilege is like having blinders. It's hard to feel unloved or unwanted because everyone wants your money, so you get the attention. I guess that isn't really what you're asking. But when everything is handed to you, there's no room to write your own story because there's no struggle. Your life becomes a story centered on accumulating things, all these things you own, instead of about the struggle to live, or the struggle to survive, or the struggle to stay in America, which is a far more interesting story than mine."

"Interesting? You think I would *choose* to go through this? Being illegal? Being deported? God, Royce."

"No, of course not, but you asked me what it was like to grow up here." He smiles at me cheekily.

"About Mason," I say.

"What about Mason?"

"He keeps hitting on me," I say. "It's creepy."

"Yeah, I know," Royce says unexpectedly, his face calm behind his aviator shades. "I'm sorry about that. When we were little, Mason liked taking away my toys and making me cry. It was his favorite game. Remember that girl I told you about? My first serious girlfriend?"

I nod. Girlfriend number five. Not one of the hand-holders, but the first girl who broke his heart.

"She cheated on me with Mason. I found out when he sent me a Snapchat of the two of them hooking up."

"That's awful," I say. "Your brother is a complete psycho."

"He likes showing me that he can have whatever I have, that he can take away everything I care about. He dumped her soon after. He got what he wanted out of her. I think it's why he went for Kayla, because you kept turning him down. Kayla was close enough to hurt you, to mess with us."

"Jeez," I say, not even able to contemplate the depths of Mason's instability.

"It's why I didn't want to introduce you to him that first night in D.C. He was a National Scholar too, did I tell you? He's smart as a whip but lazy as a dog. He got kicked out of Harvard, then Stanford, and so now he's at USC."

"Wow, he's seriously messed up."

"Yep. The price of privilege. I think someone wrote a book about it," Royce jokes, as it's a famous title and he's trying to make light of the situation.

I shake my head. "Royce Blakely, you surprise me."

"Uh-huh."

"You know that you're the smartest boy I've ever met, right?"

"Nah, unlike Mason I only got into Stanford because of my dad. But that's okay. I'm smart enough to know a good thing when I see it. Like you."

I laugh.

"Come on," he says, leaping into the pool. He enters with barely a splash. "Come on!" he yells after me again.

We swim for a while. While we're hanging by the edge, I tell him something I've been worried about since the trial. "I feel like I'll be less of a person if I move back to the Philippines," I confess.

"First of all, you're not going anywhere. Secondly, you shouldn't feel that way. Listen to what you're saying. That Filipinos are lesser? Come on. Being an American makes you feel superior. Talk about privilege."

"I guess so. When people ask me about what I'll miss, I

usually say you—and then friends of course. But I'll miss this way of life too."

"You're not going to miss me, Jas. Because I'll be wherever you are."

I so want it to be true.

"Also, I was going to ask you," he says, sounding nervous. "I wanted to do this in a more creative way, but things got busy."

"You're not going to ask me to prom are you?"

Royce shrugs his shoulders, looking guilty. "How did you know?"

I laugh. "I didn't! I was joking. Looks like you ruined your own surprise."

He curses softly, but he's laughing too. "Well, what do you say? Will you go with me? To prom?"

"Of course, if you'll go with me to mine," I say, kissing him so that I taste the saline from the pool on his lips.

Then we're out of the pool and back on the loungers.

"Royce," I say, getting his attention so he's looking at me as he dries off. "You don't have to stay with me, you know," I say. I step out and grab a towel, wrapping it around my body. "I mean if I have to leave the country, you need to go on with your life. You can't keep worrying about me."

He frowns, then takes me in his arms and wraps his hands around my towel, holding me tight. "Stop saying that," he says. "You're staying right here. I'll think of something. I promise."

I don't want to make him mad, but I can't rely on his family for a solution to our problem. We already tried that once.

39

If you can't make it better, you can laugh at it.

—ERMA BOMBECK

DAD GETS OFF the phone with our lawyer.

"What did he say?" Mom asks. She's working on some work spreadsheets. I feel bad for her. If we're really going to be deported, then she'll have to leave her job, which she loves now that she's been trained.

"I can't tell if he's stalling," Dad says. "He says he's working on it but then gives me nothing."

Mom shifts some papers around. "Maybe he's afraid to tell us the truth."

I try to play the optimist. "Or maybe he just doesn't know. Don't give up," I say. "Please, Dad, don't give up."

We have our first showing of the house this weekend. I keep trying not to think about it, but I have to prepare for the reality that I really might have to leave this country.

Meanwhile, Millie's getting better again. She's breathing a little easier. They let her go home on one condition: she has to have an oxygen mask at all times. She doesn't seem to mind too much.

Millie must be really bored, though, because she asks me to

visit multiple times a week. I'm sitting on the foot of her bed when I ask her about her health. I'm still worried about her.

"Will you have to go back to the hospital?"

"I hope not," she says. "No guarantees. Any headway on your case?"

"Haven't heard anything," I say. "*But…* I should be hearing any day now from the colleges I applied to. I really want to get into Stanford. But even if I get in, who knows if I'll be able to go. It's like the pressure of everything is about to crush me. I feel like the moon is only in the sky because I'm holding it up. And I can't much longer."

"I'm afraid you're going to have to," she says. "Just a little longer. Take comfort, Jasmine. Sometimes in the darkest times, a little light shines through."

I don't really feel like being social, but I'm hanging out at Lo's after visiting Millie because I promised Kayla this favor. All I can think about is our house slipping into the hands of some other American family when it should belong to us. I guess that's the American dream for you. Your home sold to someone else. Your job filled by another. Your dreams dissipating in a cloud of smoke.

Lo's sitting on her couch, kicking her red Converses off onto the floor. "So, Jas, you're coming to the party on Friday, yeah?"

I think of the time I was at one of Lo's parties and we thought we were being busted by the cops. What does it matter now? I'm getting deported anyway. I tell her that of course I'll be there with Royce.

Next to her, Julian strings his acoustic guitar. "Yeah," he says. "You gotta see us one more time."

"I'm not backing out," I say, though the feeling of being deported is almost a constant pain in my stomach. "I'll be there."

My friends know all about the *Politico* scandal and that Royce's dad was trying to help us but when the news leaked, he couldn't do anything anymore.

"How can you stay with your boyfriend after that?" asks Lo.

Julian turns one of the tuning knobs too far so that his string snaps and hits his fingers. He yelps, then curses. Lo doesn't even bother to look at him, she's so used to it.

"It's not Royce's fault," I say. "Although it is a little awkward with his parents right now."

"Just promise you'll be at my party," Lo says.

"I will. Promise. But there was this thing I was wondering about."

"What?" Lo asks.

"It'll be kind of weird, but I have to ask. Can Kayla come?"

"Her?" Lo asks. "I don't know about that—it's not like I don't like her. Don't get me wrong. But Dylan's my friend. I don't want to put him in that kind of situation."

"Now just wait a minute," Julian says. "Shouldn't it be up to Dylan?"

"I guess so," Lo says, backing down.

"I'll talk to him." Julian sets his guitar down. "He's in the backyard. Be right back."

After Julian walks out of the room, I ask Lo, "How are things going with you guys? You seem inseparable. I don't think there's ever a time I come over that he's not hanging out with you."

"We're going to move in together after graduation," she says. "Or maybe I can convince him to explore with me. Travel the world. Just live. You ever thought about that? Just experiencing as much as you can?"

I hadn't thought about that at all. I can't even imagine bringing that up to my parents. Am I too driven? I guess I'm not like other American kids in some ways.

"No," I laugh. "I'm looking forward to college. Even if I do have to go in the Philippines."

"You know, I have to say I'm a little excited to see what happens to you. In my opinion, Jasmine, whether you go to college or move back to the Philippines, you're going to win either way."

"How's that?" I say. "It's not what I want."

"I know it's not. But in my fantasy world I think, hey, you get to see some of the world. Look where you'll be. You'll see places most of us only dream of. And with your experiences and knowledge, you could still be whatever you were driven to become. Only now, when you're a big lawyer or whatever you end up being, you'll have an entirely different perspective on things. It's really not as bad if you think of it that way."

"I'll have to digest all of that," I say. This is what I like about Lo. She makes me think differently, consider other options. "To be honest, I'm just trying to keep my head above water."

Julian returns. We both wait for him to say something. In typical Julian style he sits and starts tinkering with his guitar without telling us what Dylan said.

"Julian," Lo says.

He looks up. "What?"

"What did Dylan say?"

"Oh yeah. He said it's cool. He doesn't care. Or—I mean, I think he cares about her, but he's pretending not to. You know? It's a guy thing."

Lo playfully slaps him on the shoulder. "Was that so hard?"

"I forgot, all right? We started talking about tour stuff."
Julian smiles.

"Like what?"

"Like how Jasmine is going to hook us up with gigs in the
Philippines once she gets the boot."

We all start laughing. It's kind of funny, imagining their
band playing some big party in Manila. They would look so
out of place.

"I'm serious!" Julian says.

"I know," I say. "At least you're planning to come visit me."

That weekend Royce takes me to his parents' house in
Malibu, just the two of us, and it's just as romantic as it
sounds. My parents don't try to stop me. They know I'm with
him. They seem resigned to the fact that I have a life outside
our house and a boyfriend.

We decide to grill on the deck overlooking the ocean and
as I watch the hamburgers cook, it strikes me how different
Royce's life will be from mine if I have to move back to the
Philippines. Thinking of what Lo said earlier, I tell him I'll
take him swimming in the pristine aquamarine waters of
Boracay, or rafting down the Puerto Princesa Subterreanean
River, or hiking up the emerald green Banaue Rice Terraces.

I try to remind myself to not be so negative about my native
country. Despite the poverty and the government corruption,
the Philippines is a place of such natural beauty. Reminding
myself of these things helps me face the fact that I may be
leaving the United States right after graduation.

"Look, Jas, I'll come to the Philippines for sure," he says.
"But it won't be because you'll be living there. We'll go together, because I want to see the country where you were
born. And I'll be taking you back home to America."

I don't disagree, because I know it makes him too upset to even think about the alternative. Also, I don't want him to burn the hamburgers. Instead, I put my arms around his back. He turns around to face me and we start kissing, getting a little carried away as usual.

The hamburgers burn. Oops.

40

Far away there in the sunshine are my highest aspirations.
I may not reach them, but I can look up and see their
beauty, believe in them, and try to follow where they lead.

—LOUISA MAY ALCOTT

ON MONDAY I tell Kayla the good news. "Are you serious?" Kayla says, banging on the metal as she tries to pop open her gym locker. "I can go to the party?"

"I didn't actually hear it from Dylan. Julian asked. But Lo said it's fine."

"Good enough for me," she says, finally opening her locker and grabbing a brush to run through her hair.

"I figured it was," I say. "Just do me a favor and stop calling him."

"I did," she says, pulling out some tangles. "He actually texted me once."

"What did he say?"

"Nothing really."

"Come on, tell me," I say, sitting on the locker room bench. "I'm just curious."

"He said he misses me."

"You don't believe him?" I ask.

She puts her hair up and closes the locker. "It's hard to feel I deserve it. I put him through a lot of pain."

"You don't have to deserve love," I say to Kayla. "You just get it."

Kayla and I head outside toward the parking lot. "Will he even talk to me at the party?"

"It doesn't really matter, because you're getting a chance. *You* have to talk to *him*. You can't expect him to do all the work," I say. If anything, that's what I've learned from my own relationship. You've got to row the boat together.

Royce drives Kayla and me to Lo's party. I tell him he has to because Kayla likes to drink, so she shouldn't be driving herself or anyone home. Also, if the party goes south for her, let's say, if she trashes a lamp or a guitar because of Dylan, then we need to be able to pull her out of there. Royce sort of thinks it's all funny, but I want him there with me. Kayla tells her family that she's spending the night at my place.

"Have to keep my options open," Kayla says in the car. "Hey, Royce, how come we never hang out with *your* friends?"

Whoa, where did that come from? Why is she attacking him all of a sudden? I'm about to defend him when Royce answers her.

"I don't have many," he says with a shrug. "I don't like a lot of people."

"Oh," Kayla says. "So how's Mason?"

"Don't even go there," I say.

"I was just curious." Kayla applies a dark layer of lipstick. She looks great. All pink. Dress, nails, everything. If ever there was a color meant for her, dark pink's the one.

"He's fine," Royce says, steering around a corner. "He's back at school."

"It's okay," Kayla reassures me. "I'm over what's-his-name."

"Just try to have fun," I say.

"I will," she says. Kayla turns her attention to Royce again. "No, I'm serious, how come you never bring any friends over? Embarrassed to take your Filipino girlfriend from the Valley around your rich white private school buddies?" she says, slurring her words a little.

"For your information, I'm taking Jasmine to prom," says Royce, sounding highly irritated.

"Kayla," I say, suddenly realizing what's going on and why she's so abrasive. "You've been drinking."

"How d'you know?" she says.

"Listen to what you're saying! You're also starting to slur. What did you have?"

"Half a glass of Dad's favorite bourbon. I drank it just before I left." She smiles.

"Oh God," I say. "You need to slow down. Be nice. Or at least play nice."

"It's all right, Jas," Royce says, accelerating as the light changes. He looks at Kayla, sitting in the backseat, through the rearview mirror. "I can handle it."

"Don't you sound grown-up?" Kayla laughs. "Big Royce, ready for college. No more school uniforms."

"Hey, you don't get to talk to him that way! And I sure am glad you're not driving," I say to her. "Kayla, get it together. I'm worried about you. Don't act like this." I'm starting to have a bad feeling about tonight.

The party is Lo's biggest shindig yet. There are so many people in her house, we have to squeeze our way through. Honestly, I don't know where her parents are all the time. There's no way I could ever have these at my house without my entire family being there too.

In the living room, members from Bob Marley Lives are

rocking out to The Clouds, a band who has traveled from out of town this morning to open for this gig. The lead singer has a sincere, melodic voice, and Lo whispers that he's recently solo-toured Australia, backpacking through the countryside for a whole year. I wish I could feel that adventurous about the possibility of moving back to Manila.

When Kayla sees Dylan, she runs straight to the bathroom.

"I'll be right back," I tell Royce, and head after her. I knock on the bathroom door. "It's Jasmine. Let me in."

The door pops open. Kayla is pale, drunk. "Why am I here?" she asks. I slip in, and she closes the door behind me. "I already threw up. Do you have some gum? No, wait." I hold back her hair as she throws up into the toilet again, then flushes. I knew this was going to happen.

I hold out some toilet paper for her to wipe her mouth. "You drank more than you said, didn't you?"

She catches her breath. "It was a pretty full glass." She heaves again, groans. "Maybe I should go home. I feel awful. I probably look terrible too."

"You can do that. We'll take you home—or to my house." I rub her back. "Or, we can go out there and get some water and hope you start feeling better. What do you say? You don't have to face Dylan if you don't want to. Come on. You done yakking?"

"I think so," she says, still breathing hard. "Okay. Let's do this… No, wait," she says, turning toward the toilet, heaving again.

When we finally return to the party, Royce is doing his usual, leaning against a doorway, watching everyone. God, he is sexy—and he's mine. What I did to deserve him, I don't know, but I thank the gods all the same. He smiles at me, then takes one look at Kayla and raises his eyebrow.

"That bad?" Kayla asks. She looks like she's about to fall over.

We go to the kitchen and I give her a glass of water. "You'll feel better soon," I say. "Drink the whole thing."

As Kayla sips out of the glass, Dylan walks over. "Hi," he says. "You okay?"

Kayla stares at the bottom of her glass. She can barely pay attention.

Dylan looks her up and down. "Is she drunk?"

"Pretty much," Royce says.

Dylan glances at Royce. "Your brother make her this way?" he says. "She hardly drank this much before. She wouldn't even share a beer with me most of the time."

"Look, man, I didn't have anything to do with it," Royce says.

"Right, sure," Dylan says, putting his arm around Kayla. "You need to lie down," he tells her. "Come on." He leads her to the nearest couch and tells the two guys sitting there to move.

"Thank you, baby," Kayla says, propped up against the couch pillows.

I turn to Royce. "I guess she's in good hands."

Royce doesn't look happy though. "What's his problem?" He cocks his head in Dylan's direction.

"Let it go," I say, not wanting him to fight with my friends.

Dylan glances toward us. "You got a problem?" he asks Royce.

"No, Dylan, he doesn't," I say, pulling him away.

But Royce responds. "I'm not Mason," he says loudly. "You know, just because my dad is who he is, doesn't mean I'm a jerk."

"It's not like that," I whisper fiercely, wishing he wouldn't raise his voice. "He was just hurt by her. Your brother's an easy target."

"I don't care!" Royce says. "I'm not my brother."

Dylan and a couple of others have noticed Royce's outburst. They come over.

"Everything okay, Jas?" Dylan asks.

"Of course she's fine—she's my girlfriend," Royce answers angrily. "What's it to you?"

"Well, Jas is my friend too, and it just so happens that I've got a problem with people like you," Dylan says, brushing his long blond hair out of his eyes.

Royce steps toward Dylan and pushes up his shirtsleeves. "And who are people like me?" He's tense, and there's a dangerous glint in his dark eyes.

I'm anxious to keep them from attacking each other. I don't want Royce to fight with my friends even if I'm proud of him for standing up for himself.

"Why don't you just get out of here," Dylan says. "You're bothering people."

"Dylan! Don't be rude!" I say. "Stop it! Both of you!"

"You have a problem with me? You don't even know me!" Royce says, jabbing a finger toward Dylan.

"Royce," I plead. I know I can't do anything about Dylan, but I can try to get Royce to calm down before the evening is ruined. "Stop. What are you trying to prove?"

"Man. You're just a fake," Dylan says, then nods toward me. "The minute Jas is shipped off to the Philippines you'll forget all about her. Guys like you are all the same."

That does it. Royce takes a swing at Dylan, who takes the hit and throws one back, connecting with the right side of Royce's face, sending him to the floor. I scream at them to stop, but Royce wipes his chin, gets up, and charges Dylan with a waist tackle.

"Stop!" I keep yelling. It always seems romantic in movies when guys fight over girls, or for their honor. But this is just stupid. I'm mad at them both for letting it get out of hand.

As they go crashing into a bookshelf I hover around Kayla. I try to cover her in case they come flying our way. "Royce!" I scream. "Dylan! STOP!" No one listens. The two are tumbling over each other. Royce lands a punch, then Dylan rolls on top and gets his own punches in.

By the time Lo rushes into the room, Dylan and Royce are on their feet again, except other guys at the party are holding them both back. I'm mortified. I can't even look at Royce.

"Screw you guys," Royce spits. "Let me go."

"Yeah, let him go so he can run home to Beverly Hills," Dylan says, bleeding from his nose.

Royce's mouth drips blood from a cut. "I'm not going anywhere."

"I'm with you," Dylan says. "Let's finish this."

Lo, fuming, gets in both their faces. "Are you losers done? The only one who's going to finish this is me, right now. I'll kick you both out."

"Man, let me go," Royce says, jerking against the guys tightening their grips on him.

"Let him go," Dylan says. "He messed up my jacket! I'm going to kill him!"

"Come get me, then!" Royce says, taunting him. "I'm right here!"

I've never seen Lo angrier. She's whirling and screaming at both of them. "I said shut up! I'm not letting either one of you idiots ruin this party. You want to fight? Go down to

Stoney Point! I don't want any fighting here. I expected better from you, Dylan!"

Royce is breathing heavily. Dylan too.

Lo gets into Dylan's face. "You're done. Got it?"

Dylan starts to complain, but she cuts him off. "Enough!" she says. "You gonna chill? Do you really want to leave your band hanging? Or embarrass yourself any further?"

Dylan thinks for a moment. He looks down, as if considering his options. "Yeah. I'm done. Sorry, Lo."

After a nod from Lo, the boys holding Dylan let go. She moves over to Royce. "What about you, pretty boy? Done with your temper tantrum? I think you owe each other an apology."

"An *apology*?" Royce says.

Lo doesn't move. "Yeah," she says. "Apologize to each other for fighting. What? Is that more difficult than throwing fists? Too complicated for you guys?"

It looks like Royce wants to punch her too for a second. Then he looks at me. With my gaze, I plead with him to let it go and do what Lo says, for me. He closes his eyes and takes a breath. "I'm cool. Sorry for making a mess of your party." He looks at me. "Sorry, Jas."

When he looks at me, I know what this is about, why he was so ready to fight. He's angry about everything—the deportation trial, the leaked *Politico* article, but most of all, he's angry about the reality of losing me and not being able to do anything about it.

The guys holding on let go. Royce stretches his shoulders a little and wipes the blood off his mouth. He walks up to Dylan, who turns wary eyes on him. "Sorry," Royce says, and it almost sounds like he means it.

"Yeah, man," Dylan says. "Sorry too. We're cool."

"Yeah, no worries," says Royce.

They briefly shake hands and miraculously, it seems everything is settled and no one is mad anymore. As quickly as it started, it's over. I'll never understand boys.

Just then Kayla wakes up. "Did I miss something?"

"No," I say. "Go back to sleep."

41

I'm an immigrant and I will stay an immigrant forever.

—JUNOT DIAZ

I GET KAYLA some more water and make sure she's okay, then I go look for Royce. I find him outside, sitting with Dylan. Wait. What?

"Man, you gotta really get out there with your music, see the world," Royce says, taking a long pull from his beer. "Ever been to Copenhagen? The music scene there is wild. You need to check it out."

"Yeah, that sounds cool. We want to tour everywhere, even Canada."

They both laugh as if this is a huge joke. It's so weird how boys practically want to kill each other one moment, then they're best friends the next.

"You guys having fun out here?" I ask drily, trying to sound annoyed.

"Hey, babe." Royce looks up. "Here," he says, tossing me his car keys.

He's way off, but I catch them anyway. "What do you want me to do with these?"

"You have to drive. I'm wasted. Both of us are."

"Really?" I ask, trying not to freak out. What is he doing? He knows I can't drive!

Dylan holds up his beer. "We were getting to know each other. You know what, your boyfriend's pretty cool, Jas."

"I can't believe you guys are so drunk. Your band is supposed to play," I say, a little exasperated.

"Not to worry," Dylan says. "I have the set partially memorized."

"Partially?" I say, shaking my head, while Royce laughs his head off.

The music is a disaster. Doesn't matter. We're all having fun. Even the guys from The Clouds are having a great time, laughing it up. At first Julian was mad at Dylan and they had a few words. But Julian figures it's just a drunken jam session at this point, and though he normally doesn't drink and perform, he ends up tipping back several beers to join in the fun. Everyone takes things easy. Kayla's even up again after having slept things off. She's still slurring her words a little, but now she seems to be doing all right.

At one point Julian pauses at the microphone. The rest of the band stops playing. "Hey, everybody," he says. "First off, I need a break from this terrible music we're playing."

Everyone laughs at him. Lo shakes her head.

"More!" says Kayla.

"You'll get more," Julian says. "But I wanted to give a big thanks to Dylan for showing both his strong and sensitive side in the same night."

Royce is drunk as hell and lifts his beer. Dylan thumps his instrument and laughs.

These crazy boys. I'll miss them. Not just Royce.

Julian still isn't finished. "Finally, I want to say congratulations to all of you high school pukes who'll soon be getting on with the next phase of your life." He takes a drink. Guzzles his beer actually, which slightly grosses me out. If this is what college is like I'll actually attend fewer parties, I tell myself. I'm enjoying the celebration, but having this much drama all the time is just too much. Julian continues, "Lo, thanks for all the kick backs. You're my number one. I love you. I'm looking forward to our many adventures. We'll probably be at some gnarly protests in the coming year."

Lo smiles. She's beaming up at him. I'm so happy for her. This is what she wants, and she's going for it. Doesn't matter that it's not the same thing I would do for myself. This is her life. And she's happy.

"And one more thing," Julian says. "This next song, though I promise you it is going to be a total mess, goes out to Jasmine de los Santos. Whether you leave or stay. We love you."

They play me my favorite Bob Marley song, "Three Little Birds." At the chorus, everyone sings along, "Every little thing is gonna be all right!"

I'm still high from the song they played. I love my friends. Kayla's less than half-awake. She and Dylan talked a little and partially made up, but I told him I wanted to bring her back to my house for the night. They can talk more tomorrow. Royce is completely awake, but there's no way he can drive his car. It's past midnight and he's downing water, sitting in the passenger seat next to me.

"You're really going to make me drive?" I blanch.

"You've driven this car," he says. "What are you afraid of?" He's taught me a little in the parking lot by my school because he insisted I should really learn at some point. What if there's an emergency?

"Yeah, around the block a few times," I say. "That's different!"

"You only have ten blocks to drive," he says. "It's nothing. Then I'll sit in the car and sober up. You don't even have to wait with me. I won't drive until I feel totally fine."

"No way, you can sleep on the couch and drive in the morning. I'll tell my parents we all just crashed."

I guess I really do have to drive, then. The dashboard lights are on. Headlights too. I haven't even gotten my learner's permit. I'm not so scared about driving the car as I am about getting caught without a license. If I get caught, will I get deported even sooner? I really don't want to drive, but there's no way out of this. I'm definitely not calling any of our parents.

"Did I already start the car?" I ask.

"You already started the car," Royce says, trying not to laugh at me. "You just need to drive."

"Okay. Yeah. I can do this," I say, taking a deep breath.

"Just drive," Kayla says. "You'll do fine. It's only how far? Thirty miles?"

"It's like a mile," I say. "Maybe two."

I start to think that maybe I should just make them walk to my house, but there's no way Kayla will make it. Her eyes are half-closed.

"Oh yeah. By the way, what happened with Dylan?" Kayla asks. "Did he and I get back together?"

"I'm not sure," I say. "But he was very nice to you."

"Oh good," Kayla says. "I should text him."

I snatch Kayla's phone from her. "Not right now. You don't want to say something stupid. And I need you to help me pay attention."

Royce knows I'm stalling. "Will you drive already?"

I take a breath. "Yes, Mr. Blakely." I turn the wheel, give it some gas. My hands are trembling. Why am I so afraid? Everyone knows how to drive except for me. If there's ever anything I'm a big baby about, it's this, but Royce has been a patient teacher. He always points out we're not doing anything wrong, since I practice in a parking lot and I'm not driving on the road.

"You can go faster," Royce says. "You're not even going ten miles an hour."

"That's scary," I say. "What if I lose control?"

"Oh my God. You're not the drunk one," he says. "You really don't want us to drive."

Still, I make the car crawl along. I *do not* want to crash a car that can be associated with Congressman Blakely. Knowing my luck, the whole awful thing would end up on the morning news.

"This could take hours," Royce growls. "You can't go this slow, Jas."

"I'm not going to go any faster," I say. "I wasn't expecting this to be driver's education with a drunk instructor."

"You should have your license already," Royce complains.

"Well, I can't fix that at two in the morning. So help me out!"

Royce leans back in his seat. "I'll teach you some more this summer," he says, forgetting or in denial that I have to leave after graduation, which is two months away.

"Why don't you just navigate," I say.

Right then I look at the rearview mirror and see a police car flashing its lights at us. I slam on the brakes, terrified, my heart in my throat.

"What the hell?" Royce says. "He must be checking on Lo's party."

I knew this was going to happen. Just like the last time.

Bye-bye, America. Bye-bye, life.

"Goddamn it! I told you I was going to screw up!" I'm terrified.

"Chill out, calm down. Pull over," Royce says as the police cruiser makes a loud *bw-w-wip*. "You weren't drinking. You're fine."

"I'm *fine*?" I say, pulling over. "I don't have a driver's license! My family could end up in a detention center. Who knows if I'll ever see *you* again?! Oh my God. Oh my God."

"Maybe I should do th' talking," Kayla slurs.

"Shut up, Kayla," Royce and I both say. Royce looks like he's sobering up, especially when he realizes what's at stake.

It feels like an eternity as the officer gets out of his car and walks up to the window. He knocks on it and I roll it down.

"Good evening," he says, eyeing all of us.

I swallow my nerves. This can't be harder than performing in front of thousands at Nationals. "How are you, Officer? Busy night?"

"I'm fine," he says cheerfully. "But your friends there don't look so hot."

"They're not," I say.

"How come? You all been drinking at that party down the street?"

Did the officer bust Lo's house? Is everyone at the party in trouble too?

"That's what they were doing," I say. "I just stopped by to get them."

"So you weren't drinking? Just your underage pals?" He looks at me closely. "Why, pray tell, were you driving so slow, then? You were twenty miles under the speed limit. You could have caused an accident."

Just then Royce opens the door and throws up in the gutter. He hacks so hard I think it's going to wake up the entire neighborhood. This couldn't get any worse.

The police officer gets a whiff. He wrinkles up his nose.

"That's why," I say. "I have three blocks to make it to the safe zone. Any false move, as you can see, will be a catastrophe to this leather interior, which will then be a catastrophe to my life. Look at this car. If anything happens to it, I'm dead meat."

The officer takes a closer look. "You know, kids, I could take the two of you in for underage drinking."

"Yes, sir," Kayla and Royce say.

I can't imagine what Mr. and Mrs. Blakely would do when they found out their *good* son was in the drunk tank for the night. Kayla's parents wouldn't be too happy either, and mine would skin me alive just for being an accessory.

"You know you're lucky to have a friend like her," the officer says, motioning to me. He holds up a finger. "You get one shot at life. Just one. And when you mess up, you need to think, 'Am I taking advantage of my friends for my own selfish pleasure?'"

I can't believe he's not asking for my license or registration.

Royce is looking especially pale again. "Yes, Officer," he gurgles.

"Looks like you need to go," the officer says. "He's not looking so good. Get straight home. And for goodness' sakes, drive safely. This is a nice car."

"Yes, sir," I say. "Thank you, sir. Thank you."

The officer shakes his head and gets back in his car and drives away. Finally, I pull away from the curb.

Royce puts a comforting hand on my leg. "I'm sorry, Jas. I wasn't thinking."

I shake my head. I'm still so scared that my heart is thumping. What does it matter anyway? We're being deported.

"It won't happen again," he says. "I promise."

It can't. It's too scary. I can't take any more risks like this. I don't think my heart can take it.

42

For unlike my mother, I did not believe I could be anything I
wanted to be. I could only be me.

—AMY TAN, *THE JOY LUCK CLUB*

IT'S FINALLY APRIL 1. D-Day. Acceptance day, when all
the colleges send emails telling us our fates. I've been admitted to two colleges so far: Northwestern and Pomona. But
neither can offer me financial aid because of my legal status.
So every time I click on an email and read that I've been accepted into a school, I don't jump around joyously, since not
one of them has determined that I'm eligible for any kind of
tuition assistance.

That doesn't mean I don't feel some kind of momentary
exhilaration. I feel proud of myself for getting this far. But it
already feels like I'm missing out, like these acceptances aren't
meant for me, but for someone else worthy of attending those
colleges. Some other person with my name.

I'm starting to feel like I'm not the real Jasmine de los Santos. I'm her doppelgänger. The one who isn't American, the
one who didn't become a National Scholar.

Then I see the one I've been waiting for. The one I want.
An email from Stanford's Admissions office. This is heavy.
Even more important to me than the National Scholarship
letter.

I click on the email and it opens.

Oh my God.

I don't believe it. "I got into Stanford!" I yell. The letter says they will be sending financial aid information in the next mailing, which brings me a crazy burst of hope, but who knows what that means exactly. Maybe they're just sending me the forms to fill out. The letter doesn't mention that I've been awarded any financial aid.

Mom has been packing boxes. She gives me a sad sort of hug and is very subdued in her response. "I'm very proud of you. I only wish I could say that you would definitely be able to go in the fall."

"If we could only stay... This would be a great opportunity. Best of all of them." *And Royce is going to Stanford too*, I can't help but think. We could be together like we've been talking about.

"Let me see that," Dad says. He's just come in to grab another box. He's been stacking them in the garage.

I show him the letter, waiting while he reads for himself.

Dear Jasmine:

I take great pleasure in offering you admission to Stanford University. Congratulations! We know that you will bring something original and extraordinary to the intellectual community of our campus. We look forward to having you as a part of Stanford. We hope you accept!

You clearly have the intellectual energy, discipline and imagination to flourish at Stanford. Your distinguished academic and extracurricular achievements captured our attention as we read through nearly 20,000 applications.

Tell your family and friends and take the time to learn more about us as you make your decision. Please thank those teachers and counselors who have been your allies, who recommended you. They are in your cheering section and have played a part in this good news.

Our warmest wishes,

Joseph M. Bellow

Dean of Admissions

Dad hands it back. "Great, Jas. Is there a college you didn't get into?"

"Lots, Daddy, but only because I didn't apply to them," I say happily. My heart is beating hard. I want to go to Stanford so bad. More than anything, I mean, aside from staying in America, *this* is what I want. "But I want to go here. This is my dream."

"I know, sweetheart, I wish I could tell you that you can," he says, waiting for Mom to tape a box. He says to her, "You going to take all day? I could take a nap while I wait."

"Maybe you should," Mom says. "You're too cranky."

Dad grumbles.

All I can think of is going to Stanford and everything it means, all the doors that are going to be open for me. This is everything I've been dreaming of since I first thought about going to college. What if I wasn't deported? What could I do then? What would my life look like? My stomach hurts with the possibilities.

Dad shakes his head at Mom for getting the tape tangled.

"But we don't have to leave yet," I say stubbornly. "Can't we wait to see if Mr. Alvarado finds anything from the judge about our visa extension?"

"*Neneng,*" he says. "We're selling the house. We'll have to be out of here no matter what. There will be nowhere for us to live."

"But even if we sell the house we can move somewhere else. We can all live in Oakland or something. You can be closer to me."

Danny and Isko are passing through. "The A's are cool," Danny says. "And the Raiders."

"Since when did you get so interested in football?" Dad asks, shrugging his shoulders. "Forget about sports. Use your brain, like your sister." He taps the letter, which I'm still holding. "Why are you so in denial?"

My comeback is fiery. "Why do you give up so easily?"

"We've had this discussion," Dad says. "Besides, how can we afford it?"

"Stanford is supposed to be need-blind even to international students," I say, smacking Danny in the head with the letter for still smirking at me. "I'm going to fill out the financial aid forms when they arrive."

"You'll be wasting your time," Dad says.

"You're so negative, Daddy," I say. "This is why you should watch sports. It's not over until time is out. I still have hope. If not for all of us, at least for me."

Dad seems a little hurt by my comment, but Danny is suddenly excited. He starts jabbering about an NHL game he was watching on television. "I've seen the Los Angeles Kings down two goals come back and score three in the last minute to win."

Dad gives Danny a look. "Why don't you go finish packing your room?"

I pat Danny on the head. "Thanks, Dan," I say. This is one of the rare moments he's come to my defense. My brothers may be quiet about deportation and show a kind of excitement for the adventure, but I know they would be happier staying here. That's how cool they are. They may act selfish, but really they just want to please Mom and Dad. It's just in our genes.

Millie is almost as happy for me as Royce is. She's glowing as she reads the letter. I've propped her up on a bunch of her pillows so she can breathe better. It doesn't sound like she's improved that much, but she doesn't have to breathe with the oxygen supplement all the time.

"This is the most beautiful news," she says. "A lifelong dream is being fulfilled with one letter. Isn't that amazing, how that happens?"

"I'm excited," I admit. "I keep having this feeling that I can actually go. But so much has to happen for it to become a reality. Every day, I wake up thinking about how, if the money doesn't come, I can still hide out somewhere and secretly attend all my classes. I'm such a nerd. I love going to school that much."

Millie laughs. "That would certainly be adventurous. But to be homeless on top of everything else would be far too difficult."

"I guess," I say, giving up the fantasy.

"But it doesn't mean you don't keep fighting, Jasmine. We experience certain things that change us for a reason. It's not what happens to us that matters. What matters is how we react to it."

43

Hope is a waking dream.
—ARISTOTLE

LOS ANGELES PRIVATE schools have their proms later than public schools, so a week later, Royce picks me up to take me to his prom. Spring has come in full bloom in the city. The purple jacaranda trees are bursting with color, and the smell of orange blossoms fills the air. A few days before, we went to my prom, hanging out with the cheer team and triple-dating with Kayla and Dylan, Lo and Julian. It was fun and low-key, at the ballroom of the local Hyatt. We all went to Denny's after. I know Royce's prom is going to be a much bigger deal.

The Eastlake Prep prom has a 1920s Jazz Age theme, à la *The Great Gatsby*. Royce showed me the dance bids when they arrived earlier. The gilded invitations are gorgeous, with black backgrounds, gold art deco designs, and bold white lettering. The thing is, though, that the location is secret. We're supposed to meet at his school, then they'll let us know where to go for the prom.

I'm expecting big yellow school buses to be lined up in front of Eastlake Prep to take us to the secret location, but instead there are rows of limousines and smaller, older luxury cars that are taking students and driving away.

For an early graduation present, Millie said she would buy

my prom dress. She took Mom, Kayla, and me all over Beverly Hills in search of the perfect dress. I don't even think looking for my wedding dress someday will be such a big deal. It took hours, but finally I found the perfect gown.

Now I'm looking at my reflection in the tinted window of a posh black Bentley that's about to take Royce and I to the dance. The dress's white beaded bodice and sequins sparkle under the streetlights. I shift a little to check the asymmetrical hemline, which is just long enough to feel formal but short enough to show a little leg. I feel like a jazz-age Cinderella.

"You look very beautiful tonight, Jas," Royce says, a serious look on his face. His hands are shaking a bit when he slips the corsage over my wrist.

I want to make fun of him for being so formal, but I take pity on the boy and just say thank-you. "You don't look too bad either," I tell him with a smile.

In his black tux with gold cuff links, he's the picture of dashing, and it reminds me of the National Scholar dinner, which already seems like a lifetime ago. He opens the door and helps me inside the Bentley, and the driver follows some of the other cars onto the freeway toward downtown Los Angeles.

Royce and I are standing on the rooftop of the Standard Hotel and looking over the gorgeous, twinkling city lights in the distance. We're taking a break from dancing. I've met a bunch of people he's friendly with, who seem nice enough, and seemed happy to meet me. I wonder if he just doesn't give anyone a chance to be his friend. He's drinking punch, but I'm sipping a glass of water. That's the only downside of a white gown. You have to be careful when you eat or drink anything, and you have to be super careful about sitting down *anywhere*.

"Remember the night in D.C.?" Royce asks.

"Of course I do," I say, smiling. "I wasn't so sure about you then."

"What? You didn't fall in love with me immediately?" He puts hands to his chest as if I'm giving him a heart attack. "Wasn't I the best-looking guy there?"

He's a little peacocky about his looks, which is endearing. "Perhaps," I say airily. "But it took me a long time to fall in love with you—a whole night." One of the best nights of my life.

Royce takes my hand and I know he's remembering too. "Sometimes I think about who I should thank that we met. God? Destiny? My uncle for getting in a car accident on Topanga?"

"That's terrible!" I playfully slap him on the arm, then pull him close. "I'm sorry I'm so difficult sometimes."

"There's nothing to apologize for," Royce says, leaning his chin on my shoulder. We're so close, I can feel his breath against my neck. "You helped me figure out what I want in life. You give me courage to be who I am."

I start to choke up. His words make me want to cry.

"Oh man," he says. "My goal was definitely not to make my girlfriend cry on my prom night."

"Shush," I say. "Just kiss me."

Sunday night, Royce's dad is in town and we're supposed to have dinner with his family. I arrive early at the restaurant, since Dad was able to drive me—he had an errand on this side of town. I sit by the chairs in front of the hostess's desk and wait. A few minutes later, I hear a familiar voice and cringe. It's Mason, and he has a smug grin on his face.

"Well, if it isn't my fellow valedictorian," he says. Royce must have told him. "What, don't look so surprised. Just because I don't look like a nerd…"

"Did you give a speech?"

"No, I actually missed my own graduation. I was passed out from a party the night before. My parents were so pissed." He laughs as if it's the funniest thing in the world.

He's such a tool. "How's USC?" I ask.

"Boring as paint. But the girls are hot. You could give them a run for their money though. What are you doing with my brother anyway? Aren't you bored yet? Did you know he didn't learn to read until fourth grade?"

"Why are you so mean to him?" I say, utterly disgusted. What on earth is wrong with this guy? "Royce is your brother."

"You serious? That idiot is related to me?" he says, getting up to say hello to his parents who've just entered the restaurant. "Sit next to me at the table," he says, as if I would ever do such a thing.

I stay quiet at dinner. I'm a little shy around Royce's family after everything that happened with the private bill and the news leak. It's awkward, but everyone is being polite. Except Mason, who keeps leering at me or laughing obnoxiously in my direction. I can tell that Royce is about to lose it, but is trying to keep the peace.

Mr. Blakely keeps boasting about Royce attending Stanford, and Royce reminds him that I got in too.

Congressman Blakely cuts off a huge chunk of meat from his prime rib. "Never hear anything negative about Stanford, do you. The place is a dream. We'll get you set up in a real nice apartment too," he tells Royce.

"I want to live in the dorms, Dad, like everyone else," says Royce.

"You're getting him a better place than mine?" Mason frowns.

"Your place is nice," Debra says. "You're practically on campus."

"It's so slummy in downtown LA," Mason complains. "I'm getting really tired of that apartment."

"You'd better not be," Congressman Blakely says. "We pay good money for your tuition and residence."

Mason winks at me. "I'm trying hard. But all the foreigners around campus really drag the whole area down."

Debra looks horrified. "Mason, your grandfather was from Mexico City. And diversity has always been a strength of LA's."

"Nice PR, Mom. You sound like some bleeding heart," Mason snickers.

I get up to go use the restroom. "Excuse me," I say. "I'll be right back."

Congressman Blakely ignores me. "Mason, did you hear back from Columbia for next year?"

I find a bench near the restrooms and sit for a few minutes, thinking about how I wish I could go somewhere alone with Royce. Just when I'm about to head back, I run into Royce looking for me.

"Let's go," he says, as if he's read my mind.

"You're walking out on your family dinner?" I ask, shocked.

He doesn't answer; he just takes my hand, and we walk out of the restaurant and don't look back.

★ ★ ★

The Ferris wheel on the Santa Monica Pier spins in rotating neon pinwheels of greens, blues, purples, and reds against the night sky. You can't see the alternating red and yellow buckets. You can't see the people in them, though you can hear everyone's ecstatic screams from below. The wheel flashes from a pinwheel into a star, pulsating over the ocean, lighting up the tides like the water really is glowing.

Royce and I are sitting on the beach together, still wearing our fancy dinner clothes, staring at the neon. Even though I'm glad we've escaped Mason's toxic company, I worry. What will Royce's parents think of me for walking out like that? Maybe I shouldn't hold on to him just because I can. I have to let him go.

It's not hot or cold here. No breeze at all. Just the sound of the ocean and a sort of stillness, except for all the happenings on the pier.

"I love this place," Royce says. "There's something about the Ferris wheel and the ocean right next to each other." He smiles at me. "Reminds me of when I was little."

"Yeah, you've told me lots of times," I say, teasing a little.

"I guess I have. But I don't think I've told you why. See, my parents weren't wrapped up in politics then. Dad was a businessman. He knew politicians, but his focus was more on raising our family. And Mason… There was a time when he wasn't like that. It might be hard to believe, but he was all right. I see that Ferris wheel, and I remember good times."

The froth of a wave washes toward us but falls short.

"It's special, that's for sure," he says. "But you're even more special to me. I want you to know that you're the love of my life." His arm around me tightens.

I should let him go, I think, my stomach twisting as my heart beats loudly in my chest. I'm being selfish, holding him to me. But I can't. "I love you too," I say, holding him closer.

"So we have to talk about the future," he says.

"What future?"

"I brought you here so you can understand that there's a part of me that loves my father even though he isn't the best father. The part of me that loves my brother, even if he can be a turd."

I lean my head on Royce's shoulder. "I do understand. I like your Ferris-wheel story."

"Me too," he says. "I'm sorry I didn't say anything to Mason at dinner. I just didn't want to blow it up."

"It's okay," I say.

"I was glad you were there. But I'm more glad that you're here now," he says.

"I don't want to be anywhere else," I say, feeling happier now that we're alone together.

And then, I'm stunned. Royce stands up and pulls me to stand too. "I was going to do this at prom the other day, but I was too nervous." He brushes the sand off his pants, then gets down on one knee. He's holding a little box, and he opens it to show me a diamond ring. "Before she died, my grandmother gave this to me to give to the person I love," he says. "Jasmine, I love you. More than anything."

My heart flies out of my chest. It's spinning around in the neon of the Ferris wheel. It sails from there through the darkness above the clouds.

"Royce! What are you doing!"

"I want you to stay with me always. Will you marry me?"

Now my breath is completely taken away. I'm literally on the verge of passing out. My legs have never felt anything like this. My stomach. My chest. My throat.

"We're both eighteen now," he says, knee still in the sand. "We're in love. And this way you can stay here in America. We can be married and go to Stanford together. You'll be eligible for all those grants and loans. I want to be with you. I don't know what I'd do without you. What do you say?" He grins, happy, so beautiful to my eyes.

My heart is in my throat. I don't know what to say. We're so young, and we're still so unsure of ourselves, of who we are, who we're meant to be. What would our families think? And what would happen to my family? Would they be able to stay if I married him?

I know I love him. I can't sleep at night unless he tells me good-night. I think about him all the time, about his happiness. I can't imagine life without him. I know why he's doing this—because he can offer this from the depths of his big, generous heart. He knows this can save me, can fix all our problems. *I'll find a way*, he promised. *I'm not letting you go.* If I were in his place, if I was the one who could do this for him, I would do exactly the same thing he's doing now.

"Babe," he says. "Um, I don't want to rush you, but my knee is starting to hurt."

I'm on the verge of laughter or tears. I love him so much.

"Say something," he says. "Before my leg cramps."

"But how? When?"

"I don't know. We elope. Right away. Within a day or two."

"Okay," I say.

"Okay. What?" he asks.

"Okay, I will. Yes, Royce, I will marry you, yes," I say, and I pull him up to stand. We're crying and laughing.

Royce shakily puts the ring on my finger and we kiss

with all those neon lights spinning like luminescent flowers through the night sky.

I love him so much.

I'm going to marry him tomorrow. We'll be husband and wife, and I'll be able to stay in the country.

Everything's going to be all right, isn't it? It has to be.

44

A woman is like a tea bag—you never know how strong she
is until she gets in hot water.

—ELEANOR ROOSEVELT

AFTER ROYCE DROPS me off at home, I lie awake all
night, tossing and turning on my bed, thinking of the possibilities of our future. Royce and I will be together. We'll
have our own home. We'll get our own things. We'll both
be in school. We'll help each other every step of the way. Before we know it, both of us will have graduated from college.
We'll have pets, a dog and a cat. I've always wanted a dog, but
my Mom is allergic. We'll have a baby at some point—babies.
But not so soon. Still, this is everything I wanted. Stanford.
A meaningful career. A handsome husband. Two kids. We
can have it, can't we? Even if we get married at eighteen? I've
seen the statistics—they aren't good. What if this is a mistake?

What will our families think? What will they do? I can't
imagine Mom and Dad missing my wedding. Will my family be torn apart if I get to stay in America and they don't?
Will this open the door to helping get them back here? I
could sponsor them once I'm a citizen. I looked up the law.
If I marry Royce, I'm immediately eligible for a green card,
and I could be a citizen in three short years.

But what if they don't forgive me for marrying so young?

Or for this reason? I know Dad certainly won't approve. Will they ever forgive me?

And what about Royce's parents? They'll be furious, won't they? No one from their world gets married at eighteen. Will they blame me for stealing their son? And if they don't support us, what then? Will we truly be on our own? Does Royce have any money apart from his family? Should I even be thinking about that? It seems wrong.

I can't sleep. The doubts start to fade, though, when I think about Royce, kneeling in the sand. I'll never forget that moment. We've been through so much together and I don't want to let him go. I want this. I want to marry him.

I fall asleep to the euphoria that nothing else matters. Only Royce's love for me. Only my love for him. Who's the romantic now? "Only us," I whisper, drifting into a dreamless sleep.

The only person I tell about the proposal is Kayla. We're hanging out in her living room the next day. She's decided on CalArts, and I'm watching her scroll through photos of the residence halls. She's been there for me and I've been there for her, through good and bad. We both know this. So I give it to her straight—Royce and I are eloping.

She sets down her phone and stares at me. "Are you sure about this?"

"I think so," I say.

"That's not a hundred percent."

"Yes it is. I love him one hundred percent and more. But I'm only ninety percent sure I should marry him right now."

"Ninety percent? Is that good enough?" Kayla wonders.

"Why are you playing devil's advocate?"

"Because there's no one else around to be that little voice in your head."

"What makes you so certain I need one?" I'm annoyed, but I desperately need to talk to someone about this too.

She sits back, sipping from her glass of iced green tea. "Because this is a bigger decision than accepting an invitation to Stanford. Going to college may be life changing, but marriage is *really* going to change your life. Look at my parents, for one."

I don't say anything. I'm surprised by Kayla's response. I thought she'd be more supportive, think that it was so romantic of us. But instead she's practical, tough.

"All right," she says. "Say you go through with it. When? How?"

"The courthouse," I guess. "Very soon. A day or two. You can be our witness."

"Great," she says. "Make me hold the shotgun."

"He *asked* me. I'm not making him do this."

"Maybe not directly," she says. "But what other choice does he have to keep you? It's not like that judge has done anything for you. Or that lawyer. Or Royce's dad. If he wants to keep you with him, asking you to marry him is his only choice."

She's right. *I'll fix this*, he'd told me. *I'll find a way.* This is the only path ahead for us, and it's a heavy one. This conversation is starting to scare me. I want to be happy about our plans. But Kayla of all people has to go throw a dose of reality in my face.

She puts an arm around me. "This is exciting for you. You feel like a princess. I know—I can see it on your face. And that is the biggest diamond I've ever seen. But as your best friend, I just don't want you to make what could possibly be the biggest mistake of your life."

"How can it be a mistake? We love each other," I say hotly,

looking at the enormous ring flashing on my right hand. I wanted to show it to Kayla but I hid it from my parents.

"Since when does love mean you have to get married?" She purses her lips like a schoolmarm.

"When it means we'd be worlds apart if we don't! At least I'll be in America!"

"But at what expense? You're both only eighteen. Do you know how many marriages fail because the bride and groom were too young?"

"I know the odds."

"And it doesn't scare you?"

"I said I was ninety percent sure, didn't I? Of course I'm scared!"

"You should be. I just can't picture you as a married woman right now. Isn't he the first boy you've kissed?"

"Pretty much."

Kayla crosses her arms smugly. "Have you guys even had sex?" she asks.

"It's private," I say, but can't help but blush, thinking of the plans we'd made for after the courthouse.

"Fine, be that way! Well, think about it, then. He's the only guy you're *ever* going to sleep with. Are you okay with that?"

I nod. "I don't want anyone else. I want him. Only him. He's the only one for me, Kay. I know it."

"But don't you think you're both forcing things a little? I know how bad you want to stay. I want you to stay too. But I don't want you to get married and wake up every morning with so much pressure on your relationship. You'll only break his heart more if it doesn't work out in the end. What if you get divorced?"

Oh God. She has a point. We can't get married this way, can we? I shudder, suddenly cold. Marriages also end in divorce. So many things can happen. Marriage is a huge step, a huge reach. We're just at the beginning. What if Royce and I think we're saving our relationship but are actually dooming ourselves? I don't want that. I want us to have the best chance of forever. "What am I supposed to do, Kayla?" I cry.

"I don't know yet. Just promise me to wait at least one more day."

45

Marriage can wait, education cannot.

—KHALED HOSSEINI, *A THOUSAND SPLENDID SUNS*

I DON'T CONTACT the media. Mr. Alvarado has bit onto my bluff. "Just a few more days, Ms. de los Santos, if you can wait this long, you can wait a little longer," he says over the phone. "I have a call in to the judge. I'll get to the bottom of this as soon as possible." But I know he knows I'm not going to talk to any journalists.

For once I don't care.

I've got my own solution. Royce. Marriage. A brand-new life. Three days have passed. Even after my conversation with Kayla, I haven't changed my mind about marrying Royce. Sure, we're taking a risk, we're gambling with our lives, but I'm confident I'm doing the right thing. This is the only way to stay in America and the only way for Royce and I to be together.

I text Kayla to meet us at the courthouse at 1:30 p.m. She hesitantly agrees. It breaks my heart not to have my family there, but at least I have Kayla. I can't think of anyone better to be there. Except for maybe Millie, whom I haven't told for fear she might tell my mother. Both of them will find out soon enough anyhow.

Royce picks me up at my house. Mom and Dad are at work,

and Danny and Isko are visiting Lola Cherry at her retirement home. I never even used to go to parties, and now I'm sneaking out behind their backs to get married. It's surreal. I'm wearing a pretty white slip dress I bought at the mall the day before. Royce wears a black suit and tie to match, my handsome groom.

I get inside the car. As I sit down, I lean over and kiss him. He kisses me back, holding my chin gently with his hand. I'm going to remember this moment forever. It's our wedding day.

"Does anyone else know? Besides Kayla?" Royce asks.

"I might tell Millie," I say. "I'm not sure. What about you?"

"I'm not telling anybody until we're ready to make an announcement."

"An announcement?"

"We'll tell everyone and have a big reception somewhere."

"We will?" I try to imagine everyone being in one hall together after finding out what we did. My family glaring at his family. Our friends, wandering around confused. "I was sort of hoping we could just keep it on the down low for now," I say. "Maybe make a few phone calls and a Facebook announcement."

"I doubt that would be good enough for my family," he says. "They'll want a huge party. Yours would too. Somewhere nice. Dinner. A full orchestra. Dancing. My dad would want to invite his friends, dignitaries. This would be pretty huge."

"It would?" I can't imagine my family at such a fancy affair. Mom and Dad like to gamble during karaoke at the annual family Christmas party. Mom gets so annoyed if she doesn't win. She's pretty bored at any wedding where she can't sing her heart out to "Can't Help Falling In Love" and "Are You Lonesome Tonight?" What would she do with a bunch of politicians? Would she rope them into a thousand-dollar pool on karaoke?

I don't even want to think about telling anyone.

My parents are going to kill me. Filipino girls from nice families aren't supposed to elope. Everyone is going to think I'm pregnant, which is so untrue, especially as I'm still a virgin!

"Don't worry." He squeezes my hand. "I'll be there to keep you company."

"I know." I smile.

The Chatsworth courthouse is gray, rounded, almost like a prison, with half a dozen palm trees staggered outside the front steps. When I see the building I feel the magnitude of what's about to happen. A *secret* marriage. Who doesn't want this? Isn't every girl's dream to be married to someone so handsome and caring? More important, Royce is someone who appreciates me for who I am. He's my best friend. He doesn't care about what country I'm from or how my family is so different from his. He loves me for me.

I glance at his profile as we walk up the steps, so proud that he's mine. We'll be married, and I'll be able to stay in the country. Soon enough I'll be an American citizen. Just like that, I'll *belong*. I won't be stuck between two countries and cultures anymore. I don't know anything else except for America. Just this country. Just me being me. This country *owes* it to me. I smile at Royce.

I should be *happy*. I try to keep smiling, but I can't mask my feelings anymore. The closer I get to the front doors, the more I feel weighed down. I can barely breathe. I don't understand what's happening. I want to scream at myself. *Keep smiling! This is the best thing that's ever happened to you! Run in there and get married to your prince!*

At the same time, I'm horrified at my thoughts. *This country* owes *it to me?* Did I really just think that? Have I really been feeling this entitled all along? Just because I'm smart? That I believe I deserve to be American and so Royce is obligated to marry me?

I start to wonder what I've really done for myself. I've been so off-putting, ramming my agenda down everyone's throat, including Mr. Alvarado, who's really just trying to do his job, Royce, my family, Kayla. Everyone. I've been so ambitious, so sure that I deserve to be here, that I've allowed Royce to throw his entire world into chaos. Am I really so selfish that I would allow our relationship to be defined by my legal status? Do I really want to keep this moment from my family, the people who have cared about me my whole life?

Royce feels me come to a sudden stop at the top of the stairs.

My hand drops away from his.

"No," I say.

He stops too. "No, what?"

"This isn't the way to do it. There has to be another way."

Royce turns to me. "Jasmine. There is no other way. We have to do this."

I shake my head. "It's not right, Royce."

"What are you talking about? We agreed to this. We agreed to get married. It's the only way to keep you here. You're going to be deported thousands of miles away if we don't."

"The extension might still come through," I say, struggling to hold on to hope.

I know Royce wants to do this for me, but the time isn't right. My family isn't here and neither is his. And this isn't the way I want us to start our official life together. We're young. Way too young to make this kind of commitment.

"We don't know for sure yet that I have to leave," I say desperately.

"What do you mean? Of course we do," he says urgently.

"It will tear my family apart," I say. "I can't do this to them, or you."

"You're not doing anything to me. I *want* to marry you," he pleads.

"I want it too, but we don't really understand what we're doing. Either of us. Don't you see? This isn't brave. This isn't part of what I have to go through. This is a quick fix, a Band-Aid. All of this is going to explode if we go through with it. Can't you see the pressure it will put on us? Our families are already stressed right now, and we need to keep them together. I have to go through this deportation *with* them. Not apart from them."

Royce takes my hand as if he's going to pull me inside the courthouse, as if in his desperation to keep me here he'll force me to marry him if he has to. "I don't want to lose you," he says, stricken. "Please, Jas."

"I don't want to lose you either, but I'm scared that if we do this now, we'll lose each other some other way later. I love you, Royce, but I can't." Tears are falling down my face, and my heart is breaking, but I know I'm doing the right thing.

I try to turn away, but he still has my arm. His face is ashen.

Kayla is in the distance coming toward us.

"Babe," I whisper. I love him so much and it's why I can't do this to him, to us. I know I'm doing the right thing. "Please let go."

Finally, he releases my arm. Then I run toward Kayla and beg her to take me far away from here, anywhere.

46

I didn't get there by wishing for it or hoping for it, but by working for it.

—ESTÉE LAUDER

IT'S LATE. The thunderstorm outside dumps rain over the house. It sounds like marbles are falling on Kayla's roof and around the patio out front.

Her mom is gone for the weekend to some hotel hundreds of miles away in Avila where she can do a day spa and not feel like she's in Los Angeles. Kayla and I are watching a movie about a young astronaut falling in love with a girl who works at a flower shop. Neither of us are really paying attention to the movie or to the rain.

"I feel so bad for running out on Royce," I say. "I think I ruined his life."

"No, you didn't," Kayla says. "You probably saved it. Jas, you're both way too young."

I'm still heartbroken, thinking of the way he was looking at me at the courthouse earlier that day. "I never thought I'd be a runaway bride," I say.

"It's not wrong to come to your senses," Kayla says. "How many times over the past year have I had to wake up from something stupid I've done?"

"I just wish I could make him understand."

Kayla doesn't disagree.

"What's going to happen with you and Dylan?" I ask.

She lets out a sigh. I can tell she's not completely happy. Maybe we've both been impatient. "We're just trying to be friends right now," she says. She eats a mouthful of Doritos. Ever since cheer ended, we've both been on an awful junk-food binge. "We're taking things slower," she adds. "We're working through the stuff that happened when I was with Mason. And I want to make sure he supports my future in dance as much as I support his band. I don't want to end up as his little groupie. We're not like Julian and Lo. It's like they're thirty-year-olds. We're barely grown-up enough to decide where to get takeout."

We both laugh. I tell her I think that's probably Royce and me too.

"Have you heard from him?" Kayla asks.

"No." His silence is deafening.

"Have you tried texting?"

"Only about a hundred times." I check my phone again just in case. "I told him I was sorry, that I still love him."

"And?"

"And nothing." I put the phone on a coffee table.

"Maybe you should tell him to come over?" she says.

"I have. He hasn't answered."

Just then something hits the window in the living room by where Kayla is sitting. The curtains are drawn, so we can't see anything.

"What was that?" I say.

She gets up. "Could be your lover boy caught in the rain. I think I saw someone pass the window. He probably thinks my mom's home so he doesn't want to be too loud."

Kayla peeks out the curtains. "I can't tell because of the

rain. Whoever it is dresses nice. That has to be Royce's coat. He's pointing toward the front door. Maybe you should go out there so you lovebirds can make up."

My heart's beating fast. I don't care that he didn't text me back all day and made me worried sick about him. I was having nightmare visions of him racing on Mulholland and getting in an accident. I'm so relieved he's here. "I'll just talk outside with him for a minute," I say.

"Take as long as you want," she says, lying down. "I might take a nap."

I slip out the front door. The outside light isn't on. A neighbor's dog barks in the darkness. "Royce?" I say, not seeing him. "Where are you?"

"Is that you, Jasmine? Where's Kayla?"

Wait a minute. I know this voice. It's not Royce. "Mason? What are you doing here?"

He steps out of the shadows like he's been in a fight. His hair and coat are rain-soaked. He stumbles over a loose brick on the walkway. He's obviously been drinking. "I came to see my girl." He spits as the rain pours behind him. "Go get her now."

"She's not your girl," I say.

"Jealous are you? I knew it." Mason grins. "Come here, baby."

"Mason, stop it!" I say, when he tries to put his arms around me.

"You think you're too good for me, don't you, National Scholar. But you're just a mail-order bride and that's all you are. I can't believe my brother hasn't seen through you. You should have been long gone by now."

"What are you talking about?"

Mason snickers. "After I sabotaged that private bill Dad

was working on, I thought for sure you'd be on a boat back to China or wherever you're from. Honestly, I don't know what's taking so long."

My anger boils up through my twisting gut. So do tears. I don't say anything. I don't do anything. I'm numb.

"What did you say?" a voice asks from behind Mason. It's hard to see in the rain, but I'd recognize that voice anywhere.

Mason addresses the darkness. "Well, *someone* had to leak the story or her illegal family might have been allowed to stay here. Even Dad was on her side, and that's just wrong, to put aside his political beliefs just for his family. No one should get what they want."

Suddenly, Royce, also soaked, is behind his brother, grabbing him by the shoulder. "THAT WAS *YOU*?" he yells. "YOU LEAKED IT?"

"Surprise?" Mason laughs.

Mason liked taking away my toys and making me cry, Royce said the other day. Is that what I am to Mason? A thing?

When you're privileged, your life becomes a collection of things. Nothing's real. Not people, not their feelings.

Sabotaging my family's private immigration bill was a joke to him. My family's life, my future, was just a toy to be played with.

Royce punches Mason in the face but Mason ducks and hits Royce in the gut, sending him falling into the bushes.

"Royce!" I scream. "Don't hurt him!" I yell at Mason.

"Come on! Get up! You've never beat me in a fight!" Mason says, dukes up.

"Mason! What are you doing here?" Kayla says, appearing in the doorway. "Stop or I'll call the police!"

Royce gets up but this time he doesn't swing or kick. Instead he speaks calmly to his brother. "This isn't about me at all, is it? Or Jasmine. It's about Dad. You leaked the article to get back at him. You're using Jasmine to make a statement. You hate when anyone else gets attention from him."

"Spare me your five-cent therapy," Mason says.

"Mason, please. Dad loves you. I love you. You don't have to do this. You don't have to be this way." I've never seen Royce look so destroyed. First I broke his heart at the courthouse and now this. I want to help but I don't know how.

Mason stumbles backward, still cursing at Royce.

But Royce is adamant that Mason hear what he has to say. "I know you've been angry ever since he started spending all his time in Washington, but he still loves us."

"What are you talking about?" Mason says. "Want me to hit you again?"

"I'm talking about your feelings about Dad," Royce says.

"Feel this!" Mason punches Royce again, who goes down hard.

I start to help Royce but he waves me off and gets up again. "He loves you, Mason," Royce says. "I know he does."

"SHUT UP!" Mason screams. "THIS IS NOT ABOUT DAD!"

But Royce keeps on talking. "I know you think Dad doesn't love you. So you take it out on everybody else. I'm telling you right now, Dad hurts for you. He's just no good at communicating with us."

Mason looks like he wants to murder his little brother. His fists are balled. He grabs Royce with one of his hands and raises his fist. "Shut up!" he says, beginning to choke up. "Just shut up!"

"I won't," Royce says. "I love you, Mason. If you need to beat me to feel better, just do it." He's crying and I'm crying too.

"Stop it," Mason croaks, pushing Royce's chest so he has to take a step back to balance himself.

"The only person you're hurting is yourself," Royce says. "You'll slip deeper into someone you're not if you don't stop. You don't even like yourself."

Mason looks like he's about to throw another punch, but he ends up shoving Royce into the side of the house and stumbling into the rain. I run over to help Royce up, and when he gets to his feet he runs after his older brother. Kayla and I follow behind him.

The rain is coming down in sheets. Mason has collapsed onto the front lawn, having completely broken down. Royce gets down on the ground and puts an arm around him.

"I don't know what's wrong with me," Mason says, sobbing. "I'm so sorry. I'm so sorry."

"It's all right," Royce says. "It's going to be okay." Holding his big brother in his arms, he squints into the rain. "Jas, help me?"

"Of course." I run to him.

Kayla and I are standing in the foyer of Congressman Blakely's house. Mason has just been taken away by his mother into another room. In a low voice, Royce tells his father what happened at Kayla's house. He doesn't hesitate to describe how Mason admitted to sabotaging the private bill.

"He did that?" Congressman Blakely asks calmly.

Royce nods. He's done with his story.

Congressman Blakely grimaces with disappointment. "Anything else?"

"No, sir," Royce says.

The congressman thinks for a moment. "Get your friends home," he says.

"Right." Royce turns and sees me standing next to Kayla. Our eyes meet, and it's like he's seeing me for the first time since I ran away from him at the courthouse. He furrows his brows and faces the congressman again. There's a look of determination on his face, as if he just remembered something. "Dad?"

Mr. Blakely turns around. He looks at his son vacantly. "What is it?"

Royce seems especially brave right now. I don't know what it is, but the way he's standing there he looks like he's matured five years in the course of five hours.

"Will you call the judge now? And confirm the visa extension for Jasmine's family? For me?"

Mr. Blakely looks at his son and nods. He takes out his cell phone and dials.

47

We never know how high we are
Till we are called to rise;
And then, if we are true to plan,
Our statures touch the skies.

—EMILY DICKINSON

IT'S THE MIDDLE of April, and by the end of the month I have to let Stanford know whether I'm enrolling in the fall. Since I never received any financial aid confirmation in the mail, last Monday I asked the dean of students, whom I'd met at the National Scholar dinner, if he could help find out what was going on. He advised leaving a message for the financial aid office asking about my package.

When the phone rings, I figure I'll let the message go to voice mail, but the phone stops ringing and Danny comes running into my room.

"It's for you," he says.

"Who would call the house phone?" I say.

"I don't know," he says. "Some guy from Stanford."

"Stanford?" I drop the bracelets I'm holding and race for the kitchen counter.

"Hello?" I say. "This is Jasmine de los Santos."

"Hi, Jasmine. This is Richard Brown from Stanford University's Office of Financial Aid. I've been trying to get in touch with you for a few days now."

My heart pounds. "Sorry, Mr. Brown. I've had a crazy week."

"I don't normally make calls," he says. "We usually send out letters to award recipients, but I had some extra time and wanted to call you and let you know personally that you are receiving a full financial aid package from our university, should you choose to enroll."

"I'm eligible for financial aid?" I whisper. "You know I'm not a citizen or a green-card holder?"

"Yes, we do," he says, as if it's not a big deal at all. "Stanford subscribes to a need-blind admissions policy, and as an international student, you've been awarded a patron grant by a Stanford alumni. There are only a few of them available."

"Wait," I say, catching my breath. "I don't understand. What's a patron grant?"

"It's a rare grant, and in your case will pay for much of your education here at Stanford. Around the same time we received your financial aid application, our department also received a grant that was specifically designated for you. You've also received several other smaller private grants and scholarships to cover your tuition. We'll be notifying you about all of those. Have you made a decision about attending Stanford? I know many students don't accept admission until they've been able to figure out the financial situation."

"I want to attend Stanford," I say like an idiot.

"That's wonderful news. You'll need to contact Admissions to officially accept. The deadline is May first."

"I'll do it right away," I say. "I'll get right on it."

Yet in the back of my mind, I'm still wondering whether I can go. There's still the matter of being able to stay in the country after all. Royce's dad called the judge and pressed for a delay of deportation and reminded him that we were supposed to get temporary visas, but as usual, we haven't heard if it was granted or not.

"Congratulations, Jasmine. This is a wonderful opportunity. We're so happy to have you at Stanford. Do you have any questions for me?"

I'm still in shock. "No... Yes. Just one question. If an alumni specified a grant for me, may I know who that person is?"

"Sure. I have that information right here..."

I can't believe what's happening. This news is so wonderful. It's as if my dreams are slowly unfurling in a breeze, only they're way up on a hill that I still have to climb. I'm so excited. At the same time, I'm feeling selfish again. If our visas don't come through soon, I don't know if I can ask my family to risk being thrown into a detainment center just because I want to attend Stanford so badly.

"Here it is," Richard Brown says. "The patron is Amelia Florence Marsh. She graduated forty years ago. She was one of the first women to graduate with a chemistry degree from Stanford."

When I call Millie to thank her, I'm glad to hear she's breathing easier. "I can't believe you did this for me."

"Did what?" she asks.

"Stanford. The grant?"

"I didn't ask them to give it to you, Jasmine. Did they tell you that? I said I wanted them to choose an incoming female student who would use her education to give back to the world. The grant committee chose you. You earned it all on your own."

Wow. I can't believe it.

"I know you're still unsure if can stay, but you know what?

Now you know you're truly good enough to go anywhere in the world. You have so many options. You just have to keep your eyes open to them."

As I hang up the phone, Dad walks into the kitchen, looking for a box to pack.

I know I need to tread on gentle ground with him right now. "Stanford just called, Daddy. I've been awarded enough financial aid to attend all four years."

I don't tell him about Millie. It'll make him think the award is pity money.

"That's great," Dad says. "Do they know you're getting deported in June?"

"No! I can't leave America. None of us can leave now! This isn't just about me getting into Stanford. This is money to attend. This is everything. This is my future."

"Tell that to the US government," he says. "We skip out on deportation, and we could lose all our assets and sit in a detainment center playing solitaire for five years."

I don't say anything. He's right. I can't expect them to live under the pressure, especially since there's a significant chance none of us may ever gain citizenship if we don't follow the rules.

"It would be worse than bad," he says. "You see those people who get kicked out? They have nothing. That's where we would be if we took too many risks. I'm sure they can take away all that scholarship money too, along with everything we own."

"But Royce's dad called the judge and asked him to change his mind," I insist. "We heard him talk to him on the phone. He said it would all work out."

"Well, where's our extension, then?" Dad finally finds a

box. He picks it up and opens the folds. "It's okay if we leave—we can eat Filipino food all the time."

I give him a weak smile. "How do you deal with all of this, Dad?" I ask. "Us leaving. Without being too sad? Without shutting down?"

"Ah, Jasmine. My girl," he says, beckoning me to come to him. When I go over, he holds me with his strong, fatherly arms. "This world is filled with families who don't have wonderful daughters like mine."

48

All happy families are alike.

—LEO TOLSTOY, *ANNA KARENINA*

ROYCE COMES OVER LATER. We still haven't had a real chance to talk since everything that happened at the courthouse and at Kayla's house, several weeks ago. I know that his family just sent Mason to rehab in Utah. They all went, and Royce just got back from the airport.

He's tired and his eyes are red-rimmed, but from lack of sleep or crying I don't know. It upsets me though. I hate when he's sad, and I'm about to make him sadder.

"Everything okay?" I ask.

"Yeah. He's going to be there for three months, Dad sprang for the full program. Mason's already joking that he's transferred to Circa Lodge instead of Columbia," he says, naming one of the most expensive rehabilitation centers in the country.

We laugh together.

"Hey," I say gently. "I got a grant to go to Stanford."

"That's awesome. Of course you did—you're amazing." His eyes are shining.

"If only the judge granted our temporary visas like he told your dad he would. I know your dad's office is working on following up but we haven't heard anything," I say. "If only we could stay."

He nods. "If only."

"I have to return this to you," I say, and remove the ring from my pocket. It seems wrong to keep wearing it. "I want you to know that you made me the happiest person in the world when you asked me to marry you."

He nods again. He takes the ring and puts it away. His lips are trembling and I can't stand it.

I put a hand on his face, feel the stubble there. "I will marry you one day, Royce Blakely. I promise."

He puts a hand over my hand and smiles, sunshine through the rain. "You're going to keep that promise."

A few days later, at home, we're all preparing for graduation. Dad buys my cap and gown and I try it on in the living room. It feels like everything is ending so quickly and I don't know where I'm going to go next.

"I have to iron it," I say.

"I don't know," Dad jokes. "It looks good all wrinkled."

"We'll iron it," Mom says.

"What are you going to wear underneath it?" Lola Cherry says. Before I can answer, Lola is already talking again. "I remember this one girl. Lilibeth Bautista. She didn't wear anything. She was painted with words. She let all her favorite boys write their name in yellow paint anywhere they wanted."

I burst out laughing. Mom's horrified. "My daughter is *not* going to do that. Stop putting images inside her head, Lola Cherry." She turns to me, looking me up and down. "You hear me? No boys are painting your treasure."

"Why not?" Lola says. "Nobody will know except for Jasmine."

"I don't want to see Royce's name anywhere either. You hear me?" my mom says.

I start laughing even harder at that. "No way!" Then I imagine what Royce would think if he did see his name written on my skin under my gown. It could be pretty sexy, put a smile back on his face. *Thanks, Lola Cherry.*

Dad doesn't say anything until now. He pouts. "My graduation was never that exciting…"

Lola starts laughing. "See? Your father understands."

"Anyway, enough about that. I need a new dress."

"All right. But no funny business," Dad says. "Mom will take you to buy one this week."

I give him a big hug, because no matter what, no matter how old I get, I'm still Daddy's favorite.

Suddenly, Lola whacks Dad in the leg with her cane.

He yelps and curses in Ilocano. "What was that for?"

"I want your attention," she says.

"You could have just asked!" he says, rubbing his leg.

"I have an idea," she says.

Dad looks very agitated. "I can see that. More like I can *feel* it."

Mom and I giggle. I hope I get to do whatever I want when I'm older just because I can get away with it.

"That's why you hit me?" Dad says. "No."

Lola swings her cane again.

This time Dad gets up. "I'm going to take that from you. It's not a weapon."

"I know," Lola says. "It's an attention getter. Jasmine says that Royce's dad called that judge and the visas were granted."

"Yeah, we heard that before," says Dad.

"Call him again. You can't just sit around and wait! You need to remind people to do their jobs!"

"We have been calling, but there's no news."

"Call him again! Call until there is news."

"She's right," I say. "Let's keep calling."

"Fine," says Dad. "What can it hurt?"

A few days later, we get a message back from Mr. Alvarado telling us to show up at his office at 1:00 p.m. We're ten minutes early. We're all getting out of our car, wondering why he needs to see us.

"Why are we here?" Isko says.

"I don't know," Dad says. "Your sister got a message from this snake of a lawyer that requested the entire family arrive. I thought we should have hidden you children in the closet before we left."

"What? Why?" Isko says.

Dad opens the car door. "This could be the moment they catch you."

Isko gets out. "Who catches me?"

"ICE," Dad says.

"Stop trying to scare them," Mom says.

She gives Dad a sideways look. He goes quiet.

"What's ICE?"

"US Immigration and Customs Enforcement," I say. "They identify undocumented people and arrest them, even in churches."

Isko ducks behind me. "They're *here*?"

"Stop it," Mom says. "Both of you. Jasmine, you know better."

Dad laughs. "I'm just messing with you. This lawyer probably just wants to say his goodbyes and have us sign a final form."

"Do we have to sign them too?" Isko asks.

No one answers him.

Mr. Alvarado greets us at the door. "I'm so glad all of you came. Have a seat."

"Where do we sign our final papers?" Dad asks as we all find chairs. He sits closest to Mr. Alvarado's desk. Mom is next to him. "Let's get this over with."

Mr. Alvarado sighs. "I'm afraid that's not why you're here, Mr. de los Santos."

"Don't tell me it's gotten worse? We're planning to leave in two weeks as required," Dad says. Our house hasn't sold yet but Lola Cherry will wire us the money when it does.

"There's been a development," Mr. Alvarado says.

"What kind?" Dad says angrily. "We've jumped through every possible hoop we could. What does Uncle Sam want now? Our savings? Do they want us to leave right now?"

Mom puts an arm on Dad's leg to try to calm him.

Mr. Alvarado is holding a pen. He taps it on the desk. "I received a phone call from Judge Reynolds," he says. Every one of us holds our breath. I feel like I'm at my first cheer competition ever, standing in front of an audience, scared to death.

It feels like the silence lasts forever. Then he says triumphantly, "Judge Reynolds has personally informed me that your deportation has been canceled."

"Canceled?" Dad says.

Mom grabs Dad with one hand. The other she puts over her mouth. "Oh my God! What changed his mind?"

"If you choose to stay in America," Mr. Alvarado continues, "your family will be allowed to live under temporary work visas until you get your employment-based immigration visas, which have also just been approved."

"What?" I say, cheering happily. "I can't believe it! We can stay! I can go to Stanford!"

"We can stay?" Isko says, jumping up.

For a second Danny doesn't move, then he gets a big smile on his face and jumps up with Isko, nearly tackling him.

I'm trying to text Royce, **Your dad did it!!! The judge reversed his decision!!! We don't have to leave!! We can stay! And I'm going to Stanford! With you! Oh my God!!!** I really can't believe it. It feels like a dream.

Royce answers back: yes!!!!! i knew it!!! YES!!!!

I don't really believe it, and it feels as if this great weight is lifted from my shoulders. I didn't realize how much stress I was carrying until it was gone. I'm so thankful.

Mr. Alvarado tries to talk over our shouting. "If you play your cards right, within a few years your daughter can apply under a different visa that has to do with persons of exceptional ability. She will of course have to obtain an advanced degree. Considering the path she's currently on, I don't foresee any problems with that. In addition, these visas mean you will all be eligible to apply for green cards, and later on, citizenship."

We're hardly listening. We're all jumping up and down cheering and hugging.

"And actually you do also have to sign some papers," Mr. Alvarado says.

We're still not listening.

"I told you this lawyer was going to pull through for us!" Dad says.

"I just can't understand how this happened?" Mom cries.

But I know how it happened. I think about Congressman Blakely and the phone call Royce asked him to make after his fight with Mason. Royce did it for me, for his family, for himself. He always offered his help, and I'm glad I finally accepted it.

Mr. Alvarado sits back and shakes his head. He's grinning like we're the most insane people he's ever met, but I don't care what anyone thinks about us. The de los Santos family will always stick together.

49

When the whole world is silent, even one voice becomes
powerful.

—MALALA YOUSAFZAI

IT'S JUNE, the month I thought I'd be dreading because it
would mean having to leave America forever. But instead,
my future, my glorious future, lies in front of me, as perfect as it was at the beginning of the year. Even more perfect, maybe, because it was even more hard-earned. The sun
shines brightly over the hundreds of people packed into the
stadium and on the field for my graduation. It's a beautiful
Southern California day, with a perfect cloudless sky and a
comfortable seventy-five degrees.

A few days before, I'd attended Royce's graduation and
watched with pride as he took the top prize in Language
Arts. His graduating class was much smaller than mine, and
the ceremony was held at the Walt Disney Concert Hall. The
girls all wore white dresses underneath their graduation robes,
like the bunch of debutantes that they are. Royce spent the
whole time texting me from the stage.

royceb: i'm so bored. glad i'm not giving a speech like you.

jasmindls: You look cute up there.

royceb: thanks you look cute from up here too. 😈

Meaning he can see down my cleavage because I'm wearing the red dress I wore to Spago, naughty boy.

Now I'm sitting up on the stage at my graduation and going over the speech in my head. From where I'm sitting, I can see that the stadium is packed with everyone's family and friends. I can barely make out my parents and brothers near the fifty-yard line. Royce is sitting with them, looking so handsome with his hair slicked back and wearing the tie I bought him with the Philippine flag on one side and the American flag on the other. When my phone buzzes, I remove it from the pocket of my gown as surreptitiously as I can. The ceremony hasn't started yet—I feel safe doing this. It's Royce, of course.

royceb: you look cute up there.

jasmindls: Wait till you see what's under my gown.

royceb: 😄 man, you're killing me.

royceb: my imagination has gone wild.

jasmindls: 😈 Good things come to boys who wait.

royceb: all right, now I'm not going to be able to listen to a word you say.

royceb: good luck, you'll be great.

royceb: who knew public schools could have such cool speeches?

royceb: just kidding.

jasmindls: Yeah, public schools even have teachers! Imagine that!

I try not to laugh as I put away my phone. The ceremony's starting, but I don't pay attention to the opening remarks or anything. I'm still going over my speech, which is different from the one I'd planned to write in November. Very different. Plus, I'm not the only valedictorian up here. I'm sharing the honor with another senior, Amanda Hiller, who's going to MIT for Robotics. If a bad bout of Valley fever hadn't made her grades dip her junior year, I probably wouldn't be standing next to her. After everything that's happened this year, I'm fortunate to be here. I had almost taken it for granted.

Amanda gives her speech, but I can't hear a word she's saying. I keep going over mine in my head, it has to be perfect. It might be my last chance to make a difference in high school.

When Amanda finishes and Principal Lopez begins to introduce me, I feel an irrational desire to jump off the stage and run away. But I square my shoulders and make my way to the podium. After I readjust the microphone I gaze out again. This time I look at the graduates. Hundreds of familiar faces. Not a single graduate is unhappy. Some are obviously bored. Their parents appear far more anxious. They're the ones who, like my parents, really understand how unpredictable the world can be.

I decide impulsively that I have to address that first. "There is so much uncertainty in the world," I begin. "We graduates often don't see this as young people. Especially today. To us, everything is attainable. We can do anything. Our choices don't matter to us as long as we feel we're moving forward. But our parents, especially mine, they're the ones who really understand that there are obstacles on our path. We all must be prepared for sudden change." I take a breath. People seem to be listening. Even Kayla, who's sitting in the third row, along with my friends from math group, cheer, even the football players. Now I can begin my actual speech, the one I worked on so hard with Royce these last few bittersweet weeks.

"Dear graduates." My voice is just above a whisper. I clear

my throat and continue a little louder this time. "I want to tell you about hope during these uncertain times of change. Many of you know that not too long ago I found myself in a situation that appeared, especially to me, hopeless. I always thought I was a legal resident of this country, someone on the path to becoming American, but guess what—I wasn't. My family was here illegally. For a while, I believed that I had lost everything. My future, my country. The barriers seemed insurmountable. Deportation loomed like a leviathan.

"We learned about Thomas Hobbes's *Leviathan* in Mr. Maynard's history class. Thank you, Mr. Maynard. We will miss your many references to the latest teen dystopian movies."

The students chuckle a little. I feel lighter. I can get through this speech.

"Mr. Maynard, like every other teacher, taught us something about ourselves. For each of us, this is a little different. We're all unique creatures. Though maybe some of you are more like monsters."

I pause while the crowd laughs, especially the parents. Somehow, people are listening. My knees have stopped shaking. My voice sounds more confident.

"I promise I won't give you a history lecture, but I want to quote a few of these bits from history, from *Leviathan*, which was written in 1651, more than a hundred years before our own Declaration of Independence. One of the things Hobbes believed in was a Kingdom of Darkness. He didn't mean Hell though. He was talking about the darkness of ignorance. True knowledge, he thought, was light. Graduates, we must not be ignorant. What you—what *all* of us—have to do in the coming years is to seek the light of true knowledge for the good of society.

"In my case, when I found out that I was going to be deported because I wasn't in America legally, I lost sight of who I was. I thought a piece of paper defined me, that I was a different person, lesser. But throughout this entire year, I've learned that who I was never changed. I let what the law said about me—that I, as a human being, was illegal, that I didn't belong in the place I'd always known as my own home—change my own perception of who I am.

"When I sat down to write this graduation speech, I thought about how these things are supposed to be filled with advice. I thought, 'Who am I to give my fellow students advice? What will I say?' And I could come up with only one thing.

"No one—not the law, not a college admissions officer, not your friends, not your teachers or parents or any other people, can define who you are. The only person who can do that is you. Even though you can't control the things that happen to you, you *can* control your perspective and your actions. There's never a moment you can't choose who you want to be.

"But we have to take that even further. Life isn't only about figuring out what we need. We need to figure out how to help others too.

"We have to ask ourselves: What can we do to better ourselves and our country? What can we do to be remembered? Who do we want to be?" I ask, echoing Suzanne's words during our trip to Washington, D.C. "Our Constitution has always been a living, breathing document capturing not just one moment of change in time, but an ongoing transformation taking place even today.

"As for me, I was lucky enough to be granted a stay of deportation and a temporary visa that will allow my family to apply for green cards and the chance to be citizens of this great nation. As a citizen, I'll fight those individuals and companies who benefit from the backs of the most disenfranchised among us, who profit from deportations, detaining and imprisoning entire families in overcrowded detention centers within our borders, deliberately destroying the American dreams of millions of people every day.

"I urge you to find your passion. Follow the light of true knowledge. Find what inspires you. Find what makes you passionate, what helps you recognize the sense of justice already burning within your heart. Give voice to the voiceless, help to the helpless, be a haven for those who have no recourse, no resources. Keep fighting—for your own sakes, and for the future of our country. Thank you."

The applause is deafening and the audience is on their feet, but I don't really see or hear any of it. I'm too busy smiling at my family, at Royce, at Kayla, all my friends and teachers, everyone who has been there for me.

Even though this moment is supposed to be mine, it's bigger than that, bigger than me. It's not just about one undocumented immigrant, but for everyone with a dream and a will to succeed. I love my country, and I won't stop until I count myself among its citizens.

50

Life is not measured by the number of breaths we take,
but by the moments that take our breath away.

—MAYA ANGELOU

THANK GOD NO one bought our house. Otherwise
where would we have my graduation party? When Dad walks
through the front door with some last-minute groceries, Bob
Marley Lives has already sound-checked and is starting a set.
Dylan is really rocking out. Julian's vocals are scratchy and
swoon-worthy.

"What is this noise?" Dad says.

I laugh. "It's music!"

"These are your friends? Did they just get out of prison?"

"No, Daddy." I hang on to him, which makes him soften.
I've always been a Daddy's girl. "Thanks for letting everyone come hang out."

Royce arrives early. He's beaming and partially hidden
behind the second-largest bouquet of flowers I've ever seen.

"Hi, baby," I say, trying to kiss him without getting pet-
als in my face.

"Am I late?" he asks.

"No, you're right on time."

Familiar faces fill the house. It seems like everyone I know
is here. Coach Davis. Mrs. Garcia. My cheer girls. Lo and

her posse. The student council. The math club. The California Scholarship Federation kids. A few guys from the football team.

Dad harrumphs. "Help your mother in the kitchen."

Mom calls to me like clockwork. "*Neneng!* I need your help. You have to take these platters out to the table. You can't let our guests starve. Haven't I taught you any better?"

I wave to Dylan and Julian as I cross through the living room. My brothers rock out in front of the band while Kayla dances next to them. She thinks they're hilarious, and I'm so happy to see her smiling and laughing. It seems like the past year has been so tense that often our laughter was forced. Not now. Not today.

I can't think of anything I'm not grateful for.

The kitchen is filled with the usual mountain of food. Mom is teaching Mrs. Blakely how to stuff and roll lumpia while Lola Cherry and Millie sit together, telling stories about their long, crazy lives. Olivia is rolling around the living room on her scooter, a little dangerous given the size of the room (tiny) and the crowd (large), but no one seems to mind. Mason is still in that rehab center in Utah.

The other day Mom found out from some friends in the hospital that the "big donor" who wanted all the undocumented workers fired was none other than Congressman Blakely. It's funny—he was part of our crisis, but he fixed it too. Things come full circle. With Royce's help, I was even able to put the book of stories together and print a few copies for the patients.

Not to mention, when I thank Congressman Blakely once again for what he did for my family, he mentions that he was able to sway the judge with Senator Lauren Silverton's help. As a high-ranking Democrat, she pulled some strings of her own. "I get by with a little help from my friends," he says with a wink.

I watch as Lola hooks him with her cane and pulls him over. "I have a question for you," she demands.

Surprised, Congressman Blakely takes her hand. "Well, aren't you a beauty?" he says.

Lola raises her eyebrows. "Why, thank you."

"What do you want to talk about?" he asks. "Health Care? Social Security?"

"Why would I care about that?" Lola shrugs her shoulders like she's confused. "I want to know about the other good-looking congressmen! Are any available?"

Millie laughs with Lola.

As he passes by the table, Dad pats Royce's dad on the shoulder. "Be careful with that one. She's worse than a teen-ager."

Congressman Blakely looks helpless.

"What do you need help with, Mom?" I ask.

"Get that thing out of the refrigerator," she waves.

I twist around to reach for the fridge. "What thing?"

"That thing!" she says.

"Ay!" I say. "You can never say what you mean." I start to open the door, waiting for more instructions, when I see a small package labeled with my name on it. "What's this?" I take it out. It's light.

Mom comes over and hugs me. "Don't you know what to do with a gift?"

I look around. Mom and Dad are smiling. The music is blasting. I tear open the package. Inside is a small box. I lift the lid to find a gold ring with a deep red stone. It's a class ring. The center is engraved with the Stanford Tree.

"Mom! Dad!" I yell. "Thank you!"

I look at Royce sitting next to Lo's friends. He winks at me. "Look on the inside," he shouts out over the music. "I told them to engrave something."

Following his directions, I find Stanford's motto etched on the band: *Die Luft der Freiheit weht.* I've been spending all my free time reading up on as much about Stanford as I can. I've already memorized the translation by heart.

The wind of freedom blows.

"We had a little extra money when we started saving up to leave," Dad says.

I start tearing up just as Kayla enters the room.

"Bawling again?" she laughs. "Pretty ring. Put it on already. Your brothers and I want you to join us."

"That music," Dad says. "We're all going to be deaf."

"I like it!" Lola Cherry yells.

"Me too," says Debra.

Mom suddenly goes frantic. She runs over to the stove. "The lumpia is going to burn!"

"Come on," Kayla says. "It's finally time to celebrate. Let's dance!"

But it's Royce I want, and I walk over to him.

"Hey," I say. "Dance with me?"

"Sure. We made it, Jas," he says, his eyes soft. "We're going to Stanford together. It's like some kind of fairy tale, isn't it?"

"So I'm Cinderella?" I ask. "And you're supposed to be Prince Charming?"

He smiles. "Something like that..." He's always been the softer one of the two of us, the more romantic one. We complement each other. He's strong where I'm weak, and the other way around. "Yup, just like a fairy tale," he says.

"Except hopefully there aren't any talking mice in our dorm rooms at Stanford."

I move to slap him on the arm, but he catches my hand. His touch still sparks everything inside me.

Royce holds my fingers up to the light, admiring my class ring. I think about how shackled I felt all year, about how hard I had to fight to get here, about the inscription on the inside of the ring—*the wind of freedom is blowing through me*—and how it perfectly sums up this moment.

"You're wrong, love. It's not a fairy tale," I say, leading him to join the party so we can dance together. "It's better. It's our life."

★ ★ ★ ★ ★

author note

Dear Reader,

While Jasmine's story of being a top student who discovers she is an illegal immigrant is not my story, it is very close to my heart and my experiences.

The National Scholarship Award in the book is a fictional creation, inspired by the Westinghouse Prize, the Presidential Scholarship and National Merit Scholarship programs. (In high school I won both the Presidential Scholarship and National Merit awards.)

My family moved to the United States in 1985, when I was thirteen years old. My father had a business/corporation visa that allows its owners to apply for a green card after three years. During this process, however, our family was scammed by a shady immigration attorney (and sadly, a friend of my father's) who never filed our paperwork with the INS. My father decided to file the paperwork for adjustment of status on his own, without a lawyer's help.

While we were waiting for approval, I was a senior in high school and applying to colleges. We were unsure if I would qualify for financial aid. My family was here legally, but we did not yet have our green cards either. My parents assured me that they would find a way to afford college no matter what, but we were hoping that I would qualify for financial aid.

Jasmine's anxiety, ambition, and determination are based on my own high school memories, and her passionate love for her country is rooted in mine.

Like Jasmine, I was accepted to several elite colleges whose offer of acceptance did not include financial aid. I was starting to get very nervous, until the glorious letter arrived from Columbia University granting not only admission but an incredibly generous financial aid package. Because I was not eligible for the Pell Grant (a federal grant that covers the neediest students), the school offered a privately funded grant.

Columbia is one of a handful of schools in the nation that offers financial aid to its students regardless of their citizenship status. It is without a doubt the single most important factor that changed my life and made me who I am today. I am here because of the generosity of wealthy patrons at my private school that funded my education at the Convent of the Sacred Heart, and the equally generous and far-reaching policies of my alma mater.

I have my US citizenship today because of the help of friends connected to congressional leadership and because I fell in love with an American guy. I was over the age of twenty-one when my parents received their green cards, which put me once again in a legal gray area (this loophole is now closed, and people who were brought into this country as children but are adults when the approval comes through now also receive green cards).

After my husband and I married in 2002, I applied for a green card. However, when our approval came, we had moved from New York City to Los Angeles and never received the letter with the date of my interview. My file was marked "dead." After I waited for a few more years and asked around for help, one of my best friends from college with ties to a local congressman asked the congressman if he could help pull my file. I was interviewed for my green card in the congressman's office, the equivalent of being moved to the top of the VIP immigration line. Two years ago, I finally became an American citizen, after twenty-eight years in this country. I will be able to vote for the very first time in this presidential election.

I hope you find Jasmine's story enlightening and moving, and that I have done justice to the story of the struggle so many millions of people experience in their journey to become American.

Thank you,
Melissa de la Cruz

acknowledgments

I AM SO grateful to so many people, but will start with my editor, Natashya Wilson, who not only asked me to write this book but helped me shape it to the best it could be every step of the way. Thank you so much, Tash, from the bottom of my heart for the opportunity to tell this story and your loving care in bringing it to light.

Many thanks to the amazing team at Harlequin, including TS Ferguson, Lauren Smulski, Margaret Marbury, Shara Alexander, Evan Brown, Olivia Gissing, Amy Jones, Ashley McCallan, Rebecca Snoddon, Gigi Lau, Erin Craig, Reka Rubin, Suzanne Mitchell, Ingrid Dolan, Kristin Errico, and especially Siena Koncsol and Bryn Collier. I will never forget our dinner at Everest and the banner as big as McCormick Place at BEA.

Thank you so much to Michelle Tan, Jennifer Abidor, Joey Bartolomeo, Laura Brounstein, Chloe Chase, Jacqueline Deval, Danielle Kam, and everyone at *Seventeen* for all their enthusiasm and support. I'm so proud to launch your imprint!

During the writing of this book, I suffered a health crisis.

I'm here today due to the incredible outpouring of love from my family and friends.

In my family, we never thank each other because the gratitude is lived in. Nevertheless, thank you to Mom, Aina, Chito, Steve, Christina, Nicholas, Joseph, Sebastian and Marie, and all our extended de la Cruz, Johnston, Ong, Gaisano, Torre, Ng and Lim families, especially Tita Odette, Tita Sony and Tito Badong, Tito Eddie and Tita Joji, Trina and Terence, Isabelle and Clark and Tina, Melanie, Mica and Maj.

Thanks especially to my mom, who was there for every scary scan and test, my brother, for the FaceTime pep talks, and my sister, Aina, who, when I jokingly asked her where my "hospital gift" was, replied: "You got to live: there's your gift." That's my family for you, always hitting the nail on the head. They're very thankful this book is not at all based on our family. (For that story, my novel *Fresh Off the Boat* was published by Harper in 2005!)

Thank you to my genius agent and dear friends Richard Abate and Rachel Kim at 3Arts.

Thank you to everyone at Spilled Ink, especially Jane Hawley and Colleen Wilson.

Thank you to my siblings from other mothers Rafi and Margie for everything, including the balloon display bigger than my house and the new food program.

Thank you to my loyal NYC gang, for endless laughs and cocktails: Andy Goffe, Jeff Levin, Tristan Ashby, Jeff Chu, Peter Edmonston and Tyler Rollins. Thank you to my fashion sister Karen Robinovitz. Thanks to my CC'93 crew—my college sisters Jennie Harman and Alicia Carmona. So happy to catch up with Thad and Gabby in Atlanta.

Thank you to the fabulous LA-NY-London crew: Tom Dolby, Tina Hay and Lady (Katie) Hawkesbury.

Thank you to my amazing mama and papa pals, who are there to celebrate or sympathize whenever the occasion calls for it; I'm so blessed to be part of our CH community: Heidi and Andy McKenna, Jill Lorie and Steve Stewart, Dawn and Dan Limerick, Tiffany Moon and Cole Hartman, Celeste and Patrick Vos, Jenni and Adam Gerber, Nicole and Chris Jones, Ava and Ron McKay, Betty and Mike Balian, Lisa and Todd Orlando, Carolyn and Bob Holmes, Bronwyn Savasta and Sean Curley, Gloria Jolley and Scott Johnson, Saher and Bassil Hamideh, Carol Koh and Tony Evans, Heidi and Sasha Madzar, Heather and Eman Kiriakou, Tim and Kathleen Von Der Ahe, Jenny and Andy Van Tuyle, Fatima Gonclaves and Auggie Ruiz, Liz Craft and Adam Fierro, Lindsay and Jason Nesmith, Michelle and Scott Bergman, Amanda and Mark Ewing, Bridget and Mike Johnsen, Vicki and Mark Haller, Ange and Dave Reiner, Dana and Charles Boyd, Maria Cina and Blair Harrison, Jen and Larry Kuklin, Jenn and Paul Davidson, Rhoda Lawrence and Marcuis Harris, Molly and Chad Ludwig, and Maggie and Robert Silverberg.

Thank you to the loving community of authors whom I'm proud to call my friends, especially my Yallfamily: Marie Lu and Primo Gallanosa, Tahereh Mafi and Ransom Riggs, Veronica Roth, Kami Garcia, Sandy London, Brendan Reichs, Leigh Bardugo, Jonathan and Lauren Sanchez, Patrick Dolan and Abbey Gardner.

Thank you to my dear author and publishing pals Jen Besser, Rachel Cohn, Ally Carter, Sarah Mlynowski and Eoin Colfer.

Thank you to my Disney Book Group and Disney Channel family for the good looking out. Thank you, Emily (Em!) Meehan, Naketha ("junior varsity") Mattocks, Seale (Eddie, darling) Ballenger and MaryAnn (MAZ) Zissimoss.

Thank you to my dear angel pal Rachel Boston.

Thank you to American Heart Association CEO Roman Bowser, who made sure I had the best doctors in LA.

I am so lucky to be so loved.

Last but certainly not least, my oldest friend Gabriel Sandoval helped get my green card, and to thank him for his friendship I asked for more help and put him on my Yallwest board. (Heh.) I can probably never thank you enough for saving my application from the "dead" zone, Gabe.

My family is the reason I get up in the morning with a smile on my face. Every book I write has all my love to Mike, Mattie and Mimi, who make it all worthwhile.

questions for discussion

1. Most Americans are immigrants or have descended from immigrants. What are the benefits and challenges of living in a country founded on immigration?

2. How does Jasmine view her parents' contributions to America before she learns the truth about their immigration status? Do her views change or develop? Point to examples from the book to illustrate your answer.

3. Jasmine's family faces suspicion and outright hostility because they are immigrants. Why do you think this occurs? Do witnesses have a responsibility to respond to this kind of behavior? Point to examples from the book to support your answer.

4. Jasmine's parents legally immigrated to the United States but were not able to renew their work visas. Why did they stay in the country? Could they have made any other choices?

5. *Something in Between* is a book about identity. How does Jasmine's view of herself change and develop over the course of the book? Does she consider herself to be more American or Filipina at times? When? Why? Point to examples in the book to support your answer.

6. What does Jasmine ultimately come to believe about herself as a person? What values matter most to her? Do her values change when she starts dating Royce? What values matter most to you? How do you think they may develop over time? Why?

7. Royce's view on immigration changes over the course of the book. How does starting a friendship and falling in love with Jasmine change his attitude and challenge his opinions? What does Jasmine show him about America that he didn't recognize before?

8. At a crucial turning point in the story, Jasmine reveals her immigration status to her friends despite feeling fear that her family could be deported. Why does she lean on her community? What are your communities that you go to for support? How might being an undocumented immigrant limit your support groups? How could those limitations affect a person's life in different ways?

9. Jasmine is proud to be a cheerleader and points out the constant false stereotyping of cheerleaders. Does Jasmine herself have personal prejudices? What prejudices do other characters display? How do the various characters develop and grow throughout the book? How do their experiences in the story shape their personal views?

10. Millie and Jasmine form a close bond during the story, but Jasmine and her family have to deal with racism on top of their immigrant status. How does Jasmine's friendship with Millie give her the courage to face her fears and stand up for herself and her family?

11. Kayla and Jasmine are best friends, but dealing with their respective family and dating problems cause them to grow apart for some time. Has this happened to you and a close friend before? What did you learn from the experience?

12. Royce's father, the House Speaker of the United States Congress, rallies against an important bill that would help Jasmine's family to start on a path to citizenship. How does she deal with dating a boy whose family's political values are different from her own? Is it possible for both sides to be able to listen to and get along with each other? Find examples from the book to support your points.

13. Are Jasmine and Royce responsible for bringing their families together? If not, why? If so, what can they do to continue to bring their families together?

14. Jasmine ultimately finds the power to believe in herself. Describe a time when you had to believe in yourself to succeed. What lessons did you learn about yourself?